P9-DFR-925

BLOOD BAYOU

KAREN YOUNG

BLOOD BAYOU

HOWARD
Fiction
A DIVISION OF SIMON & SCHUSTER
New York   London   Toronto   Sydney

Our purpose at Howard Books is to:
- *Increase faith* in the hearts of growing Christians
- *Inspire holiness* in the lives of believers
- *Instill hope* in the hearts of struggling people everywhere
Because He's coming again!

Published by Howard Books, a division of Simon & Schuster, Inc.
1230 Avenue of the Americas, New York, NY 10020
www.howardpublishing.com

Blood Bayou © 2009 Karen Young

All rights reserved, including the right to reproduce this book or portions thereof in any form whatsoever. For information, address Howard Subsidiary Rights Department, Simon & Schuster, 1230 Avenue of the Americas, New York, NY 10020.

Wendy Lawton, Books & Such Literary Agency

ISBN-13: 978-1-4165-8750-7
ISBN-10: 1-4165-8750-0

10 9 8 7 6 5 4 3 2

HOWARD and colophon are registered trademarks of Simon & Schuster, Inc.

Manufactured in the United States

For information regarding special discounts for bulk purchases, please contact: Simon & Schuster Special Sales at 1-866-506-1949 or business@simonandschuster.com.

The Simon & Schuster Speakers Bureau can bring authors to your live event. For more information or to book an event contact the Simon & Schuster Speakers Bureau at 1-866-248-3049 or visit our website at www.simonspeakers.com.

Edited by David Lambert
Cover design by The Designworks Group
Interior design by Davina Mock-Maniscalco
Photography/illustrations by Getty Images

This novel is a work of fiction. Names, characters, places, and incidents either are the product of the author's imagination or are used fictitiously. Any resemblance to actual events, locales, organizations, or persons living or dead is entirely coincidental and beyond the intent of either the author or publisher.

In loving memory of my mother, Alma Young

acknowledgments

I HAVE BEEN SO blessed in writing this, my first Christian novel. It is hard to know how to begin to thank those I should for fear that I'll miss someone in all those who have helped me along the way.

To my dear friend, Debbie Macomber, thanks simply aren't enough. You opened doors for me, Debbie, and I am truly grateful.

To Deanne Gist, who told me two years ago, "You should be writing Christian fiction, Karen."

To my incredibly talented brainstorming group, Emilie Richards, Jasmine Cresswell, Connie Laux, and Diane Mott Davidson, whose spot-on critiques during the development of my story made it better.

To the members of West Houston and Bay Area RWA chapters, thanks for your friendship and support.

To my neighbor, Jo Butler, who pops such great ideas right off the top of her head. Keep them coming, Jo.

To my superior agent, Wendy Lawton, for encouragement, knowledge, and expertise. I was blessed to land in your care as I make my way in this new career direction.

To my family, who have always understood, thank you. And

especially to my daughter, Alison, who believed in me and encouraged me and wouldn't let me quit.

To the great folks at Howard Books. You feel like family!

To Alton Gansky for terrific line editing.

To Dave Lambert, editor extraordinaire.

And finally, to my Lord, who brought me to this place, at this time, for just this purpose, I am humbly grateful.

"Conversion may occur in an instant, but the process of coming from sinfulness into a new life can be a long and arduous journey."
—Charles Colson

prologue

LUANNE RICHARD OPENED the door to her killer wearing a smile and little else. With a drink in one hand and invitation and mischief dancing in her eyes, she sensed no danger. After several martinis, her instinct for danger was hazy at best.

She'd been lounging on the patio in her bikini when the doorbell rang. It had occurred to her that a cover-up might be the proper thing, but she wasn't much into doing the proper thing. Never had been. It got really boring trying to live life properly. Now, glancing through the peephole, she saw he was alone and thought it might be fun to tease him a little. No one around, as far as she could tell. So she let him in, closed the door, and turned to face him.

That is when she saw the knife.

She sobered instantly. And when he raised it and lunged, aiming for her throat, she recoiled on instinct alone, tossed her drink at his face and somehow—miraculously—managed to evade that first vicious slash. While he cursed and blinked gin from his eyes, she turned and ran on bare feet.

She raced through the huge house wondering frantically how to escape. She cursed her carelessness in leaving the gate open when she drove home from the club. It came to her that she stood no chance while inside, so she flew through the living room and made for the den and beyond—the patio. She prayed the door was open, that she'd failed to close it when she got up and came back in.

Please, oh, please . . .

Halfway there, she took a quick look over her shoulder and screamed. He was close and gaining. He would be on her if she didn't do something. As she streaked past a very expensive Chinese vase, she gave it a push to tip it over, thinking to trip him. He stumbled but didn't go down. He picked it up, tossed it aside, and laughed. *Laughed!*

This couldn't be real. This kind of craziness happened in nightmares to other people, not to her. Hadn't she had enough grief in her life? Hadn't she tried her best to fight the demons that tormented her? Hadn't she often resisted temptation? Was she to be damned for the times she didn't?

I'm sorry, God. I'm sorry. I'm sorry . . .

No! She wasn't going to let this happen. She had a lot of life to live yet. She would change. She *had* changed. Nobody understood how hard it was for her to keep to the straight and narrow. She kept to the path. Almost always.

Once out on the lawn, she realized she couldn't make it to the front. It was too far away. He'd overtake her before she got halfway there. And there was no time to punch in the security code to open the gate. She was trapped.

Mad with fear, she ducked around lush landscaping, making for the walk that led to the pier and boathouse. She veered to avoid the cherub fountain and stumbled, twisting her ankle painfully. She flung out a hand for balance only to have it slashed on the lethal thorns of a pyracantha. Sobbing now, she dashed through a grove of wax myrtles, wincing at the slap and sting of limbs before finally reaching the pier jutting over the bayou. It was her only chance.

She looked again over her shoulder. He'd slowed, knowing she had no place else to run. The knife blade glinted brightly in the sun. She whimpered, trying to think. Blood dripped from the gash on her hand and her ankle throbbed. Scalding tears ran down her cheeks. What to do?

"Gotcha now, Luanne," he taunted. "The boathouse or the bayou, babe. What's it gonna be?"

Not the bayou. Never the bayou.

She had a fear of Blood Bayou. It had almost claimed her once. None of the romantic legends spun about it held any charm for her. The water was too dark, too still, too deep, too alive with slimy things, predatory things. The bayou was death.

She was out of breath and in pain when she remembered the telephone in the boathouse only a few feet away. Checking behind her, she saw that he was still coming, but moving almost leisurely, as if enjoying the chase, savoring her fear. Anticipating the kill?

The thought made her leap onto the pier. Hot from the August sun, the wooden planks burned the soles of her bare feet. Below the pier, black water slapped against the pilings, disorienting her. *Don't look down!* Eyes straight ahead, she finally reached the boathouse door, grabbing at the latch, fingers clawing. Panic and blood from her wounded hand made her clumsy, all thumbs, as she worked at the strange fastener. But at last she got it, wrenched it open.

Inside it was dark and dank and, like the bayou, smelled of rotting vegetation and decaying fish. But it was sanctuary and she scrambled inside, slammed the door shut, and set the bolt.

It would not keep him out for long, but it offered a few precious seconds. Her eyes struggled with the dark. It was her only chance. But one thing nagged: Why was he giving her this chance? No time to worry about that. She flew to the wall-mounted phone, grabbed the receiver, and punched in 911.

He was at the boathouse now, rattling the door. Terror leaped in her chest. With her heart in her throat, she strained to hear the ring connecting her to 911. But nothing. In a panic, she jiggled the button up and down. Listened for a dial tone. Nothing. She frantically pressed the button up and down again. And again nothing. She gave an anguished cry and slammed the receiver against the wall. The phone line was dead!

She screamed at the thunderous crash. He kicked the door open. It slammed against the wall, shaking the boathouse to its foundation. As she watched, petrified, he took an unhurried step inside, filling the doorway. With the sun behind him, he loomed as large as a truck. He paused, no doubt to let his eyes adjust to the dark interior. He took his time. Then he began to move slowly toward her. "I've got you now, sugar," he taunted, his smile grotesque.

Incoherent with terror, all she saw was the knife. She scrambled backward, desperate to get out of his reach. But he kept coming. With a bump, she backed against the sleek hull of a boat. Trapped! Below was bottomless, black water. Sobbing, she looked at him piteously. She was going to die. The bayou was going to claim her after all.

CHAPTER ONE

CAMILLE ST. JAMES stood at a podium in the college's law library facing a sea of media types. She wished she could shed her jacket. In spite of air-conditioning, August heat and Baton Rouge humidity made for sticky clothes and sweat. No other way to put it. She wished she hadn't been ordered to wear her jacket, but her boss had decreed business dress for the occasion. Now the only thing that hadn't wilted was her dark hair, which curled like crazy on days like this. Beside her, Dr. Felix Chapman's seersucker suit looked as fresh and crisp as it had two hours ago when he'd informed her that in order to capitalize on this most recent success of the Truth Project, he'd called a press conference.

She'd much rather be at her desk scrutinizing the case file of another wrongfully convicted prisoner, but positive media brought much-needed attention to Truth. Unlike Chapman, she expected a mixed reaction and, judging by the expressions on the faces of some in the crowd, she was right. There would always be people who believed every death row inmate was probably guilty of some crime, if not the one for which convicted. Therefore, in the minds of cynics, it was a public service to keep such types behind bars. Camille found it inexplicable how anyone could remain unmoved by the increasing numbers of incarcerated inmates proved innocent.

Looking over the crowd, she recognized several regular death-penalty activists. It was difficult to handle the media, but reporters were a piece of cake compared to folk dedicated to keeping or ending the death penalty. She cleared her throat and raised a hand to get the show on the road and, hopefully, over and done with.

Chapman smiled benignly, appearing pleased over this particular triumph of the Truth Project. In fact, he never missed a chance to let her know—privately—that the whole program was a pesky thorn in his side. "Pesky" defined anything that siphoned funds from projects, the ones he felt added to his stature as chairman of the Civil Law Studies department.

"Thanks for coming," Camille began. She needed no notes. She spoke easily and from the heart on this subject. "As you know, the Truth Project is dedicated to the exoneration of innocent individuals who have been wrongly convicted and sentenced to death row. It gives me extreme pleasure to announce that Truth's work on behalf of Mr. Chester Pelham has been successful. Mr. Pelham's murder conviction and his sentence of death by lethal injection have been overturned by order of the Governor of the State of Louisiana three days ago. Mr. Pelham is now a free man."

A smattering of applause eased her mind somewhat. Several hands shot up—mainly reporters, she noted—but a few activists were jockeying for her attention too. She decided to ignore everyone until she was done.

"The Truth Project chose Mr. Pelham's case after an intense examination of these factors," she said, ticking them off on her fingers. "His trial, the evidence, including DNA, and the quality of the defense."

"Eyewitness identification," she continued, "was in error here, as was botched DNA testing. Complete details of the case are available at our website. As for Mr. Pelham's future, he was released within hours of the governor's action. It was—"

"Why the delay in releasing that fact?"

Camille made eye contact with the reporter. She'd been lucky to get this far without interruption. "It was Mr. Pelham's choice. We felt that after five years of wrongful incarceration, he deserved a private departure from the prison."

"Where is he now?"

"I have no idea." She had suggested to Chester that he avoid going back to his hometown. In spite of the fact that he'd been cleared, there would always be those who rejected the truth and it would be difficult for him to start a new life under the best of circumstances. She worried that Chester would ignore her advice. He was mentally challenged, enough so that he'd been virtually incapable of assisting in his own defense. In dealing with him, Camille had found him as simple-minded as a child in many ways.

"What about those pictures?"

She sighed. This subject was bound to come up. "Chester's job, before he was wrongly accused, was yard work. In fact, he was . . . *is* gifted in making things grow and has shown superior skill in visualizing an attractive layout of plants in a yard. And although he doesn't read or write above a very basic level, he likes to sketch the landscape plans for his customers."

"Yeah, but what about the sketches of his victims? No landscape plan I've ever seen includes people, especially recognizable sketches of women."

"His customers"—she emphasized the word—"were victims

of another killer, as yet unknown. As for his sketching them, in the case of Stephanie Hill, he drew her in his plan for landscaping her yard because she lived there. He found it natural to include a sketch of her in her garden. It was as simple and as innocent as that."

Her statement was met with general mumbling and grumbling, as she expected. And what would this crowd's reaction be if they knew that Chester thought of his female customers as flowers? In interviewing him, Camille herself had been a little taken aback. The likenesses of women included in his landscape plans were eerily accurate.

"Will he get compensation for wrongful imprisonment?" a TV journalist asked.

"Again, I have no idea," she answered, glad to leave the subject of the sketches. Chester was definitely owed compensation, but with his limited grasp of his options, she doubted he would sue the state unless prompted by some opportunistic attorney. Unfortunately, such an individual would probably be knocking on his door before nightfall.

"Don't you feel some responsibility for letting these criminals out on the street, Ms. St. James?"

The question came from a woman carrying a sign that read "Victims Have Rights Too." "Mr. Pelham had no previous record when he was arrested. I don't see him as a threat in any way."

Chapman moved to her side, his smile a bit set, but still in place. "The Truth Project does commendable work in righting wrongs in our justice system. We're proud to be a part of a growing movement using forensics and the creative energy of students here at Talbot College to free these hapless individuals. I'm afraid we're unable to go further than that. After prison, Mr.

Pelham can make of his future whatever he chooses. Our work is done."

Camille managed to keep a straight face. The chairman as a cheerleader for the Truth Project was almost laughable. He was taking bows today only because they'd scored a clear-cut victory.

A reporter standing at the edge of the crowd ended a cell phone call with a snap and spoke up. "Yeah, well, it looks like Chester has started his future life by making a really bad choice right from the get-go."

Camille was confused. "Excuse me?"

"He was arrested an hour ago after stabbing another woman to death in Blood Bayou."

Camille stared at the reporter in stunned disbelief. There had to be some mistake. Chester was not capable of murder. Her mind reeled, trying to think how such a mistake could have been made.

She gathered herself enough to ask, "Where did you get this information?"

"I won't name my source, but you can check with the cops in Blood Bayou. The victim is dead from multiple stab wounds. And Pelham was apprehended still wearing bloody clothes."

The reporters began barking out questions. The few gory details were like chum thrown to hungry sharks. The reporters were in a feeding frenzy. She looked around for Dr. Chapman just in time to see him ducking out the door. The cameras would have caught that to be rerun tonight on all TV channels, she thought in dismay. But that was Chapman's problem. Hers was to get away from this crowd with her dignity intact. After this, only a miracle could save her reputation.

She was not going to have a chance to do much damage control. Not in this crowd. Even if she'd had any answers—which they must have known she didn't—her words would drown in the chaos. She realized they would hound her with impossible-to-answer questions as long as she stood there taking it. And with Chapman gone, it was up to her to make an official statement.

She assumed a stern look, lifted a hand for silence, and waited for some semblance of order. When they quieted a little, she said, "I have no statement at this time. You will be notified if and when further details are known. Thank you."

As she expected, this was met with jeers and disgust. Ignoring it all, she turned on her heel and escaped.

A few minutes later, in her office, Camille sat with her face in her hands. For Chester Pelham to be the prime suspect in a murder in Blood Bayou spelled disaster for the Truth Project. The media free-for-all she'd just survived was only the beginning.

She was still reeling in shock. There had to be an explanation. Chester Pelham wouldn't hurt a housefly. She'd stake her life on that. She had staked her *reputation* on it. Heaven only knew what would happen to Chester now.

She groaned when someone rapped smartly on the door. "Go away," she muttered. Short of the president of the college, she was not talking to anybody.

The door opened to reveal Felix Chapman's administrative assistant. She had never warmed to Sybil Moreau, whose thin-lipped smile never seemed genuine. The woman was too rigid and too impressed with her own position. "Dr. Chapman wants you in his office right away," Sybil said.

It was a summons Camille didn't dare ignore. With a sigh,

she stood, grabbed her jacket, and followed the woman. When they reached Chapman's office, Sybil opened the door and ushered her inside without another word.

"We have a problem, Ms. St. James."

Chapman sat ramrod straight at his desk, his seersucker suit still looking as fresh and crisp as ever. Was the man an android?

"I'd just like to say up front, Dr. Chapman, that I absolutely reject the idea that Chester is a murderer. There has to be an explanation."

"Sit down. Please."

Camille sat. He was clearly unwilling to hear any defense of Chester.

"I have just spoken with the police chief in Blood Bayou and confirmed the facts. Pelham was spotted at the scene shortly before the murder. When he was confronted, holed up in his bayou shack, he was wearing bloodstained clothes. I would hardly call that circumstantial."

"With all due respect, sir, it is circumstantial. But what I—"

He waved her to silence. "Hear me out, Ms. St. James. This is very bad publicity and we don't need bad publicity here in the department or at the college. As you know, I've had reservations about the Truth Project from the start. Assisting the criminal types who need such services is risky. To begin with, they're of questionable character. They're simply . . . unreliable."

"Chester Pelham's character wasn't questionable until he was railroaded by inadequate legal representation and blatant prosecutorial misconduct, Dr. Chapman. And what about the contaminated DNA? Most of all, Chester was proved to be elsewhere, contrary to the eyewitness testimony." Reading the look on his face, she took a more conciliatory tone. "You know we only deal with cases where there's clearly a miscarriage of justice. Don't these people deserve fair treatment?"

"I don't argue that. But you see how vulnerable we are in this department when things go awry. By committing murder, Chester Pelham has jeopardized the reputation of your whole program."

"I can't believe he committed murder!"

"Nevertheless, it appears he did. And it puts us, if you will, in a pretty pickle here." He picked up a few papers on his desk and shuffled them, gearing up for his next words. "I've had to make a difficult decision. I've decided to put the Truth Project on hold for the time being."

Her heart sank. "Dr. Chapman, please don't do that. This is such a worthy cause. You said so yourself at the press conference today."

"The publicity—"

"Will die down. Chester's case—it's an aberration. I'm sure there's a reasonable explanation."

He paused a long moment, simply looking at her. "You'll forgive me saying so, Ms. St. James, but I think you need some time off to put things in proper perspective. I'm aware of the effort you've devoted to your pet project above and beyond regular office hours. In fact, I'm convinced you're overworked and need a vacation. This is an unfortunate incident, but it's happened at a time that won't put a crimp in our schedule if you're absent for awhile. It's early August. Take the rest of the month off."

"I don't need time off, Dr. Chapman. Chester's case—"

"Is closed as far as this college is concerned. It's now in the hands of the police in Blood Bayou." He shoved his chair back and stood up, again ramrod straight. "I'll work on your reassignment. Returning the Tuesday after Labor Day will give you almost a full month to rest and relax. Hopefully, the furor will have died down a bit by then."

"Are you saying you're pulling the plug on the Truth Project permanently? Shutting it down completely?"

"I think that's the best course of action for the college and for this department." He walked to the door and opened it. "Enjoy your little vacation, Ms. St. James. You've earned it."

BACK IN her office, she paced. The more she thought about it, the madder she became. It was so unfair, shutting down the entire Truth Project on the assumption that Chester was guilty. Granted, it looked bad, but she knew Chester. He was a gentle soul. Five years ago, his arrest for Stephanie Hill's murder had been based mostly on an eyewitness testimony and purely circumstantial evidence. She'd had the resources of the Truth Project to unravel the case against him. She and her students had spent hundreds of hours—thousands, actually—gathering data and researching, building the case for his exoneration. Now, even if she devoted every day and night during her enforced leave of absence, it wouldn't be enough.

"Hey, how you doing?"

She looked up to see Ray Wyatt standing at the door. Formerly a homicide detective in the New Orleans Police Department, Wyatt spent considerable time in his retirement as a volunteer for the Truth Project. He'd been with Camille and her students every step of the way as they worked to free Chester Pelham. His expertise in homicide investigation had been invaluable. She was glad to see him.

"I've had better days, Ray." She rubbed at tightness in both temples.

"I hear you." He stepped inside and closed the door behind him. "As soon as I got the word about Chester, I made some calls."

"Then fill me in. Maybe you can tell me what happened. I know Chester wouldn't—"

"Right, he wouldn't. We know it, but other folks are going to see it differently." He took a seat in front of her desk. "I sure wish he'd taken your advice not to go back to Blood Bayou. When the cops figured out where he was and stormed the place, he didn't stand a chance."

She made a small sound and clamped a hand over her mouth. "He's dead? They killed him?"

"Not quite. He's at Sacred Heart. In a coma."

With a sigh, she stood and moved to the window. Sacred Heart was the hospital in Blood Bayou. "The worst choice he could've made," she murmured. "I thought I convinced him how foolish it would be to go back there. What was he *thinking*?"

Wyatt sat back in his chair, crossing an ankle over his knee. "Pelham's spent his whole life in Blood Bayou. Where else would he go?"

"He has no family left there."

"He has a house."

"A shack, Ray. A dilapidated, run-down shell of a house. Not fit for an animal."

"It's home. A man like that, unsophisticated, no skills." He shrugged. "I guess it makes sense."

"He has skills. He's worked as a yard man for years. Plants thrive in his care. He could make a desert bloom."

"Which, you'll recall, is how he came to be on the scene and arrested for murder the first time." She glared at him. "I know, I know. We proved he wasn't there."

Still at the window, her gaze fell on students moving about the campus with no apparent regard for the suffocating heat or oppressive humidity. Had she been that oblivious to weather when she was twenty-something?

"Camille?"

She turned. "Just thinking. Why would he commit murder so soon out of prison? It doesn't make sense."

He cocked his head, looking at her thoughtfully. "You appear pretty calm about this, considering."

She wasn't calm. Far from it. "Considering what? What do you mean?"

"Don't you know who was murdered?"

"No. Who is it?"

"Brace yourself, Camille. It's Luanne Richard."

Her mouth fell open. Speechless, she covered her mouth with one hand.

"Yeah, your former sister-in-law. Lucky for you that reporter didn't know her name. With your . . . ah, connection to the victim, it would have been mayhem."

"It was mayhem anyway," she said, still shaken. "And there is no connection, not now. I haven't seen or spoken to Luanne in years. But still . . . I'm stunned, I guess."

"If you think the scene with the media went south just on thinking Chester had killed again—"

"You don't know that! Stop saying it."

"Okay, okay. But think how bad it would have been if they'd known Luanne was your sister-in-law."

"Former sister-in-law, Ray." She didn't like remembering that time in her life. "And my marriage to Jack Vermillion was over seven years ago."

"You know it and I know it, but hear me on this. Since Luanne Richard is Jack's sister, there will be a big stink, wait and see. Without Vermillion's eyewitness testimony at Chester's trial, he would never have been convicted. And even though Jack's a preacher now, he's going to be extremely upset."

She nodded mutely, thinking of the effect it would have on Jack. They'd barely spoken since their bitter and soulless divorce. But she'd have to be heartless not to feel sympathy for him. "This is just unbelievable," she murmured.

"Yeah. Murder is always bad, but when it hits close to home, it's worse. Anyway, here's what I'm hearing from my connections in Blood Bayou. Pelham gets off death row, goes straight back to the town where the first murder happened and instead of going for someone on the jury—or even the judge who gave him the death sentence—he goes for the sister of the man whose testimony convicted him." Wyatt reached over and took a peppermint from a glass jar on her desk. "It'll be interesting to see how Vermillion's newfound faith handles something like this."

"It's bound to be devastating," she said, ignoring his cynicism. Wyatt was hopelessly marred by his years as a homicide detective in one of the most crime-ridden cities in America. However, she'd have to admit to being skeptical herself when, four years after their divorce, Jack was ordained as a minister. Heaven knows he'd shown precious little inclination to a faith of any kind while they were married. The driving force in his life then was rampant ambition as a lawyer, and when he wasn't working, drinking himself into oblivion.

"Pelham will find it hard to beat a conviction a second time, Camille. Vermillion will be on that guy like white on rice." He popped the mint in his mouth and tucked the wrapper in his shirt pocket. "In spite of his religion, he's still got a lawyer's instincts."

She didn't reply. Who knew Jack's skill in going for the jugular better than she? But she was unable to predict his reaction now—other than to know he would be grieving. Camille rubbed a throbbing spot on her temple. She did not want to think or talk about Jack Vermillion.

Wyatt, however, wasn't ready to change the subject. "Vermillion will be out for blood. Turning the cheek might be the rules he's supposed to follow today, but my money says he'll revert to type. He didn't get where he was as a lawyer by turning the other cheek."

"If you mean he'll demand justice, you're right. As he should."

While Wyatt droned on about Jack and Luanne, Camille struggled with the facts of the murder. If Chester had been at the scene and was captured wearing bloody clothes, it was going to be almost impossible for people to look elsewhere for a killer. It was difficult not to have doubts herself. Was her judgment that far off? She gazed out the window, thinking. If the police hadn't been on Chester's trail so quickly, they probably would have fixed their suspicions on the victim's spouse. That was routine investigative technique in a homicide.

"Maybe they should be looking to Harlen Richard as someone who might want Luanne out of the way," she murmured.

"Huh? What's that?"

She realized she'd spoken her thoughts out loud. Unable to

sit still, Camille got up out of her chair. "Chester had no reason to kill her, Ray."

"No reason except that her brother's testimony sent him to death row," Wyatt said, watching her pace.

"It's too obvious. Chester isn't too smart, but he's smarter than that. Besides, he doesn't have a vindictive bone in his body. He's . . . well, simple. And so pitifully glad to be out of jail, I just can't believe he would do anything to jeopardize his freedom."

"Maybe. I'm just saying Vermillion won't take it lightly that his sister was stabbed to death by the same guy whose fate he sealed when he testified in the Stephanie Hill murder trial. The same crazy guy we sprung from death row three days ago."

"He didn't kill that first woman, Ray," Camille said. "We proved he was elsewhere. The DNA they claimed to have was contaminated."

"Hey, like I said, you know it and I know it, but I bet you won't find three people in the parish who'll agree with you now."

"Are you one of them, Ray?"

"It doesn't matter what I think. What I'm saying is it looks pretty bad. I guess we'll know for sure if his prints come up on the knife."

"But no knife yet, right?"

"Right." He stood up. "Tell you what. Let me nose around a little more, but no matter what, it looks bad for Pelham. Blood Bayou is a small town. Luanne Richard is one of their own, the wife of a prominent citizen, the sister of the hometown boy who made good, even though he screwed up. But he's a preacher now. Plus, they will not have forgotten the murder of Stephanie Hill, same MO. Nothing short of a miracle will save Chester now."

He paused a moment and then gave a short laugh. "No pun intended."

Camille failed to find anything funny in the tragedy of a young woman brutally murdered. "But what if he didn't do it?"

"Well, I would have said you've got your work cut out for you again."

"Dr. Chapman has shut the Truth Project down."

Ray raised an eyebrow. "I should have seen that coming. I guess you'll have to leave it to the locals to prove Chester's innocence."

"Whether he did it or not, everyone will think he did." *Including Jack.* Luanne was his sister, the only relative he had left in the world. And, divorce or not, Camille had once been her sister-in-law. Somehow, it didn't feel so long in the past. At that thought, Camille felt a chill creeping down her spine. She wrapped her arms around herself. She knew who Jack would blame.

CHAPTER TWO

AFTER RAY WYATT left, Camille decided she didn't need to stay around and be cornered by a reporter, or any other hostile source. Dr. Chapman wanted her out, so she might as well go now.

But once in her car, she couldn't stop dwelling on the events of the day. Luanne was dead. Murdered. Jack would be devastated. And if he was thinking what everyone else thought—that Chester Pelham did it—he would probably feel that Camille had a lot to answer for. At the least, she felt obligated to tell him how sorry she was for his loss. It would be difficult, but it was the right thing to do.

The decision made, she glanced at her watch. The trip to Blood Bayou would take about an hour. She could go and be back in time to try to soak away the day's tension in her Jacuzzi. And maybe, just maybe, she wouldn't lie awake until the wee hours. Jack had robbed her of many a night's sleep during their marriage, but she had less at stake emotionally in this situation. Or did she? Maybe less in a personal sense, but she had a great deal at stake professionally. She heaved a heavy sigh. How had this happened?

An hour later, she was in the small Cajun town. On her first visit, she had been struck by its uniqueness and charm. That day, she'd come to reunite with her mother after an absence of nearly five years. It had been a joyous occasion. Today she felt no joy. Instead she battled a bad case of nerves.

Maybe she should have stopped at her condo and changed into something more . . . more what? She wasn't thinking to impress Jack. The suit she'd worn at the press conference would work just as well for what she had to do. Very professional. Appropriate for her mission. She glanced at her reflection in the mirror. Would he think she'd aged well? Suddenly disgusted with herself, she gripped the wheel and stopped thinking.

The bayou meandered through the heart of town, picturesque and postcard perfect. The water was a deep dark green and shaded on both sides by ancient cypress trees and moss-draped live oaks. Purple irises bloomed along the banks. A lone white heron stalked the edges, fishing for small marine life, seemingly ignoring an alligator waiting in the shadows, as still as death. Camille shivered a little and sped up.

She didn't know where Jack lived, but it was a small town, so she'd try the church. Since it was Friday, she assumed there would be someone there who could tell her where she could find him. She could call her mother, who attended Jack's church, but that would involve a discussion she preferred to avoid. She just wanted to get this over with.

By the time she'd driven around awhile searching, her stomach was in a knot. It would not be easy to face Jack after all these years. He'd called her frequently after their divorce, but she'd refused to talk to him and he'd finally given up. What was there to say anyway? What he'd done was too big, too unforgivable to get beyond. An apology—if that had been his intention—was too little too late.

At last, she spotted the church, nestled well back from the street with two gigantic live oak trees on the left and an added-on extension on the right. The church itself was obviously old, maybe even antebellum, she decided, complete with beautiful stained-glass windows and a tall steeple. It was small but appropriate for a town the size of Blood Bayou. For about the thousandth time, she marveled at the dramatic come-down for Jack: from high-powered, highly paid corporate lawyer, well known in the state and in Washington, to small-time minister in a tiny Louisiana bayou town. Was he buying forgiveness?

The heat hit her like a blast from a furnace when she stepped from her car, reminding her that it was, after all, deep summer. Leaving her suit jacket behind, she locked her car and headed toward the front steps of the church. She hoped he wasn't there. The few times she'd been inside a church, she felt uncomfortable. When was the last time?

She and Jack had married in a church because it was the thing to do, but that was in Washington, D.C., where she'd just finished law school and where she and her father had lived most of her life. Afterward, she'd been happy to move to Louisiana with Jack. She was so in love with him that she would have been happy to move to Siberia with him. The fact that it brought her closer to her mother was frosting on the cake. But the last time she was in a church? Maybe three years ago, she decided, when she'd attended a christening for a friend's baby boy.

Once under the shade of the oaks, she discovered that the heat wasn't so oppressive. To the left, beyond the trees, was a small cemetery. She quickly looked away. Cemeteries gave her the creeps.

At the top of the steps, she pushed tentatively at one of the double doors. It opened easily, soundlessly. And inside it was cool and quiet. Eerily quiet. Looking around nervously, she saw no one. But beyond the altar on each side were doors. She would have to go that way, she decided. But before she'd taken half a dozen steps, she felt a touch on her shoulder.

She nearly jumped out of her skin. Whirling about, she sent her purse flying, scattering stuff over the floor.

"It's only me, Camille."

Jack. For just an instant, words failed her. "My purse," she finally managed to say. She dropped to one knee and began to collect items off the floor: a lipstick, breath mints, her car keys, a packet of tissues, her wallet.

Jack, squatting next to her, nudged her aside. "Here, let me do that."

She rose slowly. She watched him fish a few coins from under a pew, thinking that even in khakis and a golf shirt, he looked more like a corporate executive than a minister. She wondered how that went over in a church. Weren't clergy supposed to wear a suit and tie?

He straightened up with his hands full and she had her first good look at his face. The harsh slash of his cheekbones was familiar. The stress of the day showed on his face. He was grim and unsmiling. He had aged, but the years were usually kind to an attractive man. And so they were to Jack. There was a trace of silver in his dark hair and a few age lines, which simply made him look interestingly mature. But tragedy had touched him today and his dark eyes were haunted.

Wordlessly, she opened her purse and he dumped everything inside. "Thank you."

When she closed it, he said, "It's been a long time, Camille."

"Seven years."

His gaze was fixed on her face, studying her as she'd studied him. "You look good."

"You too."

They stood mute a moment or two, both looking a bit awkward. Then Jack said, "I'm a little surprised to see you."

She glanced around, still feeling uncomfortable in a church. "After what happened, I felt I should get in touch."

"I'm in the phone book."

She nodded. "I could have called, I guess, but that seemed wrong somehow. Not for something like this." She hesitated, then said, "I planned to go to your house, but I realized I don't know where you live."

"Right here. The parsonage is behind the new annexed building," he said. "Once it was built, it blocked the house from view. But I like it. It affords me a little privacy, something you don't get a lot of in my business."

She waved a hand, taking in the pews, the altar, the stunning stained-glass windows ablaze with color from afternoon sun. "Could we talk somewhere else? I just came in here to ask someone where I could find you. I didn't expect—"

He almost smiled. "You didn't expect a pastor to be in his church?"

She shrugged. "Actually, no. It's Friday, so, well, no. But what would I know about churches and pastors?"

"Good point." Not quite touching her, he ushered her back the way she'd come and down the steps. "I wish this job allowed for taking Fridays off—or any days off, for that matter—but it's pretty much dawn to dusk, and beyond if the spirit calls."

She said nothing to that, falling into step beside him even

though her knees felt a little unsteady. Inside, *she* felt a little unsteady. She refused to think why that would be.

"My office is in the new annex. You look as if you could use
something cold to drink. We have diet cola." He paused before a
closed door. "You're still partial to diet cola?"

"No, not anymore. I've kicked the habit. It's water or iced
tea now." Once she would have said water or wine, but she never
touched alcohol now. And she assumed Jack didn't either.

"Well, no iced tea here, but bottled water we do have."

She shook her head. "I don't need anything, Jack. I just
wanted to talk to you about Luanne. Can we—"

"We can." He opened the door and she went into his office.

She looked around, curious to see Jack's new habitat. Book-
shelves lining one wall were filled to overflowing. A comfort-
able-looking sofa occupied another wall. In front of it was a
coffee table with an arrangement of bright multicolored zinnias
and a variety of magazines, among them *Sports Illustrated* and
Golf. Jack was a baseball fan and an avid golfer. Some things
hadn't changed, she noted. But surely there should be a Bible?
She watched as he moved behind his desk, which had nothing on
it except a laptop computer and a pen set. No clutter, no name
plate, not a single piece of paper, not even a phone. No change
there either. He'd always teased her for the messy, disorganized
chaos of her work area.

He didn't sit down. Instead he closed his laptop and motioned to the sofa. "Have a seat."

She slipped her purse strap from her shoulder and sat gingerly. Leaning against the edge of his desk, he looked calm, cool,
collected, while her mind teemed with nerves and memories of
their tangled past. In law school she'd been trained to conceal

nervousness, but the trick had been one of the most difficult for her to master. Whether in a practice debate then, or later, in legal arguments with dire consequences, she was always nervous. Not so Jack. He never looked nervous. He never *was* nervous. He'd once told her that revealing nervousness simply empowered your adversary. But they weren't adversaries anymore, were they? She took a deep breath and began.

"I came to tell you how sorry I am for your loss, Jack," she said. "I know how much you loved Luanne and . . . well, I . . . I'm just shocked and stunned. I'm so sorry."

"Thank you. I was wondering whether you'd acknowledge some responsibility." He paused. "That is what you came to say, isn't it?"

He knew very well that wasn't what she came to say. "I guessed you would probably be thinking that, but no," she said in as even a tone as she could manage. "Luanne was once my sister-in-law. I have fond memories of her. I'm sorry she died."

"Died? She was murdered, Camille. Are you having trouble saying the word?"

She paused, reminding herself that Jack was grieving. And angry. That he had a right to be both. Who wouldn't? She started again. "I know how devastated you must feel, losing your sister. She was your only relative. That makes your loss even greater. I understand that. I wish there was something I could do."

"You could tell me why you let that low-life out of death row."

So like Jack to go straight to the point. She sighed. "I suppose we have to talk about Chester."

"Don't we have good reason? You're here to say you're sorry my sister is dead. Well, he murdered her, Camille."

He was no longer leaning on the edge of his desk but up and pacing now. She acknowledged that he needed an outlet for his grief and by coming here she'd almost offered herself as a target. "I won't presume to think I can feel your pain at a time like this," she said gently, "but before placing blame, shouldn't we wait until we have all the facts?"

"I have these facts. A brutal murder is committed. Pelham is spotted leaving my sister's house. When the police find him, he's wearing bloody clothes." He spread his hands. "Those are the facts."

"I'm sure there is an explanation, Jack. I know it looks bad, but Chester is not a killer."

He looked at her, brows raised. "You can read his mind? Please. You finagled the release of a deranged individual on the general public, but there's no way you can know what he'll do when prison is in his rearview mirror. There's no way you can know he didn't kill Luanne."

"There's no way you can know that he did!" She stopped, realizing she was losing her cool. Gathering herself, she tried persuasion. "Think, Jack. Chester had no reason to kill Luanne."

"I can think of a very good reason. My eyewitness testimony clinched his conviction. Did it occur to you that the man might hold a grudge? That he might want to exact revenge on the person who put him behind bars?"

"I assure you that we take every—"

He put up a hand to stop her. "I watched that press conference. It wasn't really about Pelham. It was about the Truth Project. It was a blatant effort to publicize your organization, Camille. But did it occur to you that with Pelham's limited mental capacity he might not be the model citizen you made him out to be?"

"I did not make him out to be a model citizen."

"You did." He made a disgusted sound and when she didn't answer, he pinned her with a look she'd often seen him use in the courtroom. "What you did was to open the door and usher an unstable man out into the world without a thought to what he might do. And then what? You just dust off your hands and sit around feeling righteous? Does your precious Truth Project have no other responsibility beyond that?"

"Please just listen for a minute. You're jumping to conclusions about Chester. I know he wouldn't—"

"Wouldn't? Are you out of your mind?" He stared at her in amazement. "Pelham was seen at Luanne's home. When the police ran him down at his shack on the bayou, he was still wearing clothes soaked with blood. He had not been cleaning fish, Camille. And you think I'm jumping to conclusions?"

"I grant you that it looks bad, but—"

"It looks bad." He repeated her words softly, incredulously.

"Will you please let me finish a sentence?" She was not going to lose her temper, she told herself. She waited until she got a curt nod from him. "Thank you." She drew a long, slightly uneven breath. "It looks bad, I know, but I've spent hundreds of hours with Chester and he just doesn't fit the profile of a killer."

"Profiles can be wrong," Jack said bitterly. "You forget that I've been in prison. I've seen how good some criminals are at faking innocence. They're master manipulators."

Jack's incarceration was something she didn't want to touch with a long pole. "I don't doubt there are prisoners like that, but Chester isn't one of them. I can't think of a politically correct way to say this, but he's just too dumb to trick anybody. That's why it's so difficult for me to see him as a killer. I know there's another explanation for Luanne's murder."

"You know? You know?"

She winced at his sarcasm, at his outrage. His fury. Granted, he was entitled to whatever emotion he felt, and in focusing on Chester as the most obvious suspect, he wouldn't be alone. Everybody else in the town would think the same. Before nightfall, Chester would be tried and convicted.

"Can't you just consider for a moment that someone else might have done this, Jack?" she pleaded. "I urge you not to close your mind to that possibility. Don't you want—"

"What I want is to see Chester Pelham arrested and locked up again. Only the fact that he's in a hospital hooked up to a breathing machine keeps that from happening. And I urge you to remember that he wouldn't be there and I wouldn't be arranging my sister's funeral if you had let well enough alone."

Harsh words. Bitter words. And she saw he wasn't finished. Resisting the impulse to turn and walk out, she braced for whatever he needed to say to unload his grief and pain. She reminded herself that her purpose in coming hadn't been to defend Chester but to express to Jack sympathy for the loss of his sister. She blinked when he made a visible effort to calm himself and, to her surprise, he managed it.

"Look," he said in an even tone, "I grant it's a good thing to feel passionate about a righteous cause. It's good to work to free innocent people from prison. But don't you also have a responsibility not to be carried away by emotion? Don't you lose perspective when that happens?"

In the face of his changed demeanor, she took care in replying. "You're correct that the Truth Project is a righteous cause to me. It's also true that those of us who work for the release of any-one on death row are emotional, but we don't lose perspective. We'd never work to free an individual if we weren't convinced that there had been a miscarriage of justice and that that person deserves to be free."

When he didn't immediately argue, she thought maybe she was getting through to him at last. "I'm defending Chester be-cause, in the time that the Truth Project has worked on his case, I've come to know him. Now, please, just take a minute to con-sider this."

Uh-oh. She watched him cross his arms over his chest, a clas-sic pose indicating resistance. Maybe she wasn't getting through to him, but she plowed on anyway. "Suppose, just suppose, that someone else murdered Luanne. Chester could have been apply-ing to do yard work for her. Say he arrived and found her, tried to help her. He's that kind of person, Jack. That would explain her blood being on his clothes."

"Very noble," he said with a skeptical look. "But we could just as logically suppose the opposite. We could suppose he got Luanne's blood on his clothes when he killed her."

She sighed. "Okay. Neither of us knows which is true. I give you that. But I say let's wait to condemn him until the inves-tigation has uncovered the facts. Right now all we have is pure speculation."

Shaking his head, he rubbed a hand over his weary features. "Tell me this, Camille. Be honest. Are you absolutely certain it wasn't him?"

She had to be honest. "No. No more than you can be abso-lutely certain it was him."

"Yet you're still determined to stick up for him?"

"Try to understand, Jack. Chester was once convicted of a crime he didn't commit. Do you want me to do what everyone else did then? Just wash my hands and say, oh, well, tough. Stuff happens. If he didn't do this one, he probably did another one, so he's where he deserves to be?" She gave him a see-how-I'm-thinking look. "Would that be the right thing?"

"I'm still struggling to cope with what I think he did within seventy-two hours of being released."

She sighed. "I understand, truly I do. In your shoes, maybe I would be thinking the same thing."

He gave a grunt of approval or thanks. She couldn't be sure which. Clearly, she was getting nowhere. "Just consider this one last point, Jack. This crime is less than twelve hours old and only a few facts are known, yet you assume you know the killer. As a lawyer, you have been trained not to jump to conclusions. Not to assume. I'm simply asking you to remember that."

"I'm not a lawyer. I'm a minister. And I have enough facts to be convinced," he said stubbornly.

He might be a minister now, but some things never changed. Jack had world-class debating skills and knew how to use them. Years of butting heads with him should have taught her that they weren't going to agree.

She stood up to leave. "I can't persuade you that Chester isn't a killer, Jack, but I'd like you to think about this." She watched him cross his arms over his chest again with a resigned sigh. "The only way you'll get any satisfaction from the tragedy of losing Luanne is to find out for sure who murdered her. So instead of focusing on Chester, try opening your mind to the possibility—just the possibility—that someone else is the killer."

"I know the real killer. And I will not rest until I see Chester Pelham back on death row."

She simply looked at him a long moment. "You know something? I've never understood how you became a minister. When I first heard about it, my reaction was sheer amazement followed by disbelief. I felt I knew the real you after three years of marriage and you were not minister material."

"People change," he said, turning his face.

"They do indeed. Therefore, I would think that in your new life you would not be so hasty in declaring a man guilty before you know all the facts. I'm aware that losing Luanne is heartbreaking for you. But I'm really puzzled about something. Is your reaction consistent with the way a man of God"—she used her fingers as quotation marks—"deals with personal tragedy?"

She saw by his expression that she'd struck a nerve. "I'm sorry," she said. "I guess I spoke out of line. You've lost your sister. I had no right." She paused. "It's just hard for me to see you in that role."

"It's not a role, Camille. It's my life. And, with all due respect, you know nothing about my life now. You know nothing about me now. For seven years you have refused to talk to me. You have your reasons and I accept that. But when you presume to judge me on this . . . this obscenity that has happened to Luanne . . ." He stopped as if words failed him. "I should just leave it at that before I say something I'll surely be sorry for." He moved to open the door for her. "Again, thank you for coming," he said formally.

She hesitated, but found she was also at a loss for words. With a nod she turned slowly and left, feeling she'd lost something

more meaningful than just a skirmish with her ex-husband. And
she had no idea what it was.

JACK HAD spent half an hour sitting alone in a pew in the
sanctuary rerunning the first opportunity he had to talk to his
ex-wife in seven years. She was hardly out of sight before he
admitted to himself that he'd reverted to behavior that shamed
him. And his vows. One look at Camille and he had turned into
his former self, the man who'd known almost from the start that
he was killing their marriage and couldn't seem to stop himself.
His grief over losing Luanne was no excuse for the way he'd acted.
Yes, he wanted to blame someone, but deep down, he knew the
killer was to blame, certainly not Camille.

Lord, it had been so wonderful to see her, all that glorious
black hair curling around her face and framing those stunning
green eyes. She was the most beautiful woman in the world to
him. And he'd all but tossed her sympathy back in her face. One
chance handed him on a silver platter and he'd sent her away
mad and disgusted.

Why hadn't he grabbed the opportunity to say things he'd
been rehearsing in his head for years? To tell her she was the only
woman he'd ever loved and that for years he'd prayed for God
to give him a second chance with her. Now, given that second
chance, he'd squandered it. Instead of showing her how Christ
had changed him, how he was a different man from the one she'd
married, one with different values, different goals, even a different heart, he'd sounded exactly like the arrogant know-it-all he'd
once been.

But it baffled him how she could be so convinced that Chester Pelham was not the killer when everything pointed to him. He drew up his thoughts, bent his head, and rubbed at both eyes with the heels of his palms. It was all too new, too evil, and unspeakable to dwell on. None of his seminary training had prepared him for tragedy this close, this personal.

Approaching his house, he was so caught up in misery that he didn't see the woman sitting on the porch swing until he'd climbed the steps. Madge Pichon was a faithful member of his congregation and a tireless volunteer. Her job as a police dispatcher meant nothing much happened that she didn't know about. She got up, leaving the swing swaying, and approached him with her arms open.

"Jack. Oh, Jack."

Her sympathy went straight to his heart and robbed him of speech. "I came as soon as I could," she said, embracing him warmly. "I'm crushed . . . and shocked . . . and just . . ." She backed off, wiping tears from her cheeks, her smile wobbly. "There aren't any words to say what a horrible thing this is."

Jack cleared his throat. "Yeah. Same here, Madge." Revealing his grief to Madge seemed natural.

She sniffed and dabbed at her eyes with a tissue. "She was so young, so beautiful."

"Yes." He'd had the same thought when he'd stood with Harlen Richard as he'd identified his wife's body. Was it only a few hours ago?

"I can't believe something like this has happened again, Jack."

He shook his head. They both knew how, but not why. "Come inside and let's see if Jeanette has any ice tea. I could use a cold drink." With his hand at her waist, he ushered her indoors.

His housekeeper bustled up, her cheeks flushed from cooking in the kitchen. He was lucky to have Jeanette Legion. From day one of his call to the church, she'd taken him under her wing and made it her mission to keep him well fed, his clothes laundered and his house neat while keeping him in the know on the essentials of life in Blood Bayou. Along with a few others, Madge and Jeanette had smoothed his transition in town from lawyer and flawed individual to a minister of God.

Jeanette studied his face now, her button-black eyes sharp on him. "Sit down, you," she said, her Cajun accent strong. "Madge, good you came, *cher*. I've got ice tea and already folks have started bringing food. A fine pound cake I took out of the oven not one hour ago, me."

Jack dropped a folder on the antique server and sat down as ordered. "You shouldn't be baking on a hot day like this, Jeanette."

"What difference does it make, I ask, winter or summer? That air-conditioner blows air so cold it's hard to tell." On her way to the kitchen, she addressed Madge. "He installed a gizmo that's so complicated I can't figure out how to turn it off, me."

"If I hadn't, you'd be working in a ninety-degree kitchen in summer and fifty degrees in winter."

She stopped and looked at him, her hands propped on her skinny hips. "When does it ever get fifty degrees in Blood Bayou, tell me that?"

Jack smiled in spite of himself. It was hard to wallow in grief while arguing with his housekeeper. Which is probably what she had in mind. "Just bring on the iced tea, Jeanette."

"Things are in an uproar in the department," Madge said after Jeanette disappeared into the kitchen. "Chief Raines was fit to be tied that his finest had botched the job when they took off after Pelham. I can't say whether he wanted them to bring him back dead or alive. This way, he's neither."

"I was with the chief at the hospital. He came to get me to accompany Harlen to officially identify Luanne. I don't think he was serious when he suggested I might want to unplug those machines keeping Pelham alive."

"He would have looked the other way if you'd agreed."

"And in my previous life, I might have taken him up on it," Jack said wryly.

"How is Harlen? How did he take it?"

"He was shaken, but he did his duty, signed the papers, and within an hour he was working on funeral arrangements with me."

"Already? When is the funeral?"

"First there'll be an autopsy as is required in a homicide. That means the funeral will be delayed until Monday or Tuesday, I expect. Once the date is set, the wake will be the day before."

"This is just so bizarre, Jack. Pelham gets out of death row and with only three days as a free man, he kills another woman in exactly the same way Stephanie was killed. It doesn't make any sense. And why Luanne?"

"Because of me," Jack said bitterly. "I'm to blame for this."

She stared at him. "What in the name of heaven are you talking about?"

"It was simple revenge because of my testimony at his trial. He spent . . . what, five years on death row. He wanted someone to blame, someone to pay, so he murdered my sister."

She was shaking her head. "No, Jack. That's too much of a stretch. Get that thought out of your head. He had to know he'd

land right back in prison, and back on death row." She paused
a moment. "Did you see the press conference on the noon news
today? Where Pelham's release was announced?"

"I did."

She was watching him closely. "Your ex-wife is very attractive."

"Yeah. She is that."

"And a consummate professional from what little I picked
up in that spot. Her mother mentions her often and I admit
thinking Diana was biased. Now I have to say her mother might
have been too modest."

"Diana has a right to be proud."

"Did you see her face when that reporter blurted out the
news of Luanne's murder? She was shocked, you could tell, but
she sure kept her cool. She's one classy lady."

"Yeah."

Madge gave him a shrewd look. "She must be feeling awful
about this."

"She swears Pelham didn't do it."

"I didn't hear her say that," Madge said, frowning.

"I got it from her in person."

Madge's eyebrows rose, but her reply was stalled as Jeanette
came in from the kitchen with a loaded tray. Jack thanked her
and waited while Jeanette served Madge a hefty slice of pound
cake and a tall glass of iced tea. He had no appetite, but Jeanette
set cake and iced tea in front of him too.

"Eat, you," she ordered before marching back to her do-
main.

Reading the interested look on Madge's face, Jack said, "Camille looked me up at the church an hour ago. She was sorry to

hear about Luanne, but claims Pelham couldn't be the killer. Everyone else in the world knows Pelham killed her, but Camille hotly denies it. She advised me to look for the real murderer."

"The real murderer?"

"We agreed to disagree," he said with a wry smile. "We're good at that."

Madge was studying him as if seeing a new and interesting side of him that he'd been careful to keep private. Everyone in the church knew that he was divorced, which to some had been a contentious issue. Somehow—he didn't know any details or who might have championed his cause—but somehow the congregation had gotten beyond that; as they'd gotten beyond the long, long list of reasons why he should have been rejected. He knew only that after the unholy mess he'd made of his life, God had a plan for him. And it was here in Blood Bayou.

Madge wiped at a wet circle on the table before looking up again. "Diana keeps promising to introduce me to Camille, but it's never happened."

"That's because Camille is not in Blood Bayou often," Jack said, knowing the reason she steered clear was to keep well out of his world.

Madge was still watching him with a certain look in her eye. "Well, now that I've had a glimpse of her, I'd really like to meet the woman who had the good sense to fall in love with you, Jack."

He sputtered in his tea and almost choked. "Good sense? You're kidding, right?"

"You mean because you made a few mistakes?"

He blotted at tea stains on his shirtfront with a napkin. "A few?"

"Okay, a lot of whopping big mistakes, but she must have seen something real and worthwhile. I bet if she spent any time getting to know you now, she would find you as irresistible as all those ladies in your congregation do."

"Yeah," Jack said, "from your mouth to God's ear."

CHAPTER **three**

CAMILLE WAS SHAKEN by the confrontation with Jack, enough so that she decided not to swing by and see her mother. Diana had been dropping not so subtle hints to Camille about Jack ever since he'd been called as pastor at her church. In fact, Camille suspected that Diana had played a major role in the church's decision to call Jack.

But tonight she just wasn't up to fending off questions her mother might ask. All she wanted now was to go home, shed her sticky clothes, sink into her tub, and let jets of water dissolve the tension of the day. Afterward, if she was still able to keep her eyes open, she'd go to bed with a good book.

What she absolutely did not want to do was to think about Jack and the emotions stirred when they talked today. But telling herself that didn't stop her thoughts. It had been so bizarre that the two of them, who'd once been everything to each other, could stand toe to toe after seven years and passionately argue without acknowledging the past they'd shared. If she hadn't tossed that sarcastic comment about his being a man of God now, they might have finished their conversation and parted as if they were total strangers.

Once at her condo, she headed upstairs to her bedroom, kicked off her shoes, and padded across to her closet, unbuttoning her blouse on the way. And what did it mean that she'd felt bad after zinging him with that nasty remark? She shouldn't feel anything. They were divorced and with good reason. Maybe God had forgiven him, but just because he wore a clerical collar—or whatever he wore on Sundays—didn't mean she forgave him. And she bet there were still a few people out there who felt the same way.

She was bending to draw water for her bath when the door-bell rang. Muttering, she grabbed a robe, thinking there weren't three people in the universe she'd open up for. But after a look through the peephole, she gave a deep sigh, unlocked the door, and opened it.

"Hi, Dad."

After kissing her cheek, he held her at arm's length and stud-ied her face. "You look tired."

She forced a smile. "I've had a stressful day."

"I heard." He looked beyond her. "Are you going to invite me in?"

She stepped back wordlessly. Carson St. James was a tall, attractive man with electric blue eyes, a wide white mustache, and a thick mane of silver hair that had once been as black as her own. Now, at sixty, he was still as trim as he'd been at forty. He looked what he was: a power player in games with big stakes. As the senior partner in a prestigious law firm and a registered lobbyist, he had his hand in many pies and he saw everything as it related to his own interests. "Looks like you've stirred up a hornet's nest," he said. "Rotten luck, your prize pupil turning on you like that."

"Dad." She sighed and pointed him to a chair. "Do me a favor and drop the subject. I've had about as much as I can take from everyone who believes Chester got out of prison, went straight back to Blood Bayou, and murdered Luanne."

"Your ex-sister-in-law," he said, making a face. "Thank God the media didn't know that. But it will come out and then you'd better be prepared to take a long vacation."

"Dr. Chapman has the same idea and he doesn't know about my ex-sister-in-law."

"What?"

Camille spread her arms wide and gave a false smile. "Good news, Dad. Since you've never approved of the Truth Project, you'll be happy to know that it's now history."

He frowned. "What do you mean it's history?"

"Dr. Chapman has pulled the plug. And he took delight in doing it, I might add."

"Pulled the plug? You mean he's canceled the program?"

"It's over, axed, dead. And I'm on a much-needed vacation as of around noon today."

"You've been fired?" He was clearly outraged.

"As good as, it seems."

"Chapman is an idiot. I'll speak to him."

"You will do no such thing. Please, Dad." The last thing she needed was her father using his considerable influence to override Chapman. Given his powerful connections, he could probably give her boss a major headache. Sadly, at this point, no one could save the Truth Project. "Promise me you won't interfere."

After a moment's thought, Carson nodded. "Actually, now that I think about it, it's probably wise to distance yourself. Let the scandal die down a bit." He brightened. "A vacation isn't a bad idea. You've been working too hard lately. A client of mine has a condo in Maui. A month there and you'll be ready to look for work in a field more suited to your credentials."

"Stop, Dad. I'm not going to Hawaii. If I skulk off and hide, it will look as if I think Chester is guilty." She went to the fridge in her tiny kitchen and took out chilled mineral water. Her father probably preferred Scotch, but she kept no alcohol in her home. It had played a large part in shattering her marriage. She held up the green bottle. "You know I don't have any Dewar's. Will this do?"

"No." He waved it away. "Are you seriously telling me you think that scum is innocent?"

She set the bottle down with a thump. "Chester is not scum. He's uneducated and mentally challenged, and before he wound up wrongfully convicted of murder, he worked long and hard at honest labor and never caused anyone a minute's trouble."

He was shaking his head, obviously exasperated. "That's not the way I heard it. You ask me, he should be on his way back to Angola."

Camille put the bottle back in the fridge. "Like Jack, I suppose you think the few facts we do know prove guilt beyond a shadow of a doubt, so I won't bother trying to change your mind, Dad."

"Wait. Wait a minute. You've talked to your ex?"

"Yes, and it was not pretty. He was in no mood to hear my condolences."

"He called you?"

"No, I went to see him."

He looked startled. "In Blood Bayou? No kidding? Has to be . . . what, five or six years since you spoke to him, right?"

"Seven. I felt I needed to express sympathy over Luanne's death. He let me know in no uncertain terms that he believes

Chester murdered Luanne out of revenge for Jack's testimony at the trial. Nothing I said made the least bit of difference. I should have saved my breath."

"I don't like agreeing with anything Jack Vermillion says, but his thinking seems pretty logical to me."

Camille rubbed her temples and thought longingly of the bath she might never get to enjoy tonight. "Things aren't always the way they seem, Dad. Why can't people wait until the facts are known?"

"What else is there to know? I don't understand why you find it so difficult to see these people realistically. They're criminals, for Pete's sake!"

It was an ongoing conflict between them. It frustrated him that she had chose to squander her excellent career potential on worthless criminals—his view of the people whose bogus convictions she'd been successful in overturning. The Truth Project emphasized problems in the justice system. That, in a nutshell, could be embarrassing to influential people. Her father's clients were among those most likely to be embarrassed.

"Speaking of Jack," he said, "what do you make of his life now? When I heard he was a preacher, you could've knocked me over with a feather."

"I imagine a lot of folks agree with you."

"Last time I saw him was at his hearing." Carson shook his head at the memory. "My son-in-law arrested for reckless endangerment. That had to be the darkest moment of my life. My daughter married to a criminal. And no amount of effort on my part at his trial kept him out of jail."

"He would have spent more than a year incarcerated if it hadn't been for your efforts, Dad. Has he ever thanked you?"

"A dozen times. But the damage was done." Carson sighed sadly. "Jack had everything going for him and he drowned it all in a whiskey bottle."

"He would agree with you, I think."

"He was a loose cannon. I should have known it, considering what he came from. His daddy was always drunk, no mother, no discipline. Doggone it! With his brains and ability, he could have been considering a run for the governorship right about now. Instead he's got a criminal record and now he's tossed away what's left of his career to pastor a rinky-dink church in a rinky-dink town. I'm still embarrassed that I didn't see his real colors before you married him."

Jack and his wasted life was the one subject certain to cause Carson to mount his soapbox. She'd heard it all a hundred times. "But all's well that end's well, as they say, Dad," she said in a bright tone. "He went his way and I went mine—in polar opposite directions."

"Hmmph!" was the extent of Carson's reply. Actually, the failure of her marriage had been far more devastating than she wanted her father to know. And although his approval of Jack as a son-in-law had been nice, she had been so in love that nothing short of an out-and-out scandal could have changed her mind. And maybe not even that. They were married a year before she realized how serious his addiction was. And neither of them ever dreamed how tragically it would all end.

"One mistake and you're turned off marriage forever, hmm?"

"I could say the same to you." She opened a kitchen cabinet and took out a jar of peanut butter. "I haven't had any dinner, Dad. Can I offer you peanut butter and crackers?"

"No, thanks." He actually shuddered as she popped a loaded saltine in her mouth. When she headed to the refrigerator for milk, he said, "Since you need to lie low for awhile, I insist that you make plans to fly to Maui. I'll make a call to get the condo opened up. You can use the time to think about a career change."

He had not heard a word she said. She wasn't surprised. He'd always tried to run her life. When had she not been forced to fight her father for every scrap of independence?

She polished off a glass of milk. "Like I said, Dad, I think I'll stick around here. I can probably find plenty to do. My closets need cleaning and organizing. My patio plants are in need of TLC. I can actually open a few of those books I've been meaning to read. Heck, I can learn to cook."

"And wait for your mother to call?"

Her mother. In spite of the fact that thirty years had passed, Carson was still as defensive about Diana as he'd been the day of their divorce.

"I don't have to hope my mother will call, Dad," she said gently. "There's probably a message on my phone as we speak since she will have heard the news on television. I haven't checked my voice mail yet. Not to be rude, but I was just about to step into the tub when you rang my doorbell."

"Knowing you, since you won't be working, I bet you'll go straight to your mother's place," he said on his way to the door. "Don't do it, Camille. Stay clear of Blood Bayou and this Chester Pelham ruckus. Let the cops handle it."

"If Chester is guilty, as everyone seems to believe," she said, "I'll be the first to demand that he face the consequences."

She reached around him and opened the door. "Drive carefully, Dad."

She watched him stride toward his big Mercedes, his Black-Berry already in his hand. He stood in the evening gloom study-ing it. He'd said what he came to say and she was now checked off his to-do list. He would be on to other things.

So why did she care? Hadn't she learned years ago that he considered her an extension of himself and that she should fall in with his choices for her life? It was crazy to think she could change years of conflict between them. She closed the door softly and leaned against it, aware that she felt nothing much except relief that he was gone.

It was so different with her mother.

She locked her front door, put away the peanut butter and saltines, and turned off all downstairs lights. With her phone in her hand on the way upstairs to her bedroom, she checked her voice mail and, sure enough, there was a message from her mother.

"I know you've had a bad day," her mother said in her soft voice. "I hoped to catch you before you turned off your phone and settled in for some well-deserved solitude. But if you want to talk, call me. I love you, honey."

Camille listened with a faint smile, grateful that Diana seemed to know and respect that she'd be desperate for peace and quiet after the horrendous events of the day. Still holding the phone, she lifted her hair off her neck and fanned herself, debating whether to call now or wait until morning. It was a no-brainer.

Before dialing the number, she adjusted the ceiling fan and her bedside lamp. Grabbing a couple of pillows, she was settled back to make the call when the doorbell rang again.

She grumbled, then climbed off the bed and headed back

downstairs, thinking her father must have forgotten something. She turned on the porch light and, rising on tiptoe, looked through the peephole and blinked with surprise. It was Jack.

What in the world?

She glanced at her robe, which was short and silky, but decent, she decided. After cinching the belt, she turned the deadbolt and opened the door.

"I guess you're surprised to see me," he said by way of a greeting.

It dawned on her that, as her mother's pastor, he might have bad news. Why else would he be here? "Is something wrong? Is it my mother?"

He was shaking his head even before the question was out. "No, no, I'm sorry. It's not your mother. I didn't think—" He stopped. "Look, can I come in? Just for a minute? I promise this won't take long."

She hesitated for a beat or two before stepping back to let him in. Broad-shouldered and towering, he seemed to fill her small foyer. He'd replaced the golf shirt and khakis with jeans and a plain white T-shirt. His hair was a bit unkempt as if he'd been dragging his fingers through it, a habit she recalled he resorted to when he was troubled.

She closed the door. "How did you find me?"

"I've always known where you lived, Camille." He glanced at her skimpy robe. "I didn't expect you to be turning in so early. I should have called first."

"I was getting ready to soak away the troubles of this horrendous day."

"I guess I'm responsible for some of that," he said. He looked beyond her to the den. "Could we go in there to talk? I'm hoping to make it less horrendous."

With a nod, she stepped past him. Jack followed, stopping in the middle of the room to take it in. "This is a nice place," he said. "Looks like you."

She imagined seeing it through his eyes. With only herself to please, she bought exactly what she wanted. There was a lot of turquoise and brown in the furniture and accessories. She'd chosen everything to complement the art on the walls, which was good stuff, original and eclectic. Most of it she'd gotten in the divorce, but she'd been the one to insist on buying it in the first place. A big, plush sofa was inviting, bought with the idea of lazing on weekends—if she ever had a weekend free enough to laze through. All in all, the room probably was a pretty accurate reflection of her personality. He was right about that.

She motioned him to the sofa, then stationed herself opposite him, perched on one of her bar stools. "So. Why are you here, Jack?"

"To apologize." When he saw her eyes narrow with suspicion, he explained. "I acted like a jerk today. The press conference had to be stressful for you, yet you took the time to drive to Blood Bayou and see me personally. It was a really decent thing to do. Kind and considerate. I want you to know that I appreciate it even though I must have sounded as if I didn't."

For a second, Camille was speechless. The old Jack would never have lowered himself to admit a mistake. Was his newfound Christianity responsible for such a turnaround in his personality? "You've lost your sister in a horrible way. Anybody would be shocked and grieving. I can only imagine what emotions I would feel." She managed a smile. "You didn't have to make a trip to Baton Rouge to tell me that. So we're cool. No apology required."

"You mean that?"

"Of course. Why wouldn't I?"

"You've refused to talk to me or see me for seven years. I wasn't sure you'd even hear me out after the way I behaved." He didn't give her a chance to reply but plowed on. "You'll never know how many times or how many ways I've tried to think how to get you to talk to me. I know you have a lot of anger. Lord knows, you're entitled. A thousand times over. But I've needed to say to you personally how I regret hurting you. How I wish I could just erase the past." He shrugged with a sort of sheepish smile. "So, finally today I had a tiny window of opportunity and I blew it."

Seeing her expression, he gave a short laugh. "You look stunned."

"I guess I am."

"Yeah. You haven't often heard me say I'm sorry, have you?"

"I didn't hear it just now," she said.

With a short laugh, he gave himself a mock blow to his head with the heel of his hand. "I'm sorry! I guess I need more practice, don't I?"

"Don't we all? Sorry seems to be the hardest word."

"Elton John," he said, smiling at the memory. "Thanks again, Camille. I'll say it again, your coming meant more than you'll ever know."

"Got it." She climbed down from the stool, a little uncertain how to react in the face of such unexpected humility from Jack, of all people. She waved a hand, like a blessing. "So now, go in peace."

He rolled his eyes, but his smile still lingered. "You have some goofy ideas about us preachers," he told her. "I'm going to have to—"

His words were lost in a sudden loud crash as glass shattered somewhere in the front of the house. Camille instantly started toward the foyer at a clip, but Jack caught her by the arm and stopped her in her tracks.

"Hold on, Camille. Let me go first."

With her on his heels, they approached the foyer, where a huge rock lay on the floor. Camille stared speechlessly. The once beautiful leaded-glass sidelight had a gaping hole in it. Broken glass was scattered over the tile floor.

"I guess your horrendous day just got worse," Jack said grimly.

She gathered herself and, fueled by righteous indignation, marched across the foyer, crunching on broken glass beneath her slippers. The dining room window faced the street. "If they're still out there, they're getting a piece of my mind! I am not letting them get away with this!"

"Wait!" Jack threw out an arm and blocked her. "You make a good target standing there. Something else might come flying through." He moved a slat of the wood blinds and cautiously looked out. Parked opposite her house under a huge oak tree was a dark SUV. The motor was running, but the headlights were off.

"Let me see," Camille slipped under Jack's arm before he could stop her and looked out just as the driver stuck his hand out the window and made an obscene gesture while chanting, "No more killers out of jail! No more killers out of jail!" The message delivered, the driver revved the engine up, dropped into gear, and took off with a wild screech of tires.

Camille's eyes had a dangerous glint. "I don't believe this! Is he crazy?"

"No, just reckless and stupid." He touched her arm. "Watch where you step. Those slippers aren't much protection against glass."

"Just look at what he's done!" She made a pained sound and crouched down to examine what used to be art. "This was an original leaded-glass inset! I paid an artist a disgusting amount of money for it."

"It's only a memory now. Careful! We need to sweep it up before you cut yourself."

She muttered something vile about vandals and Neanderthals on her way to the kitchen to get a dust pan and brush. "Should we call the cops?" she asked when she got back.

He swept the broken glass into the pan. "Absolutely. You'll need to show that you filed a report to collect on your insurance." He paused. "You do have homeowner's insurance, don't you?"

"Yes, of course."

"As for the cops, I don't know what they could do to identify that creep, but if he's hanging around and sees that you've reported it, it may give him second thoughts about trying it again tonight."

She picked up her telephone and dialed 911. "Did you happen to get the license number?" she asked, waiting for a reply.

"No. I tried, but it was too dark. He probably planned it that way, knowing we couldn't see it." While she spoke to the 911 operator, Jack dumped the broken glass in a trash bin. When she rang off, he said, "I didn't notice any other particulars that might help identify it either."

"They're on the way," she told him. Then, standing with her hands on her hips, she surveyed the damage. "That was so tacky," she complained. "And all for nothing."

He gave her a narrow look. "What do you mean?"

She shrugged, unwilling to tell him the Truth Project was canceled and see him gloat. "A few death-penalty crusaders always get fired up when someone is released from death row. I don't know why they keep protesting. We have the death penalty in this state and there's little chance of repealing it."

"But they don't usually toss a rock through your front window, do they?"

"Not until tonight." She bent to pick up the rock, but Jack stopped her. "Don't touch it. Let's leave it for the cops. It's unlikely to have much evidence on it, but we should let them try anyway."

A police unit arrived within a few minutes and the incident was written up by a bored cop in uniform. After statements were taken from Camille and Jack, his partner took a couple of photographs and bagged the rock. But their assessment of the situation was as negative as Jack's. The chances of identifying the perpetrator were slim to none.

The cop stood with his hands resting on the heavy leather belt at his waist. "These folks know how to get in, do their dirty work, and get away without getting caught. And, best guess, this one won't be back tonight." He glanced at Jack. "But I'd take precautions with the lady here anyway. With that window breached, she's pretty vulnerable."

"It's no big deal," Camille said quickly. "I'll stick some duct tape on what's left and someone from the condo complex will repair it tomorrow."

"Well, suit yourself, ma'am." He gave a curt nod to his partner and they gathered the material they'd collected and left.

When Camille closed the door behind them, she turned to find Jack standing with his hands on his hips. "He's right about you being vulnerable to another attack with that window out. You can keep mosquitoes out with duct tape, but nothing else. Is there someone you can spend the night with?"

"I'll be fine, Jack. Go, it's getting late. I was tired before, but now I'm beyond plain tired. I'm exhausted."

She could see he wanted to say more, a lot more. He dragged the fingers of one hand through his hair. "Look, hear me out and don't refuse before you even think about what I'm saying. Let me spend the night here." He held up a hand when she instantly opened her mouth. "That rock was meant to scare you. It sure scared me. Whoever it was might be back to do something worse. I'm guessing your bedroom is on the second floor. I'll sleep on the couch and be gone by daylight when you wake up."

"No. No, indeed. That is so absolutely not necessary."

"Camille. People know you're a single woman. You've hit a nerve with this case. The lock on your door is easily reached through that sidelight."

She looked at him and felt like screaming in frustration. "I could get in my car and go to Blood Bayou and spend the night with my mother."

"Fine. I'll follow you and see you get there safely."

"But I'm too tired."

"Then I'll sleep on the couch."

"What about your church? Is it okay to be spending the night with a woman even if she's your ex-wife?"

"Let me worry about that. You go up and turn on the jets in your tub. I'll be gone by daylight."

CAMILLE WOKE the next morning to the sound of a power saw. She stumbled down the stairs to find the handyman for the condo complex busily repairing the sidelight. She glanced at the couch. Empty. The blankets and pillow she'd given Jack last night were folded neatly and placed on the ottoman. He'd been as good as his word, gone by daylight.

She went into the kitchen to make a pot of coffee, after which, she told herself, she'd call her mother. She filled the decanter with water and poured it into the pot. When she reached for the coffee canister, she spotted the sticky-note with Jack's familiar bold handwriting.

C. I arranged for the handyman to repair the sidelight. You mentioned going to see your mother last night. Until things quiet down, that's a good idea. J.

Camille dropped the note in the trash. So like Jack. The whole time they'd been married, he had never given up trying to tell her what to do. She spooned ground coffee into the pot and punched the button to turn it on. While it dripped, she dialed her mother's number.

"Hello!" Her mother's voice, breathless and upbeat.

Before Camille had a chance to reply, she heard screams and what sounded like a crash. It would be the twins, Ryan and Bryan, Diana's five-year-old grandsons. "Camille, I know it's you," Diana said. "Don't hang up."

The twins were a reminder to Camille of what might have been if her marriage had succeeded. She'd longed for children when she married Jack and now wondered if she'd ever be a mom. In the background, she heard her mother mediating some kind of territorial conflict, and then a clatter as the receiver was picked up again.

"Hello again and please excuse that commotion."

"Hi, Mom."

"I'm so glad you called, Camille. I sent the twins to look for their swimsuits. They want to get into the pool."

"Is this a bad time? I can call—"

"No, no. Looking for their swimsuits will occupy them for at least five minutes. Allen and your brother left to go to Home Depot and no sooner had they left than Janet had a call from a patient who has gone into premature labor, so here I am holding the fort."

"Home Depot at eight a.m.?"

"Yes, do they ever close?"

Camille smiled. "Do Robert and Janet know how fortunate they are to have grandparents living within a ten-minute walk?"

Diana chuckled. "I think that's why they gave us tickets for that cruise last summer, don't you? Oh, no, not again. Hold on a minute." While she waited, Camille poured a cup of coffee and moved to the fridge for cream. What would it be like, she wondered, if at the end of a horrendous day, she came home to rambunctious children and a husband who was just as beat from his job? In her fantasies, it would be wonderful. But in reality, she simply didn't know.

More clatter as the receiver was picked up once again. "They're changing into swimsuits now," Diana said. "They'll spend the next couple of hours in the pool. I'm out on the deck, so I can watch them. Maybe we can talk uninterrupted for a few minutes. Or better yet, maybe Robert and Allen will show up. How long does it take to pick up a few nuts and bolts?"

"You love having them, Mom."

"True. Now," she said briskly, "I thought I might hear from you last night. I saw you blindsided by that reporter at the news conference yesterday. What a dreadful way to learn there'd been another murder here. Thank goodness, he didn't say the victim's name. Poor Luanne. I'm shocked, as is everyone. And so sorry."

"Yes, so am I. It would have been more horrible if I'd known it was Luanne. But it got worse, Mom. Dr. Chapman has canceled the Truth Project altogether."

"Oh, you can't be serious."

"It's true. And I'm to take a hike for awhile, keep a low profile, and hope that folks will forget the role the college played in releasing a killer who headed right back to his lair and killed again."

"Oh, my, I don't know where to begin. If Truth is canceled, Chapman is simply covering his backside. But what's this about you taking a hike? He didn't terminate you, did he?"

"No, I'm to learn what my new job is when I return from my quote-unquote vacation."

"Well." Her tone was brisk again. "I see this as good news and bad news. It's bad that Truth is canceled, however, I'm guessing that's a temporary panic-induced decision and will be reversed when calmer heads prevail. And the good news is that you can pack your bags and visit me for the duration."

WITHIN AN hour, Camille was on the road. She felt less stressed than yesterday. Slowing her car to a crawl passing the bayou, she looked closely, trying to spot an alligator. It was a bit of self-torture since she was scared to death of the beasts. And there it was—or was that a log? No. No log moved like that. She watched it glide smoothly across to the other side and disappear into shadow. She would frankly never get used to the sight of the primitive animals considered by townsfolk to be a normal and ordinary phenomenon. To her way of thinking, alligators were fierce, predatory, ancient creatures meant to stay hidden deep in swamps and not lazily cruising the civilized banks of a town's pretty bayou.

But there it was. Rather, there he was. Had to be a big male monster. As always, she shuddered and turned her eyes back to the road.

Her mother lived in a subdivision near the small state university where she taught piano. To get there, Camille drove past an antebellum plantation, a barn converted to an antique store, and acres upon acres of sugarcane. She'd stopped in that antique store a couple of times and been treated to an oral history of Blood Bayou by an ancient Cajun whose English was liberally sprinkled with the French patois commonly spoken. At first she'd been almost unable to understand him, but soon her ear was acclimated and she was charmed by the old gent.

Now, still on the main road, she spotted Jack's church. Today it looked pretty quiet. Maybe Saturday was his day off, she thought. And for a moment, she wondered about his sermons.

He had already honed his speaking style to perfection by the time she first met Jack at a legal conference in D.C. when she'd been in law school. To her dazzled eyes, he'd radiated confidence and charm as well as an amazing gift for keeping his audience spellbound. But at the time, thanks to her father, she believed herself immune to the force field of charismatic men.

What naïveté. Even before that conference ended she'd been half in love with Jack.

She drew up her thoughts and shot past the church. But leaving behind the ghosts in her past wasn't so easy. She'd put Jack and their ruined marriage behind her long ago, but Luanne's death had put him front and center of her life again. And last night, in her house! Maybe having that rock tossed into her foyer had temporarily deranged her.

A minute later, she pulled in her mother's driveway. Diana was out and heading for the car before Camille parked.

"Here you are and just in time for lunch. Allen and I waited so you could join us. I hope you haven't eaten a big breakfast. But even so, you'll be hungry because that was hours ago. I made—" She stopped and clamped a hand over her mouth. "I'm blathering. I'll hush, I really will. I'm just so glad you're here." She gave Camille a breathless hug. "Come inside. Allen will get your luggage."

"Hi, Mom." She felt a rush of pure, unadulterated love. Having been deprived of her mother's presence for most of her childhood, it was always a treat being with her now. "Thanks for having me. I hope I won't be in the way."

"I won't dignify that with a reply it's so ridiculous. I hope you can stay a month. A year!"

"I'll try and keep it to a few days," Camille said. "Where are the twins?"

"They had a birthday party. That's about the only thing that makes them willing to get out of the pool. Here's Allen."

Allen Fontenot was smiling a welcome as he held the door wide to let them in. Her stepfather was a tall, quiet man with salt-and-pepper hair, horn-rimmed glasses, and a bit of a stoop that made him look like a slightly absent-minded professor. He was anything but. Behind those horn-rimmed glasses, Camille often sensed he could see right through her. And maybe he could. He was a psychologist.

He gave her a warm hug and kissed her cheek. "I hope your luggage will keep because I'm starved. Your mother would only let me have a sliver of cantaloupe, while she kept nibbling because she was doing the cooking."

"I offered to let you cook," Diana said.

Allen winked at Camille. "Because she knows I can't boil water."

Camille laughed. "Lunch sounds great. I'm starved too." It was so good to be here, so different from the tension that was always present when she was with her father. She fell into step between them and they headed for the kitchen.

"WE'LL NEED to go to the wake, you know."

Camille made a sound, something between a squeak and a wince, and closed the dishwasher with a solid clunk. "No, Mom, no way. I've said how sorry I am about Luanne and, as difficult as it was, I said it to Jack in person." She punched the start button. "My duty is done. Period."

"She was your sister-in-law, Camille," Diana said gently. "Don't you feel you should pay your respects?"

"And set myself up to be attacked by the natives? These people think I'm responsible for her death. So, no, thanks."

"Is that what Jack said to you?"

"Pretty much." She found she wasn't quite ready to reveal that Jack had made the trip to Baton Rouge to apologize last night. Her mother would want to know details. Besides, he hadn't apologized for thinking her responsible for his sister's death, albeit indirectly.

Diana leaned against the counter, folding a dish towel. "Jack had just learned about his sister, Camille. He spoke out of grief and anger."

"I understand that. But Jack made crystal clear what he thinks. So if he believes that, other people are going to see it that way too." She crossed her arms over her chest. "I'm not going."

Diana hung the dish towel on a rack and gave Camille an affectionate little hug. "You'll come around, darlin'."

CHAPTER four

TWO DAYS LATER Camille, her mother, and Allen arrived at the funeral home for Luanne's wake. No matter how intensely Camille had argued, she'd failed to persuade Diana that skipping the wake wouldn't be interpreted as dishonoring her ex-sister-in-law. So, here she was.

It surprised Camille to learn that the autopsy had been completed within a day of the murder. Such things normally took much longer. She assumed the nature of the murder and the amount of press surrounding Chester Pelham's release and presumed guilt had lit a fire under the medical examiner.

The parking lot was overflowing. A huge crowd had turned out to pay their respects to Luanne. "I still think this is a bad idea, Mom," Camille said from the backseat.

"My goodness," Diana said, surveying the crowd. "There is a nice turnout. Harlen will be pleased."

Her mother talked as if the wake were a social occasion. Allen glanced back and Camille gave him an imploring look, but all she got in return was a quick thumbs-up. No help there.

Allen found an empty stall and parked the car. When Camille made no move to get out, Diana opened the door. "Now, don't worry, Camille, it's going to be fine. All you have to do is smile—you have a lovely smile—and say a sympathetic word to

Harlen and Jack, of course. Then you'll have paid your respects and show the folks here in Blood Bayou what you're made of. We don't have to stay over thirty minutes."

Camille exited and closed the door with a bang. It was going to be thirty very long minutes. Flanked by Diana on one side and her stepfather on the other, she decided she had no choice but to make the best of a bad situation. Her stomach twisted into a knot. It was getting to be a regular thing.

Once inside, they were directed to a room. A card propped on a tripod stood by the door: "Guests honoring Luanne Vermillion Richard." Bracing herself, she went with the flow.

It was indeed a nice turnout. The place was packed. Diana and Allen probably knew many of the people, as more than a few nodded friendly greetings. But to Camille's eye, their friendliness did not extend to her. What she saw was open hostility. When her mother suggested she sign the guest book, she did so quickly. The act gave her something to focus on. After she'd scribbled her name, she drew a deep breath and looked up . . . right into Jack's eyes.

He stood greeting guests beside Luanne's husband and acknowledged her with a slight nod and the arch of an eyebrow. Was that a knowing light in his dark eyes? As if they shared a secret. Which they did, she had to admit. She sighed, thinking that her life had suddenly become very complicated.

She was determined to make nice. She was not going to get into it with anyone here at Luanne's wake, no matter what was said to provoke her. So she fell in with the crowd lined up, tucking herself between her mother and Allen. If attacked, she wanted moral support.

To distract herself while inching forward, she took a minute to study the man Luanne had married. It was the first time she'd ever seen Harlen Richard and was surprised to see that he appeared older than her father, at least sixty. She knew Luanne to be thirty-three and tried to recall when Luanne had married him but drew a blank. It had been after she and Jack were divorced.

He was not a tall man and she sought for a word to describe him. Dapper, she decided, noting the statement he made in an Italian suit, dove gray shirt, and designer tie. His styled hair, a rich dark brown, was obviously dyed and his skin artificially tanned. With his wife so much younger, maybe he felt compelled to try to shave off a few years? As she got closer, she looked for signs of grief—or any emotion, but if he felt anything, it was masked with dignified cordiality as he greeted and thanked guests offering condolences.

Camille's mother introduced her. "Harlen, I don't believe you've met my daughter, Camille St. James."

"I'm so sorry for your loss, Mr. Richard."

"Thank you. But please, it's Harlen. And I feel as if I know you, Camille. Your father and I are old friends. In fact, Carson and I have collaborated in several ventures. It's good to meet you."

Camille murmured polite thanks while digesting this startling news. Her father hadn't mentioned knowing Harlen Richard. But she didn't have time to think why, as Jack was up next.

For two long beats, both were mute. She was aware of curious eyes watching from the crowd, adding awkwardness to the moment. They had not lived in Blood Bayou while they were married, but these people knew their history. Now, looking at Jack, she could see that he was going to keep up the pretence that she was simply another visitor come to pay her respects to his sister. As with Richard, nothing showed on his face, at least nothing these people would be able to read. It occurred to her that he could be thinking it might be easier on her to play it that way considering she was a stranger here. She put out a hand and he took it, his clasp warm and strong and familiar.

"Thank you for coming," he said formally, as if she truly was just one more in a line of near-strangers. But deep in his dark eyes, she thought she saw something.

Relieved not to have to pretend anything other than polite sympathy, she murmured, "I'm sorry for your loss." And quickly withdrew her hand. With so many people looking on, nothing else came to mind to say to him, and thankfully her mother relieved the awkward moment.

"Hello, Jack." Diana reached up and gave him a warm hug. "This is such a tragedy. I'm so sorry. Luanne will be missed."

"Thank you, Diana. And thanks for coming."

Not even thirty minutes and it was over.

Well, not exactly. According to Diana, they couldn't just turn around and leave without first wandering around a bit. A wake was a lovely opportunity to greet people she hadn't seen in years. So, unless she wanted to argue with her mother, Camille was forced to go with the plan.

For the next few minutes she trailed behind Diana, smiling when introduced to a few people who didn't seem outright hostile. Finally she asked her mother about a tall woman she'd noticed watching them with more than casual interest.

"That would be Madge Pichon," Diana said. "Someone you'll want to meet." She lifted a hand to beckon her over while whispering in Camille's ear. "Madge knew Luanne as well as anybody here. She also worked with Stephanie Hill."

Camille studied the approaching woman. Thin as a pole with dark, nearly black hair, she appeared to be about the same age as Diana, who had to reach up to hug her. "Madge, hello, I was hoping to see you, but not on such a sad occasion."

Madge's eyes filled. "I just can't believe it, Diana. First Stephanie and now Luanne." She touched the corner of her eye with a tissue. "And for Jack it's just terrible. He's totally alone now."

"It certainly is sad. Two young women, such violence."

Both women went silent as if puzzling over inexplicable tragedies in life. Diana then turned to Camille. "I want you to meet my daughter. Madge is an old friend, Camille."

With Madge's smile, some of the sadness in her eyes eased. She put out a hand with nails painted blood red. "Well, Diana, you certainly can't deny this child," she said. "You two could be twins."

"Give or take twenty-five years," Diana said dryly.

"Hello, nice to meet you," Camille said, wondering how to get her hand back.

"I'm so glad to finally meet you," Madge said, finally letting go with a friendly squeeze. She blotted her eyes with the tissue again and blew her nose. "Once Diana starts talking about her daughter's latest accomplishment, we've all learned to just sit back and let her go until she winds down."

"Should I be embarrassed?" Camille asked.

"Not unless you're embarrassed to be the best and brightest and most beautiful daughter God ever made."

Camille rolled her eyes. "Oh, please."

"Madge is a longtime dispatcher at the police department," Diana explained.

Instantly Camille's antennae went up. "That must be an interesting place right now."

"Another murder has certainly shaken us up," Madge said. "Until Stephanie was killed, we'd never had a murder—if you don't count barroom stabbings or shootings done in the heat of an argument, that kind of thing. To have a second one with the same MO has sent a major shock wave through the town." Her eyes filled again. "Luanne . . . it's just such a shock."

"In that case, I hope the police do a better job finding Luanne's killer than they did finding Stephanie Hill's."

"I think you can count on that," Madge said, mopping at her eyes again. "Chief Raines is determined to handle this case personally."

"And is he like everyone else, convinced that he already knows who the killer is?"

"I can't speak for him, but it does appear to be a pretty cut-and-dried case to almost everyone."

"Sad but true." Camille sent a sweeping look around the room. "All you have to do is listen to the buzz from this crowd. Their minds are made up. It's poor ol' Chester. Case closed."

Madge followed her gaze, nodding. "It looks that way, unfortunately." She paused, studying Camille thoughtfully. "I take it you don't agree with conventional wisdom."

"I like to have proof, especially when the crime is as serious as murder."

Madge took time to consider her reply. "For what it's worth, Camille, the evidence offered by the prosecution never convinced me that Chester murdered Stephanie. What convinced me was Jack's testimony. He saw Chester at the scene. It was hard to get beyond that."

"Jack was simply mistaken. We proved that. Chester was at Stephanie's house doing weekly yard maintenance that day, but it was early in the morning, long before she was murdered. The official time of death was wrong. It was decided by an inexperienced medical examiner. We found a parking ticket issued to Chester in New Orleans. So he couldn't have been in Blood Bayou when Stephanie was murdered. Which means Jack couldn't have seen him. It must have been someone he mistook for Chester."

"Is that the crux of your investigation at the Truth Project?"

"No, that's only a piece of it. And I won't bore you by going into details right now. But someone murdered Stephanie and if it wasn't Chester, then who?"

"Well, that's a scary thought."

"Isn't it. Which is why I think it's so risky for everyone in Blood Bayou to assume he murdered Luanne. Because if he didn't, that means a killer is walking the streets of your town." She stopped, shaking her head. "I'm sorry. I shouldn't be having this conversation now. It's inappropriate."

"Don't apologize," Madge said. "You make a lot of sense. BBPD was so embarrassed by Chester's exoneration that Chief Raines is determined not to make the same mistake this time."

"They should be embarrassed. Along with Chester's lawyer and the prosecutor and the judge. There's blame enough to go around." Too late, Camille realized Madge could take her criticism of the department personally. "I'm sorry, no offense intended."

"None taken," Madge said, unfazed. "Let me just say one more thing and please don't take offense. To BBPD and a few others, you're a reminder of the fiasco. It's one thing to say the things you just said to me, but I'd advise you to use discretion talking to others. Folks are riled up, they're scared. You'll find a lot of them downright hostile."

Camille was nodding before Madge finished. "Thanks for the warning, but it's not necessary. I'm done. I'm on vacation. Someone else will have to be Chester's defender this time."

"Well, that sure sounds definite," Madge said, glancing at Diana, who shrugged and said nothing.

"I mean it."

"Okay." Madge wiped her nose with a fresh tissue and tucked it into a tiny jeweled bag. Drawing a breath, she seemed to come to some conclusion in her mind. She looked at Camille. "I was friends with Luanne and I worked with Stephanie, did you know that?"

"Mom mentioned it."

"So I feel I have sort of a personal stake in all this. Stephanie and I were both dispatchers at the department. She was a good friend. I still miss her." Her voice wobbled again, but she mastered it without tearing up. "I think something was bothering her that last week before she was murdered, but when I asked her what was wrong she wouldn't tell me."

Camille frowned. "Were you questioned about that by the detectives on the case?"

"Yeah, but they treated it like girl's gossip. They had their prime suspect. They didn't look any further." She glanced up and waved to someone across the room before turning to Camille again. "I'm telling you all this just in case you get bored and decide to take a look at Stephanie's case. Or Luanne's."

"Which isn't going to happen."

"And if I can be of any help, I'd be happy to try."

She held up a hand as Camille firmly shook her head. "I

know, I know, you're done. Finished. But you never know. And Diana has my number. Just in case."

"Oh, look, Madge," Diana said, spotting an acquaintance across the room. "It's Gay Lynn, looking absolutely stunning. I do believe she's had some work done. Camille, can you circulate while we head over there?"

"Sure, absolutely." And as they made their way toward Gay Lynn, Camille peeled off in the direction of the ladies' restroom.

Inside, she took a deep breath, glad for a moment's solitude. A sofa and several comfortable chairs were grouped around a low table. Flowers—artificial and a bit dusty but flowers nonetheless—were artfully arranged in a pretty vase. And every surface had a box of tissues. It was clearly a place to escape if one needed a private moment.

Looking about, Camille felt ashamed that she hadn't shed a tear over Luanne's death, but hardly anybody in the crowd, with the exception of Madge, seemed sad either. Maybe the tone was set by Harlen Richard's emotionless demeanor and or by how remote Jack seemed. But she knew Jack was anything but unfeeling over his sister's death. Beneath that set look and his haunted eyes, he was hiding a whole host of emotions.

She thought a minute about Richard, who had been very cordial to her. In fact, he'd been more than cordial, downright friendly. Could be he was one of the few in Blood Bayou who didn't think she was responsible for Luanne's death. That would be nice. Or was his attitude a result of his connection to her father? And why hadn't Carson mentioned that he knew Harlen Richard? She couldn't wait to ask her mother a few questions about that.

A blessed ten minutes ticked by as she perched on the edge

of a chair, wondering how long she could stay holed up before she would have to go out and face—whatever. She was on her feet to leave when the door opened and a trio entered, two streaky blondes and one brunette.

She'd noticed them huddled together earlier. All three had the look of country club types, smartly "snappy casual." All were size 4; all sported tennis tans and very large diamonds that set off French manicures. Nobody looked friendly. Instead, they looked to be on a mission. When they blocked her escape at the door, she reminded herself that she was here to pay her respects, nothing more.

The tallest seemed the spokesman for the trio. "You're Camille St. James."

"That would be me," Camille said, flashing a bright smile.

"We want to talk to you."

"Were we introduced?" Camille gave what she considered a friendly shrug. "I'm terrible with names."

"I'm Michelle Maison and this is Janice Laux." Michelle gestured to the other blonde with classically beautiful features, who nodded.

"And I'm Terri Chartrain," said the petite, blue-eyed brunette. "We saw you on TV announcing that you'd let that criminal out of jail."

Camille resigned herself to a conversation that didn't promise to be friendly. "Actually, Chester is out of jail precisely because he isn't a criminal." She kept a smile on her face.

"I don't know how you can be so sure of that," Terri said, "but he's a criminal now."

"Yeah," Michelle piped up. "And another Blood Bayou person is dead. First Stephanie Hill and now Luanne."

Camille sighed. "Look, ladies—"

"She was our friend," Terri said. "She was our *dear* friend. We were in a book club together, we played tennis with her, we took trips together, we did Pilates and yoga with her. She was great."

"I'm sure you'll miss her," Camille said. "It's always—"

Janice interrupted. "And she'd gotten it together finally after Jack was called to our church. She wasn't doing all that stuff anymore. She was—"

"What Janice means," Michelle said, stopping her with a look, "is that Luanne was special to us."

"I do appreciate your affection for your friend." Camille paused as a woman opened the door, gave a quick look, and ducked back out. Camille longed to follow. She felt as if she was in a bad movie and if it hadn't been a wake, she might have laughed. "I really don't see where you're going with this," she said, still polite, but it was taking more effort now.

"Then let me put it this way," Michelle said boldly. "This is a wake for a person we cared about. We know she was once your sister-in-law, but in all the years we knew her, we never heard her mention your name. Not once."

"With all due respect," Camille said, "Jack and I have been divorced for seven years. Most of the time we were married, Luanne was in college. That doesn't mean I didn't care for her, but I'd simply lost touch as people do after a divorce." She shook her head. "But I still don't understand why you feel you need to tell me this. What am I missing here?"

"Just this," Michelle said. "We don't think it's appropriate for you to be here at all considering your role in setting up the circumstances that led to her murder."

Camille sighed inwardly, tired to death of defending her role in the Truth Project. She struggled to sound reasonable. "Ladies. I am not responsible for Luanne's death."

"We think you are!" Terri said. "You let Chester Pelham come back to Blood Bayou, didn't you?"

"You heard what I said on TV. My answer is unchanged. No one controlled what Chester did after he was exonerated. He was free to go wherever he pleased."

"And he came right back here and murdered Luanne!"

"Actually, you don't know that," Camille said gently.

"Everybody says he did it!" Terri said.

"Excuse me, but that doesn't make it so."

"Luanne is dead because you let a killer out on the street," Michelle said, stepping in as Terri looked ready to attack. "This is a wake for people who *cared* about her! And because of that, we think you show some nerve pretending you do."

"I guess that's a not so subtle request for me to leave." Camille hitched her shoulder bag a little higher, hoping to part the trio and be able to get to the door. But nobody moved.

Michelle's mouth twisted. "If the shoe fits—"

Camille's temper finally snapped. "You know what, leaving sounds like a fantastic idea to me too. So, if you'll excuse me . . ." She stuck her arm out to forge a path through them, aiming for the door, but Terri stopped her by clutching her sleeve.

"Hey!" Camille jerked free, grabbing at her purse, which slipped off her shoulder in the scuffle.

"We aren't done yet!" Terri cried.

Camille truly had had enough. "Oh, yes, you are." She faced them straight on, still struggling as the only rational person in the room. "You've ganged up on me, you've insulted me, and now you've assaulted me. I don't know about good manners in

Blood Bayou, but where I'm from, that's rude." Nobody argued, possibly because of the dangerous edge in her tone. "However, I'm going to ignore this silly episode and as soon as I possibly can, I will find the people I came with and leave." She turned on her heel, slammed a palm against the door, and on her way out ran smack into Jack.

He caught her by the shoulders. She looked up to find the corner of his mouth quirked, the closest he'd come to a smile all night. "Need any help?"

"No, I don't," she said, batting his hands off. She was breathing hard, absolutely furious. "I can handle those . . . those . . . kindergartners!"

"Come on, let's get you away from the war zone," he said. Taking her arm, he guided her down the hall toward another door, which he pushed open to usher her inside. "Melanie said you might be in trouble."

"Well, I wasn't." Now that she'd caught her breath, she reached for the neckline of her sweater and jerked it into some semblance of its original shape. "Who's Melanie?"

"The lady who peeped into the restroom and had the good sense to back out. She gave me a heads-up, but from what I heard, you gave as good as you got."

She realized that he'd taken her into a small chapel and was guiding her to a pew. Without putting up a fuss, she sat down. In spite of giving as good as she got, she was more than a little shaken by the fracas. "If those women are typical Blood Bayou females, it's plain to me how the town got its name."

Jack sat down beside her. "They're shocked and grieving over losing Luanne. They're looking to blame someone."

"Yeah, I should be getting used to that." She drew a deep

breath and looked around at the religious symbols and felt uncomfortable. "I want to go home, Jack. Have you seen my mother and Allen?"

"Yes, Diana is making the rounds greeting folks she hasn't seen in a while and Allen, as always, is patiently waiting until she's done."

"Well, I'm sorry to cut the social hour short," Camille said, "but I'm just not up for anymore abuse tonight."

"I overheard a bit of what was said, but I didn't hear what they said to provoke you."

"It was hardly original. I let a killer out on the streets and now their *dear* friend is murdered and Chester Pelham did it and it's all my fault. Oh, and the Truth Project is an abomination. They claim I had no business attending Luanne's wake and demanded that I get out. Now. Which suits me fine." She stood up abruptly. "I am so out of here."

He stayed in his seat, wearily rubbing a hand over his face before looking up at her. "You're right to be offended, Camille. Here, of all places, it was inappropriate. I'll speak to them."

"Forget it," she said, stepping out into the aisle. "I can take care of myself."

"No argument there. I can see it. But you're running into some real hostility here. They're Luanne's friends, but some of their anger might be on my behalf."

"The pastor of their church? Is that what you mean? Their protective instincts kicking in?"

"It's possible." He got to his feet slowly. "I'm really sorry. I would have stopped them if I'd known what they were up to."

"Wow, a string of apologies within a few days. I don't think I got that many the whole time we were married." She waved a hand, taking in the chapel pews and altar. "If that's what all this does, it's cool stuff, huh?"

He said nothing for a moment, but looked at her long enough to make her uncomfortable over her flip remark. It was the same icky feeling she got the day she'd taunted him about being a man of God. In the ensuing silence, she tried to come up with something, if not an apology, then *something*. But before she could, he spoke.

"You know," he said in a quiet voice, "I think it's best to end this conversation before both of us say things we won't be proud of later. So I'll just say good night. And, again, thank you for coming." He walked to the door and held it open for her. "Don't forget your purse."

CHAPTER five

SHE FELT A mix of complicated emotions as she threw herself into the back of Allen's car and snapped the seat belt into place. Jack had succeeded again in making her feel as low as a snake. But those witches who'd attacked her were partially to blame. She'd been so incensed by their assault that she hardly knew what she was saying. She'd known it was a bad idea coming to Luanne's wake. These people hated her. The town was poisonous. Tomorrow she was packing her bags and getting out.

She groaned when her cell phone rang, tempted to ignore it. But the screen read Ray Wyatt, so she answered it. "Please give me good news, Ray."

"Fresh out," he said. "I've been trying to reach you all evening. I went by your place, but your neighbor said you'd been gone for several days."

"I'm staying with my mother for a while. Why, Ray, what's up?"

"I knew you'd want to know. I've been nosing around the department trying to find out what's developing in the case against Pelham. I'm not exactly welcome there after we made them look stupid over their handling of the Stephanie Hill case, but luckily I have a pretty reliable contact."

"Pretty and female?" Camille asked. Ray was known to have a way with women.

"I never kiss and tell," he said. "The thing is, they're keeping a tight lid on this investigation, but they're all over it. They don't want to be accused of the same incompetent police work that happened with Stephanie."

"Well, that's good news. I guess we can take some credit for that," she said dryly. "Thanks for calling. If you hear anything else, just—"

"Wait. That's why I called. There is something else. They found the knife."

"Oh?"

"Yeah. You'll hate hearing this. It was at Chester's shack, hidden up in the porch rafters. A kid would have done a better job hiding it."

"Chester is a kid in some ways, Ray," she said. But she felt a miserable sense of doom. The case against Chester was building.

"The blade was clean," Wyatt said, "but it's close to impossible to remove all trace of blood where the blade is fastened to the handle. Sure enough, they got enough to type it. Of course, it's too soon for DNA. That'll take weeks."

"Wow, you must have some source over there."

He chuckled. "Yeah, it took me awhile, but I think I can rely on the info."

"Who is it, Ray?"

He laughed again. "No way, hon. If I told you, I'd have to kill you."

She was in no mood for jokes. "Do they have the blood type results?"

"Uh-huh. And it matched."

She held her breath, guessing the answer. "Matched who, Ray? Give me a name."

"Luanne. It was the same blood type as Luanne's."

THAT NIGHT she was in her pj's when her mother tapped on her bedroom door. Camille had gone straight to her room once they reached the house. The phone call from Ray Wyatt clinched her vow to leave Blood Bayou bright and early the next morning. Diana would be disappointed and would do her best to talk her out of going, but she'd had it with Blood Bayou.

"Come in, Mom."

Diana slipped inside, but stayed in the doorway, making no move to cross the room. "I guessed you would be packing."

"I'll do it tomorrow. After that fiasco, I'm too mad to do anything but sit here and steam."

"And you're worried over what Ray Wyatt told you."

"Another nail in Chester's coffin. Poor guy, if he comes out of that coma, he might wish he hadn't."

Diana hesitated, but after a moment seemed to make up her mind. She walked to the bed and sat down beside Camille. "How can I talk you out of it, darlin'? What words can I say?"

Camille steeled herself to resist her mother. She'd been so deprived of Diana's presence in her childhood that she treasured every minute she had with her now. But this was different. After what she'd just experienced, she'd have to be a masochist to stay in this miserable town.

"I don't want to defend the Truth Project anymore, Mom. I don't want to defend Chester Pelham anymore. I don't want to

defend *myself* to these people anymore. It's plain to see that their
minds are made up. To them Chester is a killer. Even though I
proved he didn't kill Stephanie, everyone's convinced he killed Luanne. No matter how I argue, they can't see beyond the fact that
another one of their own has been murdered. And they see me as
the person who paved the way for the killer. No, I'm leaving."

Camille gaze went to their reflections in the mirror, both so
alike, the same green eyes, the same dark, curly hair. The only
difference was at Diana's temple where a dramatic silver streak
had recently appeared. Camille hoped she inherited that too, but
she was willing to wait a couple of decades for it.

"Do you really believe he's innocent?" Diana asked.

She met her mother's eyes. "I do. Well, I did at first. Now,
with all that's happened, the bloody clothes, the knife with her
blood type on it, his being seen around the time of the murder . . ." She gave a bleak shrug. "I'm the only person who even
has a seed of doubt."

"But you do? In spite of all you just said?"

"Mom, he just isn't a violent man. I can't get beyond that.
Please don't think I'm stupid or naïve, but he's too sweet to be a
killer. He doesn't even kill snakes or spiders or any other crawly
things he finds in the yards he maintains. He relocates them."

"Some serial killers love animals. They cherish their dogs.
Or cats."

"I know."

"So I take it you've decided to go back to your condo and let
the police handle the case?"

Camille gave a short, humorless laugh. "Whoa, that's a scary
thought." In more ways than one. But she didn't want her mother
to know about the rock thrown through her window.

"Seems to me, from what you say, that the case is close to being wrapped up. If Pelham survives in the hospital, he's sure to be back on death row. Barring any hitches in the investigation."

"That's exactly what'll happen and it just makes me sick!" Agitated now, Camille sprang from the bed and began to pace back and forth in front of Diana.

"But you have your doubts?"

She stopped. "I do. Sort of. Anybody would, considering the evidence—which is all circumstantial at this point. But in spite of that, deep in my heart I find it so hard to believe Chester is a killer. The Truth Project demolished the case against him for the murder of Stephanie Hill." She looked at her mother. "Why does everyone deny that fact? I keep trying to tell them. By sticking their heads in a hole and fixating on Chester, they run the risk of leaving the real killer free to kill again."

"But you're washing your hands of it. You're going home."

"Well . . ."

"You could consider putting your excellent investigative ability to work and looking into Luanne's murder yourself. You may come up with other persons of interest and then you'd have the last laugh."

"If they didn't run me out of town on a rail first."

"And you'd have at least one ally—not counting Allen and me, of course."

"Who?"

"Madge," Diana said. "And she would be your ace in the hole, darlin'. She knows some stuff in this town."

With a quizzical look at her mother, Camille stared at the floor for a moment, then smiled. "How do you do that?"

Diana blinked innocently. "Do what?"

"I'm glad I didn't spend any time packing up," she said as she sat on the bed again. "I'd just have to unpack."

Diana clasped her hands together at her chest and grinned. "You'll stay a little longer?"

"A little. But I'm steering clear of the country club. Those gals have claws!"

Still smiling, Diana crossed her legs as if settling in for an even longer chat. "So, enough of Chester Pelham. Let's change the subject."

Camille gave her a wary look. "To what? Or should I say to whom?"

"Let's talk about Jack. How are you two getting along?"

Getting along. She fell back on the bed and looked up at the ceiling. Her mother did have a knack for understatement. She drew a deep breath. "Now, there's a question, Mom. We aren't getting along. We've just called a temporary truce and that only because of Luanne's death. As you put it, I'm bound to do the decent thing."

"I'm sure he appreciates your thoughtfulness."

"Mom." She looked at Diana. "He's like everyone else. He blames me for letting a killer out on the street who murdered his sister."

"He'll come around on that," Diana said confidently. "Right now, he's too caught up in his grief. What I meant was how do you feel seeing him again?"

Coming from anyone else on the planet, Camille would consider such a question too personal and nobody's business but her own. But not coming from her mother.

She sat up. "Oh, gosh, let me count the ways. I feel awkward and confused and resentful and angry and suspicious and—"

"Suspicious?"

"Yes! Jack, a minister? It's almost ludicrous, considering."

"You don't think people can change?"

"Not to the extent that he claims to have changed. Do you realize that in the last year and a half we were married I hardly saw Jack sober? He was out of it so much that I didn't have a husband. And I can't count the many times he embarrassed me in front of people. Or he embarrassed himself at work and it got back to me. I don't know how he managed to keep his career on track. Sometimes I wonder if the accident hadn't happened, if he'd still be working and hiding his addiction; if he'd still be a menace to other people."

"Yes, it's amazing how he managed to function at such a high level while drinking," Diana said. "I admit I held my breath waiting for disaster."

"He may have managed to forget what he did, but I can't. I can still see it, Jack backing out of our driveway in a drunken rage, striking down a talented young person with a bright future. And one of the students that I was mentoring too! That boy is now a quadriplegic. Whatever contribution he might have made to the world is wiped out, gone, vanished."

"As you say, Jack left a lot of damage in the wake of his journey to sobriety. And no matter what he's made of his life since, he must live with that on his conscience." She saw Camille's skeptical look. "You don't think Jack lives with the weight of that every minute of every day and night of his life?"

Camille set her mouth in a stubborn line. "I don't know, but I think he should."

"I take it you doubt the sincerity of his conversion and his call to the ministry?"

"Well . . . duh." She made a disdainful sound. "I think he's found a slick way to buy forgiveness. Or respectability. It's pretty difficult to put a positive spin on your résumé if you've spent a year in prison. He had to do something to appear halfway honorable again. Maybe preaching was his only option."

Diana reached over and gave her a hug. "You'll have to allow him to tell you his story someday."

"Huh! When hell freezes over."

JACK HAD a conflict on the time Harlen chose for Luanne's funeral the next day. He agreed, though it fell at the hour when he should be at Sojourner House. But Harlen, like everyone else, knew nothing of Jack's commitment to the extended care facility. So he'd arranged the services without consulting Jack, as was his right, Jack told himself.

Luanne's funeral service had been one of the most difficult tasks he'd ever performed as a minister. It was still a blur. Luanne had been a troubled soul, but for her to die so brutally made the usual message he delivered at funerals sound empty and meaningless. Given a choice, he would have asked someone else to conduct the service, but Harlen had insisted that Luanne would never want anyone but Jack to do it.

Consequently, he was late arriving at Sojourner. From his first visit four years ago, he'd tried to arrange his schedule so that he never missed. Usually, he stopped in to spend a few minutes with different patients, and he usually wound up with Ron. But today, after a quick peek, he found the boy's room empty. At this hour, the patients were already at supper. The administrator, a stickler about maintaining the patients' schedules, made no allowance for glitches in visitors' lives. That included funerals.

He heard the rowdy clamor long before he reached the dining hall—laughter and babbling and whining and strange shrieks—a cacophony of human sounds coming from people who weren't burdened with doing the polite thing as they dined, if you could call the act of consuming food as best they could dining.

He spotted Ron right away, struggling to eat what had been placed in front of him on a tray. Much of it was scattered around his plate. In spite of intense effort in the two years he'd been at Sojourner and Jack's attempts to reacquaint him with the purpose of a spoon, he just couldn't do it.

As Jack walked over and Ron spotted him, the boy yelled with delight and bounced in his wheelchair. "How're you doing, Ronnie?" Jack said, managing to connect with the boy's awkward high five.

He listened, smiling, as Ron released a babble of excited sound, nodding and gesturing, trying to articulate some idea, some thought that nobody could possibly translate.

"Yeah, how 'bout them Tigers?" Jack replied as if he did understand. Ron was an avid LSU fan and might well have played for the famed college team but for the drunk driving accident that had resulted in brain damage. The driver, Ron's father, and his mother, had died in the accident.

Jack picked up a spoon, loaded it with mashed potatoes, helped Ron get his fingers around the handle, and then guided it to the boy's mouth. "So, they treating you okay around here?"

Ron nodded vigorously and smiled a big goofy grin.

"Let me see you pick up that spoon, Ron." Jack positioned the spoon at his hand. And because he wanted to please Jack, the boy struggled to comply.

"Come on, you can do it," Jack coaxed. But Ron couldn't do it. Picking up a spoon was a skill simply beyond his damaged brain to perform.

Rehabilitation at Sojourner House was effective in many cases, but in spite of Jack's efforts to coach him, Ron wouldn't be one of those to graduate and live a nearly normal life. And neither would David Bergeron, the young law student whose life he'd destroyed seven years ago. Jack's requests to see David weren't always approved. He had no family except his grandmother and, in spite of the incredible fact that David and Jack had a solid relationship now, she wasn't as forgiving. And who could blame her?

"We almost gave you up tonight, Reverend."

Jack turned to find Angela Berthelot behind his chair. "You were almost right," he said to the administrator. "How're things going around here?"

She waved a hand over the rowdy group. "As you see." She paused, studying him shrewdly. "How are you doing?"

"I'm okay."

"I was so sorry to hear about your sister." She pulled out a chair and sat down. "I intended to attend the funeral today, but we had a little emergency."

Jack frowned. "What happened? Could I have helped?"

She smiled. "It wasn't a legal problem or a spiritual one. The air conditioner quit during the night."

"I've been expecting it." Without AC, especially at night, it would have been miserable, but to Jack, it seemed cool now. "What did you do?"

"I called a repairman, Jack," she said with irony. "And fortunately, he was able to crank it up again."

"One of these days," he said grimly, "no one will be able to crank it up again, Angela. You need new equipment."

"My thought exactly, then I looked at the budget. Somehow I just couldn't find an extra twenty big ones."

"There has to be a way. How about a fund-raiser? We could invite—"

She touched his arm before he finished. "You mean, as in a wine-and-cheese, black-tie affair to generate tons of money? That was in your other life, Jack. This isn't a country club or a museum. We can't even assess the patients for an extra hundred dollars. Most of them—or their families—don't have enough income for their upkeep here in the first place." She sighed. "We'll manage as we always have. When it quits for good, something will turn up. Some good soul will write me a check."

"I'm going to write you one right now," he said. "My checkbook—"

She tightened her hold on his arm to keep him from rising. "No, you do enough. God knows, you do enough. I'm going to talk to the board members."

He made a face. "We both know they'll hem and haw and come up with ten reasons why there isn't enough money."

"Most of the time there isn't."

"I can appeal to my congregation."

"And let the cat out of the bag? You've been coming here every week for four years and so far your congregation is clueless."

He didn't feel comfortable letting his parishioners know about his commitment to Sojourner. To some of them—those church members who were most judgmental—it might appear self-serving that he spent time with youngsters who were in the

same boat as David Bergeron. And some would never believe he
was sincere. So he'd rather not have to explain himself.

He handed Ron's tray to an orderly. "Air-conditioning is as
necessary here as the roof or the kitchen," he told Angela. "I'll
think of something. Give me a little time."

He stood up and moved behind Ron's chair. "Meanwhile,
the next time the board meets, be sure and shut down the AC.
The best way to change their thinking is to spend an hour or two
trapped inside the building in August when the temp is in the
upper nineties. They'll come around."

She laughed, rising from her chair. "That's not a bad idea."

"And if it doesn't work, you'll let me know?"

"Only as a last resort." She hesitated, then fell in step beside him. "David asked that you stop in today. Do you have the
time?"

"Of course. Absolutely." He maneuvered Ron's chair over an
uneven tile. "How is he today?"

Her features somber now, she shook her head sadly. "To tell
the truth, Jack, I don't think he'll make it much longer." She saw
the look on his face and squeezed his arm in sympathy. "Don't,
Jack. His kidneys are failing, but not because of the accident.
We both know it's genetic. He was born with this condition. It
would have cut his life short no matter what."

"Yeah, but who knows how many years he would have had a
healthy body if he hadn't had the bad luck to be in my driveway
that day."

They stopped at Ron's room; Jack looked beyond Angela to
the elevator. "Has his grandmother been in today?"

"She spent most of the morning with him."

"She knows he asked to see me? She's okay with that?"

Angela smiled. "It's been a while since she objected to you visiting David. Here, let me get an orderly to settle Ron back in his room." She brushed at his hands and took his place behind the wheelchair. "Spend twenty or thirty minutes with him. As weak as he is, that's about all he can handle. But it'll be the highlight of his day."

Angela's smile faded as she watched Jack make his way down the hall toward David Bergeron's room. Penance, she thought, for one reckless moment, and consequences to both Jack and David that would last a lifetime.

CAMILLE HAD attended Luanne's funeral alone, slipping into a rear pew of the church and leaving a minute or so before the end of the service. She hadn't wanted to take a chance on another awkward confrontation. She'd found herself tearing up as she listened to Jack's message and wondered at his strength in being able to conduct this final good-bye for his sister. It struck her that the man who spoke so eloquently definitely wasn't the man she had divorced seven years ago. She was intrigued and recalled her mother's remark. Maybe it would be interesting to hear how he'd managed to turn his life around.

But today she had other fish to fry.

An hour later she was at her father's office in downtown New Orleans. Carson was on the phone. He motioned her to a chair while he concluded his conversation. That done, he rose and came around to give her a kiss on top of her head.

"I was going to call you today," he said. "I'm glad to see you've wrapped up the visit with your mother. I've been talking to a couple of people about adding you to their practice."

"Dad—"

"Of course, they're located here, so you'd have to sell your Baton Rouge condo, but it's in a great location so I don't think you'd have a problem. And wait'll you hear the starting salary. It's more than twice what you're making at the university."

She put up a hand to stop him. "I wish you'd grant me the courtesy of asking before you do these things, Dad. I'm not interested in going to work for your friends."

He gave her a long, puzzled look. "I'm trying to understand how a daughter of mine could be so obstinate. Do you realize what an opportunity like this would mean to anybody else?"

"No offense, Dad, but please find someone who will appreciate that opportunity and stop trying to run my life." She sighed. "I hoped you would have learned that about me by now."

"I'll never give up. I live for the day when you come to your senses."

She almost laughed. "Okay. So now that we have that behind us, here's why I came. Luanne Richard's funeral was today." She watched him as she added, "I thought you might be there."

He frowned and moved to stand in front of a full-length plate-glass window. With the glare of sunshine behind him, it was hard to see his face. "Why would I?"

"Out of courtesy to her husband, your good friend," she said deliberately. "Why didn't you tell me you knew Harlen Richard?"

"Didn't I?" Carson turned and adjusted the blinds. "I know a lot of people, honey."

"But according to Richard, you two have collaborated on quite a few business ventures."

"How is it that you've been in conversation with Harlen? Isn't he caught up in settling his wife's affairs?"

"He told me as I went through the receiving line at Luanne's wake."

"You went to the wake? That surprises me."

"Yes. And I was embarrassed, Dad. He made it sound as though you were not only business partners but pretty good friends."

"He exaggerates. That is to say, we do business together, but that's the extent of it. I wouldn't call him a good friend."

Her father's wiliness was irritating, but she was gifted with a few of those same genes herself. She wasn't going to let him dismiss her questions without first getting a few answers. "Tell me what kind of business you are in together."

As he moved away from the window to go to his desk, she saw that he was smiling. "Ah, now you sound like a real lawyer."

"And I'd like a real answer."

He waved a hand. "Oh, we're 'collaborating,' to use your word, in a venture in the state capital. It's no big deal. I managed to acquire the property and his company is the building contractor."

"And that's it?"

"More or less."

It didn't sound like the kind of project Carson would have kept quiet about. She decided to take another tack. "How well do you know Harlen Richard, Dad? Personally, I mean. Do you have a gut feeling about him as an individual, about his character?"

"What kind of question is that?"

"Pretty straightforward, I thought. Have you ever been out socially with Richard when Luanne was with him?"

"Sure, several times. And before I answer any more questions, I want to know what you're getting at."

"Do you know the first rule of any homicide investigation?"

He shrugged. "Secure the crime scene, I guess."

"Besides that. You try to figure out why a person would have been murdered. And if possible, you zero in on a suspect."

Now he had a wary look on his face. "Go on."

"First person the cops look at is the victim's spouse."

Carson sat straight up and gave her a ferocious frown. "Oh, come on! If you're thinking Harlen—" He stopped. "It's ridiculous! You can't be serious."

"I didn't say I thought Richard murdered Luanne," she said patiently, "although someone did. I'm just trying to piece together information about him. About their relationship. Since you know him, I thought it reasonable to start with you."

"Camille, tell me you aren't poking and prying into this case on your own like you did with the Stephanie Hill thing. Because everyone knows who murdered Luanne and it wasn't Harlen."

"It wasn't me poking and prying into Stephanie's murder, it was the Truth Project."

"Which is defunct, in case you've forgotten. I mean it, Camille. I don't want you involved in this thing. You let the cops in Blood Bayou take care of cop business. I want you to go home, put together a new résumé and get on with your life. You hear me, girl?"

"Do you have anything else planned with Richard?"

Carson swore and hit his desk with the flat of his hand. "As your father, I'm telling you to butt out, Camille."

"I heard you, Dad, but I'm still asking."

Furious with her, he waited a moment before replying. "I always have plans and Harlen might be included in some of them. Or then again, he might not. There, are you satisfied?"

"Hardly. But I can see you aren't going to tell me much more. It just made me curious that you didn't reveal your connection when we discussed Luanne's murder. I wondered if the thought of Richard doing it occurred to you too."

"It most certainly did not! And I'm curious about why you needed to go to a wake where you were sure to cause a stir. I bet that's what happened, isn't it?"

"I was not the most popular guest." He would probably say I told you so if he knew what had actually happened. She stood up and moved to the door. "Before I go, I'll ask once more. Can you tell me anything about the Richard marriage? Did he ever say anything—do anything—that seemed out of line to you?"

"No."

She held his gaze straight on until he huffed and looked away. "Harlen Richard is not a killer."

She pulled out her car keys. "I need to go, Dad. I want to get across the bridge before rush hour starts." She was almost to the door when he stopped her.

"Wait. You aren't heading back to Blood Bayou, are you?"

"I'm still visiting with my mother." She gave him a wicked smile. "I'll tell her you said hello."

"Instead of visiting with Diana, you should be thinking about your next career move."

" 'Bye, Dad."

CHAPTER SIX

"HERE, MY TREAT." Camille signaled to the server as an iced latte was passed to Madge Pichon at the local coffee shop.

Madge smiled. "Is this a bribe?"

"You bet." Camille gave her credit card to the server. "Besides my mother and Allen, it's like pulling teeth trying to get folks around here to even speak to me, so for the sake of a little civilized conversation, I'm happy to buy your caffeine fix for the day."

"That bad, huh?"

"No matter where I go—the grocery store, the mall, the library—I'm like Typhoid Mary in this town."

"And you want to talk about what?"

"Luanne's murder." Camille signed the credit card slip and tucked the card back into her wallet. "But so far I don't know any more than I did at the wake."

"Here, let's get out of the traffic." Madge steered her to a corner table blocked from view of other customers by a display of gourmet coffees and fancy insulated cups. She took a long drink of latte and, with a sigh, closed her eyes to savor the taste. "Hmm, that is heavenly. So, you've decided to do a little investigating on your own. I thought you nixed that idea."

"I'm a glutton for punishment, I guess." Camille took a sip

of her drink. "Which doesn't matter because I may as well be invisible. People see me coming and they run the other way."

"Which wouldn't be possible if you were invisible." Madge studied her face for a minute. "Could be they're doing you a favor, Camille. To use your own words, if what you believe is true and Chester didn't kill Luanne, the real killer is walking around and probably aware of what you're doing. It could be risky."

Hearing that, Camille saw her best chance for an inside source slipping away. "So I guess that offer you made to help is off the table."

Madge touched her lips with a paper napkin. "You're sure you want to do this?" At Camille's nod, she gave a resigned sigh. "I sure hope I won't regret it. Or that I ruin my friendship with your mom."

Camille made a zip motion across her lips. "I won't tell."

"So, let's hear what you've discovered so far."

Camille felt like hugging her. She scooted her chair a little closer. "Here's what I've got: Luanne married Harlen four years ago; he was sixty, she was twenty-nine." She stopped, waited.

"That's it?" Madge said. "You could have found that out from records in the courthouse."

"That, so far, is my only source except for eavesdropping. I overheard someone at the wake saying Luanne's job right out of college was working in one of Harlen's businesses in New Orleans. I'm thinking that has to be when their relationship began."

"True."

"But did she marry him for money? He probably has pots of it."

"Not really. I mean, he is rich, but I don't think Luanne married him for that reason." Madge's red nails did a thoughtful rat-a-tat on the table. "Here's my take on it and I know this sounds like so much psychobabble, but in Luanne's case, it fits. She spent her life looking for a father in all the wrong places. Then along comes Harlen, who fit the bill. And what he wanted was a beautiful wife to display to the world. It was a match made in heaven."

"So they were happy?"

"I didn't say that. I meant the circumstances that brought them together worked to the satisfaction of both."

"So they weren't happy?"

"I didn't say that either." Madge studied her nails thoughtfully. "Luanne and I worked out together at the gym and sometimes I felt something was seriously wrong, but she'd had problems before."

"Drugs?"

"Not so much." She turned her face toward the front window for a long moment, then said, "You were married to Jack when Luanne was in college, so you must have known she was troubled."

Troubled was putting it mildly. Many times Luanne and Jack had fought fiercely over what he considered her scandalous behavior, but with his own problems, he didn't have much credibility when he lectured her. Camille sought for words that wouldn't seem harsh or judgmental. "Jack worried that she had a tendency to make bad choices," she said carefully.

"As in her sex life," Madge said, looking at her for confirmation. "Good, I'm glad I don't have to worry over revealing things about someone who can't defend herself. But yes, she—that is,

I know she seemed to have—encounters with men, sometimes total strangers."

"Did that happen even after she was married?"

"I think she was bored, Camille. For the most part, Harlen neglected her until he needed her. I know for a fact that he liked parading her around at big events, social and political. She looked good on his arm. She really was a beautiful woman." She took another sip of her latte. "That was probably why she'd get restless every now and then and have a little fling, you know? It was meaningless, at least she claimed it was, but—"

"But dangerous?"

"Yeah. And I told her so . . . frequently. Working at the police department, I knew firsthand the consequences when girls—women—engaged in that kind of thing." Madge shook her head, frowning. "It was as if she couldn't help herself."

"Did Harlen know?"

Her shoulders lifted in a who-knows shrug. "If he did, she never told me."

A promiscuous wife might drive some men to violence. But murder? Camille decided to probe a little deeper, but before she could ask, Terri Chartrain stopped at the table.

"Hello, Ms. St. James."

Camille forced a smile and hoped being in public would prevent another stinging attack from the petite brunette who'd invited her to leave town. "Hello, Ms. Chartrain." Clearly the woman didn't think Camille meant it when she was told not to come within ten feet of her again or else.

Madge must have read the look on her face because she hurriedly spoke. "Terri, you're looking fresh and cool on such a hot day. How's everything?"

"Fine," Terri snapped, her eyes locked on Camille. "I thought you'd be back at your university looking to free another criminal, Ms. St. James."

"Actually, I'm on vacation, Ms. Chartrain."

Terri's lips thinned to a bloodless line. "So you don't plan to leave us."

"Not in the foreseeable future, sorry," Camille quipped. "In fact, I'm having such a good time enjoying Blood Bayou hospitality that I'm thinking of extending my stay."

"Hey, look who's here!" Madge half rose from her chair and waved at Ray Wyatt making his way toward them carrying iced tea. She smiled brightly at Terri. "Join us, hon, or let Ray have that chair you're not using."

Terri made a play of looking at her watch. "I've got a committee meeting in ten minutes." With a last hard look at Camille, she left.

"Hi, Ray." Camille spoke between her teeth.

He grinned. "I don't know if it's safe to sit with you two. That little lady looked ready to claw some eyes out." Drawing up a chair, he gave Camille a knowing look. "What have you been up to?"

She threw up her hands. "Nothing! Really. At least, nothing to warrant her bad manners." She related to Madge and Ray the confrontation in the ladies' room at the wake. "I honestly think she may start a petition naming me a nuisance, sort of like a litterbug or someone who parks illegally in handicapped spots, then she'll be the one to escort me out to the city limits."

"Here's what your star student's been up to," Madge said to Wyatt. "She's been asking questions around town about Luanne, ticking off the locals."

Wyatt gazed at Camille's face over his cup. "Have you learned anything interesting?"

"Nothing that should irritate Terri," she said.

"Well, not yet." Madge dabbed at her lips with a napkin. "But maybe she's afraid you may discover something."

"About her personally?" Camille was quick to pick up innuendo. "Like what?"

"Everyone has secrets, Camille." Madge finished off her latte and squashed the cup. "Isn't that so, Ray?"

"After fifteen years in homicide, you need to ask?"

Camille resolved to ask a lot, but later. Now she looked at them both. "Have you two met before?"

"Sure."

"Yeah."

Both spoke at once, then Ray graciously deferred to Madge. "Ray has known some of the guys on the force for years. You also have relatives here, don't you, Ray?"

"Yeah, one or two."

"Plus, when representing the Truth Project digging into Stephanie's murder, he was a pretty constant presence at the station." Madge gave Camille a knowing look. "But after exposing a few of the department's shortcomings in that case, you could say he sort of wore out his welcome."

"Ouch," said Camille.

But Madge's smile seemed friendly enough when she turned back to Ray. "This time I bet you're here for the fishing rodeo, right?"

"Staying for a few days with Bennie, my brother-in-law," he said. "He took the trophy for a big grouper last year, but I've got new gear and a guide who swears he knows where the granddaddy of all groupers hides. And for what he's charging, he'd better come through."

"This is serious business," Madge explained to Camille.

"You better believe it," Ray said.

Camille gave him a stern look. "Is a fishing rodeo more important than finding Luanne's killer?"

Wyatt leaned back and crossed his long legs at the ankles. "Whoa, she's on a tear," he said to Madge. "I guess my timing's good. Maybe I could ease up a little on chasing that grouper and devote myself to keeping Camille out of trouble."

"Uh-huh," Madge said, collecting her cup, napkin, and stirrer. "And maybe you'll have more luck than Jack. He claims trying to head Camille off once she's on a scent is like banging your head against a brick wall."

Wyatt's gaze was fixed on Camille's stubborn expression. "Interesting."

Madge rose to her feet. "So I'll let Camille fill you in. I'm late for an appointment to get my nails refilled. See you, hon."

Ray waited until she was out of earshot before saying to Camille, "So, like the lady says, fill me in. What's happening?"

At last, a person who wouldn't tell her all the reasons why she shouldn't be poking and prying into the mystery of who killed Luanne Richard. Lowering her voice, she moved closer to him and began talking.

THAT NIGHT Camille went with her mother to a piano recital of Diana's younger students. One of Camille's deepest regrets was that she hadn't learned to play the piano. Had she grown up with Diana rather than Carson, she surely would have.

The recital was great fun even though she had to sit alone. Allen begged off, telling Diana that he had a backlog of patient files needing attention. The kids' talents ranged from the awful to the very awesome. Camille found herself laughing at the antics of the boys, cringing in sympathy when a little girl flubbed up and ran from the stage crying. Next she teared up as her mother and a child with exceptional talent played a duet. If she had a child, her mother could teach him to play the piano. It was a lovely thought.

"Why didn't you force Dad to enroll me in piano lessons?" Camille asked as they drove home.

Her mother's lips curved in a smile. "Me? Force Carson to do anything? Are we talking about the same man?" She reached over and patted Camille's knee. "No, darlin', it was all I could manage to persuade him to let me see you now and then. Piano lessons were out of the question."

"He didn't want me to do anything that reminded him of you, Mom."

"Probably. Sadly."

She gave her mother a quick look before turning her gaze back to the road. "I don't understand how you aren't just boiling over with anger at him. Yet you never say a word against him. He sure said plenty against you."

Diana laughed but without humor. "You should have heard me in those first few years. I ranted and raved and cursed and stormed. I'm ashamed to admit that I fantasized about boiling him in oil. It didn't do any good, of course, and eventually I came to accept the inevitable. As he knew I would."

"When did that happen? I mean, when did you learn acceptance?"

"After I turned it all over to God."

Camille waited a long minute deciding whether to follow up on that. But she was curious. "What does that mean, Mom, turning it all over to God? Dad literally stole your daughter, he did his best to sully your reputation by accusing you of having an affair, he caused severe damage to your career, and you just sat down and had a talk with God, who told you . . . what?"

Diana sat for a minute thinking. "God has a plan for every person's life, Camille. Yours, mine, Jack's, everyone's. And everything happens according to His plan. We like to think that means He will shield us from all harm or pain. But God doesn't promise that. What He promises is to be with us during the storms that life inevitably brings. When I realized that, and accepted it, I was able to find the strength to build a new life." She smiled at Camille. "You should try it sometime. It works."

Turn her anger at Jack over to God when it was Jack's behavior that destroyed their marriage? Turn over the unhappiness she felt after years of being deprived of a mother? It would be nice not to have those ugly emotions rear their heads so often. And just for a fleeting moment, Camille considered asking how one did that, but shied away and went in another direction.

"Can I ask you a personal question, Mom?"

Again, Diana didn't reply immediately. "You can ask, but I don't promise to answer."

"I've always wondered why you married Dad. You two are so unsuited. I mean, I love Dad, but he's domineering and controlling and so driven. He had little time for me. It must have been the same for you. You, on the other hand, have a warm and outgoing personality. You're openly affectionate and he's just the opposite. If you did have an affair, I can understand why. But didn't you know how he was before you married him?"

"Don't you think I asked myself that question a million times? I was in love. And love truly is blind. I was mesmerized by the sheer power of his personality, his bigger-than-life persona. And I didn't have an affair."

"I wasn't hinting to know that, Mom."

Diana waved a hand, but her gaze was fixed straight ahead. "Carson accused me of having an affair with Allen, but I wasn't. Allen was a very good friend but not in a romantic sense, not then. He was always there for me, not like Carson, who was frequently absent because of business commitments, travel and such. Then one evening while I was setting up for a recital with Allen's help, Carson appeared unexpectedly. I'd just learned that one of my young students had drowned while on a vacation in Hawaii. I was crushed and grief-stricken. Allen was comforting me. His arms were around me and . . . and Carson . . ."

She drew in a shaky breath. "Carson would not believe it was innocent. He filed for a divorce the very next day."

"Oh, Mom." Camille was stopped at a red light. Picking up her mother's hand, she brought it to her cheek lovingly. "I'm so sorry. It must have been so hurtful for you."

"The divorce and being asked to resign from the university were nothing compared to giving up my only child," Diana said, showing the first hint of bitterness. "That was excruciating."

Camille drove silently for another mile or so, mulling it all over. "Think of the consequences. Dad let me grow up thinking you'd been unfaithful. And you know how kids are, I imagined I was somehow to blame, that because you'd given me up, you didn't love me."

When Diana made a wordless sound, Camille went on, "When I got into my early teens, that's the reason I stopped going to see you. It was my decision. Only later did I realize Dad had orchestrated the whole thing." She struck the steering wheel with her fist. "How could he, Mom?"

"Long ago, I gave up trying to figure out why Carson does anything. And I'm wondering whether I should have told you all this now. It's so much water under the bridge, Camille. And my life with Allen has been wonderfully happy and fulfilling."

"When you married Allen, Dad must have been convinced that his initial suspicions were true: that you were having an affair."

"Probably. But by then, I didn't care a snap what Carson thought. And Allen was everything your father wasn't. Besides giving me Robert, he helped me cope with the pain of Carson's rejection and the feeling that I'd failed. But I don't have to tell you about the trauma of divorce. You've experienced it first-hand." She stopped. "I'm sorry, here I am going on and on when I should just hush."

"Please don't stop, Mom. I need to hear this."

"Well, by way of full disclosure, there is just one more thing you should know," she said in a tone rich with irony. "Allen claims Carson had reason to suspect an affair because he saw in Allen what I didn't: that even then Allen was in love with me."

"Was it true?"

"Yes. I, of course, hadn't a clue. And Allen's code of honor would never have allowed him to speak of his love as long as I was a married woman."

"Aw, Mom, that's so sweet. He seems the quintessential ab-sentminded professor, but underneath he's a romantic. I love that." Camille was smiling as she turned into the driveway at Diana's house.

"I don't know about that," Diana said, "but he's definitely absentminded." She looked at the front of the house and huffed with impatience. "For instance, I told him to be sure to leave the porch light on for us. The sidewalk is uneven and twice already I've broken a heel on good shoes. So be careful."

"I'm not wearing heels, so I'm good to go," Camille said, taking her mother's elbow. "You're the one who's dressed up, so watch your step." She was smiling as they climbed the steps to the front door.

"And wouldn't you know," Diana said irritably, "after all the nice things we just said about him, he hasn't even remembered to turn the lights on in the foyer. That man!"

As Diana fished for the house key in her purse, Camille tried the door and found it unlocked, which ratcheted Diana's temper up another notch. "Anybody could have just walked in here tonight!"

"They would have had a hard time getting around," Camille said. "It's dark as pitch."

Diana snapped the switches on the wall and flooded the living room, foyer, and stairs with light. "I'm going to give him a piece of my mind," she declared, storming off in the direction of the den. "He gets caught up in whatever he's working on and zones out."

"Wait. First let me get to my room and close the door," Camille said, taking the stairs two at a time. "I don't want to see bloodshed." She was smiling as she entered the guest bedroom and flicked on the light.

Instantly her heart dropped to her feet. The room was in

shambles and reeking of perfume. Her overnight case was emptied and the contents scattered on the floor. Hand lotion had been squirted on the carpet, the furniture, the walls. Clothes from the closet were strewn about, some ripped to shreds. Camille put her hand to her throat and sank down on the bed, unable to make a sound. Only then did she see the blood-red words scrawled across the mirror.

LEAVE OR YOU WILL PAY

She stared, shocked. Nausea boiled in the back of her throat. Someone had been in her mother's house, someone who had managed to slip by Allen and—

Oh, Lord, Allen! Where was Allen?

She sprang up just as her mother screamed. Terror sent her sprinting from the room to the stairs. Was someone still in the house? She leaped from the bottom steps and burst into her stepfather's office. Her heart plummeted. Allen lay on the floor. Diana was beside him on her knees, blood all over her hands as she cradled his head.

"Mom, is he—"

"I don't know. *I don't know!* Call nine-one-one."

CHAPTER SEVEN

HOW COULD IT take so long for an ambulance to make a two-mile trip? Camille didn't know anything—anything!—about what to do for a traumatic head injury. While Diana sat with Allen, she hurried to the kitchen for a clean towel to stanch the bleeding. *So much blood!* Next she dragged an afghan from the den and spread it over Allen's unconscious body, tucking it in gently, carefully. But with that done, she knew nothing else to do. So she paced the foyer, waiting for the ambulance.

Her mother was pale with shock. To go from an evening of innocent young children making music to the stark evil of an attack on her husband had left Diana shaken. Allen lay still, gray-faced and bleeding.

Finally Camille heard the ambulance siren down the street. She hurried out the door and onto the porch, waving frantically as they pulled up. "He's here! Hurry, hurry!"

Two paramedics got out of the ambulance with bags in hand and quickly climbed the steps to the front door. Camille took them to the office, where Allen lay on the floor with his head in Diana's lap. One of the paramedics knelt beside her.

"You need to let us take over now, ma'am," he said, carefully lifting Allen's head. His partner took her arm and gently helped her to her feet.

"Please say he's going to be all right," Diana begged, wringing her hands.

"We'll do our best, ma'am. What is his name?"

"Allen," Camille said. "He's my stepfather. This is my mother."

"Okay. Now, it'd be best if you could go with your mom into another room and let us get to work here."

"He needs to go to the hospital," Camille cried. "Right now!"

He fitted a blood pressure cup on Allen's arm while his partner examined Allen's head. "We'll be doing that as soon as we can. You can help by taking care of your mother."

Diana was reluctant to leave, but Camille managed to lead her out of the office and into the den. She looked ready to keel over. Camille crouched in front of her. "I'm going to get you a bottle of water, Mom."

Diana looked at her with tears in her eyes. "I couldn't get him to wake up. He's . . ." She pressed trembling lips with her hands, unable to finish.

"Allen is going to be all right," Camille told her in a bracing voice. She rose just as two uniformed policemen appeared. Startled, she put a hand to her chest. "Oh! I didn't know you were called."

"We respond to all nine-one-one calls, ma'am." He glanced toward the paramedics who were transferring Allen to a stretcher. "What happened here? We got a report that you'd had an intruder."

"Someone broke in tonight and attacked my stepfather." She was hardly aware of what she said. Her attention was fixed on the paramedics. "My room upstairs was trashed."

"You have any idea who would do anything like that?"

"No." She moved aside to allow the paramedics to roll the stretcher past. "You can look, but I'm leaving with the ambulance right now. My mother needs to go to the hospital with Allen and I need to be with her."

"We'll need a statement, ma'am. This is a crime scene. You shouldn't mess around with anything until we've completed our investigation."

While he spoke, the paramedics expertly maneuvered the stretcher down the porch steps and out to the ambulance. Camille put out a hand to stop her mother, who clearly wanted to go with Allen. "Just a minute, Mom. We'll go in my car."

To the cop, she said, "Whatever you need to do, do it. We have to go now." She grabbed her purse and without looking back helped her mother down the steps to follow the ambulance to the hospital.

CAMILLE HAD never been in an intensive care unit. It was a scary place. She'd visited friends having babies, or surgery, or some other area, but never the ICU. There were no flowers, no proud new fathers, no jovial nurses teasing patients and visitors. And no sound except the occasional moan or whispered prayer to accompany the steady hum and beep of machines monitoring heart and breath while death hovered nearby, waiting to claim the next victim.

She stood beside Allen's bed, her heart a lead weight in her chest and her hands in a white-knuckle grip on the raised bars. He was so pale, almost as colorless as the bandages wrapping his head. The gentle man who'd smiled and waved her and her mother off to the recital seemed shrunken and lifeless. His eyes were sunk in their sockets, his cheekbones sharp and prominent. An IV line taped to the back of his hand snaked up to a plastic bag filled with medication. A machine beside the bed blipped in time with his heartbeat and pulse while a monitor displayed squiggly lines and incomprehensible numbers. Guilt for her role in this appalling crime rose in her like a tsunami.

Almost as painful to Camille was the look of her mother hovering on the other side of the bed. Diana was a ghost of the vivacious woman whose loving personality blessed everyone who knew her. Camille had never felt so helpless, so wretched.

She spoke softly. "I've called Robert, Mom. He's in Houston for a business meeting, but he's catching the next flight home."

Her mother nodded but didn't speak, didn't smile. One hand touched Allen's face, cupped his cheek. She closed her eyes and silently moved her lips. Camille realized her mother was praying.

Camille drew in a shaky breath. Her brother had reacted as expected when she told him that someone had entered the home of his parents on the night of Diana's recital, probably expecting it to be empty. He had asked a dozen questions for which she'd had no answers. One thing she did know and was able to confess: She was the reason the intruder had been in her mother's house. The incident was meant to convey a threatening message to her. So it was her fault that Allen now lay in ICU.

She spotted the young resident who'd examined Allen in the ER coming toward them. With her heart in her throat, she moved to meet him just out of earshot of her mother.

But Diana saw him too. She stepped away from the bed and spoke anxiously. "Dr. Kendall, can you tell us anything? How serious is it?"

"Hard to say. He's sustained a nasty concussion. But the CT scan will tell us more. What we worry about is blood leaking into his brain."

"Is that happening?" Camille asked in horror.

"I prefer that you talk to a neurosurgeon to get an expert opinion. I've called Dr. Duncan. He will be looking at the scan, after which he'll be able to answer your questions."

"I know you can't answer definitely, but why hasn't he regained consciousness?" Camille asked. "How long before he wakes up?"

He offered a sympathetic smile. "I wouldn't hazard a guess. If I did, it would be just that—a guess. Dr. Duncan's the one to talk to you about that. I'm sorry." Seeing Diana's stricken look, he added, "I will say this. Your husband is in excellent physical shape, Mrs. Fontenot. He's not young, but he's strong and he has no other medical problems. Those are positives."

Which told them exactly *nothing*, Camille thought in frustration. Putting an upbeat spin on a horrible situation wasn't enough to relieve her mind. Or her guilt.

But when he walked away, she smiled optimistically at her mother. "You heard him, Mom. Allen has a lot going for him. He's strong, he's a man in his prime. We just have to—" She stopped when her lips trembled.

"Yes." Diana whispered, squeezing Camille's hand. "We just have to pray."

"You need your minister at a time like this," Camille said

suddenly, surprising herself. *Where had that thought come from?* "I'm going to call Jack."

Diana gave Camille a grateful smile. "Thank you, darlin'."

IT WAS almost midnight, but the good thing about a small town, Camille thought as she pulled into the driveway at Jack's church, was that it was small. The trip had taken only ten minutes. Trouble was, in this small town, bad things were happening. She'd been a little leery of going alone to her parked car at this time of night, but if her mother wanted Jack, she would get him, even if she had to drive to New Orleans.

She would have preferred calling Jack rather than ringing his doorbell so late, but her mother didn't have his number and she got a voice mail when she called the church. Now all she had to do was figure out where, behind the new building, she might find his house. Thank goodness it wasn't on the same side as the cemetery.

Using a sidewalk that led to the nether region beyond the new building, she tripped a security light and was grateful that it flooded the area with a bright white glow, making it easy to follow the walk to the house.

She didn't know what she expected, but it wasn't what she saw. The house was a classic French Creole cottage design, set up off the ground about two feet, which was a practical feature to aid in ventilation in times past, before air-conditioning. A full-length gallery with a waist-high railing stretched along the entire front. Twin gables were inset on the low, sloping roof. Tall windows on each side of the front door went all the way to the floor. Camille wished it wasn't nighttime, as she'd like to see it better. It was absolutely charming.

But she wasn't here to admire the architecture of Jack's house. She hurried up half a dozen steps and across the porch. Then, taking a deep breath, she rang the doorbell.

When nothing happened after a couple of minutes, she was on the verge of giving up, then she heard sounds behind the door. She felt a rush of relief when the lock turned and the door opened.

She saw that he'd been in bed. No surprise there. He wore pajama bottoms and nothing else, no shirt, no shoes. Reading glasses were perched low on his nose. His hair was a mess and he had a surprised look on his face as he gazed at her over the glasses. "Camille?"

"I didn't know you wore glasses," was her inane greeting.

He reached up and took them off. "What are you doing here?"

"I know it's late. I'm sorry. Did I wake you?"

"I was reading." He held up a book, marking his place with his fingers. "What's wrong?"

"It's Allen," she said, suddenly choking up. "He's been hurt." She felt tears welling in her eyes. She blinked hard and cleared her throat. "He's at the hospital. I thought my mother might need you. You know, as her minister."

He reached out and pulled her over the threshold. "Wait here while I throw on some clothes."

She stopped him when he would have closed the door and looked back as if she could see her car. "I have to get back. He's in ICU and I don't want my mother to be alone."

"It won't take three minutes," he said, tossing his book and glasses on a small table on his way down the hall. "I'll drive and you can fill me in."

He disappeared toward what she assumed was his bedroom. She could leave anyway, she thought, wiping at tears with her fingers. But somehow the idea of going back with Jack was better. She took a moment to pull herself together, arms hugging her midriff, and let her gaze roam about the room.

Jack's world.

She'd seen his office and now she was in his home. It looked orderly and quite uninspiring. A chocolate brown leather sofa was matched with two comfy-looking chairs upholstered in a co-ordinating tweedy fabric. There were two end tables, each with a lamp. A low table was placed in front of the sofa, nothing on it, nothing—zip, nada. No knick-knacks, no green plants, no color-ful throws or cushions. It was all very practical and, to her eye, very sterile. She'd always been the decorator in their home and he'd always seemed okay with her style. Style sure didn't figure much in this room. But what did she know about a minister's home décor? What was it supposed to look like?

She walked over to peek at the book he'd been reading, a thriller by a best-selling author, one she'd read a month or so ago. He'd always loved a good mystery. Apparently, he still did. Besides the Bible, what was a minister supposed to read?

From the bedroom, she could hear him moving about. A door closed. The closet? The bed creaked and she imagined him sitting on it, putting his shoes on. And then the light was flicked off and he came toward her dressed in a dark T-shirt, well-worn jeans, and running shoes. It truly had taken only a few minutes.

"Let's use my car," he said. "You can explain on the way."

Catching her arm, he steered her through the house and out the back way to a garage. "If you need to leave before I do, I'll drive you to Diana's house and I'll see that your car is returned to you wherever you say."

It was eerily familiar, Jack making decisions with lightning speed and expecting her to go along with them. Tonight she was too worried to argue. Without a word, she climbed in when he opened the passenger side door for her and buckled up.

"Now," he said as he backed out, "tell me what happened."

"Someone came into my mother's house while she and I were at a recital and attacked Allen. We think they expected the house to be empty, but Allen didn't go to the recital."

"How is he hurt? Was he shot?"

"No, he has a serious head injury. He must have been struck hard with something. There was blood all over. He's sure to have a concussion. And then whoever it was trashed my room, slashed my clothes, and left a message for me on the mirror written in red letters, paint or lipstick. I didn't check."

Jack's features were grim, but whatever he felt, it didn't show in his voice as he asked, "What kind of message?"

"It wasn't a love note, I can tell you that. It said something like, 'Leave or you will be sorry . . . or you will pay.' I can't recall the exact words. I only had a moment to look at it because about that time my mother screamed and I ran downstairs scared to death."

"You called the police?"

"I called nine-one-one. Allen was unconscious and bleeding, as white as a ghost. We were terrified. We thought he might die." Her voice broke, but she cleared her throat and kept going. "We still don't know how seriously he's injured."

"The ER setup here has a fine reputation. He's in good hands."

"I hope so. He's had a CT scan. They did that right away, but the specialist to interpret it hasn't arrived, or hadn't when I left to get you. I thought my mother needed someone. I mean, as her minister, I thought you might be able to comfort her."

"I'm glad to go," Jack said quietly, "but you're the person she'll need most right now."

"I feel awful about this. It's my fault Allen is hurt. The whole thing was aimed at me; to get me to turn tail and run."

Jack pulled into the parking lot at the hospital but didn't shut off the car. He shifted in his seat to look directly at her. "What exactly have you been doing, Camille?"

Guilt and worry made her defensive. "Nothing to warrant an attack on my stepfather or having my room vandalized and almost everything I own destroyed!"

"I wasn't suggesting that. I'm just wondering, why would someone want you to turn tail and run?"

She turned her head, fixed her gaze on an arriving ambulance. "Because of the questions I'm asking about Luanne, I guess. The whole town seems to resent it."

He groaned and bent his head, rubbing his eyes with thumb and forefinger. "How many people have you talked to? Better yet, exactly *who* have you talked to?"

"Very few, directly. But not because I haven't tried. Still, they know." She turned and gave him an exasperated look. "It beats me why people are so determined to ignore the fact that a killer might be walking the streets in this town."

"If that's true, Camille, it's all the more reason for you to be cautious."

"I happen to think this proves it's true."

"Then you could be in real danger. That rock tossed through your window was probably some kook activist. This sounds a lot more serious."

"I can handle it, Jack." She reached for the door handle but stopped before opening it when he didn't move. "Are you coming inside to be of some help to my mother or are you just going to sit there and lecture me?"

A few seconds passed. Jack seemed torn. In the past, he wouldn't have considered giving in until he'd argued his point of view and won. But now, he simply got out of the car.

Neither said a word on the walk to the hospital entrance. But as they approached the elevators, Jack said, "You'll need to report this to the police. The house is a crime scene. The sooner they begin processing, the better."

"That's happening now. They were at the house when we left to go to the hospital. And I told them I'd give them a statement, but only after I felt comfortable leaving my mother with Allen."

He looked down at her. "I thought you said you didn't call them."

"I didn't have to. They came when I called nine-one-one." The elevator door finally slid open. "You don't need to take over, Jack. I didn't come to get you for that. You're here because my mother seemed to need . . . something."

But standing beside him in the elevator, fear lodged in her chest again. What if Allen had taken a turn for the worse while she was gone? What if Allen died? It would be her fault. How would she be able to live with that?

She must have made a distressed sound because suddenly

Jack put an arm around her shoulders. "I know you're scared, but Allen is right where he should be. These people know how to treat head trauma. And he's pretty fit."

Stiff and unyielding at the feel of Jack's arm around her, she shook her head. "But we don't *know* if that matters. He may have brain damage."

Jack's tone lightened. "Hey, I play golf with him. I know he's got a hard head."

Only seconds ago, they'd been arguing, falling into the familiar destructive habits that had destroyed their marriage. Now he was offering reassurance, trying to tease her out of her fear. She hesitated for a minute. She had been the contrary one. Jack had been surprisingly restrained.

"I'm just so scared, Jack," she whispered. "If he dies, I don't know if I can bear it."

He didn't tell her that her fears were silly. Or that Allen would be fine. Or that he knew what the next few hours would bring. He didn't say anything. He simply turned her toward him and put both his arms around her. That it was Jack didn't seem to matter. She gave in and clung, desperate and scared. At the moment, she needed what he had to give.

JACK SEEMED to be recognized by much of the ICU staff, Camille noted as they headed toward Allen's cubicle. He spoke softly to the nurses, nodded to a physician at work by a patient's bedside, and waved to an orderly attending a very old man. She had only a moment to process yet more glimpses of this new Jack because Diana had spotted them and immediately hurried to meet them.

Camille saw with a rush of relief that her mother's color was markedly improved. When Camille left, Diana had looked fragile to the point of near collapse. Now she saw light in her mother's eyes and a spring in her step. And she was smiling.

"Oh, thank you for coming, Pastor," Diana said, giving him an enthusiastic hug. "You must have been praying, because Allen woke up a few minutes ago. He says he has a horrendous headache and the doctor said he might have some memory loss, but he hasn't. First thing he wanted to know was whether Camille and I were okay. He worried that the intruder might still have been in the house when we got home."

She stepped back, catching Jack's hand to lead him to Allen's cubicle. "Come over and let him see you. He's not going to be out of ICU for a day or so, Dr. Duncan says. Allen objected to that and tried to get the doctor to say he could go into a regular room, the silly man. Dr. Duncan put his foot down and said absolutely not. He has to be watched closely for at least forty-eight hours. Next thing, he'll be asking to go home, wait and see. He can be mule-stubborn."

"Whoa, take a breath," Jack said with a smile, while allowing himself to be hustled toward Allen's bed by Diana's nearly drunken exuberance. Both seemed to have forgotten Camille. She stood back, watching while they talked with Allen.

But after a while, Diana seemed to remember her and motioned her closer. "Come here, darlin'. Let Allen see that you're okay too."

Camille approached warily, and when Allen reached out for her, she put her hand in his. "I'm so sorry, Allen," she said. Tears rose in her eyes. "This is all my fault. I just never dreamed anything like this would happen."

He frowned. "Why would you think it's your fault?"

She glanced from his face to her mother's. "You didn't tell him about my room?"

"I haven't had a chance," Diana said, passing her a tissue. "As soon as he woke up, Dr. Duncan appeared, and when he left, you came back." She turned to Allen and told him what happened in Camille's bedroom.

"Ah." Allen still held Camille's hand. "Looks like you've stirred up a hornet's nest, young lady."

"I've already given that lecture," Jack told him in a dry voice. "I suggested she leave investigating to the cops."

"And I can imagine her reaction." Allen tightened his hold when, with a huff, Camille tried to pull free. "I'd listen to the reverend if I were you, honey. And meanwhile, don't let me hear any more talk from you about this being your fault." Allen squeezed her hand again. "Nobody's to blame except the thug who walked in our home uninvited."

"Speaking of that," Jack spoke from the other side of the bed, "did you see who attacked you, Allen?"

"No. Diana can tell you that I tend to zone out when I'm working. I was listening to music on my iPod. I guess that explains how he was able to come up from behind and hit me."

"It was a man?"

"Well . . ." He tried to think back. "Tell the truth, I don't exactly know. One minute I was bent over paperwork and the next I woke up in here. I'm just assuming it was a man." Without thinking, he reached up to touch his head, then changed his mind. "Judging by the size of my headache, I'd say it was a man."

"And you were out a long time," Camille said.

"I've been meaning to ask." Diana eyed Allen sternly. "How

did he get in? Were the doors locked? I know I locked the back, but you promised you'd lock the front."

"I guess I forgot," Allen said, assuming a shamefaced look. But he recovered quickly and said to Camille, "See, there's the proof that it's not your fault, honey."

Nobody noticed the nurse approaching until she stopped at the foot of Allen's bed. "We have rules here, folks. Only two visitors at a time are allowed."

She smiled as Jack put up both hands, palms out. "I'm leaving, Monette."

When he didn't move, the nurse looked pointedly at her watch. "And when would that be, Reverend?"

"Right now." His gaze moved to Camille. "Are you ready to go to the police? They'll want your statement while it's fresh in your mind."

Camille realized Allen and her mother were agog with curiosity. "Do you need me to stay, Mom?"

"No, darlin', you go with Jack. In all the excitement, I purely forgot we need to make a formal statement."

When Camille still hesitated, Diana gave her a brisk hug. "Thank you for being so brave, Camille. I would have gone to pieces but for you." She gave her a little push toward Jack. "Now, go. It'll still be a long night for you. They'll probably have a million questions since you were the target of the man's violence. Allen was what they call collateral damage."

"Are you sure?"

"I'm sure. Go."

Jack took her arm.

She shook him off, talking to her mother as she backed out of the cubicle. "Call me on my cell if anything changes."

"I will," Diane said.

Camille and Jack stepped from the cubicle. "I don't like being hustled that way," Camille grumbled as they headed to the elevator.

"Sorry, but Monette Comeaux doesn't like people who break ICU rules," Jack said, watching as she punched the down button. "Not only were we one person over the limit but you're only allowed one ten-minute visit each hour in ICU."

"It must be nice having friends in high places."

Jack chose not to comment as the elevator doors slid open.

"I was so worried about Allen," she said, stepping inside ahead of him. "He could have been killed."

"But he wasn't," Jack said as the doors closed. "And he went out of his way to relieve your mind."

"I heard what he said, but that doesn't change what we both know. What happened is my fault." And Camille knew she would have to live with that fact.

CHAPTER eight

SHE DECIDED LATER she could have saved telling the cops altogether, considering their attitude. They showed little enthusiasm about taking her statement. The lead investigator opined that the incident was probably an act of teenage vandalism gone awry. Most likely, he told them, the kids had heard of Camille's support of Chester Pelham and, assuming the house was empty, had set out to teach her a lesson. Stumbling upon Allen, they overreacted "as kids will do."

She left the police station in disgust and made no objection when Jack wanted to stop by the house and take a look. In her concern for Allen and getting him to the hospital, she hadn't been able to see it in all its gory detail. Surveying the damage now, she was appalled and more incensed than ever at the cops for dismissing it as the work of teenagers.

"Can you believe those incompetents!" she fumed. "They think a bunch of teenagers got together for a little fun, assaulted my stepfather, trashed my mother's guest room, and, just for kicks, wrote me a vile message." She would have paced off her agitation if there had been room enough on the floor to pace. As it was, she could hardly move, let alone pace, since her belongings were strewn everywhere. "What does it take to excite the cops around here?"

"Murder," Jack said, holding up a scrap of scarlet bikini.

She snatched it away from him. "That's my swimsuit! Or what's left of it. Do you know what that cost?"

"Considering the amount of fabric," Jack said with a droll look, "about a dollar ninety-eight?"

"Eighty-five dollars!" But suddenly the fire went out of her. She swept aside a mountain of stuff from her bed and sat down. "You realize this means I can't stay here anymore."

Jack was studying the letters scrawled on the mirror and frowning. At her words, he turned to look at her. "I'm glad to hear you say that. Whoever did this, . . . it's worrisome. Makes you wonder what they might do next."

"Worrisome to you, maybe, but infuriating to me." She picked up a pillow that was soggy with liquid makeup and, making a face, tossed it on the floor. "The linens on this bed are ruined. The furniture will have to be professionally restored." She stared down at a dark stain. "This carpet will have to be replaced. I'll pay for all that, of course, but they could try again. I can't take that chance. I don't want my mother or Allen to be victimized on my account."

"I think you're right to go back home," Jack said thoughtfully. "If it wasn't vandalism, then the next threat may not be a message written on a mirror. It could be something a lot worse."

He hardly had the words out before she pounced. "Who said anything about going home? No way. I'm not giving up. I'm on to something and I'm staying until I figure it out."

"I'm confused," Jack said. "You aren't leaving, but you aren't willing to risk more trouble for your mother and Allen?"

"No, I'm going to a motel. I'd prefer a hotel, but since there aren't any, it has to be a motel."

"A motel."

"Or a bed-and-breakfast. Do you know of one? Or can you think of anybody in this town who'd put me up? I'm not exactly the most popular person, in case you haven't noticed."

"Camille, you shouldn't go anywhere except back to your condo. Or preferably, move in with your dad, which is where you'd be safest of all. Let the cops do their job."

She pounced again. "Are you agreeing with them?" With a sweeping gesture, she indicated the trashed room. "You think it was a bunch of kids doing this?"

"Probably. But whether it's kids or not, it's mean and vicious."

She stared, nearly speechless. "Which means you still think Chester killed Luanne and this obscenity that we're looking at doesn't mean I've alarmed somebody."

Jack took his time replying. "You've definitely irritated somebody, but I just can't get beyond the facts, Camille. And I'm betting when we get the DNA analysis on that knife, it'll be Luanne's."

It made a compelling case, Camille had to admit. But why was she urged to get out of town? She couldn't believe it was a bunch of kids. Kids would have backed off once they realized Allen was at home. Instead, the intruder had attacked him and then set about doing what he came for: delivering a message meant to scare her off. Why did it all make so much sense to her, but nobody else could see it?

"It's four a.m., Jack." Weary to her bones, she stood up. "Thanks for coming out. My mother needed you. It must be nice to be able to do that for people. Can you have someone drive my car over here tomorrow morning? I'll need it."

"No problem." He stepped aside at the door to let her pass. "It won't be long before the sun is up, otherwise I wouldn't want you to be here without someone in the house with you."

"Why? I'm hardly in danger from a bunch of kids. Right?"

He ignored her sarcasm and, without comment, followed her downstairs. But at the front door, he stopped. "I'm thinking about what you said a minute ago, thanking me for going to your mother when you thought she might need her minister. I'm really glad you were able to get beyond our differences to do that."

Camille shrugged. "It was about my mother, not me. Besides, what are ministers for?"

"I'm not just any minister, Camille. We both know that. I'm your ex-husband. There's bad history between us. I hurt you too much, and if you never spoke to me again, I would understand."

"It was a long time ago, Jack. Time wounds all heels." Almost before the words were out, she hurriedly said, "I'm sorry. That was tacky. I guess I'm tired."

She thought for a minute, wanting to get right what she had to say. "Just because we're talking now doesn't mean the issues that separated us no longer exist. Maybe your new life helps you bury that stuff and pretend it's over and forgotten. For you, maybe even forgiven. Well, that's your new life. I'm still living my original one and stuff keeps boiling up. If my attitude isn't what you want, you'll just have to live with it."

His smile was a little crooked and definitely sad. "I hope someday you can forgive me, but the past can't be buried and forgotten. So I can only try to make amends now."

"That sounds like one of AA's Twelve Steps."

"What can I say?" He lifted both hands in a you-got-me

shrug. "One of the steps is to make amends, but that wasn't my intent just now, although I would make amends in a heartbeat if I had a clue as to how to do so. I'm just glad I have a chance to tell you that in spite of the fact that we still wind up going at it like two cats in a bag sometimes, I'm happy that at least we're talking. Happy that you got beyond whatever you feel and knocked on my door tonight."

"I guess the decent thing to say is thank you for responding. My mother apparently really respects you."

Now he was openly smiling. "And you don't get it."

She gave him a gentle shove, pushing him over the threshold. "Good night, Jack."

He was halfway to his car when she suddenly remembered something. She opened the door and called out to him from the porch.

He stopped, looking back. "What?"

"Shh, don't wake the neighbors." She motioned him closer and went down the porch steps to meet him. "I want you to find out something for me, will you?"

He angled his head, looking at her narrow-eyed. "And that would be . . ."

"Find out where Harlen Richard was tonight when my room was trashed."

In a split second, he saw where she was headed. "Are you serious?"

"As a heart attack. Since the cops are focused on Chester as their prime suspect, I bet they haven't bothered to look at Harlen."

"Harlen didn't murder Luanne, Camille. You're way off base there. Give it a rest, for Pete's sake!"

"If you really think he's beyond suspicion, then you won't have a problem just finding out where he was between eight and ten tonight, will you?"

"Other than he's my brother-in-law and I'd feel sneaky as a snake on top of the fact that I don't believe he's capable of murder, no, nothing other than that."

"Oh, come on. You can ask without arousing suspicion and I can't. You just said you'd do anything to make amends." She tilted her head, looking at him expectantly. "Well, yes or no?"

He looked to be counting to ten, but he finally gave a quick jerk of a nod, which she took to be a yes, and stalked off to his car. She was smiling as he sped off into what was left of the night.

THE NEXT morning Camille woke thinking she heard the telephone ringing. Assuming it would be her mother with news about Allen, she groped for the phone on the floor beside the couch where she'd spent what was left of the night. But after picking it up and getting a dial tone, she realized it was the doorbell.

She wrapped an afghan around herself and stumbled through the house to the front door. A woman was visible through the leaded glass, but she couldn't tell who it was. She twisted the dead bolt and opened the door a crack.

"Madge? What . . ."

"Coffee, that's what," Madge said, stepping inside. "You look like you haven't had any and neither have I."

"No." Camille put a hand over her eyes. "I just—I mean, Allen is in the hospital and I—"

"I know. And hey, I bet you didn't expect this much excitement when you decided to spend a few days with your mama, did you?"

Camille looked around for a clock. "Give me a minute. What time is it? And how did you know about Allen?"

"Jack, of course. He sent me. It's Sunday, so he's at the church. And it's ten-thirty. But first things first. Take your shower and when you're done, we'll talk over breakfast."

"Wait, I need to call the hospital," Camille said, looking around to locate the telephone.

"You can, but Jack was there to check on Allen early this morning. He's fine, nagging anybody who'll listen to let him check out. The doctor won't hear of it and Diana won't either."

Camille hesitated but gave in. She'd feel better able to cope after a shower. Hopefully, she could find something to wear that wasn't ripped to shreds or soaked with lotion, perfume, or liquid make-up.

Halfway up the stairs, she was hit with the stench. Perfume mixed with the rest of her toiletries combined into a putrid pot-pourri. Bracing herself, she opened the bedroom door and found it even worse in daylight than it had been the night before. Cleaning it up would be a mammoth job.

But not right now. Right now, she needed to root through the mess to try to find something to wear. She tossed aside a shredded blouse, found several T-shirts soaked in something green and disgusting, and three pairs of pants cut to ribbons. She grimaced upon spotting the bottom half of her scarlet bikini swimsuit. Last night when Jack held it up on one finger and gave her that look, for just a moment she'd felt—

She quickly stuffed the red scrap in a drawer. Whatever she'd felt, it meant nothing. Nothing.

"Aha," she muttered, finally pulling out a pair of capris that had somehow survived. If she couldn't find a top, she'd raid her mother's closet. Now, closing her eyes to the destruction, she went into the bathroom and turned on the shower.

Once out and dressed in the capris and a white shirt of her mother's, she used her cell phone to call the hospital. Allen was fine, Diana assured her. He had a headache, but he'd been persuaded to take some pretty heavy medication, so he was resting. Robert had arrived, which relieved Camille. Diana would be in good hands with her son beside her.

A few minutes later, she went downstairs, lured by the delectable aroma of brewed coffee. She stopped short. The table was set and Madge stood at the stove, dishing up something that looked a lot like an omelet.

"I apologize for waking you up," she said, setting the treat in front of Camille, "but I have a good reason."

Camille blinked at the enticing plate loaded with an omelet, toast triangles, and fresh blueberries. She loved breakfast. Unlike tons of people she knew, she never skipped it. "I forgive you," she said sincerely, savoring the first taste. "You can wake me up any day, any time, if this is how you apologize."

"Jack said you loved breakfast." Madge pulled up a chair and sat, wrapping fingers around a mug. "I'm here to make an offer you can't refuse."

"Oh, please." Camille put down her fork with a clatter. "Jack sent you, didn't he? I'm not leaving, Madge. I told him that. He can send the mayor, the town council, and the chief of police—he can send the governor. I'm not leaving."

Madge spread orange marmalade on a piece of toast and

handed it over. "Will you please hear me out before throwing me out?"

Camille had the grace to look chagrined. "I'm sorry. I'm being rude to you when it's Jack I'm irritated with. He's always done this to me, Madge, making decisions without consulting me, assuming his judgment is superior to mine, preaching what's right for me." A smile flashed. "No pun intended."

She bit into the toast and munched awhile before adding, "Anyway, those days are over. He'll just have to put up with me staying here whether he believes it's wise or not."

"Staying here means moving into a motel?"

She shrugged. "Unless you know a good bed-and-breakfast. I can't stay here and put my mother and Allen in jeopardy. Plus I don't want to be responsible for more vandalism at their house. You wouldn't believe the mess upstairs. The furniture in the guest room will have to be repaired by a professional and I think the carpet will have to be replaced. Oh, and whoever that creep was, he even knocked holes in the Sheetrock."

"We can clean it up today," Madge said, finishing off her coffee. "I'm not a professional at restoring antiques, but I know a guy who is. And I know a carpenter who can repair the Sheetrock. He'll find a painter. As for the carpet, I bet you'll find it can be shampooed."

"What do you mean, 'we can clean it up'? I couldn't let you do anything like that."

"I just thought the sooner we get it done, the sooner you can pack up what's left of your things and take them over to my place."

Camille paused. "What?"

"I live on the bayou. I have an extra bedroom and two large German shepherds who are better than any security system, although I have one of those too. I promised to help you poke and pry a little around here and maybe throw some light on who may have killed Luanne. I think I know where we can begin."

"So you agree with me it wasn't Chester?"

"Not necessarily. I just agree that we should explore other possibilities."

"Great. Wonderful." Camille leaned forward. "Tell me."

"We start with Harlen Richard. In law enforcement, we always look at the spouse first. Seems to me, BBPD hasn't done that."

"I quoted statistics on that to Jack and he almost blew a gasket," Camille said. "I figured he'd be the best source to go to about his sister's relationship with her husband. He was not pleased that I asked."

"I know a better source," Madge said, studying her red nails.

"And that would be . . ."

"My cousin, Alafair Menard, formerly the Richards' maid."

"No kidding? And she's willing to talk to me?"

"To us. For the past couple of months, she's been in Minnesota, where her pregnant daughter lives. Alafair quit her job to be on hand for the birth of the baby and to help out for a few weeks after. She's back in Blood Bayou now." Madge paused, looking very pleased with herself. "You know what they say, 'Nobody knows you like your maid.'"

"I don't have a maid."

"Me neither, but Luanne does. Did." Madge's look turned somber as she folded and refolded a dish towel. "I'm not doing this just out of the goodness of my heart, Camille. Stephanie Hill was a close friend of mine. We worked side by side for over ten years. I loved her. I miss her. And when they arrested Chester for her murder, I was never quite convinced that he did it. Bottom line is, I'd like to see justice done on her behalf and the best way to do that, I think, is to start with the mystery of Luanne's murder. They have to be linked."

Camille was still a little dubious. "And Jack sent you over, knowing all this? He approves?"

"Not exactly." Madge hung up the towel. "Let's just say his habit of thinking he knows best doesn't always sit well with me either."

Camille burst out laughing. They both raised a hand and high-fived. "Okay, let's do it!"

CLEANING UP the room was not as overwhelming as Camille feared. With Madge helping, they made good time. After putting things in as good order as possible, she packed up the meager remains of her clothes and cosmetics and put them in the trunk of her car. While Madge contacted the antique furniture restorer and the carpenter, Camille went to the hospital. Jack had been as good as his word about returning her car. As it was Sunday, it must have been very early. She guessed Sundays were pretty busy for him.

She found Allen half awake but relaxed and drowsy from a narcotic taken to dull the pain in his head. Her mother hovered at his side. She felt a pang of conscience looking at Allen; he had smoky smudges beneath his eyes and his color was off. But when she asked, he said he felt fine.

"Anybody would after getting a shot of morphine," Diana said after giving Camille a hug. "And don't I recognize that shirt?"

"I'm sorry, Mom, but it was all I could find to wear. I'll have to drive back to my condo or buy a few things here to tide me over."

"I was teasing. You know you're welcome to anything in my closet." She moved back to Allen's side. "Jack came by this morning and told us about the mess in your room. I'm so sorry."

"I'm the one who's sorry." She crossed the room to hug Robert, who had risen from a chair when she came in the room. "I'll pay for the damage to your walls and furniture and the rug, of course."

"You'll do no such thing," Diana said. "It is not your fault. Besides, the insurance will cover it."

"After a hefty deductible, I bet. I will definitely pay that, Mom. Please let me. I'll feel even worse if you don't."

"Here, sit." Robert motioned her over to sit beside him on the settee. "And tell me what you've been up to, Sis. Is it as naughty as I've been told?"

She rolled her eyes. "I'm just asking a few perfectly reasonable questions about Luanne."

"Which is apparently making the natives restless."

"The cops think it's teenage vandals, but I'm not so sure."

Robert studied her thoughtfully. "You're sticking with your theory that Luanne's killer isn't Chester?"

She shrugged. "Doesn't it make sense? If my poking and prying is making the real killer nervous, wouldn't that be reason enough to run me out of town?"

"Which means the real killer doesn't know you very well."

Robert's smile, so like Allen's, flashed. "And if you're replenishing your wardrobe, I guess that means you're not going quietly."

"No."

"Then tell me it's just a crazy rumor that you're planning to book into a motel," Robert said.

"I told Robert I wouldn't permit it!" Diana spoke in a fierce whisper to keep from disturbing Allen. "I wouldn't sleep a wink knowing you were in a motel, Camille."

"And I wouldn't sleep a wink knowing I'm a threat to you and Allen," Camille said. "Don't you see that?"

"Here's what I see!" Diana interrupted. "I see news reports of single women being assaulted in places like that. Or worse yet, murdered! No, indeed. You'll stay right where you are, Camille."

"I don't want to be responsible for another break-in at your house, Mom. Unlike Jack and the Keystone Cops, whose investigation was a joke last night, I don't think it was teenage vandals who did this. I think it was Luanne's killer."

"All the more reason for you to stay at home with me," Diana said, now pleading instead of commanding.

"No, Mom. Thank you, but I just can't expose you and Allen to that threat." She placed her hands on her hips. "And I won't be scared off. I'm staying."

"She means it." All three turned when Jack walked in. "I tried talking her out of it last night."

"Hey, bro!" With a big grin, Robert was out of his seat and across the floor to shake Jack's hand. "Good to see you."

Jack's grin matched Robert's. "How was your trip?"

"Same old, same old. I was glad to cut it short."

Jack's gaze went to Camille. "You've talked to Madge?"

"She made breakfast for me and helped me clean up the mess in my room."

"You'll be staying with her?"

"Yes."

Diana's gaze sharpened. "What's this?"

"You didn't give me a chance to tell you," Camille said. "Madge has offered to put me up." She lifted a hand to stall her mother's protest. "She has two German shepherds, Mom, and a security system. I'll be safe. Don't worry." She flicked a wicked glance at Jack. "Jack thinks it was a bunch of teenagers doing mischief, so there's really nothing to worry about, is there?"

JACK WAS close behind when she left a few minutes later and caught up with her at her car. "You're up to something," he said, as she fished in her purse for her keys. "I know that look. What's going on?"

She stopped, keys in hand. "What is it with you, Jack? What do you care? Go back to your church and plan your next sermon or something and stop trying to give me advice I don't need."

"Just tell me this. Is Madge in this with you?"

"Did you hear me? Butt out, Jack."

"She's a frustrated cop. The thought of the two of you getting together worries me. Worse yet, it worries me more if you don't stick together."

For a heated moment, she gazed over the roof of her car at nothing in particular. Then, coming to a conclusion, she said, "We're going to see Alafair Menard. Since you were unwilling to talk to me about Luanne and her marriage, Madge suggested her cousin might be more forthcoming. There. That's the plan for today. Are you satisfied?"

His frown told her he was anything but satisfied. "You're still thinking Harlen murdered Luanne?"

"No, I'm thinking I want to eliminate him as a suspect," she said with exaggerated patience.

Before she finished, he was shaking his head. "Harlen would not murder Luanne, Camille."

"Maybe. Maybe not." She opened the door and tossed her purse across to the passenger seat.

Jack's measuring gaze lasted a long time. "Do you ever give up?"

She met his look head-on. "Once I did. Not anymore." She shook her head. "No, never."

CHAPTER **nine**

A LAFAIR MENARD DIDN'T look old enough to be a grand-mother. Pretty, slim, and petite in white shorts and a pink T-shirt, she didn't look much like a housekeeper either. And she certainly didn't look as if she was related to Madge, who was nearly six feet tall in stocking feet. The only similarity Camille found between the two cousins was their partiality for outlandish nail polish. Alafair's toenails, she noticed, were also blood red.

"So how's that new grandbaby?" Madge wanted to know after introducing Camille.

"I've got pictures," Alafair said, jumping up to get them. And for the next ten minutes, they were treated to a slew of photos of a cute little black-haired baby girl, over which they oohed and ahhed, as required. She was a beautiful baby, Camille thought wistfully. Maybe one day.

The photo show over, Alafair put the pictures away some-where in the direction of the kitchen. When she came back, she set a bowl of mixed nuts on the coffee table and took a handful for herself. "Can I get y'all something to drink? Ice tea? Pepsi? It's diet."

"Nothing for me, thanks," Camille said.

"Too close to lunch," Madge said. "We need you to tell us about Luanne, *cher*."

Alafair settled in a large armchair and popped a cashew into her mouth. "I couldn't believe it when I heard what happened to her. To be murdered like that, stabbed and left at the water's edge, bleeding out right into Blood Bayou." She shivered and rubbed her arms briskly. "It's really creepy, isn't it?"

Her words echoed what Camille thought, but she kept it to herself for fear of shattering the housekeeper's expansive mood. Madge too, was silent.

"And here's the really odd thing . . ." Alafair leaned toward them as if sharing a secret. "Luanne might not have been surprised to be murdered. I know that sounds crazy, but she sort of expected the worst to happen to her. When she'd get in a mood, she'd talk about having bad karma. She believed that about herself."

Camille had noticed a few strange-looking pieces of art in Alafair's house—Creole or Cajun, she couldn't tell. She knew some Creoles practiced ancient rituals handed down for generations. She hoped she wouldn't find that Luanne had been dabbling in that kind of thing.

"Why would she believe that?" Camille asked.

Alafair let out a long breath and paused as if weighing her words. "You're Luanne's former sister-in-law, right? You were married to Jack?"

"Yes."

"So you probably know that Luanne sometimes acted . . . ah . . ."

"Wild and crazy," Madge said, helping herself to nuts. "You don't have to tippy-toe around the facts, Alafair. Luanne had a racy reputation before she married Harlen. What we'd like to know is what kind of relationship they had after they got married."

"I don't like to speak ill of the dead." Alafair paused, letting her words hang.

"Oh, please." Madge rolled her eyes. "She wasn't exactly the perfect wife, which is what you told me at Monette Comeau's shower. You said she sometimes . . ." Madge paused. "What word was it you used? Oh, yes, she sometimes strayed."

"But she was alive then, Madge."

Camille spoke before the conversation got out of hand. "Was she having an affair?"

"No." Alafair slipped out of her sandals and got comfortable in the big chair, tucking one foot beneath her. "That was what was so odd about it. She wasn't having an affair. She'd just pick up men. Occasionally, not too often. It was crazy. And I told her so."

"Dangerous too," Camille said, thinking Madge's take on Luanne was similar. "Did Harlen know?"

"She wanted him to know. She wanted to defy him, anger him, anything to make him notice her. He married her because she was so gorgeous and then he neglected her something awful. But acting out the way she did—like a teenager, you know—it just made him think she was immature and silly." She paused, thinking. "Actually, Luanne was a teenager, in some ways. She and Jack—" Alafair looked at Camille. "You'd know this, Camille. She and Jack had a very dysfunctional childhood, no mama and their daddy was an alcoholic. He used to bring women home and some would stay and some wouldn't. Luanne once told me she used to try thinking up ways to make them stay. Of course, they never did. Anyway, could be her escapades were a way of just trying to connect with another human being. Or maybe searching for a replacement daddy." She gave a big sigh. "Who knows? I'm no psychologist, but that's my take on it."

"And Harlen just let this happen?" Camille asked in amazement. "He didn't care that her behavior—besides being dangerous—might be embarrassing if people found out? Or, here's another thought. She was at least twenty-five years younger than Harlen, so he might be perceived as a man who couldn't satisfy his woman at home. Not many men would just blow that away."

Alafair studied her brightly painted toenails before meeting Camille's eyes. "I need to be discreet here."

"Understood," Camille said. "I'm just trying to get a picture of Luanne's life. Somebody murdered her and I, for one, don't think it was Chester Pelham."

Alafair's eyes grew big. "You think it was Harlen?"

"I don't have a clue. Not yet."

"Okay." Alafair straightened a little, put both feet on the floor, neatly together. "Okay. Harlen reacted just about how a husband would whose wife is cheating on him." She looked at both women, as if expecting them to guess what she meant.

"He threatened to cut off the money, keep her on a lean budget" was Madge's guess.

"No," Camille said, "he had a bigger ego. He was a big fish in a little pond here in Blood Bayou. I'm guessing verbal abuse. It's not hard to imagine what he'd say to her. And it wasn't pretty, right, Alafair?"

"It was worse than you can imagine. My word, the things he'd say, what he'd call her." She shuddered with distaste. "Worse yet, he knew I was in the house and could hear it. And he didn't care."

Because he knew Alafair's job depended on her discretion, Camille thought. And a housekeeper's opinion didn't matter to him.

Madge shoved the bowl of nuts far out of her reach. "That was verbal abuse. Did he ever get physically violent?"

"Did he ever!" Alafair said. "And lately it was just horrible. Something had to give. I thought she'd get up enough nerve to leave him, but . . ." She frowned. "She never did. To tell the truth, I didn't think he would kill her."

"You actually saw evidence of physical abuse?" Camille asked.

"No way not to. I'd see her in the morning before she put on her makeup. Luanne was a genius with makeup. She'd have a purple bruise on her cheek when I got there, which was around eight a.m. But by lunchtime, when she met those pals of hers at the country club, nothing showed. I've known her to take a handful of painkillers just to be able to walk. Sometimes I'd have to drive and drop her off."

Camille had a sick feeling in her stomach. "Did she ever need medical treatment?"

"Well, he never broke a bone that I know of. But twice I drove her to a clinic in Lafayette."

"Yes!" Madge gave Camille two thumbs-up. "We can get records if we need them."

"No," Alafair said with a half-smile. "She used my name, my driver's license, and paid with my credit card. She didn't file insurance."

Camille studied Alafair's dark hair, dark eyes, and petite stature, same as Luanne. Except for the age difference, it would probably work. Alafair was a very young-looking grandmother in her late thirties, most likely. Luanne was thirty-three. Yes, it would work.

"But would he kill her?" Madge asked as the silence stretched.

"He could. In a rage. Yes," Camille said. "Domestic violence can turn deadly. But stabbing her and just leaving her lying at the edge of the bayou, I don't know. It doesn't seem to fit somehow." She tapped her finger against her lips, thinking. "And how would he have managed to plant the knife at Chester's place?"

Madge spoke. "We need to find out where he was when Luanne was killed and whether he had time to plant the knife."

They both stood up together. Camille gave the housekeeper an appreciative smile. "Thank you, Alafair. You've been a big help. In fact, let me give you my cell phone number. If you think of anything else, please call me."

"I hope I don't get in trouble," she said with a worried look.

"You won't. Everything you've told us is in confidence. You have my word."

"And mine," Madge said.

"That's good," Alafair said, then added, "But you can tell Jack. In fact, I wish you would."

Camille stared. "Excuse me?"

"Luanne was his sister. He should know." She stood up and walked with them to the door. "He's a minister and a strong Christian, so he won't betray a confidence. He should be on the lookout for this stuff. You know, in his congregation. I begged Luanne to tell him, to ask him for help. But she wouldn't. Maybe if he knows, it will help him pick up signs of abuse in other women."

CAMILLE AND Madge drove in silence after leaving Alafair, each wrapped in her own thoughts. "You knew Luanne," Camille said finally. "Did you ever suspect anything?"

"About the abuse? Never. And I'm feeling pretty stupid that I didn't."

"It's funny that nobody has mentioned any of this," Camille said. "You'd think otherwise, considering Blood Bayou is a very small town. If this kind of scandal isn't an open topic, then rumors are usually red hot beneath the surface. And we've heard nothing."

"She's a hometown girl," Madge said. "Folks around here tend to keep something like that quiet now that she's gone."

Camille was thinking back. "I seem to recall that Ray Wyatt said something about Luanne being a hottie when we first learned she'd been murdered, but I think he meant before she was married."

"If anybody suspected, it would be her buddies at the club," Madge said.

Camille laughed shortly. "You can kiss good-bye the possibility that they'd talk to me. I was told that she's their dear friend, their tennis, bridge, and golf partner now murdered by Chester Pelham and sorely missed. That's a direct quote."

Madge frowned, thinking. "There must be somebody."

Camille snapped her fingers. "I just remembered! When we had that confrontation in the ladies' room, one of them started to say something, but she clammed up at a look from another one. What was it? What was it?" She drummed her fingers on one thigh, trying to recall. "Something about Luanne having finally gotten it together and she wasn't doing that anymore." Camille looked over at Madge. "I wonder what she wasn't doing anymore."

Seeing Madge hesitate, Camille pounced. "And you. You mentioned something about Terri Chartrain when she showed up at the coffee shop. You said everybody has secrets. What's Terri's secret?"

"I was afraid you'd remember that," Madge said. "And I don't really think it means much, but we got a call at the station one night about a domestic disturbance in progress at the Chartrains'. The story we got is that Joe Chartrain had been out on the town and was too drunk to drive home. Guess who gave him a ride?"

"Luanne."

"None other than. So instead of just opening the car door and shoving him out, Luanne helps him get all the way to the front door, rings the doorbell herself, and personally delivers him right into Terri's arms." Madge was shaking her head at the memory, trying not to smile. "After which there commenced one really mean scene. I mean, Terri's a little bitty thing, but she made a big, big stink. She yelled and screamed and called Luanne names I'd never heard spoken at the station, and I've heard some pretty raunchy stuff. It was Joe himself who called the cops. Of course, he wouldn't if he'd been sober, but he told us he was afraid Terri was going to go inside the house, get his gun, and kill Luanne. Or him."

"Wow." Camille was turned in the seat staring. "And you didn't think to mention this before?"

"Nah." Madge signaled and stopped at the curb. "If Terri did it, she wouldn't have used a knife. Too risky. She might cut herself, besides stabbing is too messy. Might get blood and stuff on her designer outfit. No, she would have used Joe's gun."

When Camille recovered from her amazement over the goings-on in small towns, she realized Madge had pulled in front of Jack's church. "Why are we stopping here?"

Madge put the car in park and pointed toward the church. "Look, isn't that Jack? Now's your chance to talk to him."

Camille looked but saw no one. "Why would I want to talk to him? Besides, I need to do some shopping at that little boutique in town." She looked down at herself. "I need to buy a couple of outfits until I can go home and pick up a few things. I can't wear this again tomorrow. Everything I own is ruined."

"You want to talk to him because Alafair asked you to tell him about Luanne's abuse and she had a good reason."

"You can't honestly believe he doesn't know, Madge. Every time I mention Harlen or ask about Luanne in a personal sense, Jack gets all uptight. That makes me think he knows but doesn't want to share with me anything that might reflect badly on his sister."

"You can't blame him for wanting to protect her name."

"Of course not. But I wouldn't repeat anything damaging to Luanne and he should know that." While she talked, she'd been looking at the church. "Anyway, I don't see him. He's probably inside doing something holy."

Madge hid a smile. "I guess a stroll through the cemetery could be considered holy, which is where he is. I saw him going through the gate. This is a good time to catch him."

"No way. I don't like cemeteries."

"Oh, come on." Madge gave her a friendly shove toward the door. "It's broad daylight. You're perfectly safe. Everybody's dead."

"Now you're a comedienne? I mean it, Madge." Camille looked warily at the snowy white crypts, all raised above ground to accommodate a low water table. "There's something unnerving about those things. You're supposed to bury people in the ground, not shove them in a slot where some other dead people have been stashed. It's just weird."

Madge rolled her eyes. "This comes from being raised in Washington, D.C., so I guess you can't help it. And what would you prefer, that we dig a hole in the ground which would instantly fill with water and just let the casket float?" She laughed at Camille's expression. "Come on, I bet if you pluck up the courage to go over there, you'll find it pretty interesting. For instance, Allen Fontenot's ancestors from way back are entombed in the Blood Bayou cemetery. Jack's too. Lots of Vermillions in there."

Camille turned to look at her. "I didn't know Jack had any relatives. Other than Luanne and his father."

"Camille. You were married to Jack for three years and yet there's so much you don't know about him personally. Didn't you two ever talk?"

"I don't think you'd call those shouting matches talk," Camille said dryly. Still, she was intrigued. Now that she knew of Luanne's abuse and he knew she knew, he might tell her more. And she had promised Alafair.

"Okay," she said, and reached for the door handle. "But since I'm not in my car, you have to come back in thirty minutes to pick me up. Do not let me down."

"Deal." Madge smiled as she put the car in drive. "It'll be close to sundown then and you wouldn't want to be near that cemetery in the dark, right?"

"Very funny." Camille climbed out and didn't look back when Madge drove off.

She approached the cemetery warily, as if the sound of her footsteps might disturb the residents. The flagstone walk leading to the gate was shaded by a pretty mimosa tree with feathery fernlike foliage and clusters of pink puffball flowers. But it took more than a pretty tree in bloom to make a cemetery anything except a place for dead people to her. She paused at the gate, a work of art with its elaborate design wrought in cast iron, and searched the sea of white crypts looking for a sign of human life. If she didn't spot Jack in ten seconds, she told herself, she was out of here.

But there he was. He stood at a crypt that was overflowing with still-fresh flowers. Luanne's tomb, she assumed. He was utterly still, his head bowed, hands clasped behind his back. With her hand on the gate to push it open, she realized she was intruding on a private moment and should leave. But something— possibly his catching her out of the corner of his eye—alerted him to her presence. He hesitated only a heartbeat before lifting his hand. He didn't smile or welcome her, yet she found herself pushing the gate open, undeterred by the eerie squeak of hinges, and walking to him.

In spite of her unease, she was aware of the serenity of the place, but not because it was silent. There were sounds: birds calling from the depths of magnolia trees, water trickling from an unseen fountain, deep summer insects humming, and, faintly, organ music. Apparently, someone in the church was practicing.

"I'm intruding," she said to Jack as she drew closer.

"No." He gestured vaguely at the crypt. "I was just . . . I don't know. I haven't yet come to terms with losing Luanne like that. She had a lot of problems, but she didn't deserve such a violent death."

"Nobody does, Jack."

He looked fully at her and frowned slightly. "Has Allen taken a turn for the worst?"

"No." She decided to delay bringing up the subject of Luanne's miserable marriage. "What is that smell, sort of sweet and citrusy?"

"Sweet olive." A hint of a smile played at his mouth. "It's a shrub that was traditionally planted in cemeteries in the Deep South in times past, before embalming was common." At her blank look, he stepped a few feet away and broke off a sprig from a small shrub nearby. When he handed it to her, she saw tiny flowers. "Take a sniff," he said.

It was very fragrant. "What does it have to do with embalming?"

"When sun strikes sweet olive flowers, they give off that pleasant fragrance. Long ago a person who died in the summertime would be placed in one of the crypts without being embalmed. You can imagine folks looked for ways to mask the smell." He was smiling outright now. "You might say that sweet olive was the very first room freshener."

She dropped her jaw. "That's gross!"

"And fortunately not necessary anymore."

She waved a hand at the crypts. "I've never been in a cemetery quite like this one. Madge mentioned Allen's relatives were buried here."

"Mine too."

He hitched his chin in the direction of a crypt adorned with an angel. "Just beyond that angel are a bunch of Vermillions, my grandparents, my great-grandparents, uncles and aunts and cousins. My dad." He was quiet a minute. "Lots of stories buried here."

She put her hand above her eyes, shading them from the sun. "Why did you never talk about your relatives, Jack? Why did you let me assume you had no one in the world but Luanne?"

"There were no close relatives in any place you and I lived. And when Luanne and I were kids in Blood Bayou, most Vermillions were long gone. My dad was considered the black sheep of the family and pretty much disowned."

"Surely that didn't include his children?"

"I guess it did as we never had any contact."

"Wasn't that 'visiting the sins of the fathers on the heads of their children'?" she asked. "Isn't that what your Bible says?"

"Not my Bible and not quite accurate, but I take your point."

"Well, I think it's beyond cruel." She was genuinely outraged. "It was hardly Luanne's fault or yours that your father was less than perfect."

"Less than perfect." He chuckled. "That's an understatement. He was a hopeless drunk. And I mean hopeless. He lived in such misery that he didn't have anything left over to offer his kids."

Then why have children, she wondered. But she was fascinated. Jack had never openly talked like this. "I seem to recall that your mother died giving birth to Luanne."

"Yeah. Maybe that was a factor in Dad's downward spiral, but I struggled accepting that, even after surrendering to the ministry. Many people overcome much worse tragedy than losing a spouse and they still step up to the plate. They get on with life, they shoulder their responsibilities."

Especially if they have two young kids, Camille thought. It was a miracle that Jack had eventually managed to build a productive life, considering. Her own sterile childhood left a lot to be desired, but it paled in comparison to what Jack and his sister had lived daily.

She studied him thoughtfully. "You were never forthcoming about your childhood . . . or anything that happened before you entered law school."

"Because my life was pretty sordid before then," Jack said, meeting her eyes. "Tell the truth, Camille. Wouldn't you have run screaming if you'd known my background?"

"It wasn't your fault. We don't choose our parents, so I don't know what I would have done . . . had I known."

Jack made an impatient sound. "Why are we talking about this? I sound as if I feel sorry for myself when I don't. It's ancient history and I survived it. Eventually." He touched her arm to turn her around on the path leading to the gate. "Since I've been dry for seven years, I know more about addiction now. Unfortunately, my epiphany didn't happen before Dad died. I might have been more understanding. I might have helped him."

He pulled the gate open and motioned her to a bench set in deep shade beneath one of the sprawling live oaks. "You say cemeteries are creepy, so let's head this way." When they were both seated, he said, "Have you talked to Alafair yet?"

"Yes, and she was nothing like I expected."

"Pretty, petite, and stylish," he said, smiling. "No apron, all her teeth, and no Cajun French sprinkled in her language."

"I hope I don't come across as that silly, but maybe I did assume she'd be a bit more . . . matronly."

He laughed. "Matronly. Alafair would get a kick out of that." He was still chuckling when he said, "I bet she filled your ears. Harlen is not one of her favorite people."

Camille gave him a sharp look. "Does that mean I shouldn't believe what she told me?"

He shooed away a mosquito. "Depends on what she told you."

Camille's eyes strayed to Luanne's flowery place in the cemetery. "I don't like talking about this so near Luanne's resting place. It seems . . . sacrilegious somehow. Or, at the least, disrespectful to her memory."

"Luanne is not here anymore, Camille," he said gently. "She's truly in a better place."

"Any place would be better for Luanne," she muttered under her breath.

But Jack heard. His gaze narrowed. "How so? What did Alafair tell you?"

Camille watched a dragonfly light on the arm of the bench. She'd been so eager to pry open the secrets in Luanne's marriage . . . if there were any. Now, armed with a boatload of stuff, she found herself reluctant to share the dark truth with Jack. If he didn't know, would it be better to leave him with his illusions intact regarding his sister's marriage?

"Camille?"

Still uncertain, she looked into Jack's eyes. "Do you believe Luanne had a good marriage with Harlen?"

Now it was Jack's turn to think about his reply. Camille could almost see the wheels turning. It was a look she recognized. He was weighing options, considering what to say and how to say it.

"I never considered Harlen good husband material for Luanne," he said finally. "I tried to caution her before she married him. I pointed out their vast age difference, her insecurities versus his supersize ego. This obvious plan for her to play the role of trophy wife, all of that. But she wouldn't listen. You were right when you said she needed a protector, someone to offer the kind of safety and security neither of us had as children. She saw all that in Harlen."

"And do you believe you were right, that he turned out not to be a good husband?"

He studied her face as if trying to read into her words what she wasn't saying. "Where are we going with this conversation? What did Alafair say about their marriage? That Luanne was unfaithful?"

"It's funny . . . I mean, it's odd that you would assume Harlen the victim," Camille said. "The scenario you just described sets the stage for Luanne to be the victim."

"Then it was Harlen who was unfaithful?"

"I have no idea."

"It's not what Alafair said that's troubling you?"

"Do I look troubled?"

He looked on the verge of swearing. In their other life, Camille thought, her cagey replies would provoke a string of profanity. Now he was frustrated, obviously, but he held himself in check.

"Tell me straight out what the woman said, Camille. And don't start again about it being within earshot of Luanne. She can't be hurt by anything Harlen has done anymore. So spill it, please."

"Alafair asked me to tell you this so that you can possibly use it in your ministry," she said, poking at an acorn on the ground with the toe of her shoe. "I know that sounds weird, but she thought when you talk to other troubled women in your congregation, you might pick up . . . certain signs." She looked up at him. "I mean, if you aren't already aware of this kind of thing."

"What I am is in the dark," he said with an obvious edge in his tone. "I don't have a clue whether I'm aware of anything or not."

She studied him, hunched over, elbows on his knees, looking down at his feet. "Tell me that you suspected something not being right in your sister's relationship with Harlen. Tell me that, Jack."

A good half a minute ticked past. "Yeah, I guess I thought there might be something wrong, especially in the last few months." He settled back, looking at Camille. "Luanne wouldn't tell me anything. She flatly denied being unhappy."

"You had to know she was occasionally . . . indiscreet," Camille said, choosing her words carefully.

"Promiscuous. She was promiscuous."

"I wasn't sure you knew."

"That's why I tried to get her to open up to me. I'm no longer the total dunce I once was when it comes to reading the people closest to me. So I could see she had serious emotional problems. Every day I have people sitting in my office pouring out their troubles, but I couldn't get my sister to say anything. When we were together, she was Little Miss Sunshine. It was frustrating. But there was no forcing her."

"Alafair tried to reason with her about her behavior too, but she didn't get anywhere with her either." Camille leaned over and picked up the acorn. "Maybe when I tell you what was really going on, you'll understand why she couldn't bring herself to ask for help."

It must have been difficult, but Jack managed to wait her out while Camille studied the acorn in her palm, wondering how to say the words. Finally, she looked up at him. "Harlen was routinely beating up on Luanne, Jack."

She saw that he was stunned. Nobody could fake that look. "It's not unusual for women to hide their abuse out of a mistaken sense of shame or fear," she told him. "Or to protect the person who's abusing them. Which do you think applies to Luanne?"

He stood, clearly shocked. "That can't be true. There would have been signs." He paced a few feet away, then turned back to look at her. "I've counseled abused women. They're a mess. They have a certain look. I never saw that in Luanne."

"Maybe she was a good actress."

"You can't hide bruises or a black eye or broken bones or—"

"You can hide a multitude of stuff under makeup that's skillfully applied, Jack. Trust me on that."

"You're saying he beat her up frequently and yet she never needed treatment? That she was able to hide everything?"

"When it was bad enough to require treatment, Alafair took her to a clinic in Lafayette."

"Then there will be a record. I'm going to check. I'm—"

"There is a record, but you'll have to look for it in Alafair's name. Luanne was so determined to keep her secret she used her housekeeper's name." She paused, watching him try to take it all in. "They're similar types, Jack, Luanne and Alafair. Same height, weight, coloring. It worked. Check it out yourself."

"I'm positively going to check, you can count on that."

She played the acorn from one hand to the other. "I guess this isn't a good time to ask if you've checked on Harlen's alibi?"

Instead of a reply, he simply stared at her. She'd pushed him about as far as he could go, she decided. Still, it was a little surprising that the man she knew as king of the acid comeback was suddenly mute. "And I guess you didn't mean it when you promised to do that."

When he still didn't reply, she drew in a long breath and spoke with as much patience as she could muster. "Jack, think about it. Chester's conviction for the murder of Stephanie Hill has been thrown out. And it wasn't too difficult, considering the incompetence of both the Blood Bayou PD and the prosecution. Do you really trust them to investigate Luanne's murder?"

She paused, searching for a way to break through his resistance. "Don't you want to know beyond a shadow of a doubt who killed her? If it wasn't Chester, then some individual in Blood Bayou is going scot-free thinking he's gotten away with murder—again."

"It is not Harlen," he stated flatly. "I know that."

"And maybe you're right. As for me, I'd still be interested to hear where he claims to have been when his wife was being murdered."

With a glance at her watch, she tossed the acorn away. "Madge is due to pick me up. I apologize for being the one to tell you this, but I promised Alafair."

"Yeah. And what was her reason again?" He spoke between his teeth.

"It was not meant as a criticism of you. She just wanted you to be on the lookout for women in your congregation who might be victims like Luanne."

"And you think I don't know an abused spouse when I see one?"

"I don't know what you know or don't know in your new profession, Jack. I'm quoting Alafair, which makes me, in this instance, just the messenger. I guess I'm lucky we're not in bib-lical times or you'd have to kill me." She looked beyond him to the street. "Here's Madge now. I'm going."

He made no move to stop her and she was glad.

"WELL, THAT went well," Camille said facetiously once she'd buckled herself in the car beside Madge.

"He wasn't cooperative?"

"He was downright hostile. I think he took Alafair's sug-gestion as a personal criticism of his ministerial ability. Or lack of." As they pulled away, she looked back and found Jack still watching. Something about the way he stood, shoulders a little down, hands just hanging at his side, caught at her heart. She'd unloaded a lot of bad stuff on him, and for just a tiny moment she wished they weren't always fighting and parting angrily. He appeared to need a hug and she wished she could give him one.

For just one tiny, fleeting moment . . .

CHAPTER ten

JACK DECIDED, AS he entered the local police headquarters, that it didn't matter much how big or how small the town or what demographics existed, police stations were all alike, even down to the smell. Cigarette stench was embedded in the Sheetrock walls; walls that seemed always to be painted a sick green. The dingy floors reeked of pine-scented mop water. All of it mixed with the odor of unwashed bodies and stress.

In the ebb and flow of cops going about the business of law enforcement were people waiting in chairs for who knows what, or pacing with anxiety or anger or fear, all adding to the look of the place as somewhere you didn't want to be.

Nowadays, when he had occasion to go into a police station, he felt profoundly thankful that he had a legitimate reason, but it hadn't always been that way. As a kid, he'd had more than a few run-ins with the cops as a consequence of drinking in his early teens. Back then, the police in Blood Bayou knew him as Vincent Vermillion's wild boy, keeping to the family tradition of drunkenness. But he was most embarrassed to recall the times when as an adult he'd been hauled into police stations scattered over various parts of the country. Until that one last traumatic arrest. Bottom line: he didn't like police stations.

Today, in spite of his past, there was nothing but genuine respect in the face of the grizzled desk sergeant behind the counter as Jack approached.

"How's it going, Boyd?"

"Couldn't be better, Reverend. I got a fine new pirogue, me. You tell me when you want to go fishing, we'll search out some *sac-a-lait* hiding places, then have a party, yes."

"Sounds good, Boyd." Jack had enjoyed several dawn excursions on the bayou with Boyd Soileau, who had a reputation to maintain as the local champ fishing for the small, freshwater perch. But now Boyd's smile faded as he studied Jack's face.

"Sorry to hear about your sister, Reverend. That was sad, very sad."

"It was that, Boyd. Thank you." He glanced down the hall at the office labeled Private. "Is the chief in yet this morning?"

"Oh, yes. Been holed up in there since before shift change." Boyd walked back to his desk and punched the intercom. Bending down, he spoke into the old-fashioned box. "You got a visitor, Chief."

The chief's reply was an unintelligible squawk, at least to Jack, but Boyd seemed to understand and waved him on. "You can go in, Reverend, no need asking if he'll be glad to see you. A man of God is always welcome here, *mais oui*."

To get to the police chief's office, Jack had to walk past various squad rooms. Midway down the hall was the break room, reeking of burnt coffee and stale doughnuts. As he passed, he glanced inside and was surprised to see Ray Wyatt talking to a rookie female cop. Jack frowned, searching his memory for her name. Her parents attended his church. Styles, that was it. Theresa Styles. The retired detective appeared to be spinning a tale that Theresa found hysterically funny. Besides that, she looked flushed and flirtatious. The guy had a way with the ladies, Jack decided.

He knew from Madge that Wyatt was a volunteer for the Truth Project. That he'd spent a good bit of time at BBPD working the Chester Pelham case. It seemed odd to Jack that Wyatt wasn't shunned by the department after his role in unraveling their case against Pelham. He also found it odd that a man retired from a career in homicide chose to spend his retirement doing something so grim. Maybe the old maxim was true, he thought—once a cop, always a cop.

Wyatt, noticing Jack, wrapped up his story with a teasing wink at Theresa, then stepped out in the hall. "Hey, Jack, have you got a minute?"

Jack hesitated, curious. He nodded, deciding that his conversation with Chief Raines could wait.

"Coffee's old and the doughnuts are gone," Wyatt said, motioning to the break room, "which means it'll be private. Let's talk a minute."

Private? Jack's curiosity went up a notch.

Inside, Wyatt closed the door. Jack refused coffee, but watched Wyatt pour himself a cup, then grimace at the taste. "Whoa, that's bad," he said. "Sure you don't want some?"

"I've had enough today. What's on your mind, Wyatt?"

"Luanne's murder." He stopped, looking pained. "Sorry. That sounded blunt, but I'm a blunt kinda guy. You spend twenty-five years in homicide, you learn to cut to the chase."

"What about Luanne's murder?"

Wyatt leaned casually against the metal table, cupping the vile brew. "You're aware that I worked real close with Camille's group in proving Chester didn't kill Stephanie Hill?"

"Several people mentioned it," Jack said.

"Yeah, well, you would know how she can be when she gets an idea in her head, right? I mean, you were married to her."

Jack had no intention of discussing Camille with this character. He looked at his watch. "The chief's expecting me, Wyatt. What's your point?"

"Hey, no offense," he said, holding up one hand, palm out. "What I'm trying to say is that she's one stubborn lady and she's got the bit in her teeth about Chester being railroaded."

"I'm aware that she believes Pelham is innocent."

"Yeah. Which is not doing anything to endear her to the folks here at the station since they're dead certain he's guilty. I hear talk. They're ticked off at her. I thought you might be able to persuade her to back off, you know? Let the BBPD handle the case."

Wyatt as a spokesperson for the department? Jack had serious doubts. More curious than ever, he asked, "What if he really is innocent?"

Wyatt looked startled. "You don't believe that, do you?"

"What I believe isn't the issue," Jack said. "And I don't have one iota of influence where Camille is concerned. If the guys here at the station want her to back off, they'll have to tell her so."

"It's never a good idea to have the cops mad at you," Wyatt said. "They're still sore that she made them look bad when Chester was exonerated."

Jack's dislike for Wyatt grew with every word the man uttered.

"And they weren't sore over your role in helping her?"

"Big time," Wyatt said in a wry tone. "And I've had to work hard to try and repair my image, you know what I mean?"

"Starting with Theresa Styles?"

Wyatt shook his head and grinned. "I had to start some-where." Losing his smile, he said, "I'm serious about Camille backing off. I wish you'd have a talk with her." He set his cup aside, unfinished. "Look at it from their perspective. They were made to look incompetent by a woman, and what I'm hearing is that they don't like her messing around in Blood Bayou police work this time."

"Afraid she'll made them look bad again?"

"Right. And because we're friends, Camille and I, I felt I should try to head her off at the pass, so to speak."

"That's big of you, Wyatt."

"I'm serious, Rev. Why don't you try reasoning with her? Or you could tell her mother to send her back to Baton Rouge. For her own good."

"Uh-huh."

"That incident at her mother's house was meant to tell her that she's making folks mad. Because she's used to city life, she doesn't understand small towns and how they see interference. You know what I mean?"

With a pointed glance at his watch, Jack moved to the door. "I'm short of time, Wyatt. And I still need to see the chief." He glanced at the coffee pot. "You should watch drinking that stuff. It's lethal."

He was still irritated when he got to the chief's office. And puzzled as to why Wyatt had approached him instead of going directly to Camille. But he pushed it to the back of his mind to be reconsidered later. Right now he had another mission.

Jack was reminded of a monkey when he looked at Chief June Raines. The man was barely five and a half feet tall and might weigh a hundred and thirty on a good day. If there had been a contest for looking the most Cajun-like, June Raines would win it hands down. He had nut brown skin; sharp, button-black eyes; and coal black hair. But what was truly impressive about him—besides his awesome temper—was his mustache. It was as black as his head hair, thick and lustrous with both ends curled up crisply. Jack wondered how much time it took each morning to achieve that effect.

Raines was already on his feet behind a huge and imposing desk as Jack entered. Smiling a welcome, he extended a hand over the vast desktop, shook firmly, and pointed Jack to a chair. "Sit, sit. Good to see you, Jack."

"Same here, June."

Jack took the chair as directed, thinking there had to be a platform to elevate Raines, otherwise the man couldn't possibly see over the desk once he sat down.

"No need in me asking why you're here, Jack. You'll want to know how the case is progressing. We have the knife with Luanne's blood type on it, but you already know that. It'll be a couple of weeks before we get the DNA back from New Orleans. We don't expect a surprise there. Makes you wonder why Pelham didn't toss it in the bayou, his shack being built right over it. Almost more trouble to stick it in the rafters in plain sight than to just sink it where it'd never be found."

The same thoughts had dogged Jack till the wee hours. Chester Pelham was short a few bricks of a load, but was he that stupid? Jack hated to let his thinking be colored by Camille's low opinion of BBPD's expertise—or lack of—in investigating the case, but it was hard to find logical answers to the questions she'd raised.

"How is Chester doing in the hospital?" he asked.

"Hanging on, hanging on." Raines reared back, lifted his booted feet, and propped them on the corner of his desk. Jack hid a smile, noting the heels added about two inches.

"They tell me he's in a drug-induced coma," the chief said. "It's something they do now while the brain restores itself, so they say. What it really means is they won't let him die. Some folks around here might object to that, but . . ." One shoulder went up in a shrug. "That's the way it is."

"I was at the hospital when they brought him in," Jack said, recalling Chester's head as a bloody mess. "I don't see how anybody could survive looking like that."

"Yeah, he caught a few bullets that day."

"How exactly did it happen, Chief?"

"Tell the truth, I was pretty upset with my men the way it went down. In a situation like that when you've got a suspect cornered, the least thing can cause a rookie to panic. Jimmy Labat hadn't been out of the academy a month, so he shouldn't have been on the scene at all and he wouldn't except he was in a patrol car when the call came in and just scatted over there to get in on the action. I've suspended him."

Jack said nothing, wondering at Camille's reaction if she ever learned exactly how Chester came to be shot.

"So it was Labat who spooked," Raines continued, "and next thing, there's a hail of bullets flying and Chester's the target." He shook his head, looking regretful. "Not that he didn't deserve to die for murdering Luanne like that, he did. But me, I prefer him sitting on death row in his right mind, weak as it was. Instead, he'll be a ward of the state if he survives and waited on hand and foot."

"So you're convinced it was Pelham who murdered Luanne?"

Raines's look was one of pure amazement. He swore, quickly
apologized, and sat up, boots flat on the floor. "Well, heck-fire,
Jack. Who else would want to kill your sister?"

"Why would Chester want to kill her?"

Raines looked disgusted. "A half-wit like that, they don't
need a reason." He paused for a moment as a thought struck.
"You been talking to your wife, right?"

"I don't have a wife, June."

"Your ex-wife, then." Raines picked up a folder, rose, and
walked around his huge desk to hand it to Jack. "She was here
early this morning nagging me to let her look at the crime
scene photos. I held out for a while, but I'm telling you, she's
pretty persuasive. You ever noticed that? Being married to her,
I mean?"

Jack let that one pass, but opened the folder to get an idea
of what Camille might have seen. But on taking a look, he was
at first revolted and then anguished at the way Luanne's life had
ended.

Unable to stomach it, he closed the file. "What did Camille
say she was looking for?"

"Well, it's like you say, she doesn't believe Chester did it, so
I think she was looking for some bit of evidence that might have
been overlooked by my people, which is why I wanted to know
if you agreed with her." He was back behind his desk now but
still on his feet. "You think we've got a killer on the loose here,
Jack?"

Jack took his time replying. He didn't want to add to the
chief's irritation without proof. And at this point, there wasn't

any. "I'm not sure, Chief. If that's the case, we've got a very smart and cunning killer. He's played it so that Chester looks so guilty we aren't even looking at anybody else."

"Well, I am sure, Jack. The evidence points to Chester and I never argue with evidence." He sat down and scooted his chair close to his desk. "Now, I know you're divorced from Camille, but you're not the man you were when that happened. She's bound to recognize that and you'll have some influence using your clerical collar, so to speak. Why don't you ask her to just back off a little? Let us do our job. You think you could do that, Jack?"

First Wyatt and now the chief. "I'll give it a shot, but I'm not promising she'll listen." His smile took on an ironic slant. "She's not much influenced by my clerical collar."

When Raines saw that Jack didn't rise to leave, he studied his face, narrow-eyed. "Something else on your mind?"

The question Jack had come to ask was framed in his mind now and he'd been given the opening he needed. He might be a welcome visitor in the chief's office today, but not afterward if his question was taken the wrong way. "I was wondering, Chief, whether or not your investigation had led you to ask Harlen where he was at the time of Luanne's murder."

AFTER THREE days at Madge's Cajun-style cottage, Camille was in love with it. The floor plan was classic shotgun, a straight shot from front door all the way through the house to the back porch, bedrooms on one side; kitchen, dining, and living on the other. Raised on tall pilings, it was set back from the water about twenty yards, which made for a gorgeous view of Blood Bayou. After dinner, Camille was in the habit of settling on the back porch swing to enjoy that view and listen to the oddly harmonious medley of night sounds.

Tonight the sky was clear and dotted with a million stars. Moonbeams sparkled on the still, dark water. A cypress tree stood like a tall, straight sentinel, limbs dripping Spanish moss. At its base, cypress "knees" stuck up out of the water. Camille started when out of the dark came the call of a bullfrog, deep and full-throated, instantly echoed by another. And another. Until there was a chorus of sound.

But instead of enjoying the primeval show, she couldn't quite banish the gory image of Luanne's body at the water's edge. After studying photos of the crime scene where her ex-sister-in-law was murdered, the moss hanging from the tree was more creepy than picturesque. The sounds were scary. And Blood Bayou seemed more eerie than beautiful. Its name was a bit too menacingly apt.

She'd had to do some fast talking to Chief Raines to get access to the photos. Her hope had been to spot something, some tiny detail overlooked by the detectives working the case, but in spite of her intense study, she'd found nothing. All she'd taken away was a grisly mental picture of Jack's dead sister.

She heard a clock inside strike the midnight hour. She'd felt no qualms when Madge left at ten o'clock for a swing shift at BBPD after reassuring Camille that her two German shepherds, Ben and Jerry, were on guard and trained to repel anyone they didn't recognize coming too close to the house. Both slept at her feet now, looking as angelic as kittens. Still, she wondered if she'd feel secure enough to sleep. There were neighbors, but too far away to be of any help if she needed help.

Get a grip, Camille!

She stood up abruptly, mostly to rein in her overactive imagination. Madge told her that the dogs were to remain outside when she went to bed. And sure enough, on her way to the door, both dogs lifted their heads and watched her go inside. Neither made a move to rise.

After punching in the security code, she undressed in her room in the dark, feeling somehow that she needed to keep a view of the bayou within sight. A pier extended thirty feet or so over the water and she could see it clearly. Nothing moved, which should have reassured her but didn't.

She was brushing her teeth when the dogs began to bark. She paused, toothbrush in hand, guessing they'd spotted some night creature and were warding it off their doggy territory. However, on second thought, Madge had told her they were trained not to react to the appearance of wildlife common to the area. Clearly something had spooked them.

She hurriedly donned a shirt and shorts, grabbing her cell phone on the way to a window where she'd have a view of the front yard. The dogs were frantic now, barking nonstop. She suspected they wouldn't carry on so without reason. Moving the curtain aside cautiously, she was just in time to see one of the dogs sail over the fence like a deer. Heart racing, she flipped a switch that lit up the front yard and opened the door. Immediately the security alarm went off, setting up an earsplitting racket. She quickly closed the door and managed to punch in the code with shaky fingers. When she opened it again, the dog at the fence was barking madly and she could hear the other in the distance, apparently giving chase. Suddenly a man yelled. And instantly two gunshots rang out, brief, staccato bursts of sound. Unmistakable sound. Then abrupt silence.

With a gasp, she stumbled back and slammed the door. Truly terrified now, she turned the lock and retreated toward the bathroom, pulling out her cell phone on the way. Thank God, Madge had given her the number. But before she had a chance to call, it rang in her hand.

"What's wrong, Camille?" Madge asked. "Why was the alarm triggered?"

Camille sagged with relief, pressing a hand against her racing heart. "Someone is outside, Madge! I heard gunshots. And the dogs are barking like crazy. One of them, I mean. The other jumped the fence and disappeared."

She heard Madge repeat her remark about gunshots to someone nearby, then she was back. "That would be Jerry who gave chase," she said. "Ben is trained not to leave the yard. And don't go outside. Wait in the house. A unit is on the way. They'll check the area, but whoever it was is probably gone now."

"I don't know, Madge," she said, looking out a window. "Ben isn't acting like he's gone. He's almost throwing himself against the fence."

"But you don't see Jerry?" There was note of concern in her voice.

"No. And I don't hear him barking anymore either. But I'm not sure I could anyway because Ben is so loud. Should I try to call him back inside the house?"

"No! Don't even think of cracking that door. Wait for our guys. You should see the unit any minute now. They'll take care of the dogs."

Just then headlights swept across the room as a car pulled up and parked on the street in front of the cottage. Camille's knees went weak. "They're here. I'm hanging up," she said.

She moved to the door, but before opening it, she waited until she heard footsteps on the porch. Closing her eyes, she tried calming herself. When she faced her rescuers, she didn't want to appear as near hysterics as she felt.

Minutes later, Madge's property was overrun with Blood Bayou's finest. In addition to the original responders, three more police units were on the scene to work the call. A meticulous search of the property was in progress while Camille was questioned by a detective whose name tag read "Duval." But it was almost impossible for her to concentrate, as Jerry still had not returned. Ben must have felt the same concern for his partner; he was pacing the fence line and whining, clearly distressed.

"No," she told Duval for the third time, watching him scribble notes on a yellow pad. "I didn't see anything, just Ben and Jerry going crazy. Then Jerry jumped the fence to chase him, I guess. I heard a yell just before two gunshots rang out."

"To chase him? How do you know it was a man?"

She gave a shrug. "I can't be sure, but it sounded like a man." Still shaken, she wrapped her arms around herself. "I'm really worried because Jerry's not back. I'm wondering if he caught up with him and if he did, I'm afraid those gunshots mean that he's hurt. Or worse." She looked at Ben pacing. "See, Ben knows something's wrong."

"We're searching the woods, ma'am. They'll find your dog."

"It's Madge's dog!" She heard hysteria in her own voice and tried to master it. "Sorry, I'm not used to this kind of thing. My room at my mother's house is trashed, now someone tried breaking into this house, gunshots . . ." She shuddered.

"Take heart," Duval said bracingly. "He didn't get to the house. In fact, thanks to the dogs, it doesn't appear that he even managed to get in the fence. But, there's no getting around it, he intended to do just that. You're sure the gate was closed when you turned in for the night?"

"Absolutely. And it was still closed when I looked out. I know the dogs scared him off before he got inside the fence."

Duval paused a moment, surveying the layout of the house and grounds. "Your neighbors are too far away to have heard anything." He noted that fact on his yellow pad, then looked up from his notes as a cop approached.

"Sergeant, we found something."

"Such as?"

"Looks like hamburger meat." Holding up a plastic bag. "Found it outside the fence. Whoever it was came prepared to feed it to the dogs, but looks like they didn't let him get close enough."

"Bag and label it," Duval ordered. "Then see that it gets to the lab. If it contains something to put the dogs out of commission, we want to know that."

Camille's heart took another dip. The dogs poisoned?

Seeing her expression, Duval said, "Don't worry, neither of these dogs would have eaten it. They're trained not to. Madge adopted both from the K9 team, which means they're smarter than the average thug."

Camille wanted to believe him, but that didn't change the fact that the dogs had been in jeopardy on her account and one of them was still missing. In spite of good training, a well-placed bullet would take care of the smartest guard dog.

"Sergeant!" one of the cops called from outside the fence. "We found the dog."

Camille put her hand to her mouth and felt her knees go

weak. A cop was leading Jerry slowly toward them. The dog was unsteady on his feet and limping, but he was alive. Ben dashed over to him, barking a joyous welcome, dancing around him, whining and wagging his tail. Camille felt like doing a jig too.

"What happened to him?" she asked anxiously.

"Not sure yet," the cop said, guiding the dog carefully up the steps. "When we found him in the woods, he seemed dazed. If he was shot, it missed anything vital. Could be he wasn't shot at all but kicked or struck with something. He's bleeding from some kind of wound on his head, but it was hard to tell how bad out there with just our flashlights to check him out."

Camille bent down, extending the back of her hand. When Jerry licked her fingers weakly, her eyes filled. "I'll take him to a vet right now. Oh, I can't believe this has happened. Madge will be so upset. *I'm* so upset!"

"We already radioed for Doc Watson. He'll come out, and if Jerry needs other treatment, he'll take him back to the vet hospital."

"I'll get something for him to lie on until the vet arrives." Camille dashed inside and scooped up a thick rug on the floor beside her bed. When she brought it out to the porch, she spread it on the floor. "Down, Jerry," she said gently, giving the dog a familiar command. Well trained, he did as told, but it was obvious by the slow and painful way he obeyed that he was injured.

Duval bent closer to have a look at a bloody patch near the dog's ear. "This is just a guess," he said, straightening up, "but I bet when our guy shot and missed and Jerry kept coming, he used his gun to whack him upside his head. Hopefully, he took a chunk out of the guy's rear end."

Just then, another cop checking the fence line called out. "You might want to take a look at this, Sergeant."

"Hold on," Duval said to Camille.

She watched as Duval joined the group clustered at the gate studying something of interest. After a few minutes, she was curious enough to see for herself. Leaving Jerry lying on the mat, she headed out to see for herself. As she approached, a young cop moved to head her off, but Duval waved her through.

"I think we can safely say your intruder had a good reason to yell," Duval said, with a nod at what one of the investigating officers held in his gloved hand. Moving closer, Camille saw that it was a piece of torn fabric, denim, she thought.

"Jerry must have overtaken him before he was injured. This looks like a piece of his clothing," Duval said.

"Do you think those gunshots were aimed at Jerry?" she asked.

"Looks that way. I bet he was at the gate planning to entice the dogs with a little red meat, but Ben and Jerry were too well trained to be enticed. He took off when they put up such a ruckus, but Jerry's training kicked in and he went after him." He gave the denim a wry look. "I'm guessing that fabric comes from an embarrassing part of his anatomy."

His remark produced chuckles all around from the cops.

"Is there any blood on it?" Camille asked. "If so, we have DNA."

"Unfortunately, no," said Duval. "But we'll send it to the lab anyway. Can't tell, maybe there'll be something."

With the investigation complete, Duval walked back to the porch with Camille. "I'll be leaving a unit with two men out here, Ms. St. James," he told her. "It's not likely you'll have any more trouble tonight, but better safe than sorry." He looked up at the eastern sky showing the first pale streaks of dawn. "It'll be daylight soon anyway."

Camille glanced at the pink sky. "Madge's shift is supposed to end at seven, but she'll be concerned about Jerry. Can she leave before her shift is up?"

"Maybe not, depending on whether anybody can come in early and relieve her. But she'll be all over us to find the lowlife who did this. You don't want to mess with Madge or her dogs."

Camille put out her hand. "Thank you for such a prompt response, Sergeant."

"No thanks required, ma'am. Just doing my job." But after letting go of her hand, he added, "I read the report of the vandalism at your mother's place a few days ago, Ms. St. James. If you really believe that incident is connected to your interest in Luanne Richard's murder, then you probably think this one is too."

"I do."

He scratched his head thoughtfully. "No offense, but you should leave this business to the cops. Whoever it is would probably back off then, 'cause it's plain that somebody wants you to leave Blood Bayou, ma'am."

"It's pretty plain to me too."

"Well, then, does that mean you'll be leaving?"

"No. From now on, I'll just be extra careful."

THE VET arrived while the police were still milling around. Camille hovered while he examined Jerry thoroughly. That done, he sat back on his haunches and told her that the dog had bruised ribs, probably kicked by the assailant, but he could find no other injury except the obvious wound on the dog's head. But it was a hard lick too. Like Sergeant Duval, he guessed it was most likely the perpetrator's gun. It had probably knocked Jerry out briefly, or close to. Camille was to watch him for a couple of days, try to keep him less active than usual, feed him lightly, and keep him well hydrated. Just as a little kid with a mild concussion, there wasn't much else to be done. Camille breathed a sigh of relief and was glad to see the whole crowd climb back in their vehicles and leave.

But there was no sleeping after that, and when Madge came home an hour early because of Jerry, Camille had cooked break-fast as an act of penance. While they ate, she suffered through a lecture from Madge, scolding her for opening the door when the dogs were obviously in attack mode.

"It was stupid," Camille admitted, pouring herself a glass of orange juice. "I don't know what I was thinking. Well, actually, I wasn't thinking. I knew the dogs weren't supposed to bark except for a good reason, so I opened it to see what I could see." She shrugged sheepishly. "Really stupid, huh?"

"Well, let's just say I'd never react like that."

"I'm so sorry Jerry was hurt," Camille said. "How can I make it up to you?"

"It wasn't your fault that he gave chase." Madge buttered a second piece of toast. "He did what he was trained to do. And he'll be okay." She glanced over at Jerry, lying in the corner on the rug. "Won't you, sweet boy?"

She smiled as the dog wagged his tail weakly, then said, "I'm probably too paranoid about security due to what I see every day in my job."

"You'd think that a town as small as Blood Bayou would have very little crime," Camille said, getting up to clear the table.

Madge handed over her plate. "Small towns have all the sins of big towns, just not as much of it."

"Two unsolved murders in five years," Camille observed. "You'd think the cops wouldn't rest until the killer is found."

"They think he is found," Madge said. "As we know. But it's plain that you poking and prying into Luanne's murder is giving someone severe heartburn. Which means staying alone here at night even with Ben and Jerry on guard is too risky."

"Oh, Madge, are you going to try to talk me into going home too?"

"Would it do any good?"

"Probably not. Definitely not." Smiling, Camille gave a shrug. "At least not until I'm forced to admit there is no other suspect besides Chester. And you don't need to worry about me. I've called the one and only motel and reserved a room. To tell the truth, when the clock struck midnight, I did feel a little spooked. So staying where there's security twenty-four/seven seems the smart thing to do."

"You're not going to a motel," Madge said, moving to the sink. "And since you're determined to stay, I've put in for vacation." She held up a hand when Camille began to protest. "Hear me out. I've got so much time accrued that a couple of weeks won't make a dent in the total. The pay is lousy at BBPD, but one of the perks is the amount of vacation and sick leave we get."

"I can't let you do that!"

"You can't stop me. It's done." She refilled her coffee cup. "The way I figure it is that if we haven't come up with anything concrete after a couple of weeks, I'll go back on the day shift while you keep our investigation going. That way, I'll be here at night."

"We? Our?" Camille repeated. "Do I have a partner now?"

"You do." Madge stirred sugar into her coffee. "This way he's forced to keep an eye on both of us. At least we'll keep him busy trying to figure which of us to torment next." She headed out of the kitchen, making for the bedroom. "And now I'm going to bed. Wake me when it's time for lunch. A late lunch."

Madge might joke about it, but Camille was still a little unsettled over being the target of an unknown tormentor. "Let's hope he's satisfied with tormenting and doesn't decide to do something a lot meaner," she muttered to Madge's back.

CHAPTER eleven

MID-MORNING SHE WAS on the porch swing, jotting down the facts of Luanne's murder as she knew them in a spiral notebook. In police homicide parlance, such a tool is called the "murder book." And in all Truth Project investigations, Camille had found the process of recording every detail, no matter how minor, invaluable in keeping focused.

She studied her notes now, all too few, then sat back for a minute, swaying gently. As always, her gaze strayed to the bayou. For the past half hour, a gray heron had been fishing at the water's edge. The huge bird with its long legs made barely a ripple, high-stepping in the shallows. She watched, thinking how peaceful and still the bayou appeared, how beautiful.

She recalled asking her mother how Blood Bayou came to have its name. Diana had been only too willing to tell her. "Sometimes, at just the right moment," her mother said, clearly enjoying herself, "when the moss-draped branches of the trees along the edge are shot through with setting sun, some say the water seems to turn an eerie blood red."

"You're kidding!" had been Camille's response.

"No indeed. Cajun legend has it that it's the bloody stain of a curse stemming from the desecration of the bayou by big oil and greedy folk." Diana had smiled at Camille's expression.

"Don't look so appalled, darlin'. Most say it is simply an optical illusion."

"I vote for that," Camille said with feeling.

"On the other hand, scientists claim it's a mix of algae, heat, and swamp gases."

"Logic. I like that one even better."

"Hmm, no romance in your soul?"

Not with the image in her head of Luanne's body bleeding out in the dark water, she thought now. And at the moment, she was glad it was broad daylight and that the sun was high overhead. After all that had happened lately, the legend was more than a little creepy.

When Ben and Jerry, sleeping at her feet, suddenly stirred and began to bark, the startled heron spread its wings wide and lifted up in a splendid display. Ben scrambled up and clambered down the steps, making for the front of the house. Jerry followed, with a little less energy. Only then did Camille hear the sound of a car. And in spite of the fact that she didn't think she was in any danger from anyone arriving in broad daylight in full view of God and the world, she went inside the house and locked the door behind her as she'd been cautioned to do by Madge.

At the front window, she saw that Ben was frantically throwing himself at the gate, holding a wary Ray Wyatt at bay. Jerry stood well back, as if aware that he was less able to do his part. Apparently they didn't recognize Ray.

With an exasperated huff, Camille opened the door and went out onto the porch. "Ben! Jerry! Come!" When the dogs did not respond, she clapped her hands together smartly. "Here, boys, here. Come!"

They ceased barking, but reluctantly, as she went down the

steps and hurried to the gate, but both still stood their ground. She caught both dogs' collars, yanking hard on Ben's. "Stop it, both of you!"

Both settled, but the hair on their backs still bristled and both were growling low and with real menace. "Sorry, Ray, but Madge says they're trained to repel strangers. I guess you're a stranger."

"I guess." Wyatt held his position a safe distance from the closed gate, still eyeing the dogs warily. "And I'm not sure I want an introduction."

"They'll be okay once you're introduced as a friend." She turned to the dogs. "Sit," she commanded. "Stay!"

Both sat obediently, but looked anything but welcoming as they watched her lift the gate latch. "Come inside and let them get your scent."

Moving cautiously, Wyatt kept an eye on the dogs while inching through the open gate. "You sure they're okay?"

"They're lambs—except when they aren't."

"Funny."

Oddly, both dogs seemed to have taken a dislike to Wyatt, but at her command they allowed him inside the gate and both stuck close to her side protectively as she and Ray made their way to the front porch.

"I'm sorry about this, Ray," she said, going up the steps. "This must be a bit of leftover aggression from the ruckus we had here last night."

"I heard about it," he said, following Camille while still keeping a safe distance from the dogs. "But could we talk someplace where your bodyguards aren't?"

"I'll close them inside the house and we can talk on the back porch. It's beautiful out there this morning." She swept up the murder book from the floor. "I'm glad you're here. I was just putting down on paper the few facts I've gathered on Luanne's murder."

He glanced at the spiral notebook in her hands. "Keeping a murder book, eh?"

"You know I always do." She opened the front door, ordered the dogs inside, then closed it. She made a face but ignored them as they whined and scratched at the door.

"Follow me," she told Wyatt, tripping down the steps. "We'll go around the house to the back. I wanted to talk to you anyway to ask if you have any thoughts to share about the case. I've just about exhausted all angles as to why anyone would want to kill Luanne. I welcome anybody with a fresh perspective."

"I'll be glad to look at what you've got, but that's not why I'm here, Camille." As they walked, he studied the layout of the cottage on the grounds and, once they rounded the corner and the bayou came into view, the proximity of the house to the water. He was shaking his head as he spoke. "This is an open invitation to do you harm, woman! I see what the guys meant."

"What guys?"

"The uniforms who responded to your nine-one-one last night."

"I didn't call nine-one-one. Actually, Madge called here because I tripped the alarm."

"Same thing. As for the department, they downplayed the vandalism last week at your mother's house, but last night proved someone really is harassing you. Gunshots they can't ignore."

"Do you think it's just harassment? Is it just a mean-spirited attempt to scare me, to force me to leave, or . . ."

"Or what?"

"Or would he have done something worse if he'd been able to get past the dogs? As it was, he could have killed Jerry."

Wyatt took a seat opposite the swing. "Who knows? That's the scary part, Camille. You don't know what his intentions are, so in my opinion you can't afford to take any more chances. You've got to give this up and go home."

She pushed the spiral notebook into his hands. "Do me a favor and let's not argue. I get enough of that from just about everybody I know." She motioned at the notebook with her chin. "Take a look at my notes and tell me if you think I've missed or overlooked something. I've spent so many hours figuring so many angles that there could be a clue right in front of my nose and I'm not seeing it."

He ignored the notebook. "Did you hear anything I said?"

She sighed. "I won't be alone after today. Madge is starting a vacation. She must be a frustrated detective, because she's decided she wants to work with me." She gave a what-can-I-say shrug. "Who would dare threaten Madge Pichon? She's a match for almost any crook."

"This is no joking matter, Camille."

"I know. Really. But we'll be okay, Ray. For now, just take a look at my notes on the case, will you? I'm trying to find out where Harlen Richard was at the time of Luanne's murder. I'll bet you anything the cops are giving him a pass even though clearing the spouse of a murdered woman right out of the box would be the first priority of any homicide investigation."

"Even if they're absolutely convinced they know who the killer is?"

She nodded. "Even if."

He studied her at length, then asked, "What makes you think it could be Richard?"

She pointed to her murder book. "Just take a look, then we'll talk."

For the next hour, they brainstormed possible scenarios to explain why anybody would want to kill Luanne Richard, but they wound up with nothing much. Before Wyatt left, Camille made a second attempt to introduce him to Ben and Jerry, but both dogs remained very prickly. Camille waved him off at the gate with a dog on either side of her, bristling.

SHE WAS preparing lunch when Ben and Jerry started up again. Drying her hands, she again went to the front window, but this time, when the driver got out of his car, instead of going into attack mode, both dogs wagged their tails madly and danced around Jack Vermillion in a frenzy.

She was surprised to see him. The last time they talked, she'd been the messenger of bad news that he hadn't taken well. Now, curious as to why he'd want to talk to her, she opened the door and went out on the porch. Whatever his purpose, she was determined not to let him rile her. She'd had enough drama for one day.

"Hi," he said from a distance, his eyes on hers.

"Hi yourself."

He climbed the porch steps with Ben cavorting around him and Jerry clearly adoring but less frisky. "Looks like you've got ample protection here."

"I definitely do," she said, eyeing the dogs fondly. "If a stranger shows up, they turn into mean, lean, barking machines. And worse."

"That's good."

"You'd think so. But a while ago, they wanted to do more than just bark at Ray Wyatt."

"Because they don't know him."

"Apparently. I tried to introduce him, but it didn't seem to make much difference. No matter how I coaxed, they weren't buying."

He bent and had a close look at Jerry's injury, then, without comment, straightened and looked up at Camille. "Early to have a visitor, wasn't it?"

"Ray is helping with the case."

He nodded, but whether he approved or not, she couldn't tell. "Where's Madge? You're not here alone, are you?"

"No. She's sleeping. She worked last night."

He took a minute to survey the properties on either side of Madge's house. "After last night, you must see it's risky for you to stay here, Camille."

She wasn't sure whether he meant here in Blood Bayou or here in Madge's house, but whatever he meant, Jack didn't make decisions for her anymore. She watched the dogs still competing for his attention. It was no wonder they liked him. With all that rubbing and tussling he was doing, they were like two puppies again. "How did you know about last night?"

"June Raines called me. A day or so ago, he asked me to use my influence with you to persuade you to go home." He looked up at her, smiling. "Beats me why he thought I had any."

"But you're going to give it a shot anyway."

"Uh-uh." He was shaking his head, still smiling. "Lost cause. You'll leave when you're ready and not a minute before."

Pleased and surprised, she moved to the front door and held

it open. "In that case, you can come in. Want some iced tea? It's mango-peach."

He rose, dusting doggy hair from his pants. "Anything with ice in it sounds good. Thanks."

She led him through the cottage to the kitchen and filled a glass with ice and the fruity tea. After refilling hers, she opened the French doors leading to the porch overlooking the bayou. "Let's sit out here. It's so peaceful and beautiful."

She took a seat on the swing, while Jack chose to stand at the porch railing. With the frosty glass in hand and his gaze on the bayou, he seemed lost in thought for a few moments, but she could see that something was on his mind. If not another lecture to send her home, she wondered what it was.

"Luanne didn't find anything peaceful or beautiful about Blood Bayou," he said finally. "She hated it."

Camille's eyes followed his to the bayou. With morning sun sparkling on the surface and birds swooping to capture insects, there appeared to be nothing sinister about it. "I was thinking about her last night. I remember when she was in college and made one of her rare visits to us. She told me she'd once fallen into the bayou and nearly drowned." She turned to look at Jack. "That's a pretty classic reason to fear it."

"She was about three years old when that happened," Jack said in a voice devoid of emotion. "Dad left us in the care of some woman he'd met in a bar. I don't think she realized she was going to be saddled with two kids when she moved in. I was about eight and full of anger, so I was probably a terror to try and discipline. That day she wanted to watch soaps on TV, so she sent us kids outside, putting me in charge. Luanne was a tiny little thing, barely out of diapers."

"Where was your father?"

"Good question. I don't know—still don't—but he wasn't there. I was supposed to watch my little sister and see that she didn't fall in the water."

"What was she thinking!" Camille said. "Kids can be in danger in the wink of an eye near water."

"Tell me," Jack said grimly.

"Is that what happened?"

"She toddled out on the pier and fell into the bayou. I jumped in to try and save her, but her shirt caught on a nail sticking out from an underwater pier post. I couldn't get it loose. Last thing I remember is swallowing water and choking, then the world went black."

Camille felt the horror that both must have suffered. "Who saved you?"

"Two teenage kids were waterskiing and just happened to pass at the right time. Luckily, they'd had a class in school where they'd learned CPR. I came around on the pier after they'd pumped me dry, not too damaged from the episode. Luanne was hospitalized."

"And traumatized," Camille murmured. "It's a wonder you don't both feel the same about the bayou."

"I have no fear of a body of water, which is, after all, God's creation." He studied the tea remaining in his glass before looking up at her. "But I wish I could say the same about my feelings toward my father. For too many years I was bitterly angry."

Anyone would be, Camille thought to herself.

"Why bring two kids into the world and then shamelessly neglect them? What if we'd both drowned that day? If he didn't want to be bothered with two kids, why didn't he send us to his

relatives? Or, failing that, give us up for adoption?" He tossed
the dregs of his tea and ice into the shrubs. "I swore that if I ever
had kids, I'd be a better father since I knew firsthand what it
meant to have a bad one."

It struck Camille that she'd learned more about Jack in the
last few days than she'd known in the three years they'd been
married. With so little constructive parenting, maybe it was understandable that he'd had a difficult time behaving as a responsible adult. When she didn't say anything, she looked over to
find him watching her.

"No comment to that? You must feel profound relief that we
didn't bring a child into the world, considering what a rotten
husband I turned out to be."

Instead of a comment, she simply lifted a shoulder. With
these illuminating glimpses at what made Jack tick, she found
she had no desire to pile on. It appeared that he carried enough
emotional baggage.

"Did you have any special reason for coming out here today?"
she asked.

He relaxed against the porch railing. "I'm not as stupid as
I must have seemed to you yesterday when you tried to tell me
that Harlen had abused Luanne."

"I never thought you were stupid. I could see you were
shocked."

"You know what they say about closed doors," he said. "Nobody knows what really goes on except the two people behind
those doors."

"And I wouldn't want to," Camille said, "unless somebody
is being brutalized."

He looked directly at her. "I can't believe I didn't have a clue as to what was really going on with my sister." Pain and bewilderment were on his face and in his voice.

"Because she didn't want you to know, Jack."

He straightened up and drove both hands deep in his pockets. "In my work, I see all kinds of horrors. You won't believe what people tell me, what they've done, how they've suffered. And now, when it's too late for Luanne, I learn she didn't trust me enough to even confide in me when I might have helped her."

Camille, without an answer, could only shrug helplessly.

Jack was clearly mystified as well. He turned to look out at the bayou. After a long minute, he spoke in an unsteady voice. "What kind of minister am I? How can I think of myself as God's messenger if I'm blind to the suffering of my own sister?"

Camille knew his questions weren't meant for her but for himself. Or maybe for his God. But, even as she was murky on that subject, she found it impossible to witness such a painful display of self-doubt and feel no sympathy. She couldn't see his face, turned as he was away from her, but she knew he was in need of something.

She rose and tentatively touched his shoulder. He was instantly tense and, to her amazement, actually trembling. He was obviously in the grip of profound emotion. This was a Jack she'd never seen.

"Jack," she murmured, beginning to stroke his shoulder gently. "You are not at fault here. Luanne took great pains to keep you from knowing."

"Wrong." He shook his head in denial, still turned from her. "I should have known. After what we went through as kids, I should have known the signs that she was in trouble."

"What? You were supposed to read her mind?"

He finally turned to look at her with tortured eyes. "Yeah, I should have read her mind. I was the only one who could. And I didn't."

She studied his face and then withdrew her hand and gazed out at Blood Bayou. Jack had never tolerated failure well. That, at least, hadn't changed. Still, for this new Jack who seemed to be carrying so much pain, she found that she wished to somehow ease his suffering.

"I'm certainly no philosopher, Jack, but I see this as one of those 'what if' moments in life. Everybody has them. What if I had acted differently? What if I'd made another choice? What if I'd taken that other fork in the road?" She brought her gaze back, looked into his eyes. "So, you're human. I guess that doesn't change even if you're a man of God."

A minute passed while his gaze roamed her face as if some answer was to be found there. And when he spoke, it was in a tone that was low and filled with regret. "It was so senseless, her dying that way."

She nodded. "Yes, it was."

"She was so messed up."

"She was."

After a minute, he drew in a deep breath. "I was the lucky one."

She tilted her head, questioning. "How so?"

"I was born into the same hell, but by the grace of God, I was able to climb out."

She reacted almost instantly with unease and Jack saw it. "Talking about that makes you nervous, doesn't it?"

About God? About grace? She opened her mouth to deny it

but couldn't. It was true. While she struggled to come up with some answer that wouldn't make her seem a total heathen, he reached out with one hand and tucked her hair behind one ear. In doing so, he touched the tiny ruby earring she wore.

"It's okay," he said. "There will be a right time when you'll let me tell you and you'll listen." He bent then and, catching her off guard, touched his lips to the jeweled stud. "I gave these to you when we celebrated our third anniversary, do you remember?"

She gave a little nod, intensely aware of how close he was, how intimate this moment could become if she wasn't careful. But she didn't stop him, not even when he settled his hands at her waist and gently drew her close, resting his chin on her head.

"I knew even then you were going to leave me."

She was. By that time, the naïve just-out-of-college girl he'd married had experienced too much ugly reality.

"Your mind was made up," he said sadly. "But I was hope-lessly ruled by so many demons that I couldn't change. My thinking then was that I wanted to give you something to tell you what you meant to me. Ruby earrings filled the bill."

"I always liked them."

She felt him smile. "A wife of noble character, who can find?" he quoted. "She is worth more than rubies."

"Who wrote that?" she asked, trying to keep things from getting out of hand. "It sounds familiar."

"It's in the Bible," he told her. "Proverbs."

"You knew a Bible verse back then?"

"I didn't, but the salesperson in the jewelry store suggested it when I told him I was looking for something special for my wife."

"Well, I don't know about the 'noble character' part," she said dryly.

"Running the Truth Project is a noble endeavor," he told her, still holding her and now swaying gently.

Both went silent then. She found herself going along as they moved together in an embrace that wasn't entirely comfortable to her, but that, oddly, she felt little inclination to end. She thought about the demons he mentioned. What answers had he found to be profound enough that he'd been able to banish them? Had someone influenced him? She, as his wife, had never been able to.

He again settled his chin on top of her head, this time with a sigh of deep satisfaction. "Holding you feels so right, Camille."

"That's because you probably aren't allowed to make passes at the ladies in your congregation."

He laughed softly. "No. I mean, no, I don't fool around, but that's not why this feels so right." He pulled back so that he was looking at her with eyes that were serious. "It's because you're the love of my life."

As with his remark about God and grace, she felt instant unease. She quickly made a move to step back, to break away, but he stopped her, not forcefully, but with a gentle tightening of his hands at her waist so that she found herself looking up at him. "You own my heart, Camille. There will never be anyone but you. Ever."

Something, some part of her that had been as dead and cold as yesterday's ashes, stirred to life as she gazed into Jack's eyes. What was it? She searched his face, looking for something that explained the change she sensed in him.

"What is it?" he asked. "What are you thinking?"

"I don't know you anymore, Jack."

A fleeting smile softened his dark eyes. "I know. Because I'm not the man I was when we were married. I hope someday you'll let me tell you why and how I'm changed."

She looked at him suspiciously. "Is it this religion thing?"

"It is." And smiling fully now, he caught her up in a fierce hug. Her first reaction was surprise. But then she felt the deep breath he took when he buried his face in her hair, knew he was filling himself with the scent of her even as she did the same with him. It was all so familiar. She hesitated when she might have pulled back, rejecting any touch from Jack. But her emotions were in turmoil. She'd never felt a scrap of emotion for another man, only Jack. That was then, of course. Not now. She'd spent seven years in pain over their failed relationship, over all they'd had and lost. He might harbor leftover feelings, but she didn't believe there was anything left of that sweet lost love.

Which is why she should have stopped what was happening right then and there. But she didn't.

"I want to kiss you," Jack said, holding her tight.

She heard arousal in his voice, felt the tension in him. And uncertainty. Jack, uncertain? Instead of giving him a flat no, she said, "So, now you're a minister you have to ask?"

"No, now I know the value of what we once had and I've lived seven years regretting that I didn't recognize it at the time, that I was so careless with a gift so precious."

She resisted the emotional tug to her heart that came with his confession, telling herself there were too many memories. Bad memories. But there was no denying his sincerity. So, on sheer impulse, she reached up and kissed him.

She felt the shock of it run through him and knew she'd put

a torch to tinder. With a wordless sound, his arms tightened around her. He took the kiss deeper. The hunger in him stunned her. Her own hunger stunned her. It was as if they'd both been in a dark, cold room that was suddenly filled with sunlight. And promise.

It did feel good. It even felt right. But it wasn't right, she reminded herself. She braced her hands against his chest and pushed back roughly. "I don't want to do this, Jack."

Breathing hard, he let her go, dropped his face in his hands for a long minute, and then met her eyes with a look of chagrin. "I'm sorry. I got caught up in the sheer delight of touching you. I was out of line. But I have to be honest here, Camille. I want so much more than just to kiss you."

She turned away with a murmured protest.

"Please don't do that. Now that we're here"—he looked around, waved a hand at nothing in particular—"just let me take a second to say what I need to tell you."

No. She didn't want to be forced to deal with whatever he wanted to say. Just finding herself caught up in a situation that had put Jack back in her life was difficult enough. Whatever he wanted to tell her was bound to be something weighty, something to do with his new, made-over, too-incredible-to-be-real self.

She studied his face for a long time and finally decided it would do no harm to hear him out. But she wasn't going to be drawn into Jack's world, not even on the edges. "What is it?"

"I'm sorry," he said.

And when she instantly made a sound of impatience and moved to put more distance between them, he reached out to stop her. She shook him off. "Just say it, Jack."

He hesitated, as if he might give it up in the face of such open irritation, but in the end he took the opportunity she'd handed him. "I'm sorry for everything, Camille—for being a rotten husband, for subjecting you to so much pain, so much unhappiness, so much shame and embarrassment and neglect. I know sorry is a puny word for everything I did, but it's all I have to offer."

"It's all in the past, Jack. I've tried to forget it." She was turned away from him now, her body language screaming rejection.

"Some things can't be forgotten," he said quietly, gently, "but they can be forgiven." He paused, searching her profile as if trying to judge how she might take his next words. "Can you ever forgive me, Camille?"

When she was silent too long, he sighed and then said, "Can you at least try?"

"Jack—"

"Can you at least try?" he repeated.

Camille gripped the porch railing hard and berated herself for letting her guard down. She should have known that giving Jack an opening meant he'd mine it for everything he could get. Behind that minister's garb he was still a lawyer, still able to spot a weakness, still quick to seize a moment. And what had she been thinking to let him get so close?

She turned and looked at him. "This was a mistake, Jack. Don't try to make it more than it was. We're two healthy adults. It was an emotional moment."

"Camille—"

She put up both hands to stop him. "We know we click in a physical sense, but we also know how abysmally inadequate that proved to be when nothing else was right between us."

"We can change that, Camille."

She turned to look at him. "No, we can't," she said.

He looked so downcast that she found herself thinking what it might cost her to give him what he wanted: forgiveness, absolution, redemption. No, she told herself, that kind of thinking belonged in his bag of tricks. She had to stick to logic and coolheaded reason. And that dictated that she send him on his way. Right now.

She picked up his empty glass. "Can I make you a to-go cup?"

CHAPTER twelve

WHATEVER JACK MIGHT have replied was lost when the dogs suddenly exploded in frenzied barking. Camille leaned over the railing in time to see Ben running flat out toward the front of the cottage, with the handicapped Jerry trailing.

"What now?" she muttered. "How Madge can get any rest around here is beyond me." Jack was already through the French doors and heading for the front of the house. When he opened the door, Camille peered over his shoulder and instantly recognized the big black Mercedes. "Oh, no."

"Yeah, it's Carson," Jack said. "Do you still want me to go? If you take him up the front steps, I'll wait underneath until you get inside, then leave."

"I'm not the insecure twenty-something twit I once was, Jack. I don't keep secrets from Dad now. If he doesn't like seeing us together, tough. I think we can both weather the lecture." She gave him a meaningful look. "At least I can."

He was studying her with his head cocked to one side. "You really have changed, haven't you?"

"I could say the same about you." She turned her attention back to the ruckus going on out front. "But right now, it looks like Ben and Jerry consider Dad a stranger and are giving him the same treatment they gave Ray. Could you try to subdue them? Since they're gaga over you, they might respond better to a command from you."

With a nod he opened the door and called a stern command to the dogs. Both responded instantly and sat with eager looks and tongues lolling as he approached the gate and unlatched it.

Camille suspected that the reason for the dark look on Carson's face was Jack, not the dogs, but she chose to ignore it. Instead, she greeted him with a bright smile and a quick hug. "This is a surprise, Dad. And guess what, you're just in time for lunch."

Still warily eyeing Ben and Jerry, he didn't respond to the invitation or acknowledge Jack, who was keeping the dogs in check. "Are they friendly?" he asked, keeping his distance.

"Jack seems to be able to control them," she said.

At that, Carson shifted his gaze to his former son-in-law. "It's been awhile, Jack." There was little warmth in his voice, but he accepted Jack's hand and shook it. Briefly.

"How are you, Carson?"

"I'd be a lot better if I didn't have to worry about my daughter." He turned to her. "Let's go inside. I've got good news."

"That's nice. You can tell me over lunch," she suggested, falling into step beside him. Jack followed behind them to keep the dogs under control.

Carson glanced at his watch. "No time for that, but I'll take a nice tall glass of something cold. It's hotter than Hades out here. You'd think being in sight of the bayou it would be cooler."

"It's August. We're in the Deep South, Dad. It's hot." She opened the door and waited for him to go inside. Jack smiled at her, saluted her smartly, and headed around the house with the dogs. Deserter, she thought. She braced herself for a tug-of-war.

Whatever turned out to be her father's good news, they would probably argue over it. Drawing a fortifying breath, she prepared herself for battle.

"So what's the good news?" she asked, reaching for a glass.

"In time," he said. Moving to the French doors, he peered out. "Where's Jack?"

"With the dogs. He'll be up in a minute."

"Why's he here, Camille? What's going on with you two?"

"Nothing." She felt an involuntary blush and turned away from her father's piercing eyes to get ice from the fridge. "Do you want sugar in this?"

"No. I don't want you mixed up with him again, Camille. You two have nothing in common now. You would stick out like a sore thumb in his life."

She stared at him. "What are you talking about, Dad? Jack and I are not getting 'mixed up' again. He's here because—" She stopped, unwilling to give him any details about her and Jack. It was none of his business.

"Because what?" he demanded.

Actually, she wasn't sure why Jack had come over. She pushed the ice dispenser in the refrigerator door and filled the glass, all the while casting about in her head for a reply. "He and Madge are old friends."

He went narrow-eyed. "Are they involved?"

"Involved?" Was he serious? "Madge and Jack? Of course not."

"So where is she?" he asked, watching Camille pour tea over the ice.

"Sleeping. She worked the midnight shift last night."

"Humph. Wasn't here when the excitement started, was

she? So much for you being safe in her little cottage by the bayou."

Just then Jack let himself in at the French doors, but Camille was focused on her father. "What excitement?" she asked.

"The attempt by an intruder to break into the house, Camille," Carson said in his most disapproving fatherly voice. "I can't tell you how shocked I was to hear about it. And scared stiff. What if he'd gotten past the dogs?"

She frowned. "How is it that you know all about this, Dad? It only happened a few hours ago."

"What does it matter who told me? What matters is getting you away from this place."

She looked at Jack, who stood leaning against the kitchen table with his arms folded over his chest. "Did you call Dad?"

"Me?" His arms fell to his sides. "No."

She looked at her father suspiciously. "Is that true?"

Carson shrugged. "He's a preacher. They don't lie. Supposedly."

"Forget it. So what's your good news, Dad?"

"Hmm?" Carson frowned and then his expression cleared. "Oh, that. I was getting around to it." He raised the glass and drank. "Hmm, that is good. Nice and fruity."

Camille noticed for the first time that Carson's face was flushed, as if he'd had too much sun. Or was the flush something more? It seemed impossible that her father could be ill. He was invincible. "Are you okay, Dad?"

"What do you mean, am I okay? I'm fine." He held the glass against his forehead for a second. "This has got to be the hottest August on record. I don't know how folks survived down here before air-conditioning."

"Your good news?" she prompted.

"Oh, that." He put his empty glass on the counter and gave her a smile, showing too many teeth. Camille's brief concern for his health was forgotten. She knew something bad was coming when Carson conjured up a large smile. "I've found the perfect job for you, sweetheart," he said. "It's an opportunity any lawyer would kill for."

She gave a heavy sigh. "Dad. Please. We've had this conversation."

"Now just hear me out, missy."

When he called her missy, she knew they would wind up in a battle royal. "How many times do I have to tell you? I don't want you finding jobs for me."

"This is a position that is connected to the governor, Camille! It's being offered to you on a silver platter."

"I don't care if it's connected to the president and offered on gold! If I wanted a job other than the one I've got, I'd put out my résumé and, believe it or not, I'd be able to find something. And just so you'll know, it would be something I like, Dad!"

Carson's face was now an alarming shade of red. "No daughter of mine should be satisfied with just something."

"Is this your way of shooing me out of Blood Bayou? Because if it is, read my lips: I'm not going."

"You're chasing a dream if you think you'll clear that animal's name!"

"Chester is not an animal, Dad."

"People who murder are animals."

She strove for patience. "Nevertheless, I'm going to try and clear his name. And I've got help doing it now. Ray Wyatt has volunteered and so has Madge."

"Did I hear my name?"

Madge appeared, resplendent in a top with a bold red, black, and white print and crisp white pants. Barefoot she was tall, but in three-inch platform wedgies she towered over everybody in the room except Jack, who straightened from his slouch against the door to receive her hug and kiss on his cheek.

"Did we wake you up?" he asked.

"No, sugar." She rubbed a spot of lipstick off his cheek, then turned to Carson. "I'm not surprised to find Jack in my kitchen since he can't stay away from Camille, but finding you really is a surprise. How are you, Carson?"

"I don't get a hug and a kiss?" was her father's sarcastic reply.

Madge laughed softly, walked right up to Carson, and kissed him full on the lips. Camille's astonished gaze went to Jack, who shrugged and looked amused. Carson was, for once, flummoxed.

"Gotcha!" Camille murmured, hiding a smile.

Madge, looking satisfied that she'd defused a sticky situation, stepped back, rubbed her hands together briskly, and asked, "What's for lunch?"

WITH HIS mission foiled, Carson was testy and after a few minutes left in a huff. There had been times when similar scenes with her father had given her a headache or made her so worried that she was unable to concentrate and lost a day's work. Thankfully, he didn't have that much power over her anymore.

"I made quiche and a salad," she told Jack and Madge. "Let's eat outside on the porch."

"Sounds good to me," Madge said. "Jack, you'll stay for lunch, won't you?"

He looked at Camille, eyebrows raised in question.

"There's more than enough," she said, shoving place mats and napkins in his hands. "You can set the table while I get the quiche. It's keeping warm in the oven. Madge, you just take a seat. I know I never want to do anything when I first get up in the morning."

"Yes, ma'am. But first, I've got to ask," Madge said, watching from the open French doors as Jack set the table, "is your daddy always like that?"

"Pretty much," Camille said. Using oven mitts, she carried the warm quiche out to the table. "And I can't tell you how hard it was to learn to stand up to him. Because he thinks everything he does is for my own good." She placed the quiche on a trivet. "But what I hear when he's arranging my life is 'I don't quite trust you to make decisions for yourself, therefore, I'll decide for you.'" She stood looking over the table. "What are we lacking out here? Oh, the salad."

"I'll get it," Jack said. "Both of you, please, take a seat."

Camille and Madge exchanged an amused glance, then sat. In moments, Jack appeared with the salad, set it in the center of the table, and even produced salad tongs.

"You've been domesticated," Camille said, shaking out her napkin.

"And you've been liberated," he said, doing the same. But as she reached for the bowl heaped with fresh salad makings, he held up one finger. "Join me in a word of thanks, please?"

For a heartbeat, she hesitated. "Oh, okay."

"If you'll just give me your hand." When she complied, he took it in a warm clasp. Madge, without coaching, reached for Camille's other hand and Jack's, then all three with linked hands bowed their heads while he asked a simple blessing of thanks for the food and the one who prepared it.

"Amen," Madge said softly when it was over. And after a moment of hesitation, Camille murmured a soft amen too. In her head.

For the next few minutes, they busied themselves filling their plates. When they settled to eating, Jack said, "I talked to Chief Raines."

Camille paused with her fork halfway to her mouth. "Oh?"

"I wanted to know if in the investigation he'd checked on Harlen's whereabouts at the time of Luanne's murder." He passed the salad to Madge. "Did I forget to bring the salt and pepper out?"

"Jack!"

He stood up. "Back in a minute."

For the second time Camille and Madge exchanged a look, but this time there was more exasperation than humor on Camille's face.

Upon returning, Jack began grinding pepper over his salad. "Here's the deal," he said. "Apparently, Harlen has no alibi."

Camille, sipping water, sputtered and set her glass on the table with a thump. "See, I told you! Oh, this is just great. Just peachy." She blotted her lips with a napkin. "They ignore the classic suspect, who has a motive to kill his wife even though they find he has no alibi. And still they stick to their conviction that Chester is the killer." She leaned back and wagged her head in disgust. "I don't know why I'm shocked. This is so not a surprise."

"I don't know why you assume Harlen is the killer based on the fact that he has no alibi," Jack said calmly.

"Actually, I don't." At his confused look, she added, "I don't assume anything."

"You want to explain that? You've pushed and pushed to know Harlen's whereabouts that night because you consider him a prime suspect, and now you don't?"

"Yes and no." She picked up her fork again. "It's classic investigative technique to vet the spouse of a murder victim. So naturally I'm curious as to where Harlen was when Luanne was murdered. But, realistically, I don't believe a man like Harlen would do it himself. Too risky. He'd hire somebody."

Jack sat back, looking at her. "Then why bother to find where he was? Why does his alibi or lack of one even matter?"

"It's obvious, Jack." She leaned forward. "Look, even though I may think he'd hire somebody, what that does is it opens another can of worms. Who'd he hire? Meaning we've still got a killer on the loose in this town. So I'm simply suggesting we should know a lot more about Harlen before we eliminate him as a suspect."

"Okay, with that somewhat convoluted theory in mind, I'll go talk to him."

His ready agreement took some of the wind out of her sails. "Oh, well. Okay." She cut a piece of quiche but didn't taste it as another thought struck. "And while you're at it, I wish you'd poke around to see if he knows anything about my room being trashed."

Jack almost laughed. "Somehow I can't see Harlen, who is always slicked out in a thousand-dollar suit and five-hundred-dollar shoes, scribbling a message on your mirror with lipstick."

"I agree. But if—and I emphasize *if* here—he hired someone to kill Luanne, he'd want me out of town and out of his hair, wouldn't he? So he'd get someone—maybe that same person—to scare me off."

"And he's going to admit it?"

"No! Of course not." She strove for patience. "You would just be on a fishing expedition, Jack. Looking for suspicious behavior, a misspoken word, a guilty look!"

"Oh, I get it," Jack said, deadpan. "If he skulks or turns a whiter shade of pale, I'll know I'm on to something."

Madge snickered.

Camille ignored her and loaded her fork with quiche. "And while you're at it, ask if she had a diary. That would really be helpful."

Jack leaned back with a resigned look on his face. "Anything else, Sherlock?"

She picked up her napkin. "Yes. When are we going?"

They argued over that for ten minutes as Madge looked on with amusement. But in the end, Jack relented. "I must be losing my touch," he told Camille. "Either that or you've learned a lot more about how to get what you want than you used to."

Her first reaction was to want to annihilate him with a few well-chosen words, but she caught the humor dancing in his eyes and simply poked him on the arm—hard. "Get used to it, buddy."

Jack winked at her. "I look forward to it, sugar."

Madge suddenly clapped her hands in applause. Both looked at her, startled. "That was beautiful," she said. "Nothing like a nice knock-down-drag-out between formidable adversaries and when it's over, both are left standing and nobody's bleeding."

To which both rolled their eyes.

Another debate ensued over whether to confront Harlen at

his office or wait and try to talk to him in his house, where he'd be more at ease. Camille argued for going directly to his office, but Jack managed to persuade her that on his own turf, Harlen would be less likely to oust them when he realized what their questions implied.

"Trust me," Jack said, "he doesn't want me wondering if he had anything to do with my sister's murder. He'll try to lay to rest any suspicion."

"If you say so," Camille said, unconvinced. "But okay, I'll meet you there. What time?"

"Let's go together." When he saw her gearing up for a third argument, he said, "Hear me out. It'll be dark when we're done and if you take your car, you'll wind up having to drive back to Madge's place alone. At night. That road is too dark and deserted to be safe. You've been the victim of two unpleasant acts already. Let's not give anybody a chance to make it three."

Camille set her mouth in a stubborn line, but there was a twinkle in her eye. "If I cave, that makes one for me and two for you."

Now it was Madge rolling her eyes.

AFTER LEAVING them, Jack had a jam-packed schedule. Among other things, it was Thursday, his regular day to visit Sojourner House. Then, as sometimes happened, everything that could go wrong did. So, by the time he left his office to go to Sojourner, he was cutting it close. He didn't want to be late meeting Camille. He considered his time with her a gift, a direct answer to prayer. But he considered his mission at Sojourner a sacred pledge. Above all, he wanted to spend time with David Bergeron today. He might not have many more opportunities.

It always hit him straight in the heart to see David. He knew he would never get to the point where he could walk in the room and not be devastated at the sight of the twenty-one-year-old quadriplegic. Today David was upright in his chair, thanks to a variety of ingenious devices fastening arms, chest, and head in place as he watched a video monitor suspended from the ceiling at eye level. Keeping him alive were tubes, a shunt, numerous medications, and prayer. But from the look of him now, nothing short of a miracle would help much longer.

In spite of all that, David slowly turned his head and smiled in genuine delight when Jack knocked softly on the open door. "Rev! It's about time you showed up. I've finally"—he paused to take a labored breath—"conquered this piece-of-trash video game you brought me last week."

"Hah! Bragging again as usual." Jack drew near and lightly punched him on one skinny arm. "It's going to be embarrassing for you, big guy, when I take you down in about three minutes."

The contest was on. It had a NASCAR theme; a passion of David's. He'd once confided that as a kid he'd dreamed of being a NASCAR driver. But, he said he never could figure out how to do both law and competitive racing.

Today Jack played hard. David was a computer whiz kid. Video games were truly child's play for him. In the beginning when they played, he had spotted Jack pulling his punches to let him win. He'd quickly and angrily demanded fair play. Now it had become a challenge for Jack to win a game.

Today David took him down in an embarrassingly short

space of time. "I don't get to practice as much as you," Jack complained.

"Lame, lame," David said, grinning. "Tell it to somebody"— he stopped, struggled for oxygen for his starving lungs—"dumber than me."

Not only was David very weak but his color was off. Never healthy and pink, today his skin was pasty, nearly gray. He'd hoped Angela's prognosis was mistaken, but he worried that it was on the mark. He glanced at his watch and saw that his visit was going on thirty minutes. David was fading fast. Jack dragged his stool a little closer. "I've stayed too long, Dave. But I'll be back checking on you in a day or so. You want to pray with me now?"

David's smile was weak but genuine. "Don't I always?"

No, he hadn't always. When Jack first met with David, he'd been without faith of any kind. He'd been bitter and angry over the hand he'd been dealt, over the sheer unfairness of what had happened to him. Who wouldn't? It had been a source of heart-rending pain to Jack, mixed with crushing guilt. Only after David's conversion had he found peace and acceptance of the tragedy that had stolen his future. Today, with his heart aching and guilt weighing on him like a stone, Jack covered the bony, too cold hand, bowed his head, and prayed with the young man whose future he'd destroyed.

A few minutes later he headed for Ron's room. No smile greeted him there. Ron was having a bad day. Sometimes, as a result of his brain injury, yet without anyone knowing quite why, Ron's mostly sunny outlook turned surly and even violent. Today was one of those days. Jack spent some time trying to interest him in several things, putting together a simple puzzle with large pieces, then making a game of working out on some of the equipment in the physical therapy room. Finally, he took him outside on the grounds, thinking fresh air and the tranquillity of the bayou might calm him. He squatted beside the wheelchair, pointing out an alligator cruising in the water some distance away. Nothing worked. Ron was clearly agitated, in no mood to be entertained.

"Okay, buddy, let's go back inside, get you something to eat. Maybe that'll make you feel better."

Jack leaned across Ron to release the brake on the chair. He made a solid target when the boy suddenly drew back hollering, "No!" Jack never even saw the hard right that landed on his cheekbone.

For a few seconds, Jack literally saw stars. Leo, a longtime orderly, rushed over and quickly secured Ron in restraints, then turned his attention to Jack.

"You okay, Reverend?"

Jack's ears were ringing. He shook his head to clear it. "Yeah, I'm fine."

"You sure?" The attendant eyed him narrowly. "You're gonna have a beaut of a shiner there."

Jack worked his jaw as he watched the attendant preparing to remove Ron, who was now sobbing with remorse and bewilderment at his own behavior. "Wait a minute, Leo."

Jack approached the boy, going down on his haunches beside the chair. Ron reached for him but was unable to lift arms now locked down in restraints. Jack leaned in and, with a hand on the boy's neck, pulled him into an embrace. Resting his forehead against the sobbing boy's temple, he whispered, "It's okay, Ron. You're having a bad day. You just need a little time out."

"You . . . you'll . . . never . . . come baaackkk!" he wailed.

Jack knew that kind of fear all too well. Ron was afraid he'd driven away the one person he loved and needed above anyone in his world. It was not an unreasonable fear. Jack was far more than a casual visitor to Ron. Outside Sojourner, everybody who might have cared had forgotten the boy existed. At least David had his grandmother.

Jack spoke in a firm voice. "Don't you worry, buddy, I will be back next Thursday, as usual. I promise."

He stood up then and watched Leo roll the boy down the walk, still sobbing and looking back at Jack piteously.

"It was my fault," he said a few minutes later to Angela Berthelot, who insisted on personally applying a cold compress to Jack's eye. "From the minute I got here today, I saw that he was having one of his bad days. I should never have tried to tease him out of whatever demon had taken hold of him."

"You didn't want to disappoint him."

"It would have been better if I had."

She dropped the compress in a pan. "You won't be able to do for him what you did for David."

Jack touched his eye gingerly. "No, but Ron's not a lost soul as David was. From the moment of his birth, Ron belonged to God."

"And thanks to your ministry and faithfulness to David, his soul also belongs to God now." She stood back, considering the bruise with a critical eye. "Well, Leo's right. You'll have a shiner very soon. So, how will you explain it to all those people who don't know anything about your visits to Sojourner?"

He chuckled. "I guess lying is not an option, is it?"

"Preachers aren't supposed to."

"I'll think of something," he said, looking around for his sunglasses, which had gone flying when Ron connected.

"Here they are." Angela bent and picked them up from the grass. "And still in one piece, amazingly. I guess it's not a good time to tell you the news, so I'll just e-mail you. Don't forget to check it when you get home."

He peered at her over the sunglasses. "As if I'd leave after you drop a line like that."

She smiled and put out a hand, pushing the sunglasses onto his nose properly. "Then let's take a walk, provided you don't have posttraumatic stress syndrome after what you just experienced. We don't have any vacant beds."

"Everyone's a comedian," he said, falling into step beside her.

Outside, strolling along the path that paralleled the bayou, both were quiet for a while, taking pleasure in the serene sunset. They took a seat on a bench under a huge oak.

"I think of your sister when I look at the bayou now," she told him in a quiet voice.

"So do I."

"I hope in time it won't hurt so much for you, Jack, but it was a terrible thing. Two murders in our town. I'm a Christian woman, but I'm human too, so I find myself wishing terrible things befalling that evil man."

"What if he didn't do it?"

She gave him a quick look. "Didn't do it? I thought it was a foregone conclusion that he did do it."

He tossed a pebble into the still water. "I'm beginning to wonder, but don't ask me how or why since I don't have any answers yet." He suddenly shifted on the bench, checked his watch, and brushed briskly at the grit on his hands. "I need to be back by six. What was it you wanted to tell me?"

"Someone wants to buy Sojourner House."

"Oh?"

"I mean, someone wants to buy the land that Sojourner House sits on."

"Meaning if you sell, you'll have to relocate." He studied her face. "You refused?"

"Actually, I'm thinking about it."

"You'd dismantle Sojourner, close it up? What about the patients?"

"I wouldn't dismantle it, as you put it. I'd rebuild bigger and better. The offer is for a lot of money, Jack. Far more than the land is worth, in my estimation." She looked out over the water. "Of course, a lot of it fronts on the bayou and it is beautiful property, but I was still flabbergasted by the amount that was offered."

"So you're leaning toward selling?"

"I have to present the offer to the board, of course. But yes, I am thinking of recommending they accept the deal." She reached over and patted his hand. "Don't look so distressed. I'm going to recommend a pretty ambitious plan for expanding Sojourner. Some of these patients have been here for years. It's their home. But it will be nice not to have to worry about the air-conditioning breaking down. Or the plumbing backing up. Or the roof leaking."

He squeezed her hand. "You had me worried there for a minute. Do you need me to appear at the board meeting with you?"

"Absolutely. A recommendation coming from you makes it a

done deal. And by the way, thank you for the check to repair the air conditioner. Where did it come from, if I may ask?"

"You may not."

She huffed out an exasperated sound. "It had better not be from you personally. I know how much your salary is at the church and I know you can't afford to write a check as large as that one."

"It was an anonymous donor, Angela." He smiled and stood up. "Someone with a guilty conscience. I'm personally acquainted with a lot of those types." He glanced again at his watch. "And now, I've got to run."

"A hot date, huh?"

"In a way," Jack said. "I'll be with my wife. Say a prayer."

CHAPTER thirteen

AT SIX O'CLOCK, Camille was at Jack's house. A small and wizened woman with bright, near-black eyes, welcomed her inside, introducing herself as Jeanette Legion, Jack's house-keeper.

"You would be his wife, Camille, no?"

"No. His ex-wife," she corrected, but with a smile. "We were divorced seven years ago."

"Yes. Very sad, that," Jeanette said, clucking her tongue. "Our Jack, he has had some very sad things happen in his life. But you would know these things, yes?"

"Well, I—"

"Come inside. He will be back in a few minutes. He's sometimes held up when over there." She made a face. "Things happen."

"Excuse me?"

Jeanette closed the door. "I talk too much. You will have lemonade?" She took a step, saying over her shoulder, "I make it fresh squeezed, me."

"Jack isn't here?"

Jeanette stopped, turned. "I did say that."

Camille looked at her with suspicion. "He went without me, didn't he?"

"Pardon?" Jeanette looked confused.

"I should have *known*!" Camille whirled around and reached for the doorknob. "Ooo, this is so like him. When will I ever learn?" Furious, she pulled the door open, but then turned back to Jeanette. "You can give him a message for me. Tell him—"

"Stop, stop! You are so mistaken. He said you should wait."

"Mrs. Legion—"

"Jeanette."

"I don't think you should lie for him. And I don't think a *minister*"—she almost spat the word—"should ask you to lie. And I plan to tell him so—if I ever speak to him again."

"*Mais non*, no, no." Jeanette took her arm and gave it a firm shake. "Jack, he would never lie and he would never ask Jeanette to lie." She drew herself up like a small queen. "And I would never do it, me."

Camille was suddenly mortified, realizing she'd insulted this woman. Instantly ashamed, she spoke quickly, "I'm sorry. I'm so sorry. I didn't mean to imply you are a liar."

"You say things you don't mean?"

Camille felt her face flame. "I guess I do, Jeanette. Sometimes. It's a character flaw and I know it, but I'm working on it. I hope you'll forgive me, but it is so upsetting that Jack left without me when we agreed to do this together."

"Here, come, you need lemonade." Leading Camille by the arm, Jeanette gently pulled her away from the door and through the house to the kitchen. Not wanting to insult the woman further, she felt she had little choice but to go along.

"Now sit, *cher*," Jeanette said, pulling out a kitchen chair. "Calm yourself."

"Now I'm embarrassed," Camille said. Sighing, she rubbed

at her forehead. "Nobody can make me as mad as Jack can, which doesn't concern you, I know, so I do apologize. But I'll just say this. There will not be a next time for him do this to me."

"*Cher. Cher.* No more apologizing. I tell you truly. Jack will be back soon." She set about loading a glass with ice and filling it to the brim with lemonade. "He is at that place and there is probably some problem he must deal with. I tell him always, you give them too much of yourself."

Before setting the glass on the table, she used her apron to brush the spot in front of Camille it as if some unlikely crumb might have escaped notice. "This will taste very nice to cool your temper on a hot day."

Truly chastened, Camille took a sip of the tart, sweet drink. "After the way I acted, you shouldn't offer me anything except an invitation to leave."

"As if it's a bother to pour lemonade for Jack's wife!" she said, settling in a chair opposite Camille.

Camille didn't bother to correct her again and took the moment to look around. The kitchen was so neat and clean she suspected surgery could be performed on the countertops. The pedestal table was made of golden oak and beautifully restored. The walls were painted a cheerful butter yellow. Pots of herbs thrived on the windowsill. She thought of the sterile look of the living room and wondered at the contrast.

She'd nagged Jack when they were married about failing to hang his clothes or keep his side of the bathroom neat. She'd never understood why he couldn't keep their home as neat and orderly as his desk and work area.

"You are thinking this room looks nothing like the rest of the house, *cher*."

"No. I mean, well, the living room is pretty spare."

"Jack tells me I can do what I like with the kitchen, but the rest of the house, it needs a woman's touch, no?"

"In the form of a decorator, for sure," Camille said.

"No, a reverend—a shepherd with a flock—could not bring in a decorator." She smiled slyly. "But he could bring in a wife. And that is what I told Jack this very morning."

"Uh-huh." Camille was busy trying to imagine Jack as a shepherd.

Jeanette studied an area beyond the kitchen. "This house it has no flowers, no knickknacks. I think that time in prison when he was confined in a small room, it marked him." She rose to pluck a napkin from a drawer and handed it over.

"Thank you," Camille said. "You mentioned Jack being 'over there.' And that sometimes things happen. Is there an emergency? A church thing? Maybe I should leave. What we were going to do could wait."

"No, no," Jeanette said quickly. "He called just before you came. As for the emergency, isn't there always one at that place?"

"What place would that be?"

Jeanette's shrewd gaze rested on Camille's face for a moment, as if she was working through a problem. "Jack would be very upset with me if he knew I told you this. No one knows, not in his church, none of his friends, not even me until recently when that woman called in a panic which forced Jack to have to tell me."

That woman. For a second, Camille stared in shock at Jeanette. Of everything happening now that Jack seemed to be back in her life, the possibility that there might be another woman had never occurred to her. And it surprised her that it would matter. But it did, enough to worry her. Drawing in a deep breath, she set her glass down carefully and stood up. She should leave. Jack could call her when he got back.

Or she could wait for him and hear what he had to say about that woman.

"Ah, *cher*." Jeanette, reading something on her face, spoke gently. "Don't go. Jack is at Sojourner House. Do you know what that is?"

She shook her head. "No."

"It is a . . . how do you say? A place for rehabilitation, a place where people, patients, stay who are not sick in an ordinary way, but who can't care for themselves. Some of the patients there, they are in wheelchairs, some are not. How can I say this? They are not right in the head."

"Oh." More shock. Without realizing it, her hand went to her heart. "I didn't think . . ." What didn't she think? That Jack was the kind of person capable of selflessness? That he had moved beyond the tragic consequences of his actions that fateful day and thought nothing more about it?

She found herself sinking down in the chair, a dense, almost painful feeling growing in her chest. "How . . . I mean, does he . . ." She cleared her throat. "What did you call it? Sojourner House?"

"Yes."

"Where is it?"

"It is not so far, but still out of town. It is on the bayou."

"The bayou."

"I think one reason he wanted the Blood Bayou church is so that he would be near Sojourner House."

"How often does he go?"

"Regular as a clock, he goes on Thursday afternoon. Today, I know he planned to be back before you got here, but something must have come up. That woman, she calls for every little thing."

"What woman, Jeanette?"

"Hmm, is that a green-eyed look I see? I don't think you would get that look if you did not still feel love for our Jack. Am I right?"

Camille repeated firmly, "What woman?"

"The one in charge. Angela Berthelot. I want to tell him she will suck him dry, but I'm not allowed to say a word to criticize, not me."

Camille fixed her gaze on the green plants at the window. Who was this man? What could have turned the dissolute, addicted, ambition-driven man she'd married into the person he was today?

"I have shocked you, yes?" Jeanette's eyes were shrewd, but soft with something. Sympathy? Understanding?

"Yes." Camille gave a short laugh. "Shocked is an understatement."

"You must not let Jack know that his secret is told. He must tell you in his own time."

"Yes. I mean, no, I won't say anything."

Jeanette stood up suddenly. "And you must put on a different face quick. I hear his car now. Jack will take one look and think something bad has happened."

Camille rose. "Thank you for telling me. And thank you for the lemonade. Where is the bathroom?"

Jack was coming in the door as she made her way toward

the front of the house after freshening up. She hoped she didn't look as rattled as she felt, but it would take more than a few minutes to wrap her head around yet another revelation of her ex-husband's new life. And character.

He met her at the arched entrance to the living room with a welcoming smile. "I'm sorry I'm late," he said, looking as if he'd like to hug her. "Something came up. Have you been waiting long?"

"Ten minutes." She kept her distance but gasped as he removed his sunglasses. "What happened? You have a black eye!"

He touched it gingerly. "Would you believe I ran into a door?"

"No."

"I didn't think so." Beyond her, he sent a telling look to his housekeeper, who whirled about on one heel and headed back to her kitchen. "I was in the line of fire when a . . . friend lost his temper. And in my line of work, I'm bound by confidentiality, so I really can't say any more."

She took her time before replying. "I guess I didn't realize your calling could be dangerous."

"I was never in danger," he said wryly. He cocked his head, looking her over. "You look absolutely gorgeous today."

"In this?" She wore a simple white man-tailored shirt and black linen capri pants.

"In anything. And I'm a mess." He pulled at the trendy golf shirt he wore and made a face. "I'll just take a second to change my shirt and we'll be on our way."

She decided to try to see if he would tell her where he'd been. And if he'd mention the woman Jeanette disliked. "If you didn't have that black eye, I'd think you might have spent the afternoon playing golf."

"I wish. I haven't been on the course in some time."

"Shepherding your flock gets in the way of fun stuff, I guess."

He gave her another one of those looks. "Let's just say the compensation is worth it," he said gently, and then turned to go down the hall. "Back in a jiff."

Watching him disappear, she wondered why she kept making those tacky little remarks. She really didn't mean to mock him. In fact, she admired him for the changes he'd made in his life. She moved to the window and gazed out thoughtfully. Apparently Jeanette was right and, in spite of showing up with an injury, he didn't intend to reveal his secret. At least, not to her. And why would he, she wondered, watching a line of egrets in the distance. She wasn't in his life anymore, so why should he reveal anything of a private nature to her?

Jack reappeared in another golf shirt embroidered with a famous logo. "Ready?" He glanced at his watch. "Actually, I called Harlen when it looked like we wouldn't be able to make it as scheduled and it turns out that he has a conflict too. So we've got about an hour to kill."

She scooped up her purse from a chair. "What was his reaction when you said we'd like to talk to him?"

"He was curious, but he didn't hesitate to make the date." He reached to open the door. "I thought we could pop in at the hospital and check on Allen first. He's got to be ready to get out of there."

"Good idea. I meant to drop by today, but time got away

from me. Mom says they're hoping he'll be discharged tomorrow. It isn't the concussion keeping him hospitalized now, it's
fluctuating blood pressure. They think they've finally gotten it
under control."

On the way, she was quiet, thinking about what Jeanette
told her. The Jack she was seeing was not the man she'd married.
What was it her mother had said the night of Luanne's wake?
That one day she should hear from Jack himself exactly how or
what changed him.

"You're quiet," Jack said, giving her a sidelong look. "Something on your mind?"

She decided to ask straight out. "Tell me how you decided to
become a minister."

He glanced at her in some surprise. "You really want to
know?"

"Yes, Jack. That's why I asked."

"And I'm glad you did." He paused, as if gathering his
thoughts. "It wasn't like when you're in college and looking at
your options, weighing the pros and cons and choosing the one
you're best suited for, which is how I made the decision to go to
law school. I was in prison when I realized God was calling me
to the ministry."

She sat very still. She'd never been able even to think about
Jack in prison. It was simply too horrible.

"I was teetering on the edge of a dark precipice and I knew I
would fall into the abyss if I didn't surrender." His voice took an
ironic edge. "Before that, some might think there was so much
turmoil in my life that I was already in a bottomless pit. The
real problem was that I was addicted to alcohol even in my early
teens and in deep denial about it."

He looked at her. "That doesn't come as much of a surprise to you, right?"

"Not really."

He cruised through an intersection on a green light. "I managed to keep my addiction under control, sort of, to get an education. Later, as a lawyer, I was so driven by ambition that I had to control it to keep up the crazy, mindless pursuit necessary to succeed the way I wanted to."

He went quiet for a minute as if choosing his words carefully. "Generally it's believed that we alcoholics have to hit bottom before we're ready to withstand the struggle for recovery. For me, the low point was that day when I struck David Bergeron down and wiped out his future."

He gave Camille a quick look when she made a small, anguished sound, and then he turned his gaze back to the road. "It's a dreadful memory for you too, isn't it?"

"Yes," she whispered. She had watched in horror as Jack's car slammed into the boy. She would never forget that sickening sound or sight.

As he came to a stop at a red light, he spoke in a voice that was low, tortured by the memory. "I don't know if you or anyone can understand my everlasting shame and regret."

Oh, she did. She did. Over the years, she'd spent countless hours wondering about her own role in the accident. She'd known that her nagging fueled Jack's urge to run away, to escape. Maybe if she'd just shut up that day, Jack wouldn't have stormed out, wouldn't have gotten in his car and backed up so recklessly, wouldn't have struck down that young life.

"He's now confined to an institution," Jack said. "Did you know that?"

She nodded mutely.

"You walked out then. I knew you'd been thinking about a divorce. The only surprise to me was that you'd put up with me as long as you had."

She knew why. Love dies hard, she could have told him. She had been thinking about leaving him for months, but as she stood in their driveway and watched the EMTs working on that boy's broken body, her decision to divorce him crystallized. In that moment, her marriage was over.

Waiting for the light to change, Jack looked straight ahead, but his thoughts were clearly focused on that fateful day in his life. "For the first time I couldn't talk my way out of a bad situation. I was arrested and charged with DUI and aggravated assault. Worse, my wife was gone, my marriage destroyed, and I discovered that I didn't have any friends either. My position in the firm was suddenly nonexistent. I was a disgrace to my partners and to the practice, something that I learned was truly unforgivable. So I got what I deserved, a prison sentence."

"It sounds awful when you spell it all out like that," she said.

"It is awful. It was awful. But, Camille, it took something awful to wake me up. And, believe you me, once the jail doors clanged shut behind me, I was suddenly wide awake. I was one sorry, messed-up piece of human garbage." He drove through the intersection. "But prison is not a place where a man can sit around wallowing in self-pity. You'll find yourself in some really unpleasant predicaments doing that."

"Were you scared?"

"Scared out of my mind." He sped up to pass a slow-moving pickup. "But one good thing happened: I sobered up.

They had an AA program and I went, mostly as a way to fill the endless stretches of empty time. In prison, you have nothing to do, and in my case no one to talk to, as I'd alienated everybody who might have helped me. I had plenty of time to think. So I was open to anything that kept me from dwelling on all I'd lost."

He signaled a left turn as they neared the hospital. "AA counsels turning a person's life over to a Higher Power," he said. "I didn't know what that meant. But there was this one man who came around regularly. I didn't know until months after I met him that he was an activist working for prison reform. He had the ear of the governor and several bigwigs in Washington and he's written several books."

"Are you talking about Malcolm Holifield?"

He looked surprised. "Yes, do you know him?"

"I do. He's been very supportive of the Truth Project. In fact, I think he was instrumental in approving the funding for it, but I could never get him to admit it. He's a prince of a guy."

Jack was smiling as he approached the parking garage. "And they say there's no such thing as coincidence."

"I'd expect you to say it was the hand of God having both of us indebted to Malcolm," she said.

"I would, which is what I believe, but I thought you might bristle if I said it." He stopped, waited for the barrier to lift. "As for me, I tend to think of Dr. Holifield as an angel. He saw something in me when I was so down-and-out that I honestly didn't know if life was worth living."

"Oh, Jack . . ." There was real dismay in her voice.

"And that is when I turned my life over to the Lord."

Camille considered that in silence for a minute or two. "My

mother said the same thing," she said finally. "When her life was at its darkest, she turned everything over to God."

Jack smiled. "It's a pretty tried-and-true solution to big problems and it worked for me." Now inside the parking garage, he pulled into a spot reserved for clergy. "Here we are. I'll save the rest of the story for later."

She looked at him. "There's more?"

"Oh, yes," he told her. "A lot more. The best part." He opened the door and got out. "But right now, let's go check on your dad."

CHAPTER fourteen

DIANA WAS IN the room with Allen when they arrived. She jumped up, hugged Camille warmly, and turned to Jack. She stopped midstride at the sight of his bruised face. "Oh, my, Jack! Whatever happened to you? That's a perfectly beautiful shiner!"

"He won't tell," Camille said. "He cites professional confidentiality."

"A very appropriate attitude," Allen said, holding out his hand to shake with Jack. "I never thought about it, but I guess lawyers and preachers do have a lot in common."

"How are you doing, Allen?" Jack asked, smiling.

It was Diana who answered. "He's been simply awful today, so thank heaven you've come to give some comic relief."

"A joke or two in this place would be welcome," Allen said darkly.

Diana ignored him. "He's been so bad that the doctor finally said he could go home just to get rid of him. You almost missed us. Right now we're waiting for the orderly to wheel us out. Rules, you know."

"At this hour?" Camille looked at her watch. "I thought patients were released in the mornings."

"Not anymore. As soon as they think you can make it down to your car without fainting, they kick you out. You're not even expected to be able to walk."

Allen sniffed. "I could have made it to my car days ago."

Diana, standing at the head of the bed where Allen couldn't see her, mouthed silently, "No way."

Allen's gaze narrowed, looking at Jack and Camille. "What's up with you two? I mean, it's nice to have you visit, but you look like people on a mission."

"You're so wrong," Camille said. "Our mission is to visit you, Allen." To say they had a date to talk to Harlen Richard would provoke a round of questions she wasn't ready to answer, along with cautions from her mother that she'd rather avoid.

"After which, Camille wants to look in on Chester Pelham, too," Jack said.

Camille shot him a surprised look, then quickly recovered. Seeing Chester wasn't something she'd thought of, but she was definitely up for it. "Yes, indeed. Wouldn't it be something if Chester came out of his coma and started talking?"

"It would if it made any sense," Jack said.

Allen barked out a laugh and immediately winced with pain. Diana made a *tsk* sound. "You know what happens when you do that, Allen," she scolded, but her hand was stroking his tenderly. She looked at Camille and Jack. "He forgets he's had a concussion, but every once in a while he has a nice reminder, such as when he laughs."

"I haven't had much to laugh about in this place," Allen said.

"He's looking so much better," Camille said to Jack fifteen minutes later as they waited at the elevator. "I don't know what

I would have done if there had been lasting damage. I was so afraid. How would I ever have forgiven myself?"

"You never had anything to forgive yourself for," Jack said, ushering her into the elevator. "Allen's injury was solely the fault of the thugs who attacked him."

Instead of letting Jack select their destination, she quickly punched the button for the second floor. "That's where ICU is," she told him. "I wasn't sure you really wanted to check on Chester or were just deflecting questions from Allen and Mom."

He glanced down at her. "These days I mean what I say, Camille."

She was effectively silenced at that. He was good at saying stuff that took her off stride lately.

"And here we are," he said.

The elevator doors slid open. Camille's earlier unease at being in a hospital had been replaced with healthy respect. After seeing the exceptional care Allen had received the night of his assault, ICU was no longer a scary place. It was a place of healing. These people were in the business of saving lives.

They headed for the nurse's station, circular in design and situated so that the patients' beds, arranged like spokes on a wheel, were always in view. "I hope there's someone around who'll talk to us," Camille said as they approached the counter.

A nurse looked up. "Reverend Vermillion! Nice to see you again."

"Nice to see you too, Monette. How are you?"

"Just about to end my day." She glanced at the clock on the wall. "Seven o'clock and I'm gone. Who are you checking on today?"

"Chester Pelham."

"You're in luck. He's not allowed to have visitors on orders of the police chief, but the doctor's with him now, along with two people from the police department." At the sound of a curtain being drawn back, she looked beyond them. "Ah, yes, here they come now."

Three people were moving away from a patient's bed. One was obviously a doctor. Another was a cop in uniform. The third was Ray Wyatt.

"Ray," Camille exclaimed. "I didn't expect to see you."

He greeted her with a smile and a wink. Jack was acknowledged with a nod. "I probably had the same idea as you, checking on our guy." He glanced at the doctor. "I was just getting an update from Dr. Kendall here."

"We were told Pelham was not permitted to have visitors," Jack said to the doctor.

"Mr. Wyatt was cleared by the police department," Kendall said. He put out a hand. "Good to see you, Jack. We miss you at the club. I shot an eighty-six last week. You should have been there."

"You and me both. I miss playing, Pete, but it's been crazy lately." He glanced toward the cubicle where Chester Pelham lay, hooked up to tubes and gadgets recording his vitals and displaying them on a beeping monitor. "How's he doing?"

Kendall followed his gaze. "When he was first admitted, I would have said he wasn't likely to survive. Today, well, he just might."

"But in what condition mentally?" Camille asked.

Kendall shrugged. "There's no way of knowing that. We'll just have to wait it out."

A few minutes later, Camille left ICU to wait for Jack, who

had stayed behind briefly to talk to Chief June Raines, who'd showed up to check on Chester.

Ray Wyatt caught up with her in the hall. "What do you think?"

She shook her head. "You mean about Chester? I don't know. But I'm hopeful that he'll be able to tell us something when he comes around."

"If he comes around." Wyatt moved to a window overlooking the hospital parking lot. "I'd sure like to be here when he does."

"How did you get in here, Ray? Were you really cleared to have access to Chester?"

"I keep telling you, sweetheart. I've got a nice connection with the police. All it took was a phone call." He reached back and touched the wallet in his pants pocket. "And if that fails, it doesn't hurt to flash my badge."

"Is it legal for you to carry that?"

He grinned at her. "I didn't hear you ask that question."

"Come on, Ray."

"Whatever it takes, Camille. We want to solve this crime, don't we?" His smile faded. "What's up with you and the reverend? I thought you two were blood enemies."

"I never said that, Ray." She realized that such a characterization of her relationship with Jack was wrong, but she wasn't sure exactly how to describe it. "I guess you'd say we've called a truce long enough for me to try to get a few answers to questions that Blood Bayou's finest have ignored."

"Such as?"

"It appears that I'm more suspicious about Harlen Richard as relates to Luanne's murder than the cops around here. Tonight,

Jack is going with me to talk to him after we leave here. Not because he agrees with me. He's convinced Harlen is innocent." She paused, thought a minute. "But then again, he sees the good in most people nowadays."

It was true, she realized. In his other life, as she called it, Jack had been cynical and suspicious of most people and their motives. His embrace of a Christian life had made staggering changes in him. It was all very interesting.

"Then why is he giving you a shot at Harlen?" Wyatt asked.

"Maybe to convince me he's innocent."

"Ah, I get it. And then you'd look elsewhere, meaning Pelham."

"Probably." She smiled.

"Why do you think Harlen is a good suspect?"

"You saw the notes in my murder book, Ray. He has motive and, if he doesn't come up with an alibi, opportunity. However, if he wanted to get rid of his wife, I don't think he'd do it himself. I think he's the type who'd hire someone to do it."

"Interesting. And if true, finding his hired gun will be tough. Take it from me. I spent years in the back streets of New Orleans trying to nail people like that. They know how to survive on the edges, they live in dark places and they're slippery as snakes."

"Lovely," she murmured, and was glad when, at the sound of footsteps in the direction of ICU, she saw Jack headed their way.

"Here comes your hero," Wyatt said. "Oops, he's with the chief. I don't want to push my luck." He began backing off. "And, Camille, don't forget to clue me in after your talk with Harlen. Until then, you be careful. I still think you should let the cops work this one, whether you respect their methods or not. I don't like the feeling I'm getting about this place."

She waved him off with a smile. "I'll be okay, Ray. At least I have a lot of people listening to me now: Madge, Jack, you. I'm not an idiot. I will be careful."

A SECURITY code was required for access to Harlen Richard's estate. Jack spoke into the intercom box announcing their arrival. There was no verbal response, but almost instantly the ornate gate swung slowly open to reveal a winding driveway.

"No chance of unwelcome visitors," Camille commented.

"No. Luanne gave me the code when she and Harlen were first married, but she told me later that Harlen objected and had it changed."

"The killer got inside," she said. "I wonder how."

"Good question."

"Wow, this is something else," Camille breathed. They'd gone several hundred yards along a winding, brick-paved drive and still had not reached the house. "I didn't realize it was so splendid. Whatever Harlen's business, it must be lucrative. I'm more curious than ever about how he and my dad are connected."

"You won't get any answers from Harlen on that," Jack said, as he stopped his car on a curved driveway in front of the house. "And I bet Carson isn't talking either."

Camille looked over at him. "Does that mean you think they're into something illegal?"

"I have no idea, but I know them. Whatever their connection, they both like to keep their cards close to their chests. Which makes sense for most businessmen at their level of wheeling and dealing."

"Loose lips sink ships, huh?"

He laughed as he got out of the car. "Something like that."

She was out by the time he walked around to her side of the car. "You ought to know."

He closed her door. "What does that mean?"

"You never talked about your cases. I used to just burn with curiosity, because you were involved in some really interesting things with interesting people. But you wouldn't talk." She walked beside him to the steps. "To tell the truth, I used to wonder if everything you did was strictly legal."

"To tell the truth," he said, with a hand at her elbow, "your suspicions were pretty much on point. I'm not proud to admit that I skated very close to the edge more times than I like to recall. I'm glad I'm not tempted to get back into that kind of game. I just wish I could erase the stain on my reputation."

"Your work as a minister is a good start, isn't it?"

He looked down at her. "There are people in my past who will never believe any remorse on my part is genuine. Or enough. I just have to live a life now that is free of that kind of behavior and trust God to deal with the rest." He rang the doorbell.

"When we get to the good stuff," he said, "let me do the talking, okay? You promised."

"Okay, okay." As for his God-centered life now, what was there for her to say about it anyway? She lived her life relying on the law as a moral code. She didn't know what Jack's moral compass was before his conversion, or even if he had any. Clearly he now relied on God's law.

The door opened and she found herself eye to eye with Harlen Richard. She was struck again by how short he was. Luanne, who had been at least five feet eight, must have towered over him when she wore heels. Camille remembered her as partial to three-inch platforms.

"Jack, come in, come in. Good to see you," Harlen said heartily, and stepped back to let them inside. "Camille, you look lovely, as always. Welcome."

He ushered them into an enormous foyer and across a sea of black and white tiles. They passed a stunning formal living room and wound up in a den that could have been featured in *Architectural Digest*. Three walls were paneled in what she guessed was weathered cypress. The fourth was all smoked glass, from floor to ceiling. Beyond a huge patio was a view of the bayou. Ordinarily, she would have found it breathtakingly beautiful—if she hadn't recognized it as the spot where Luanne was murdered.

After seeing them seated, Harlen stood before them, briskly rubbing his hands together. "Now, since it's the cocktail hour, what'll you have to drink? You name it and I've probably got it."

"Nothing for me," Jack said, removing his sunglasses.

"Holy smokes!" Richard eyes went wide with surprise. "Is that a shiner you've got there, Jack? What on earth happened?"

"I accidentally stepped in front of a fist."

"Well, you need to watch the company you keep, man." He peered closer. "Or failing that, watch where you step."

"Point taken," Jack said.

"I bet you wish you could have a shot of good Scotch, but now that you're dry, I guess you have to settle for stuff that isn't alcoholic. So name it."

"I'm good, Harlen. But Camille might want something. Thanks anyway."

"I'll have sparkling water," Camille told him.

"Excellent. I'll just be a minute." He disappeared into the bowels of the house, and the minute he did so, Camille got up and began prowling around the room. She would have liked a tour of the whole house. If it matched what she'd already seen, it was probably gorgeous. She wandered over to the glass doors. "I hear some fabulous wind chimes," she said, tilting her head to catch the deep, melodious sounds.

"They're special," Jack said. "Luanne bought them in Key West. She loved to sit out on the patio and listen to them." He watched her stroll back to the couch. "Did you really want sparkling water?"

"Nah, I'm just nosy and wanted to look around a little." She gave him a wicked smile, lowering her voice to a stage whisper. "Harlen may be tempted to pour it over my head once he realizes what we're here for."

"Shhh."

"He can't hear us. This house is humongous."

Jack pulled her down beside him on the couch and silenced her with a playful tug on one of her black curls. Consequently, she was struggling to control a giggle when Harlen reappeared.

"Here we go." He handed Camille the bottled water and a frosted glass. "I'll just let you serve yourself, Camille. How's your dad?"

"Hale and hearty," she said, pouring the fizzy water. "And still trying to fix me up with any job other than the one I have."

"He's lucky to be a father." Harlen had settled into a sumptuous leather chair. Crossing his legs, he leaned back, sipping at something she guessed was Scotch. "It was always a dream of mine."

"Really?"

"Yes, indeed." He studied the glass in his hand. "But somehow Luanne never conceived. We considered in vitro, but you know how it is. You make plans, but things happen to distract you. Now I really regret that we never followed through."

"I didn't know Luanne wanted a child," Jack said.

"I think she wanted a baby for the wrong reasons, if you want the truth of the matter. She had a terrible childhood, which of course you'd know. She wanted to relive it through a baby, giving it all the things she never had and correcting all the wrongs she'd suffered as a little girl."

What a crock, Camille thought. She didn't believe a word of it. For some reason, Richard was trying to rewrite history, manufacturing an image of Luanne and their relationship that was nothing like the dysfunctional mess it really was. But understandable from his point of view. A dysfunctional mess might reflect on him and tarnish his public image.

"This is a side of Luanne I never knew," Jack said. "Tell me more."

Camille looked at him to see if he could possibly be serious. Was he buying this? "Better yet," Jack said, "let's start with the day she died. Do you think she had any idea she was in danger? Was there anything going on that suggested she was fearful about anything?"

"Absolutely nothing." Harlen replied instantly. "Why would she think she had anything to fear? Which might explain how the killer got inside the gate. She knew Pelham because he'd been her yard man before he killed Stephanie Hill. She must have let him in that day because you saw for yourself how secure that fence is. A stranger would have to know the code to get in."

"Excuse me," Camille said, "but we know now that Pelham didn't kill Stephanie."

"Whatever," Harlen said, dismissing her point. "Although I personally have doubts. No offense, you understand, Camille. But all that aside, the fact remains that Pelham was our yard man as well as Stephanie's."

"If it was someone other than Pelham," Jack said, "maybe she thought it was you coming home and she opened the gate from inside the house."

"She knew I wasn't due home until much later."

"You were out of town?" Camille asked.

Harlen shifted, set his glass on the table beside him. "I was."

Before Camille could follow up, Jack gave her a speaking look and then turned back to Harlen. "It occurred to me," he said, "that if it wasn't Pelham, then the killer might have known your plans that day, otherwise, he was taking a very big risk in the event you showed up unexpectedly."

Harlen frowned. "It sounds to me as if you're having some doubt whether it was Pelham who murdered Luanne, Jack." He glanced at Camille. "Again, no offense, honey, but everybody in this town knows you're Pelham's biggest fan. We all know you don't believe he did it. I, on the other hand, am totally convinced that the police have the right fellow. I'm torn between wishing him dead as dirt and wanting him to survive so we can shoot him up with a lethal injection and watch him die."

Camille managed to keep her smile in place. Ignoring Jack's warning look, she said to Harlen, "Let's just take this as a hypothetical. Say Chester really didn't do it. That somebody else did." She paused, waiting for his reluctant nod. "So where were you that the killer knew you would not walk in and foil his plans to murder your wife?"

CAMILLE DID not need streetlight reflecting on Jack's set face to see that he was furious. A sure sign was the controlled way he'd ushered her into his car after Harlen ushered them—none too politely—out of his house.

"I told you to let me do the talking," he said.

"You were just going to schmooze him forever, Jack! Did you believe that nonsense about Luanne wanting a baby?"

"I don't know. I didn't know she was a battered wife either," he said bitterly. "She kept so many secrets from me, why not that too?"

"Well, she didn't want a baby. I'd bet a million on that. And if you want to check it, have a talk with those witches who cornered me in the bathroom at her wake. They'd know." She sat back in the car with her arms crossed and her mouth set stubbornly.

"Face it, Camille. You blew it. He now knows you, for one, consider him a suspect. If you hadn't revealed yourself, we might have learned where he was, assuming he wasn't here in Blood Bayou."

"He was never going to tell us anything because—"

"Because he killed her? You don't know that." He roared away from a traffic stop. "You don't have nearly as much evidence, even circumstantial, to point to Harlen as the cops have to believe Pelham killed her."

"I keep telling you I don't think he would have been the one to kill her! But he had reason to want her dead. She was an embarrassment. Worse than that, she flaunted her affairs. That's motive for a man like Harlen. I'd just like to know why he isn't willing to furnish an alibi. If he has one."

"Not one he's willing to tell you. And, after tonight, me."

"And we know the cops don't care."

"Camille. They have no obligation to keep you informed of their investigation," Jack pointed out.

She responded to that with a grunt. "Don't I know it."

Both went silent for a while, busy with their own thoughts. In the distance, heat lightning flashed, revealing low clouds. It would probably rain sometime tonight, Camille thought.

After a few minutes, Jack said in a mollifying tone, "Let's not argue. Let's both sleep on it tonight and tomorrow maybe I'll go see Harlen again and try to get him to talk. Without you."

A peace offering. The new Jack. "Okay," she said. "I guess I did come on a bit strong."

"Are you hungry? We could stop and get something before I drop you at Madge's place. In case she hasn't prepared anything."

"No, but I'd love a cappuccino. I don't want to leave Madge alone too long."

"Sounds good to me too."

Half an hour later they were back on the road, but not one she recognized. They'd left the town behind and were now on a secondary highway, but to call it a highway was an exaggeration to Camille's way of thinking. One side was thick with tall, canelike growth, cattails, she thought they were. On the other side, palmetto and elephant ears grew right up to the pavement. It was fully dark now but seemed darker, as vegetation encroached so much that in some places the road narrowed almost to a single lane.

But it was hard to see much of anything. As they were out of the town limits, there was no light and no other traffic either. Except for the headlights on Jack's car, the world was as black as pitch. And when the headlights flashed on a curve, she saw the trees were draped with moss and standing in water. It dawned on her that they were driving through a swamp!

"Where are we, Jack?"

"On an old oil company road. There's something going on at the college tonight and traffic tends to back up, so to avoid it, I've taken the scenic route, you might say. Don't worry, we'll get to Madge's place eventually."

"Well, I might be able to appreciate the scenic route if it was daylight." She cast a wary look through the side window. "To me, the swamp seems spooky at night."

He paused to consider what she said. "I guess it could be if you aren't used to it." After a minute, he chuckled. "I could always tell you a story to distract you."

She settled back. If he wasn't concerned, she supposed she shouldn't be either. "That reminds me," she said. "You never finished telling me the rest of your story. I know a person can't just decide to become a minister and walk into a church. You have to attend seminary, don't you?"

"Yes, but I had a lot of soul-searching to do before that. Believe me, it was not my plan to be a preacher, even though God was giving me signs right and left. My plan was to get out of prison, stay sober, and somehow try to pick up the pieces of my life. I'd decided on a career in business. I wasn't going back to being a lawyer even if I managed to get my law license back. But God had other plans."

"Really?"

"Really. And in case you think it was an easy transition from first-class sinner to soldier for Christ, let me tell you about the months and months I spent stubbornly resisting."

"What made you cave?"

"Surrender, Camille," he said softly. "The word is surrender. But to answer your question, prayer mostly. And Dr. Holifield. And a sense of impending doom if I didn't. I don't know. All of the above, I guess. I just know that the night I surrendered was the longest night of my life. It was worse even than when I crashed and ruined that boy's life. It was worse than waking up in jail the next morning and realizing everything I'd worked for, including you, was gone."

"It doesn't sound like a happy thing."

"I guess it doesn't, but the instant I surrendered, a weight was lifted from me in the most profound way. I've never felt anything like it. The only way to describe it is that a sort of heavenly peace descended on me. Settled in me. And I felt this awesome rush of relief." He paused as if the memory gave him pleasure, then added with irony, "None of which lasted long, because I realized that I knew nothing about being a minister."

"I was thinking the same thing."

"Yeah. Luckily, God put Dr. Holifield there to buck me up. He was instrumental in approving my parole and then in helping me get into the seminary." He glanced over and smiled at her. "The rest is history."

"That is pretty incredible," she said.

"God is pretty incredible," Jack said.

She wondered if she'd ever get comfortable hearing him speak so casually and often about his God. And she realized she'd like to know more. She was sorting through ways in her head to ask when she glanced in the side mirror and got a view of headlights several car lengths behind them. "Well, look at this. We've been alone out here for miles and now there's finally a car behind us. If a swamp creature jumps out at us, maybe we'll have some help."

He laughed. "You're really spooked, aren't you? I guess I'm used to it as I'm on this stretch of road pretty often. I have a . . . oh, call it a mission . . . located a few miles beyond Madge's place."

"A mission? You mean your church is sponsoring a smaller congregation way out here? Something like that?"

"Not exactly."

"Then what exactly? Or is it a secret?"

He paused as if considering what to say. "Let's just leave it for now, okay? I can say this. It's an important part of my ministry."

But still a secret, although she guessed his "mission" was Sojourner House. Camille was surprised to feel a pang of disappointment. Surely she wasn't hurt. After sharing the story of his conversion, why would he keep the Sojourner part from her? She, more than anyone, knew why he'd be committed to such a mission. And why should she care that Jack was reluctant to share anything about his present life? But she found that she did care. What she needed to do was to work out in her mind why it mattered.

"One day I'll take you out there," Jack was saying. "Actually, in daylight this area is really beautiful. But developers are a problem, always looking for waterfront property to throw up more houses. And, of course, oil companies have sites any and everywhere. But so far this area has escaped desecration. It gives me hope. The ecology here is delicately balanced. It needs protection."

"It must have looked this way millions of years ago," she murmured as lightning flickered ahead of them. In a few seconds, off in the distance, thunder rumbled softly. It was definitely going to rain. "It's almost primordial to look at," she said. "But, to me, still a little spooky."

Jack glanced at his rearview mirror, frowning. "Whoever this is behind us, he's way too close now. I hope he doesn't try to pass—we're coming to a narrow bridge that has no guardrails."

Camille turned in her seat to try and see the driver, but with the high beams on, she couldn't see much. "It's a truck, I think. Omigosh! He is really tailgating us, Jack. Another few inches and he'll actually run into us. Is he crazy?"

"I don't know what's going on, but I'm slowing down. The bridge is just ahead. It's not safe to cross it at this speed."

Camille clutched the armrest on the side door with one hand and her seat belt strap with the other, bracing herself. "Maybe we should stop, let him get around us," Camille said.

"Not a good idea," Jack said grimly. "If he's up to no good, we don't want to just hand ourselves over."

"What do you mean, no good?"

"I don't know." He glanced at her, then her seat belt. "Okay, the bridge is coming up. As soon as we get across, I'm speeding up."

She looked behind once again. "Looks like he's dropped back."

"Good. We need to get away from this idiot if we can. Here's the bridge."

"Jack!" She was turned in her seat, watching. "He's speeding up! He's coming up behind us just flying!"

Whatever he said in reply was lost in a deafening crash as the truck slammed into them from the rear. Camille screamed as the car went airborne, then dropped like a ten-ton stone into the bayou. The force of impact stunned. Pain exploded in Camille's head.

Seconds later, she was dazed but conscious. She came fully to herself when she realized that water was pouring in at her feet and rising fast. The car was in the bayou! Terrified, she fumbled at her seat belt, thinking only to escape from the car. She didn't know how deep the bayou was, but the water was already past her ankles. But wasn't there some rule about exiting from a submerged vehicle? With growing panic, she realized she couldn't remember what it was.

Just then, Jack leaned over, caught her face in one hand, and forced her to look at him. "Don't panic, Camille," he said calmly. "We'll be okay. We can get out of here."

"How? The water is pouring in!" Her voice rose, nearing hysteria.

"Just do what I tell you, love. Are you hurt?" He released her seat belt and began running his hands over her arms and legs, checking for injury.

"My head."

"I see it. Do you think you can swim?"

"Yes, I can swim." She had to in spite of a blinding headache.

"Are you sure?"

She touched the spot at her temple and winced with pain. "I'm okay, I think."

"Not dizzy, not feeling nauseous?"

"Stop talking and let's get out of here, Jack! Look, the water's coming in fast." It was past her knees now.

"We can't open the doors yet," he said. "We have to wait."

"No!"

"Yes," he said in a firm voice. "I know what to do, Camille."

Of course. That was what she couldn't remember about escaping from a submerged vehicle. Something about equalizing pressure. The force of the water outside kept the doors sealed shut, or something.

Her teeth began to chatter with fright. "I was never very good at waiting," she whispered.

"I know that, love." Incredibly, he smiled and reached for her. Now that the water was up over the console, it was easy to pull her across to him. And there was room because, as she remembered, Jack's long legs forced him to push the seat back to its limit.

She realized that, with his arms around her, some of her fright faded. He was big and solid and safe. She hoped it wasn't just illusion since the water was waist-high now. And cold. And there were probably *things* in it. *Live things.* "Are you sure you know what to do when something like this happens?"

"I do."

"But have you ever done it?"

"Do I have to tell the truth?"

"No, just let me keep thinking you know how to save us."

"God is going to save us, love."

She closed her eyes as water reached chest level. "Do you mean that literally or figuratively?"

He laughed softly. "Both. But just in case it's figuratively, I want you to know that I love you."

"Don't say that! It sounds like a farewell speech."

He hugged her tightly and kissed her on the mouth. "Now would be a good time to pray."

"I don't know how!" she wailed as water sloshed around her neck.

"I'm going to open the door. When I do, we will push out of the car. Together. I'll be holding you and I won't turn you loose. Once out, I'll boost us up to the surface, you got that?"

"I'm really scared, Jack."

While water lapped at her chin, he took her face in one hand again, forcing her to look at him. "Say after me, Our Father, who art in heaven . . ."

She felt an astonishing rush of relief. "I can say that. I know it. Our Father, who art in heaven."

"Good girl. Now, when I get the door open, it'll be like a tidal wave as the water gushes in. It'll be over our heads instantly. When I tell you, take a good, deep breath, okay? Hold on now. Here we go!"

And with that, he gave a mighty push with his shoulder against the door. "Now, Camille!"

Instantly, water thundered in. Camille panicked as it crashed into her and swallowed her up. In spite of all Jack's instructions and his apparent calm, she was terrified. And utterly disoriented. It had been dark before. Now it was pitch black. Even with Jack's arm about her waist and knowing he was dragging her free of the car, instinct made her want to save herself. But her struggles were in vain. He held her in a grip of iron, propelling her strongly and confidently up, up, up. Would they never get there?

It seemed forever, but then they broke the surface, both gasping for air. For a few seconds Jack held onto Camille, then with a keen look into her face, he asked, "Are you okay? Do you think you can make it over there to the bridge?"

"I don't know. I guess. Eww! What is this stuff?" While trying to stay above water she raked at her face and hair and neck, trying to rid herself of clumps of weblike something. And horrible stuff floated around her legs.

"It's duckweed," Jack said. "It's harmless. Right now, we want to get to the bridge. Can you make it?"

"Yes. And even if I thought I couldn't, I would out of sheer fright. I know there're alligators in this bayou!"

"Trust me, none are hanging around here now. After that crash, they'll be scurrying for calmer water." He reached toward her ear and plucked something off. She didn't want to know what. "Our problem's not duckweed or alligators; the surface of the bayou at this point is choked with water hyacinths. They're thick and hard to swim through, but we must to reach the bridge."

She gave a panicked look around and saw that the path to the bridge was covered with the lily-like plants. "Is anything going to be lurking underneath there? Like snakes? Or crawfish?" She'd never liked those little creatures waving their pincers like tiny weapons.

"Again," Jack said, "they're more leery of you than you are of them."

Just then a sudden bolt of lightning struck with a thunderous boom. Camille instinctively squealed. "Can you believe this! Now we're going to be electrocuted."

"No, we aren't. C'mon." Jack gave her a good shove toward the bridge, which pushed her into a thick floating island of hyacinths.

"I hate this!"

"Go! I'm right behind you."

It was horrible. Who knew water hyacinths could be lethal? She would never look on a bayou and admire the beauty of the lavender blossoms again. Tangled roots dangling in water brushed at her legs, her body, her arms. It was like trying to swim in a net loaded with squirmy snakes. She forced that thought out of her head and focused on making it to the bridge. And ignoring the possibility of being struck by lightning.

It couldn't have taken as long as it seemed, but finally she bumped against a wood piling, which presented another problem. There was nothing she could grab onto and haul herself up out of the water with. The pilings were encrusted with years of marine growth. What was worse, she wondered, drifting in the hideous hyacinth plants or slashing her body on razor-sharp barnacles? Then, to her amazement, her fingers found a large bolt sticking out from the piling. She grabbed it gratefully and shared it with Jack.

"How are we going to get up to the bridge?" she asked him.

"I'm going to the shallows. It'll be knee-deep mud and choked with elephant ears and more hyacinths, but I'll be able to walk out. You stay here. Don't let go of that piling. I'll go up on the bridge and pull you up out of the water."

She gave a quick look around. Except for occasional flashes of lightning, it was black dark, which meant excellent cover for someone lying in wait for them. As close as Jack was, she could barely see him. Anything beyond three feet might as well have been three miles.

"Wait, Jack! What if somebody's watching and decides to finish the job?"

Jack was already making his way to the water's edge. "I don't think he'll take that chance. This was supposed to look like an accident. To finish us off, he'd have to use something that would not look like an accident. Doesn't matter. We have to get out of the water."

"Hurry, I'm still worried about snakes!"

Although it was barely a minute and Jack was on the bridge above her, it seemed more like ten.

"Here, give me your hand." He lowered himself flat on the bridge and leaned over as far as he could and still be able to lift her up. She reached up and let him pull her out of the water and onto the bridge.

Finally on a flat, firm surface, she needed to take a minute to catch her breath, but Jack pulled her to her feet. "Let's get out of here. I don't think our friend will be back, but he just may be crazy enough to try again."

"He tried to kill us, Jack."

"Yeah, but he didn't. Do you still have your shoes or did you lose them in the bayou?"

"I have them, but they're soaked and squishy. They were definitely not designed for swimming."

"And neither were our cell phones."

"Yours. I forgot and left mine in my car. Which won't help us. We can't call anybody. We have to walk to civilization. Please tell me it's not too far."

CHAPTER fifteen

IT TURNED OUT to be more than a mile on a road that meandered beside the bayou, thick with overgrowth and precious little shoulder. More than once Camille had taken a false step and found herself ankle deep in mud. Dark as it was, she was almost grateful for flashes of lightning which lit their way, albeit briefly. There was no sign of human habitation, but there was an abundance of sound. The swamp rang with creature noises, everything from nocturnal insects to the low bellow of bullfrogs. Angry, rumbling clouds obscured a full moon. The promise of rain made it imperative to find shelter fast.

"Last thing we need is to get caught in a summer thunderstorm," Jack said, eyeing ominous signs overhead. "We're a good five miles from the point where I would have turned off onto a main road. I hope we don't have to walk that far."

"What choice do we have?" Camille flinched as lightning flashed and moved a little closer to Jack. "There's no place to take shelter." Cypress and tupelo trees, shrouded in Spanish moss, stood in water. Once it began to rain, she wondered if the road flooded.

"I'm hoping there will be a fishing camp," Jack said, "but to tell the truth, I've never seen one. At this point, anything that has a roof would be a welcome sight."

"But will it have dry clothes?" She glanced down at her once white shirt and soggy, bedraggled capris? "And shampoo."

Jack caught her hand and gave it a squeeze. "Not unless we're very lucky."

"It's only fair that we have some good luck since we've definitely had our share of the other kind tonight." She slapped at a vine dangling from a tall tree in front of her face and squealed when a huge something suddenly flew out of the branches. "What was that!"

"An owl," Jack said, reaching up to push the vines out of their path. "How's your headache?" Jack asked.

"It's dull and throbbing, but that owl nearly gave me a heart attack."

"Not dizzy?"

"No."

"No double vision?"

"No. But I wouldn't refuse a couple aspirin. I don't suppose you'd have any in your pocket, would you?"

"Sorry, I wouldn't."

Wind gusted about them and she shivered, knowing it would rain any minute. Jack drew her close with an arm around her shoulders. He felt warm and solid.

"You're shivering," he said. "Are you cold or just spooked?"

"A little of both. And this is the first time I actually appreciate August weather. We'll be miserable when it starts to rain, but thankfully we won't freeze."

"I owe you an apology for putting you in such a predicament."

"You call it a predicament that somebody tried to kill us?"

"No, I call it attempted murder." His voice sounded grim.

"And I intend to find whoever it was and see that he doesn't get close enough to be a threat to you again, Camille."

"So now do you believe me that Chester isn't the killer? That someone else murdered Luanne and he's worried enough that I'm going figure out who? And that he has to kill me too? Are you finally convinced?"

"Yeah."

She gave him an exasperated look. "That's it? Just a flat 'yeah?'"

"A near-death experience convinced me." He hugged her against him briefly. "I chose this road knowing it's deserted at night. Cars break down, accidents happen. I should have considered that."

"We have cell phones for that kind of thing. You couldn't have anticipated that somebody would follow us and do what he did." She started when lightning flashed a little too close for comfort, but it did give them a glimpse of the road. "Every time that happens," she said, "I hope to see something, but it looks like we're in the Twilight Zone."

"Not quite," Jack said, "but I admit I'd like it better if I could see."

"But does anybody ever actually use this road? What are the chances that somebody will show up—other than someone who wants to kill us?"

"Not much, I'm afraid. And even if someone did come along, we'd have to duck for cover on the chance it could be him again."

She gave the swamp a wary look. "I don't know what's worse, having to get off this road or having to stay on it." She made a squeaky protest as she felt the first few raindrops. "Oh, no, it's starting to sprinkle."

"We need to pick up our pace," Jack said, tightening his arm about her. "I think we're about two hours away from the main road, at best. Once we're there, it'll be safe to flag down a ride." Before he stopped talking, lightning struck in a spectacular display, followed by a deafening boom.

Camille stopped abruptly and grabbed his arm. "Jack! Look! I think I saw something. See, through the trees?"

"No. How could you see anything?"

She tightened her hold on his sleeve. "I don't want to lose it. Let's wait and at the next flash, look where I'm pointing."

On the heels of her remark, lightning lit up the world again. Jack said he saw nothing, but in the next dazzling strike, Camille saw, clearly, a cabin about fifty yards away.

"There it is! Did you see it?"

"I did." There was a note of wonder in his voice.

Camille felt her knees almost give way in a rush of profound relief. Thank goodness it hadn't begun to rain in earnest; otherwise they might have missed the cabin.

"I never thought I'd grateful to be outside in an electrical storm," Jack said as another bolt struck. "If it keeps up, it'll help us find a way to get to that cabin from here."

"I'm counting on it," Camille said. "I don't look forward to crashing through swamp water in the dark."

"Here it is." Jack stepped off the road onto a trail that looked to be an access lane, overgrown and easily missed except for the lightning. Tire tracks were unmistakable. "Let's hope this leads to the cabin, and watch your step. You don't want to twist an ankle out here."

"Right, I want to be able to outrun any alligator chasing me."

He laughed and caught her hand and pulled her with him on the trail. "That's my girl. Keep up that attitude and one day we'll look back on this as a great adventure."

"In about fifty years. Maybe."

THE CABIN was locked, but Jack kicked the door open. He expected to find the place musty and derelict, but it appeared fairly new. And, as campsites go, it was surprisingly clean. After a quick tour, he realized it had been replenished lately with fresh provisions. Surprisingly, it also had electricity. This was a remote location. Jack wondered who'd paid to run the line.

"Somebody's been here recently," Camille said, looking around uneasily. "I hope it's not the guy who wants to kill us."

Jack, busy opening cabinets and drawers, held up a knife. "If so, he's in for a surprise. This baby was made for gutting fish, but it can definitely double as a weapon."

Camille was shaking her head. "I can't believe any of this is happening, Jack. It's like a bad dream."

Just then, a horrendous crash of thunder shook the cabin. Instantly, the heavens opened in a torrential downpour. Rain pounded the tin roof with the force of a freight train. Windows rattled and the whole cabin trembled from gusting wind, testing the pilings beneath them.

"Nice vacation we're having," Camille said, attempting a shaky smile. "I just wish I'd brought my swimsuit. Oh, I forgot, it's slashed to ribbons." As she watched, Jack crossed the room, making for a large chest. "Wait!" she said.

He looked back at her. "What?"

"Now seems like a good time to pray there are clothes and a blanket in that chest and not a dead body."

The smile he gave her was slanted with irony. "I've been praying ever since we approached that bridge. Now, let's see what we have here."

He opened the chest and instantly pulled out a blanket. "Here you go. Step into that other room and take off those wet clothes. Wrap yourself up and take a seat over there while I check for other goodies."

"We're in luck!" she shouted a minute later from the other room. "There's a chest of drawers in here and it has clothes in it!"

She sailed a pair of jeans through the door. "Sorry, no underwear, but here's a T-shirt. I won't tell you what it says on the front."

He scooped up the jeans. "Just as long as it's extra large and dry."

"It's both."

He heard her moan, then give a dramatic sigh. "And so is mine, extra large and dry, but it feels heavenly."

He looked up as she emerged clothed in a huge T-shirt that reached her knees. Clearly it was meant for a tall man. And so were the pants, which she'd rolled up past her ankles.

She struck a pose. "How do I look?"

He grinned. "Not as stylish as when we started out tonight, but still very beautiful."

"I think you must have taken a lump on your head too," she said. "While you change, I'll look for something to eat. I don't know about you, but lunch seems a long time ago."

"It was a long time ago. That stove runs off a gas bottle, so we can at least have coffee. I found some. And there's a lot of stuff in the cabinet. Including peanut butter."

"I love peanut butter! I won't starve after all."

Jack was smiling as he changed into jeans and the T-shirt. Some things hadn't changed. Camille had once said if she was marooned on a desert island, all she'd need to survive was peanut butter.

While draping his wet clothes on hangers found in the tiny closet, he considered sleeping arrangements. There was one double bed. He'd like nothing better than to spend the night with his wife in his arms in that bed, but that delight would have to wait until they managed to work through the issues that had separated them. He wouldn't let himself think that wouldn't happen. He would just have to be patient. All in God's time, he reminded himself, not his own.

The thunderstorm was still raging, but not as fierce, an hour later. Coffee had been brewed and they'd pulled a selection of nonperishables from the cabinet. Jack was eating boned chicken straight out of a can. Camille, no surprise, went for the peanut butter.

"The crackers are stale," she said, wrinkling her nose. "I'll leave a note for the owner to do some shopping." She stopped, giving Jack a puzzled look. "What?"

"I guess you don't have a concussion."

She touched the bruise on her temple gingerly. "How can you tell?"

"You wouldn't have an appetite or a sense of humor."

She shrugged. "It's probably the euphoria that comes when narrowly escaping death. They say some people want to make love when that happens, but food is probably a good substitute."

He almost choked. "I'm not touching that one."

She laughed softly, then flinched at another huge crash of thunder. "How are we going to get out of here, Jack? I mean, your car is at the bottom of the bayou. It's still storming outside and the rain might not let up tomorrow. People will be concerned about both of us. Are we going to start walking again? What if our nemesis shows up?"

"We're leaving by way of the bayou. While we climbed up the stairs, I noticed a pirogue stored under the cabin. Tomorrow at first light, we'll launch it, if the rain has stopped, and row ourselves out of here. If it's still raining, we'll wait it out and leave when it quits." He stood up and dropped the can into a plastic garbage bag. "But until then, you need to rest. Even if you don't have a concussion, you have a nasty lump on your head."

"What about you?"

"I'll be here on the couch where I can keep an eye on the door. Our guy will probably assume there are weapons in the cabin, so I don't think he'll try anything. But to be on the safe side, I'll push the table against the door." While talking, he was clearing a path to move the table.

Camille stood up, cupping her coffee mug. "I don't know if I can sleep, Jack. I think I'll just stay out here with you."

He crossed over to her and took the mug out of her hands. "Enough caffeine." He set it aside and took her face in his hands. "Look at me. You're scared?"

"Yes!"

"Trust me, you're safe now, Camille. I'll be right out here. You'll be able to see me. I won't be sleeping. I have a weapon. You saw it."

He was still a little worried about her, but he didn't tell her that. He planned to check on her every couple of hours in the night. Although she didn't appear to be concussed, he wasn't taking any chances.

Later, thinking about it, he knew that was the moment when he should have stepped back and urged her into the bedroom away from him. But what he'd done instead was to give in to aching temptation and kiss her, to taste Camille again. The wife of his heart. His love.

He felt the little shock that went through her, but instead of stopping right there, a wave of fierce desire washed through him when she did not resist. Instead, she stepped close, lifted her arms, and wrapped them around his neck. No force on earth could have stopped him then as he was so desperately hungry for her. She was warm and soft, womanly. The scent of her was achingly familiar, the sounds coming from her, soft kitten-like murmurs, were an aphrodisiac more powerful than any drug. All spoke to him of heady pleasures, of intense need. He was a starved man and rational thought had vanished.

Outside, a sizzling lightning bolt struck near the cabin, literally shaking it on its pilings. It shook Jack too. With a gut-deep groan, he broke the kiss and caught her by her arms. "Camille—"

She gave a strangled cry, wrenching away. "What are we *doing*!"

Jack turned from her and took a minute to try to clear his head and the sexual need that raged in him. When he could speak, he said in an ironic voice, "Good question, Camille."

When he finally turned to look at her, she was breathing hard, her face flushed, her green eyes flashing angrily. On her beautiful mouth, he saw the effect of that kiss. "I'm sorry," he said before she could go on attack. "I got carried away, I guess."

She was rubbing her arms briskly. "We both did. But I can't believe you can still do that to me. I can't believe I don't have the brains of a flea when you come on to me sexually."

"I didn't mean to come on to you sexually, Camille. I didn't. I think we're both in an emotionally charged state. We've survived an attempt on our lives tonight and we reacted like—"

"Animals in heat?"

He gave a short, humorless laugh. "Not a pretty picture, is it?"

She began to pace. "I'm not sure who I'm more ticked off at, you or myself." She threw her arm out to indicate the cabin and the storm. "And as for the situation we're in, it's no excuse. I'm not a silly teenager who can't control her hormones. I should know not to get within a foot of you or you'll take a mile!"

"No," Jack said quietly and moved to the window to stare out at the rain. "If I'd taken a mile, we'd be in that bedroom now."

Some of her outrage seemed to fade at his words. "I guess you're right since you're the one who put the brakes on. As much as I hate to admit it." She paused, obviously thinking. "I'm curious. Are there rules that say you can't act like a normal man? I mean, you and I should not even consider getting involved in that way based on our history, but what about dates and a social life for you? You can't live like a monk. Can you?"

He took a moment to choose his words. Camille had no faith.

How to make her understand? "I'm bound by principles that come with my calling, Camille. One day I hope you'll let me share them with you. That means when we go to bed together, it will be as a married couple who've taken vows that honor that sacred covenant."

He turned from the window to look at her. "Does that make any sense?"

"Of course. You're just very different from the person you used to be."

He smiled. "I sure hope so."

"And who said anything about us being a married couple ever again?"

"A man can hope, can't he?"

And then, in spite of the charged emotional mood, he slipped his arm around her waist and hugged her once, quickly, then let her go. "Now, go crawl into that bed and try to get some sleep. You've had a really tough day."

At the door, she stopped and looked back at him. "You've got to get this through your head, Jack. We are not going to be married again."

When she saw he wasn't going to rise to that, she shook her head and went into the bedroom. He waited a moment just out of sight beside the door while she shed the huge pants. He knew she had nothing on under those pants and, thankfully, the over-sized T-shirt made a decent gown. Still, his imagination filled in what he hadn't seen. After all, he reminded himself, he was only human. Then, hearing the bedsprings squeak, he moved to the door and watched her settle in for the night. Because he knew she was emotionally charged and scared, he waited in a spot where she could see him. Five minutes later, she was asleep. Exhaustion, he thought. And just as well. For him, however, it would be a long night.

THE RAIN stopped sometime before dawn. Camille had slept fitfully. A couple of times when she awoke, she realized that Jack wasn't in the cabin. Apparently, he'd been as restless as she and, instead of tossing and turning, he'd spent some time prowling the confines of the cabin and, with the help of a flashlight and rain poncho, he'd even snooped around outside. Both were glad when the sun rose and they could leave.

She noticed that he seemed distracted as they prepared to launch the flat-bottom, canoe-like pirogue. "I found another poncho," she told him. "The sky is still a little cloudy, so we'll both have them just in case."

Jack tossed a bulging plastic bag into the pirogue. "That's good. Later we'll replace everything we used."

Grimacing, she pulled at her once white shirt and wrinkled capris. "My clothes aren't quite dry. How about yours?"

"Nope, they're damp, but they're mine."

Her gaze fell on the plastic bag. "I assume you're taking the clothes we borrowed in that bag so we can wash and return them. But what else is in it?"

"This and that."

Whatever, she thought. He was a man of few words this morning. "I wonder who owns the cabin," she said as they left the dock. "It's fitted out with more conveniences than your usual fishing or hunting camp."

Jack positioned the oars and began rowing with a faint smile. "And you'd know a lot about fishing and hunting camps?"

"I've seen movies."

"Well, then."

He set a brisk pace, but Camille was still a little uneasy. She felt exposed in the tiny pirogue and vulnerable. It was unlikely that anybody could find a place to watch them from the tangle of vines, moss-draped trees, and other primordial vegetation on both sides of the bayou, but what had happened to them the night before had been unlikely too. In spite of the stunning beauty all around them, she would be happy to see civilization again.

She would also be happy to forget last night's . . . indiscretion. But it would be a while before she forgot how right it had felt and how easily she had succumbed to the sexual attraction that apparently had not died with their divorce. One thing that had not been wrong in their marriage was their love life. She had to keep reminding herself that everything else had been wrong; otherwise she might find herself falling in love with him again.

Civilization came an hour later after they'd taken a fork in the bayou. Dotting the shoreline was a collection of campsites. Jack chose a prosperous-looking cabin with a wraparound porch where three men could be seen moving about. As they docked, the three looked startled at having unexpected company. They instantly offered the use of a cell phone to Jack, who called 911 and reported the incident, then asked that an EMT be dispatched and that Chief Raines be notified. While they waited, Camille called her mother and Madge, reassured both, and Jack checked in with Jeanette.

"I hope you won't argue if the EMTs want to take you to the hospital," Jack said. "You'll need an X-ray."

"I think I'm okay," she said. "A couple of aspirin seems to have taken care of my headache."

"You don't know that, so humor me. Please. Neither of us knows how to spot a concussion."

"I think I'd know how one felt," she told him. And before they launched into an argument, a cavalcade of Blood Bayou's finest arrived, three cars and the ambulance, all with sirens screaming and blue lights flashing.

"Third time's the charm, I guess," Camille muttered as they screeched to a halt in front of the camp. "Twice now I reported criminal acts and got a very tepid reaction, but when their beloved minister is involved, they pay attention."

"It's nothing to do with me," Jack said. "When an attempted homicide is reported, it doesn't matter who you are. Cops listen."

Chief Raines got out of the lead vehicle and shouldered past the gaggle of cops making their way to the porch where Jack and Camille waited. Halfway up the steps, he spoke to Jack. "What in Sam Hill is going on here?"

"Not here," Jack said, shaking Raines's outstretched hand. "It happened about four miles back on the bayou. And if I knew what was going on, I would have avoided it."

"They tell me you were on the old petroleum road. Why?"

"I decided to take the old road to avoid traffic from the ball game."

The chief looked at him narrowly. "Anybody know you were heading that way?"

"None that I know of. It was a spur-of-the-moment decision."

"Somebody must have been watching us," Camille said.

Raines shifted his gaze to her. "Doesn't look like any place in Blood Bayou is safe for you, does it, Ms. St. James? First your mother's house, then Madge's place, and now this."

"What it looks like," Camille said deliberately, "is that I'm making somebody very nervous. What we should be asking is, why?"

Jack slipped an arm around her waist as he spotted two EMTs wheeling a stretcher toward them. "She needs to be examined by the EMTs, Chief. We can talk after that." His arm tightened when Camille looked ready to balk. "Let these guys do their job, Camille. If they say you're good to go, we'll head on over to Madge's place."

"Okay, but I don't need a stretcher. I can walk perfectly well. And I'm not getting into any ambulance unless they tell me something really bad."

"Yes, ma'am." At the bottom of the steps now, he gave her a little push toward one of the EMTs. "She's all yours, Jerome."

She stopped and looked back at him. "Do you know everybody in this town?"

"She's a little grouchy, Jerome," Jack said. "A ride in the ambulance should sweeten her up."

AFTER SEEING Camille reach the ambulance, Jack climbed the steps where Chief Raines waited, then said, without a trace of humor on his face, "There can be no doubt anymore, June. Someone wants to silence Camille. Even if he has to kill her."

"And you too, looks like," Raines said. "Between the two of you, I don't know what to expect next, Jack. I got a call from

Harlen Richard and when I got to his house, he chewed my rear royally. He was so hot I thought he'd have a heart attack right there in his fancy den."

"What time was this?"

"After you and your ex-wife left his house. What were you thinking, Jack? He said you think he murdered Luanne."

"I don't think anything yet. You'll recall telling me that you hadn't been able to establish whether or not he had an alibi. Camille and I went over together to try and find out where he was when Luanne was killed. I expected him to tell us. Instead, he was furious. He threw us out."

"Humph." Raines squinted thoughtfully at the activity going on at the ambulance. "That's not exactly the version he gave me."

"Well, that's exactly what happened," Jack said. "I left there wondering why he didn't say where he was. And because he didn't, I intend to find out."

"I hear you. I had the same thought. So I asked him straight out." Raines propped a booted foot on a low rung of the porch rail. "He told me it was none of my business. Can you believe that?"

"You'd think he would know that would not work to his advantage, you being the chief of police and conducting the investigation into his wife's murder."

"He makes the mistake of thinking he has enough clout in our town to be able to thumb his nose at us cops," Raines said with a glint in his eye. "You oughta tell him to rethink that one, Jack."

"I don't think he's taking advice from me anymore," Jack

said. "But I'd like to see you follow up. It's my sister's murder we're talking about."

Raines gave him a sharp look. "If you know something, I want to hear it."

"I don't know any more than what I've told you."

"Are you suggesting it might be Harlen who shoved you into the bayou last night? If it happened when you say it did, it couldn't be Harlen. I was with him when that went down."

"Have you considered that Harlen might have paid someone else to kill Luanne?"

Raines looked at him in astonishment. "It sounds like Harlen was right. You do suspect him."

"Like I said, I don't know." Jack sighed, watching as Camille climbed down out of the ambulance, and with a wave and a smile to the EMTs, now headed back to the porch. "But I can't deny that something bad is going on in our town." He waited until Camille climbed the steps. "What's the verdict?"

"He gave me two extra-strength somethings," Camille said, "and wished me well."

Jack gave her a skeptical look.

"It's true. I don't have a concussion, Jack. At least, he didn't see anything with that bright, shiny little light he used. But I'm to seek medical help if I feel dizzy, get nauseous, or see double. Same thing you said."

"In that case," Chief Raines said, "are you willing to give Sergeant Duval a statement now?"

"Sure." She looked at Jack. "Right?"

"Yeah."

"You want to come to the station like that?" Raines gave

a quick look at her rumpled, still-damp clothes. "We can stop by Madge's place and let you get a change, Ms. St. James. The reverend might want to freshen up too. We can swing by the parsonage, Jack."

"I'm okay."

"Why can't we give our statements at Madge's house?" Camille asked. She glanced beyond him to Sergeant Duval, who stood waiting for orders. "The sergeant and I are already acquainted."

Duval moved to the bottom of the steps. "A wrecker's on the way to the bridge to haul the reverend's car out of the water, Chief," he said. "Hopefully there'll be some forensic evidence on it. Ramming into the back of a car hard enough to send it flying would have left paint scraping for sure. And maybe something else. You never know. We'll check it out." Duval looked at Jack. "Can you tell us anything about it?"

"Jack didn't see it except in his rearview mirror," Camille said. "But I did. It was a truck."

Duval gave her a keen look. "Can you tell us anything more than that? What kind of truck? What color? Big truck, a pickup, an SUV?"

She was shaking her head. "It was so dark I couldn't tell anything except that the lights were higher up than on a regular car. Oh, and there was one of those frame things on the front of it. I don't know what you call it. A grate? Anyway, a thing that's sometimes on the front of trucks to protect the grille, I assume. You know what I'm talking about?"

"Yeah, sounds like a work truck. We have one at the department that we use to push vehicles when necessary. Is that all you can recall?"

"At the moment. I didn't realize I had noticed that grate thing until just now. Maybe something else will come to me." She paused. "Oh! There was an emblem on the hood."

"Like what?"

"I don't know. It was just an emblem."

"That's why we need your statement while it's fresh in your mind, Ms. St. James," the Chief said. "Yours too, Jack. And I don't see the problem with taking your statements at Madge's house. Both of you can ride with me since you don't have a car."

"Since that's the plan," Jack said, "and we'll pass the church on the way to Madge's house, I'll run inside my house and change."

"I have no objection to that," Raines said, and headed down the steps. "So let's get going."

CHAPTER sixteen

SHE LOOKED OKAY, Jack thought, studying Camille as Madge bustled about, coddling her. After giving her statement to Sergeant Duval, she'd been plied with hot tea, coaxed into a warm bath, and given strict instructions to lie on the couch and do nothing. She'd been okay with everything except lying on the couch.

He watched as she regaled Madge with a report of their adventure, even finding humor in how the thought of alligators lent Olympic speed to her swimming ability. But Jack didn't find any humor in the experience. Someone had tried to kill Camille, someone who was so desperate that it didn't matter if he took Jack's life too.

Madge set a cup of tea in front of him. "This whole thing is very disturbing. The town will soon get wind of everything that's happening. The cops are going to have to show that they're serious about investigating this."

"And it's about time," Camille said. "Episodes one and two were scary but sort of amateurish. Each could have been done by malicious kids, or even adults who resent my connection to Chester and just intended to run me out of town." She paused. "Although since he came armed with a gun, I think he meant business. But trying to kill me takes resentment to a whole other level."

Jack reached for the sugar bowl. "But what he's done after last night is to show his hand, so now we can be prepared. He's seriously determined to stop you, Camille, and he's willing to kill to do it. You're a threat too, Madge, since you've let it be known that you're helping her."

Camille put both feet up on an ottoman, cupping the warm mug. "I've been thinking."

Jack glanced at Madge. "There was a time when I'd run and hide when she said that, but since I'm now oh for three . . ."

"Funny," Camille said.

"Let's hear it, sweetheart," Madge said.

"I really don't fault folks for not falling in with my theory that Chester didn't kill Luanne. It's difficult considering two rather troubling questions." Setting her tea aside, she ticked them off. "One, how is it that the cops zeroed in on Chester so soon? I mean, how did they know he was at his fishing camp? And two, motive. Why on earth would Chester want or need to kill Luanne?"

Madge set her empty cup in the sink. "I can answer why the cops were quick to finger Chester. I was the dispatcher that day. Someone called and asked for the chief. And after the chief talked to him, he told us this guy had suggested taking a look at Chester Pelham."

"How convenient," Camille muttered.

"Who was it?" Jack asked.

"The chief said he refused to identify himself."

"How could that be?" Camille said. "Don't you have caller ID?"

"Not from a pay phone."

Jack thought about it, stirring sugar in his tea. "Aside from dropping Chester's name, was there anything else?"

"That's it. At the time, our boys were on the scene at the Richard estate. They were busy collecting evidence. But Chief Raines immediately put out an order for all available units to head for Chester's place on the bayou. It's not every day we have a homicide in this town, so they took off with blood in their eye."

"Poor Chester," Camille murmured. "He didn't stand a chance."

"It would be useful to know who made that call," Jack said, then grimaced after tasting the tea. "What is this stuff, Madge? Did you boil your socks in the water?"

Madge laughed. "It's lapsang souchong, very aromatic and soothing to the nerves."

"It's aromatic all right." He shoved his mug to the center of the table. "I'll pass."

Camille sipped thoughtfully. "Are we agreed that Chester has no motive for killing Luanne?"

"Folks will argue that he needed no motive," Jack said. "They'll say he kills for pleasure."

"Is that what you think?"

"No, not anymore." Jack stood up. "Madge, I need to borrow your car, please. I'll get someone to return it within the hour. If that's okay."

"Sure. Be my guest." She picked up his cup and emptied it in the sink. "The keys are on that small table by the door."

"Thanks." He stopped at the door, giving both a stern look. "Do I have to remind you both to lock all doors and windows and keep Ben and Jerry close by?"

"No, you don't, Daddy," Camille said, leaning back on the couch, eyes closed.

"And once you have a car, you'll be careful where you go and what you do, right?"

"We will," Madge said, collecting cups.

He was still troubled. "About tonight." He waited until both women looked at him. "I'd prefer staying here to be sure you were safe, but some in my congregation are sure to consider it inappropriate. I'd suggest going to your parents' house, but frankly, I think Madge is a better bodyguard than Allen, fresh out of the hospital."

"Even with Allen in the pink of health, Madge is better," Camille said. She looked down where Jerry slept at her feet. "And the dogs are extra insurance. I'll be okay, Jack."

She sat up. "Here's something else I've been thinking about. Will there be any repercussions from your congregation over the fact that we spent last night alone together? I mean, it was unavoidable, we had no choice. But I would hate to be the cause of trouble for you in your church."

"I think once folks know the circumstances, it'll be okay," he said. "I'll mention it in my sermon Sunday."

"A hundred years ago," Madge said with a smile, "you would have been forced to marry her to save her good name and reputation."

Jack gave Camille a slow smile. "My tough luck times have changed."

"Didn't you say you had things to do?" she asked him.

"I did. I do." He looked at Madge. "Do you have a gun?"

"A gun?" Camille's eyes went wide. "No way."

"Actually, I do." Madge was busily sponging off the table. "I have a permit to carry it and I know how to use it."

He gave her a quick, decisive nod. "That's good."

He missed the appalled look on Camille's face as he opened the door to check the area before stepping out on the porch. "I'm calling Chief Raines to get round-the-clock protection for both of you. But until then, call me if you see anything or anyone suspicious hanging about. And don't hesitate to shoot, if necessary."

"Jack!" Camille protested.

He pretended to miss that too.

JACK WAS barely out of sight when the dogs sprang up and barked at the sound of a car. "It's Diana," Madge said, after ordering Ben and Jerry to sit and stay. "And she looks exactly as I'd expect, considering."

Camille sat up and pulled one side of her hair over the obvious bruise on her temple, then rubbed a little color into her cheeks to try to make herself look normal. "Can you see my lump?"

"No, but Diana won't be fooled by anything you do to hide it. She'll want to inspect your wound personally."

Before Diana reached the top of the porch steps, Madge had the door open to welcome her. "Hey, lady. This is a nice surprise. Come inside and out of the heat. It's a scorcher, isn't it?"

"Thank you, Madge. Good to see you too." Diana stepped over the threshold and pulled off her sunglasses. Her gaze went directly to Camille, who was on her feet. She crossed over to her daughter and caught her in a fierce hug. "You're going to be the death of me yet, darlin'."

Camille sighed. "I guess you heard. Did Jack call you?"

"No, I was at the pharmacy getting a refill of Allen's medicine and Marlene Duval told me."

"Who?"

Madge laughed. "That would be the wife of Sergeant Duval. You recall we just discussed this being a small town."

"Are you all right, Camille? Was it a concussion? Have you had an MRI? Why aren't you lying down?" She stopped herself with a hand over her mouth. "I'm going on, aren't I?"

Camille returned to the couch and patted a place beside her. "Come, sit down. I'm fine, Mom. Really. I haven't had an MRI because I didn't need one. I was examined and told to take it easy and call if anything out of the ordinary happened."

"They tell that to people who have a sprained wrist or a case of hives," Diana said. "You've been through a life-threatening ordeal. You should, at least, be lying down."

"She was," Madge said, pouring tea in a cup. "But she's hard to keep in a horizontal position."

Diana took the tea with unsteady hands. "This has been a horrible week . . . or has it been longer since the world has unraveled? It seems like . . . I don't know, a lifetime. My husband, my daughter, Jack . . . what else can happen?" She set her tea, untouched, on the coffee table. "Camille, you have to promise me you'll go to your father's house in New Orleans. You are in danger here."

"I'm aware of that, Mom. But I don't think I'll be any safer at Dad's house in New Orleans than here with Madge and the dogs. Actually, I'd be more at risk. You know Dad goes to the office, I'd be alone there."

Diana gave a heartfelt sigh, closed her eyes for a minute, and seemed to reach some semblance of calm. "Let me see where you you're hurt," she said.

Wordlessly, Camille pulled her hair back from her temple and allowed her mother to take a look.

"Well, it doesn't look as bad as I feared," Diana said. "But the whole incident is horrifying. Nearly drowning in the bayou, getting caught in a thunderstorm. Forced to spend the night in a fishing camp! I can't imagine what you must have gone through out there on that wretched old road. What was Jack thinking?"

Madge settled in a chair opposite them. "Marlene Duval didn't leave out any details, did she?"

"By the way, where is Jack?" Diana asked.

"He has a life, Mom," Camille said. "As far as I know, he's at his church where he belongs."

Diana reached out and touched her cheek. "I'm so incredibly thankful you're safe, Camille. I know you usually balk when I bring it up, but I hope you'll be at next Sunday's services. You have a lot to be thankful for."

JACK HAD a long to-do list when he left Camille and Madge. The first item was to swing by BBPD and see June Raines, who agreed to assign a unit to patrol the street where Madge lived. Next he replaced his cell phone. Back at his house, he spent a productive hour on the Internet, then called one of his deacons, who owned a car dealership, and asked for a loaner SUV. Later he'd settle with his insurance company.

Consequently, it was midafternoon by the time he left to go to New Orleans. He had a bone to pick with Carson St. James. He'd found some disturbing things where he and Camille had taken refuge. And he didn't want to share with her what he'd found. Yet.

Carson looked surprised when his secretary ushered Jack into his office. After shaking hands and seeing him seated, Carson went back to his chair. He could have shown outright hostility, considering Jack's horrendous behavior while married to Carson's daughter, but all he saw in his ex-father-in-law's face was a hint of puzzlement, and not much of that.

Carson took out a huge cigar and leaned back in his chair as if settling in for a comfortable chat. "What can I do for you, Jack? Or do you prefer to be addressed as Reverend now?"

"Jack is fine," he said, watching Carson light the cigar.

"Amazing thing, you being a preacher."

"Uh-huh. First, Carson, I'm wondering whether your sources have reported what happened to Camille and me last night."

Carson frowned through a fog of smelly smoke. "What sources? I don't follow. What happened to you and Camille last night? And don't tell me you talked her into marrying you again."

Jack's smile was wry. "No, not yet."

"Just for the record, Jack, my daughter will never marry you again. Not as long as I live and breathe."

So much for a friendly conversation. But Jack let it go. No point in arguing something that neither of them had any control over. That decision was Camille's.

"Last night, Camille and I were in my car and someone rammed us from behind as we approached a narrow bridge. We went into the bayou and were trapped underwater in the car."

"What the—" Carson's jaw dropped. "Are you serious? Is Camille okay?"

Jack recognized genuine surprise when he saw it. "I'm serious and yes, she's okay. She has a nasty bump on her head, but the EMTs say should be fine. She's been told to take it easy today."

Carson sat up straight in his chair. "Why didn't you call me when it happened?"

"Cell phones and water don't mix. Anyway, we were able to get out and make it to shore. From there we started looking for shelter, and guess where we wound up?"

He looked blank. "How would I know?"

"Would you know if I told you we were on the old petroleum road that branches off the main highway in Blood Bayou? And that the cabin we found was new, totally outfitted with all necessary provisions, complete with electricity? Would that be a clue?"

"Is this some kind of twisted guessing game? Get to the point, Jack."

"Not only did this cabin have everything I just told you but it had some very interesting paperwork stored below the main structure in a locked shed."

"How do you know what was in a locked shed?"

"I'd already taken a stroll around the grounds where I spotted several flags that appeared to be the surveyor markers. Since the location was so remote, I was curious."

"Curious enough to break a lock on private property? And you a preacher too. But how did you manage that, by the way?"

"It's a skill I learned in prison."

Carson studied the end of his cigar. "So what does all this have to do with me?"

"You'll probably want to have a talk with the engineers who are surveying the properties. And the land man who's busy collecting title information for what I'm guessing will be important to something grand that will require waterfront property. You'll want to caution him about leaving stuff around that could let the cat out of the bag." He paused, knowing he had Carson's full attention now. "You probably prefer that your secret remain a secret, at least until you've acquired title to those properties."

"I repeat, Jack, what does all this have to do with me?"

"I'm getting to that. Some careless employee left his client's business card and a few papers I found in the kitchen cabinet as I searched for something to eat. They weren't under lock and key. Turns out, it's a consortium." Jack pulled a folded document from inside his jacket pocket, spread it open on Carson's desk, then leaned back to watch his ex-father-in-law.

Carson gave it a cursory glance and pushed it back toward Jack. "So what?"

"The consortium is called Bonaventure, Limited. I looked it up using the Internet. After quite a bit of subterfuge that was designed to foil nosy people like me, I finally found the names of Bonaventure's board of directors."

Carson rose, stubbed out his cigar, and went to stand with his back to the tall plate-glass windows. With sun flooding in, it was difficult to read his face. "You always were a sly one, Jack."

"If you want to keep secrets, Carson, you need to choose your associates with caution. Someone was careless in leaving this document lying about."

"You didn't come here to wave it under my nose. You have something else on your mind. What is it?"

"Chester Pelham's property is smack in the middle of the property your consortium needs to acquire, Carson."

"Now look here—"

"And Harlen Richard is on the board of directors with you."

"As well as six other investors."

"Yes, all six of whom are in Vegas. What's the plan, a casino?" He waited while Carson chewed on his cigar, then added, "I'm puzzled as to why Harlen's wife was murdered."

Carson snatched the cigar from his mouth. "Are you out of your mind? What are you insinuating? Why would Luanne's murder have anything to do with Harlen's business interests?"

"Maybe nothing. Maybe a lot. I don't know. But Pelham's property popping up in that survey makes me suspicious. So I'm giving you notice right now that I've only begun to dig. My wife is trying to prove Chester Pelham innocent of Luanne's murder. And now someone wants her silenced even if they have to kill her to do it."

"You're suggesting that Harlen wants to kill my daughter? This is absurd, Jack."

"Yeah, it would be absurd if it wasn't so chilling. I'm still trying to figure out how all this ties in." Jack looked beyond Carson to the skyline of the city for a long moment. "My gut tells me it does."

"Are you seriously telling me you believe I would put my daughter's life in jeopardy over anything, especially some pie-in-the-sky business venture?"

"I don't know what you would do or how far you would go, Carson. I know there was a time in my own life when I skirted very close to the edge. I don't like judging other people by the wobbly principles I lived by then, but I haven't forgotten how to think that way. In fact, it reminds me of another scheme I knew about involving you and Harlen."

"Scheme is a nasty word."

"Yes, it is, Carson." Jack studied the luxurious carpet, wishing he didn't feel it necessary to keep going. If it turned out there was no connection to what threatened Camille and the business dealings of her father and Harlen Richard, he'd be on his knees apologizing to Carson.

"You'll recall that highway project a few years ago that connected bayou country below the Atchafalaya to the interstate," he said. "It opened up an area that had been inaccessible to New Orleans and Baton Rouge except on roads that flooded in heavy rains and were in disrepair most of the time."

Jack didn't see any sign that Carson recalled the project, but he saw that he had the man's full attention. "A number of old-time residents in the parish owned the property needed for the new highway. It was mostly swampland and considered pretty worthless, but a group of businessmen who had connections in Baton Rouge and Washington got wind early of the government's plans."

Jack moved over to the tall windows where Carson had stood a few minutes ago. He could see Carson's face clearly now. "These guys began buying up the land, picking it up for a song, a fraction of what the state would have offered had the original owners known about the new highway. And when that project was announced, the new owners demanded prices far exceeding what they'd paid. And the taxpayers were stuck."

Carson was now on his feet, pacing. "Nothing about that deal was illegal, Jack."

"No, it wasn't illegal," Jack said. "Just sleazy and dishonorable." He held up a hand when Carson began to sputter. "I'm the last person to cast stones, Carson. I knew about this at the time and said nothing. And don't worry, I never told Camille."

"Then why bring it up now?"

"Just this. There was a lone holdout, you'll recall. This one old Cajun wouldn't sell, so one night his house and all his posses-sions went up in flames. And so did he. Problem solved."

Outrage simmered in Carson's eyes. Standing straight as a pole with his white eyebrows drawn together in a fierce scowl, he said, "Are you seriously accusing me of having a hand in kill-ing a man?"

"No, Carson. It came to mind after I found that scrap of paper showing you and Harlen involved in another scheme to ac-quire land for some ambitious project as yet unnamed. I couldn't help but wonder how far you'd go to get Chester's land."

"That was Harlen's deal from day one. He found the land man, he paid to do the title searches, he worked the whole thing and presented the bill to the investors."

"Who was the land man?"

He shrugged. "I don't know. I told you it was Harlen's deal and, to tell the truth, I didn't want to know. But there was noth-ing illegal about my involvement or, as far as I know, the other investors'. It was strictly business."

"Nobody burns to death in a deal that's strictly business."

"Get out of my office." Carson stalked to the door and jerked it open. "You're talking a crock of you-know-what. And don't think that as a preacher, you can get away with making wild ac-cusations. I'll see you run out of Blood Bayou before nightfall if I hear that you've breathed a word of this."

Jack stood his ground for a long moment, unmoved by the threat. "I'm beyond being bullied by you, Carson, so save your breath. You won't believe this, but it doesn't give me any plea-sure coming here today." He unflinchingly held Carson's gaze before making his way to the door. "But I'm thinking there's something rotten in Blood Bayou. For Camille's sake, I pray it doesn't turn out to be connected to you. And for the sake of my sister—God rest her soul—to Harlen."

WHEN JACK left, Carson St. James moved to the tall windows in his office and gazed over the New Orleans skyline. He had a spectacular view of the Mississippi and usually enjoyed watching the river traffic. Mostly it was small marine vessels, tugs and barges, the ferry. Sometimes it was a huge cargo ship or ocean liner cruising slowly up the river. Today Carson saw nothing. Jack Vermillion had destroyed his peace of mind.

He turned from the windows, walked to his desk, picked up the unfinished cigar, and lit up again. With it clamped in his teeth, he spent a few more minutes sitting in his chair, his head in a cloud of smoke, thinking. After awhile, he reached for his cell phone, scrolled to a number, and waited as it rang. Finally, a familiar voice answered.

"Harlen," he said. "We need to talk."

CHAPTER seventeen

I T TOOK ONLY two days of captivity for Camille and Madge to develop cabin fever. They were grateful for the protection of a patrol unit ordered by Chief Raines to keep an eye on the house, but by Saturday afternoon, being unable to come and go as they pleased felt a lot like being in prison.

"I think I'll call the hospital and check on Chester," Camille told Madge. "He was showing signs of coming out of his coma the day Allen was discharged. Wouldn't it be something if he actually recovers?"

"He probably won't think so if he's railroaded back into prison." Madge held up her right hand with nails painted a grotesque, dark maroon. "How does this look?"

"Dramatic." Camille punched in the number for information on her cell phone. "Now put a white streak in your black hair and you can play Morticia Addams in a local theater production."

Madge chuckled and began painting the nails of her left hand. "Yes, we're getting a little testy being penned up, aren't we? Not that I'm handling our situation any better. How long is Jack going to insist that we stay here?"

"Until we figure out who is trying to kill us, I guess. But nothing will happen while we're under police protection. Unless the killer's very stupid, he'll wait for an opportune moment when we're least expecting it." She waited for the call to go through to the hospital. "I'm going to ask for Monette Somebody. I wish I knew her last name. Jack introduced us when we were there checking on Allen but I forgot."

"Friends in high places."

"It seems as if Jack has friends in all places in this town. But I don't know if she'll tell me anything since I'm not his lawyer or family, or Jack."

"Her name is Monette Comeaux. And I bet you're the closest thing Chester has to a relative," Madge said.

"Are you like Jack and know everybody in this town?"

"It's a small town, and working as a dispatcher at BBPD"— Madge gave a shrug and grinned—"you get to know folks."

Two minutes later, Camille clicked off on the call and shot both thumbs up. "Guess what? Since around midnight Chester has been showing strong signs of waking up. Monette told me not to quote her, but the doctor thinks he might come around any minute."

"Any idea what his mental condition might be?"

"There's no way of telling yet." She picked up her purse and dug out her car keys. "I'm going to the hospital. Do you want to go with me?"

"Jack would not like it, Camille."

"I'll call BBPD so they won't freak out when they see we're gone. But we're perfectly safe in the middle of the day, don't you think? We can't just stop living waiting for the next shoe to fall, Madge. It's unhealthy."

"Not as unhealthy as being dead," Madge said. "But I don't think he'll try anything in broad daylight. However, we won't go near the bayou. Like you, I'm definitely up for getting out of here for a couple of hours. If you're dead set on going to the hospital, I'll come too. The wife of one of the guys at the station just had a baby. I'll pop in to see her while you check on Chester."

CAMILLE STEPPED off the elevator on the ICU floor and almost collided with Ray Wyatt. "We have to stop meeting like this," she teased, giving him a smile. "Are you here to check on Chester too?"

"Yeah. And after that I was going out to Madge's place to check on you." He gave her a narrow look. "Did you clear this with BBPD? They know you're out gallivanting?"

"Visiting the sick, not gallivanting," she said. "And yes, I did call. They weren't happy, but Madge and I discussed it and decided we'd be okay in broad daylight. We'll be back in her house way before nightfall."

"You sure will," he said darkly. "In fact, I'll follow you to see that you get there safely."

"That's not necessary, Ray."

"It is. You don't know how a killer thinks. In spite of your work with the Truth Project, you're naïve when it comes to understanding the criminal mind."

"I have you to remind me," she said. "And Madge and Jack."

He studied her face for a minute. "You and your ex seem pretty tight these days. Last time we talked, I got the idea you hated his guts."

"I don't hate anybody. Well, maybe the person who's trying to kill me."

"I hear you. But just so you know, folks are speculating like mad about you two. Those guys at BBPD? They're taking bets on how long it'll be before Jack has you walking down the aisle again."

Camille crossed her arms and gave him a hard look. "Are you deliberately trying to rile me? Because if you are, you're almost there."

He put up both hands. "Just filling you in on what the townsfolk are saying."

"Well, don't." She turned and headed toward the ICU. "I'm checking on Chester. You can come with me if you behave."

"Yes, ma'am."

"Have you talked to a doctor?"

"Yeah, but he just left. I can fill you in."

"Great. I guess you heard about Jack and me getting shoved off the bridge at Blood Bayou."

"Everybody in this town has heard about it. I broke out in a cold sweat. Someone is getting very worried about what you're doing."

"It's safe to say that I've figured that out."

"No chance of you taking a long vacation to, say, Europe?"

"No chance. Which is not to say I'm not scared. I am. But I'm in so deep now that it won't matter what I do or where I go. I have definitely made someone mad at me." She nodded to the uniformed cop sitting in a chair outside the ICU. "He won't quit until I figure out who he is and why he had to kill Luanne. There has to be something in her life that we're missing. I'm thinking I should go see Alafair again. She might have recalled something."

"Alafair?"

"Luanne's housekeeper. The person who told me about Luanne being abused by Harlen." She glanced up at him. "You look surprised. It was in the murder book. Which you read when you came to Madge's house."

"I thought it was just gossip you'd picked up from busybodies around town. I didn't see any names."

"It wasn't gossip. Also, another person I want to talk to is Terri Chartrain."

His eyebrows rose in question. "And she would be . . ."

"Supposedly a dear friend of Luanne's, but there was bad blood between them, according to a reliable source."

"Madge."

"A reliable source," Camille repeated, then added with a thoughtful frown, "but the person I think who could help most, if I could get him to talk, is Harlen Richard. I just have this feeling that he's the key to all this. So far he hasn't been very forthcoming."

The cop got to his feet as they approached, but Wyatt gave him a casual wave and he sat down again. "We'll just be a couple of minutes at Pelham's bedside, Rudy."

"Okay, but you know if the chief comes around, you gotta beat it."

"You could get him in trouble, Ray," Camille said seriously.

"Not likely. He's the chief's nephew."

Inside the ICU, Camille greeted Monette Comeaux, who was in quiet conversation near another cubicle. They paused, but Monette waved them on toward Chester's bed. Camille's breath caught at the sight of him. He still appeared gravely ill, was still hooked up to several tubes, his skin remained waxy and dull, but something about the look of him was different from what she had seen when she'd visited earlier. She leaned closer and saw that his eyelids moved, sort of like a person asleep and dreaming.

"Is that how they tell that he's improving?" she asked.

"I don't know, but they claim he's showing signs of coming out of it. He's not moving now, but about thirty minutes ago, he was sort of restless, twitching, I guess you'd call it. That's good, I was told."

"But even if he wakes up, I worry about brain damage."

Wyatt's look spoke clearly of his thoughts on Chester's brain, but before he could say anything, she stopped him with a severe glance. "I know what you're thinking, Ray. Just don't say it."

She reached out and touched Chester's hand. "I just wanted to see him, just to let him know I haven't abandoned him."

Wyatt stood at the foot of the bed. "He's lucky that you care, but here's some advice from a cop, Camille. Don't take any more chances by coming here. Stay inside where you'll be safe."

CAMILLE AND Madge left the hospital together and were heading to the parking garage when Madge realized she'd left her sunglasses in the room of the woman she'd visited. "Stay right here until I get back," she ordered Camille, who was perfectly aware of the hazard of doing otherwise.

She was crossing to the large fountain in front of the hospital to wait when an SUV whipped in front of her and screeched to a stop. For a split second, she was paralyzed with terror. When the driver pushed the door open, she turned and ran flat out toward the front steps of the hospital. She could hear him behind her. Close. So close.

"Camille!"

She screamed as she was caught by one arm. She turned, clawing at his face before she recognized him, then wilted in agonized relief as her knees gave way.

"It's only me," Jack said, holding her up. "Are you okay?"

With her heart racing and adrenaline pumping, she couldn't say anything for a minute. She just clung to his shirtfront.

"Sweetheart," he said gently, "I didn't mean to scare you."

Reviving, she pushed against his arms and launched a verbal attack. "What are you trying to do to me? You almost scared me to death!"

"And you almost gave me another shiner." He looked chagrined. He straightened his sunglasses and touched a red mark on his cheek. "Am I bleeding?"

"I don't know," she snapped, not even looking. "And I don't care."

He waited a minute as she tried to gather herself. "I'm sorry, Camille. I guess I didn't realize you'd think—"

"What? After all that's happened, that a strange truck roaring up right in front of me might be reason to run screaming for help?" She shook his hand off angrily when he would have touched her shoulder. "You didn't realize that?"

He didn't attempt a reply. Instead, he waited out a few beats of heated silence. Then, with a huff and a hitch of her chin toward the fountain, she said, "I dropped my purse." She started toward it at a rapid pace. "It'll be your fault if somebody has taken it."

He caught up with her in three strides. "I've apologized, but you'll probably throw another tantrum when I tell you why I'm here."

"Let me guess. The chief called and told you I'd defied instructions. Don't bother to give me a lecture about gallivanting around town. I've already had one."

In the act of scooping up her purse from the pavement, he frowned. "Who?"

"Ray Wyatt."

"I thought we agreed that the safest place for you and Madge was at her house."

"After two days being cooped up, we were stir-crazy, Jack." Calmed down somewhat, she took her purse from him with hands that were still unsteady. "It's broad daylight. I called the police station and told them Madge and I would be at the hospital for a couple of hours."

"I don't see Madge. Where is she?"

"She forgot her sunglasses. She went back to get them." With Jack beside her, she went back to the fountain to wait for Madge. "We'll be back at her house long before dark."

"But just now, if I had been someone bent on grabbing you, it would have been easy even in broad daylight."

As much as she hated to admit it, he was right. With a weary sigh, she sat on the circular bench that surrounded the fountain. "This is so awful, Jack. I'm like a mouse caught in a trap. I can't take a walk, I can't risk driving on my own. Even if I wanted to leave, I can't. And now I've dragged you and Madge into this mess with me." She fixed her gaze on the palm trees leading up to the hospital entrance. "If I had it to do over, I'd stay far away from Blood Bayou and let someone else figure out who killed Luanne. That was my original plan anyway. Why didn't I stick to it?"

Jack sat beside her and propped his elbows on his thighs. "You may be stir-crazy, but you're not a mouse. No mouse would have reacted as you did just now and I've got the marks to prove it." He turned his head to look at her. "There's only one way to deal with this, Camille. We're going to figure out who is tormenting you. I just don't want you to be easy pickings for him, so you have to promise me you won't go sashaying off on your own again."

She set her mouth in a stubborn slant. "Sashaying, gallivanting, you make me sound like a teenage airhead."

"You said gallivanting. I only said sashaying."

"No, Ray said it. He's as bad as you for keeping tabs on me."

Jack straightened and waved at a couple descending the stairs who recognized him. "Do you ever find Wyatt overly friendly?" he asked.

"Actually, yes. But he means well."

Jack grunted, but before she could ask what he meant by his question, his cell phone rang. He turned it up, read it. "Hold on. It's BBPD."

He spoke into the phone. As he listened, his expression turned to open shock. "When was this?" With the phone to his ear and frowning, he turned so that Camille saw only his profile. "Are you sure?" he asked, listening with a grim expression that told her something bad had happened. "I'll be right there."

For a moment, he stood half turned from her, but she could see that he was shaken. "What is it, Jack?"

"That was June Raines. He was calling from Harlen's estate." He turned, meeting her eyes. "Harlen has been murdered."

CHAPTER eighteen

WHEN JACK AND Camille arrived at the Richard estate after dropping Madge at BBPD, they found the street swarming with police units and curious neighbors. A uniformed officer guarded the gate. To keep the crowd at bay, yellow crime scene tape was strung along the entire perimeter of the property. In spite of being unable to see anything, nobody showed any inclination to move on.

Jack had tried to persuade Camille to go home with Madge, but she'd refused. Raines had called Jack, she assumed, as Harlen was his brother-in-law, but Camille knew that connection would not extend to her. So she was prepared to have to talk her way into the house or at least the immediate vicinity of the house, depending on where the murder occurred. Jack had not been forthcoming with details. She understood he was reeling with shock. Harlen's murder had hit him—and her—like a bolt out of the blue. First his sister murdered, the person closest to him in the world, and now Luanne's husband, within a few days of each other.

Apparently Chief Raines had issued orders to admit Jack as they were quickly waved through the gate. Camille, sitting beside Jack in his borrowed SUV, made herself as inconspicuous as possible, but surprisingly, no attempt was made to question her right to enter.

The circular drive was clogged with more police cars, one ambulance, and two unmarked units as well as a large black Mercedes, the same make and model as her father's, which she assumed belonged to Harlen Richard. Not only were they business associates, she thought, but they also had similar tastes in automobiles.

"This is too weird, Jack," she murmured as they walked toward the front door. "First Luanne and now Harlen. What in the world is going on?"

"I don't know. But I wish you hadn't insisted on coming with me. When June Raines sees you, he'll refuse to let you inside."

"Is the body in the house? Did he tell you that on the phone?"

"He didn't tell me anything except Harlen had been murdered and seeing as I'm his only relative, he thought I'd want to be told before the news hit the street."

"Are you his only relative?"

"To tell the truth, I have no idea. But I've never heard Harlen mention having any family. And he never took Luanne to meet anybody, as far as I know." He rubbed his hand over his face wearily. "But that doesn't mean there wasn't anyone. Look at all Luanne's secrets and I never knew anything."

Camille moved a little closer and leaned into him in sympathy. "I'm shocked over this, Jack, but it must be so much harder for you."

"It's a nightmare," he said, "but it clears up one thing. There can't be any doubt in the minds of everyone in Blood Bayou that there is a killer on the rampage. They'll all be ready to believe you now."

The door stood open and they could see what appeared to be

a dozen people milling about in the spacious foyer. Some were in uniform, readily identified as police. Camille recognized Sergeant Duval at once. Others were unfamiliar.

Duval came toward them, his expression grave. "The chief says you should go right in, Reverend. They're all in the den." He frowned at Camille. "Chief didn't mention you coming, too, Ms. St. James. I'll have to check to see if it's okay. It's a pretty gruesome crime scene. You really don't want to be there."

Camille linked her arm with Jack's, hoping to bluff her way inside. "I'll just go in with Jack and if Chief Raines objects, I'm sure he won't be shy about telling me."

"Well . . ."

"You may as well give in, Duval," Jack said. "If she faints, I'll carry her out."

The den was still as gorgeous as she remembered, but it wasn't the smart décor she noticed now. It was Harlen Richard's body.

Men stood in a semicircle in front of a leather couch where he lay sprawled half on, half off the once tan leather. Even at a glance, the cause of death was obvious. The man's throat had been sliced from ear to ear, almost severing his head. Blood had created a huge dark maroon stain on the leather, oozing down the cushions and pooling on the expensive Aubusson carpet.

In spite of her shock and nausea, Camille forced herself to show no emotion as she took in the grisly scene. Chief Raines stood behind the couch, frowning at the corpse and snapping questions to a technician of some sort at his elbow who was busily making notes on a clipboard. Maybe the medical examiner, she thought. Standing by with a stretcher were two EMTs. She guessed they needed permission from Raines or the crime scene investigation team to transfer the body. Or, she wondered again, did they even have a CSI team? Weaving in and out was a photographer—the only other woman in the room—taking multiple shots of Harlen from various angles.

She was unaware of clutching Jack's arm until she felt his hand on her head turning her face into his chest. "You shouldn't be here, Camille."

It was all she needed to stiffen her spine. She straightened, swallowed hard, and took several deep breaths. "I'm okay," she said, mustering up a brisk tone.

Averting her gaze from the body, she took a moment to gather herself by looking around the room to see who else was present. And that was when she saw her father.

Her mouth fell open. "Dad!"

Across the room, Carson St. James sat in an antique Louis XVI chair. He was clearly shaken to the core. His face was ashen, drained of all color. Camille broke away from Jack and hurried over to him. "What are you doing here, Dad?"

"I found the body." His reply was shaky, so unlike his usual confident voice that she was alarmed. She crouched in front of him and covered both his hands with hers. They were cold and limp. She realized he was holding something, a small round bottle. Medication of some sort? She took it from him and set it on the floor beside her.

"What do you mean you found the body?"

He shook his head, dazed. "I . . . we . . . Harlen and I talked yesterday and arranged to meet here. He said he had a golf game today, but he'd be back after lunch. When nobody answered the door, I found it was unlocked. I just walked in and there he was."

"When was this, Dad?" she asked, rubbing both his hands to warm them.

"An hour ago. Maybe two. I guess. I'm not sure. I mean, I told the police the time of my appointment with him. It was three-thirty. Since I had to drive from the city, I gave myself ninety minutes to get here. I arrived a few minutes early." He took a distracted look at his watch. "They told me he's been dead almost twenty-four hours." He shuddered. "It was cold-blooded murder."

Camille glanced back at Harlen's body with its gaping wound and barely contained a shudder herself. "You didn't see any sign of forced entry? The lock wasn't damaged? It was just open?"

"Yes. I thought maybe it was a burglary, but the police said no. His wallet is full of cash and he's still wearing his Rolex. And, to me, it looked as if nothing was disturbed." He shuddered again and patted his jacket pockets as if searching for something. "Just Harlen, gutted like a . . . like a steer."

"How did you get through the outside gate?" she asked. "If it's not opened by someone inside, you need a code."

"Harlen gave me the code some time ago." Talking to her seemed to help him get a grip on himself, but his color was still off. He took a deep breath and pressed a fist to his midriff. "What did I do with my medication?"

"This?" She picked it up from the floor, handed it over. "What is it?"

Ignoring her, Carson popped the cap off, shook out a single tablet, and put it in his mouth. "Dad, are you taking medicine for something?"

"Isn't everyone? It's blood pressure. It's nothing." Dismissing her concern, he slipped the bottle in his jacket pocket. Looking stronger now, he sat up a little straighter in the chair and in doing so brought the people in the room into focus. When he spotted Jack approaching, his expression changed.

He frowned. "Well, Jack, are you satisfied with what you've stirred up?"

Camille blinked in surprise. She turned to Jack, who was clearly trying to silence Carson with a look, which he ignored.

"I don't know what he told you, Camille, but I tried telling him that there was absolutely nothing illegal about the way we handled that interstate deal. We bought up land legitimately. We sold it legitimately. If a few people could have made a few more dollars holding onto their land, they had that right. But by selling it off to us, they got their money a lot faster. Jack storming in my office the way he did was totally uncalled for."

"I don't know what you're talking about, Dad."

"Carson." Jack's tone was meant to silence his ex-father-in-law. "It will be better if we talk later. Right now, the chief is headed this way."

A dozen questions buzzed in Camille's head, but none could be asked in front of June Raines. She straightened as he approached.

"This is a homicide crime scene, Ms. St. James. I'm going to have to ask you to leave. We don't want to invite any criticism about the way it's handled."

She caught the irony in his voice, but after her father's angry question to Jack, she wasn't about to leave. Almost instinctively, she went into attorney-client mode. "I'd like to stay with my father," she told Raines in a firm tone. "He's had a shock. Have you taken his statement yet? Does he need to go to the police station? If so, I'd like to accompany him there as well." She gave her father a meaningful look. "Isn't that right, Dad?"

"What?" Carson seemed taken aback by the certainty in her demeanor and took a second or two to reply. "Oh, yes. That's fine."

"She's a lawyer, June," Jack said. "You'll have to allow it."

"This is all I need," Raines complained. "Three lawyers in one family. For the record, Ms. St. James, your daddy isn't being arrested. But since he found the body, we'll need to get a statement. Police routine, you'll agree to that, I'm sure. But seeing as you suspect we might mistreat him, you will want to be present. I have no objection."

"Thank you," she said formally. "And, for the record, I didn't mean to imply that he might be mistreated, Chief Raines. I just think he'll be glad to have a familiar face around as he's had a major shock. Having a lawyer is a sensible precaution." She stood up. "If you're ready to go, Dad, Jack and I will drive you to the station."

Raines put up a hand to halt her. "Now there I must draw the line, Ms. St. James. Your daddy will be driven to the police station in one of my units. You can follow."

Camille gave him a tight smile but no argument. She felt she'd gotten as many concessions out of him as she was likely to get. Even though she remained a thorn in his side, better to leave him thinking she was a reasonable woman rather than push him to the point of shutting her out of further developments. And with the murder of Harlen Richard, there would surely be further developments. Of that, she had no doubt.

IT WAS a day of surprises. To Camille's astonishment, Carson agreed when Jack suggested he spend the night in the parsonage.

At first, she put it down to her father's reluctance to drive back to New Orleans in his agitated state of mind. Anybody would be shocked at discovering a dead body, even Carson St. James. And more so considering his personal connection to Harlen.

On the other hand, there was that strange accusation her Dad threw at Jack. She hadn't yet found an opportunity to question him, but she would before the night was over. More interesting was that her father was willing to accept Jack's hospitality under any circumstances.

Once Carson was settled in a spare bedroom with Jeanette bustling about making certain he had everything he needed to be comfortable, Jack and Camille left to go to Madge's house.

She pounced as soon as they were in the car. "Jack, what did Dad mean by saying you'd stirred up something?"

"Can you wait until we get to Madge's house? It's complicated."

What did that mean? She studied Jack's face, but he was too good at concealing his thoughts. When had he seen her father? Clearly they had talked. But why? When? About what? She was beginning to feel as if her whole world was swirling in secrets and mystery. And danger.

She was bursting with questions when they arrived at Madge's house and was relieved to see a police unit parked on the street with two cops in uniform settled in for the night. "The chief was as good as his word," she said to Jack when he opened the car door for her.

"He's clocked two murders in ten days in his town," he noted. "It could easily be four if you add our assault. He's smart not to take any chances."

"I guess so." She moved ahead of him to climb the porch

steps. "But frankly, I wouldn't have been surprised if Chief Raines had balked at furnishing protection for me. He was not pleased to have me hovering as Dad gave his statement."

"He had no choice. Once Carson requested an attorney, that was it."

"Dad didn't need an attorney," she said. "I just wanted to be there for moral support."

"I'm not too sure about that, Camille."

She gave him a quick, puzzled look, but they were now at the door and she had no time to ask anything before Madge opened it.

"Finally you're back! I'm dying to find out what's going on. I can't get a thing out of anybody at BBPD. You'd think I was an ordinary citizen or something," she said. "Get in here, both of you."

As they stepped inside, Ben and Jerry went into a joyful frenzy. Camille watched as the dogs leaped and yipped around Jack, tails wagging madly, clearly preferring him. He bent, scratching ears and tussling with them for a few moments, after which they turned a little more sedately to Camille, but clearly expecting more of the same. She obliged, but when they wanted to lick her face, she drew the line.

"I've made coffee," Madge said, leading them through the house to the back porch. "Let's sit out here. Get comfortable. I'll bring the coffee."

When she disappeared back into the house, Camille faced Jack with her hands on her hips. "Okay, out with it. You can't say something like that and leave me hanging. What is it? Is it personal? Should I ask Madge to give us some privacy?"

"It's okay. Madge may even be helpful."

"Helpful in what way?" Madge came out carrying a tray loaded with coffee and trimmings, which she placed on the table.

Jack took a mug and moved across the porch to sit on the swing. He patted the space beside him. "Come sit by me," he said to Camille. "And hear me out before you start throwing questions at me."

Taking her coffee, she leaned against the porch rail. "I think I'll stay over here. So, what have you been up to?"

"After we gave our statements yesterday and I left you with Madge, I went to see Carson at his office in New Orleans." He put up a hand to halt Camille, who was instantly ready with a question.

"That cabin where we stayed is owned by a consortium called Bonaventure. While you were sleeping, I prowled around outside. I'd noticed several surveyor flags on the property. I also found paperwork revealing the names of the investors. Harlen Richard was a major investor and so is Carson."

She looked confused. "But we already knew that Dad and Harlen were business associates. Is that so bad?"

Madge sat on the edge of her chair. "What exactly are Bonaventure's plans? And why would they own a campsite on the bayou?"

"Good questions," Jack said. "They're in the process of buying up land fronting the bayou. I saw an aerial map marking property lines. And right in the middle of it is thirty acres owned by Chester Pelham."

Camille struggled to make sense of what he was saying. Her father in some kind of land deal with Harlen? And Chester owned a piece of it?

"So they need Pelham's land," Madge said.

Camille straightened from the railing and carefully set her coffee on the table. She gazed over the bayou for a few moments. Finally she turned to look at Jack. "What do you think this means?" She added, with an edge of accusation, "Unlike the two of us, you've apparently had some time to think it over."

"I don't know. Yet. I have it on good authority that Bonaventure has approached another private entity with an offer for their fifty acres. I'm personally familiar with that particular stretch of bayou frontage. I don't know what they have in mind that they need so much land. I think I would have heard if the state or federal government were planning to buy up property for a major project. Carson wasn't giving up anything, but whatever is in the works, he and Harlen are major players. It could be they're planning a casino. The other investors are all in Vegas, but who knows. I left Carson yesterday with a promise to get to the bottom of it."

"And now Harlen is dead," Madge murmured.

Camille had a sick feeling in her stomach. She wrapped her arms tight around herself. "And you felt you couldn't tell me what you'd found? Or that you planned to spring it on my father? He must have thought you were insinuating he was involved in something shady or illegal." She paused. "Or immoral."

"I didn't want to worry you needlessly," Jack said. "Maybe that was wrong, but now that I have told you, I'm worried that I accidentally triggered circumstances that resulted in Harlen's death."

"How? Just because they're in business together doesn't mean—" She stopped, frowning. "What do you think it means, Jack?"

He leaned over and set his empty mug on the floor. "I'm not sure. I don't have enough facts to put together a theory."

"You're not suggesting that Dad is a murderer, are you?"

"I'm not suggesting anything, Camille. Believe me. My reason for seeing Carson was because I discovered Chester Pelham's property was needed in the Bonaventure scheme. Think about it. If Pelham could be framed for murder, it would be easy to grab his land. In fact, I bet if we look at parish tax records, we'll find that someone—maybe Bonaventure—has been paying the property tax."

"I don't think—"

"One more thing," Jack interrupted her. "I didn't know what to think after talking to Carson. But today after Harlen was murdered, he convinced me I was right to be suspicious. Why else would he accuse me of stirring up something? What does he think I've stirred up? I can tell you this. I plan to get some answers from him before he leaves my house tomorrow."

Camille was pacing now. "This is all so crazy. I thought it was complicated before, but with Harlen's murder, it is absolutely baffling." She stopped and asked, "Any idea how Luanne's murder is connected to all this?"

"None, no clue," Jack said, "but I'm convinced it is."

"And probably Stephanie's murder too," Madge said. "I was never comfortable with that investigation."

"It's possible that all three murders were committed by the same person," Jack said.

"For land?" Camille was shaking her head. "I can't accept that."

Jack gazed thoughtfully toward the bayou, dark and still in

moonlight. "If only Luanne had felt able to talk to me," he said softly. "Maybe she'd be alive today."

Camille thought he looked so sad and her heart went out to him. "We could talk to Alafair again," she suggested, trying to inject a positive note. "So far, most of the important stuff we've learned about Luanne came from her. Maybe she knows something she doesn't know she knows."

Hearing that, Jack shook off his mood. "Don't go out there unless I'm with you, Camille. Better yet, ask her to come into town and meet you here."

"I'm okay with that," she said.

Madge rose and began collecting empty cups. "Relax, Jack. Trust me, we're both convinced it's healthier to stay holed up and out of the killer's reach."

But you have to promise you won't go without me, Jack," Camille added. "Don't do what you did with my dad and sneak off to talk to her on your own."

"I can't go tomorrow anyway. It's Sunday and I'm pretty booked up on the Sabbath."

He spoke with a touch of irony and Camille was immediately contrite. As a result of the time he'd spent with her in the past few days, he had probably neglected his church responsibilities. "You should leave now, Jack. Shouldn't you be preparing a sermon or something?"

"Actually, yes," he said. "But I've decided on the basic theme. I'll work on it a couple of hours tonight and again in the morning."

"I feel guilty about taking you away from your work."

He smiled and stood up. "You couldn't do that, sweetheart."

He bent to pick up his mug on the floor. "Madge, can I help you clear these dishes?"

"No, I'll do that," Camille said firmly. "You need to go."

Madge lifted the loaded tray. "I don't mean to sound like an alarmist, but am I the only one concerned about Camille's daddy? Until we know why Harlen was killed, isn't it logical that he might be in danger?"

"Not as long as he's at the parsonage," Jack said, taking the loaded tray from her. "I asked the chief to assign a unit to patrol that area tonight."

Camille put a hand to her heart. "Do you think that's a possibility? That Dad could be in danger?"

"Again, I don't know," Jack said. He set the tray on a counter in the kitchen. "But until we figure out what's going on, we have to be prepared. I'm confident he's safe for tonight."

"Safe as church," Madge said.

Jack held out a hand to Camille. "Walk me to the front porch?"

Madge began loading the dishwasher. "Since we're confined to quarters, I guess I won't see you at church tomorrow, Jack. But I'll be there in spirit. G'night."

Camille was thoughtful walking with Jack through the house and out onto the porch. She took a quick survey of the street and was relieved to see the patrol car again. In spite of all precautions, however, there was still the bayou, dark and eerily foreboding at night and no barrier between it and Madge's house. Not for the first time lately, she wished Jack could stay. What was happening, she wondered. Was she growing to trust Jack in spite of their tangled past? If she was, it had to be because of the dramatic difference between the person he used to be and the man he was today.

She moved a little closer to him. "Have you thought that someone in a boat could breach all our security and be on Madge's property before those cops could even get out of their car?"

"I have." He took a moment to check the yard, and then slipped an arm around her. "Remember, you've got Ben and Jerry on guard. They'd sound an alarm before anybody even got out of a boat. Those two German shepherds are better protectors than the two cops." She saw the hint of a smile on his face as she looked up at him. "But don't tell the chief I said that."

"Plus, there's Madge with her gun," Camille said dryly. "And she claims she isn't afraid to use it."

"There is that," he said. "But just to be on the safe side, lock the doors and keep the phone handy."

His tone took on a somber note. "I know you're worried now, Camille. I wish I didn't have to leave you. Better yet, I wish I could take you home with me."

"That's all you need to send your congregation into a tizzy," she said. "I'm already concerned that people will talk knowing you've spent so much time with me in the last few days. As a minister you have to be careful to avoid even a hint of impropriety."

It was dark and his face was now in shadow, but she could tell he was smiling. "And you speak with authority on this subject because . . ."

"Because . . ." She balled her fist and gave him a little punch on his arm. "I'm an expert on human nature, that's why. I may not be a churchgoer, but I bet your congregation is like the rest of the human race. If you give them reason to gossip about you, they will."

He caught her hand and brought it to his lips. "Thank you

for that sage advice. I'll keep it in mind, but not if it means I have to stop seeing you." His voice went deep with feeling. "I have to play this thing out, no matter where it ends, Camille. I can't let anything happen to you."

They stood for a minute without saying anything. Camille was again struck by the drastic change in Jack. Was it his calling? Was it his God?

"You're so different now, Jack. I keep trying to fit the person you were when we were married into the man you've become. I'm just so puzzled."

He paused, obviously thinking how to reply. "I am changed, Camille. It has everything to do with my relationship with Christ. And I could not have done it without Him. And believing in His promise that all my mistakes, my sins, all the pain and suffering I'd caused others would be washed away and forgiven. That He would take them all upon Himself and I'd be cleansed. Once I accepted that, accepted that He was able and willing to do that for me, then I had a new life. In Christ."

"I don't think I understand that kind of . . . faith, I guess you'd call it. And you talk about being forgiven. I have a problem with that. I see the changes in you and I believe they're real. And if you tell me that you've been forgiven by your God, fine. But I know you need to hear me say I forgive you for all that happened in our past. And yet I don't know if I can. I haven't experienced what you've just talked about."

"Here, let's sit down." Still holding her hand, he led her over to the porch steps. When they were settled, he said, "I don't expect you to understand until something like this happens to you. You may be thinking it could never happen, that you just don't think in that way, but I'm going to keep praying that it will."

"And I keep wondering about forgiveness," she said. "What I assume by the way you talk is that your God will forgive anybody, even people who have done terrible things. That doesn't seem right to me. You're an awful human being and suddenly you aren't?"

"We're offered forgiveness, Camille, even though we don't deserve it and we can never earn it. Our debts were been paid by Jesus Christ when he died for our sins."

"That's a lot to swallow."

He smiled, stood and put out his hand to help her up. "Indeed it is. And that's enough for tonight. Just by asking you've taken the first step to understanding. That gives me hope. And don't think I'm pushing, but why don't you consider coming to my church tomorrow?"

"I don't know." She gave a shrug, but the idea wasn't unappealing. "Maybe I will. I'll think about it."

"It would make a lot of people who love you very happy."

She laughed. "Oh, now, that's pushing."

He lifted his hands, palm out. "Then I'll say no more."

She stood thinking for a minute. And Jack waited. "I guess I could give it a try."

"Really?"

"Yes, really." She could see that she'd surprised him. "You've just given a very moving testimony to explain incredible changes in your life. It stands to reason that out of sheer intellectual curiosity I should do a little investigating." She gave him a teasing smile. "You forget, investigating is what I do best."

"You are incredible," he said. And then, as if he couldn't help himself, he bent and quickly kissed her.

"Whoa," she said, pushing him back.

He backed off but didn't let her go, not quite. His hands on her waist were gentle while he roamed her face with loving eyes. She was flushed and her heart was in a flutter, but what she didn't feel was anxious or wary about risking some kind of healing between them. He must have read something of her thoughts in her face.

"Why?" he asked simply.

She lifted her hands, resting her palms on his chest right over his heart. He was warm and strong and familiar. "I'm not sure I know why yet. I'm content, just now, to go with what I'm feeling. When I get the answer, you'll be the first to know."

"That sounds good to me."

She looked up into his face. "Keep my father safe tonight, Jack."

"I will."

Rising on tiptoe, she gave him a soft kiss. Before he had a chance to take it further, she pulled away and went back into Madge's house.

CHAPTER **nineteen**

WHEN HER CELL phone rang early the next morning, Camille was out on Madge's back porch watching the sun rise. Bright rays slanting through the cypress trees were quickly dissipating the mist hovering over the bayou. She found it hauntingly beautiful.

She reached in her pocket for her phone, thinking it was probably her mother, who needed frequent reassurance that Camille was safe. But when she read the number displayed, she answered with a smile in her voice. "Good morning," she said to Jack.

"Is Carson over there?"

No cheer in his voice. It was terse, all business. She glanced around as if she might spot her father lurking about. "Where?"

"There. With you. Is he?"

"No, Jack. It's six a.m. Nobody's here but Madge. And she's not even up yet." She heard him mutter something beneath his breath, which she guessed was as close as he ever came to swearing. "Did you check to see if his car is gone?"

"It's gone. I think he left sometime in the middle of the night."

"How? Weren't cops watching the house?"

"I don't have a clue as to how. And I plan to find out. I

checked on him when I came in around eleven, then I worked on my sermon until one or two a.m. He was sound asleep. Or appeared to be. But when I got up this morning, he was gone."

Camille's gaze drifted back to the bayou. "He's probably on his way home. I was surprised that he agreed to stay with you in the first place."

"He stayed because he was afraid he'd be next on the killer's list," Jack said grimly. "And he thought nobody would look for him at a church."

She sat carefully on the swing. "You're scaring me, Jack."

"I'm sorry, but I think we'd better face facts. Another thing is that he knew I was going to be asking questions he might not want to answer."

"But where would he go?" she cried. "If he really believes he's in danger, he can't go to his house or his office."

"Beats me. I hoped he'd be with you, but since he isn't, I'm hoping he'll decide to contact you. And if he does, try to impress upon him how urgent it is to get back here. He can't go far enough to escape whatever he's running from."

He was calming down now, but still she heard frustration in his voice. "I'd hoped to talk to him this morning, Camille. To try to persuade him to tell me what he's mixed up in, if he's mixed up in anything. It's possible that this was Harlen's show all the way."

"Let's hope so," she said. He was silent so long that she thought they might have been disconnected. "Jack? Are you still there?"

"Yeah, just thinking. I'm sorry to give you a fright so early in the morning. I hope it doesn't make you change your mind about coming to church today."

"No, I'm thinking church is the safest place I could be. And don't keep bad news from me because you're afraid I might be too fragile to handle it."

"You are not fragile, Camille. You never were."

He wouldn't say that if he knew the current state of her nerves. There were so many questions.

What did the killer think they knew? What was he worried they might discover?

"Camille? What is it?"

"Like you, just thinking. I'm wondering what to do next, Jack. I'll try to reach Dad on his cell phone, but until he calls, I don't see that there's anything we can do. Am I right?"

"I'm afraid so."

She heard the rustle of paper and the squeak of his chair at his desk as he stood. She sensed him moving restlessly, probably mentally organizing his to-do list for the day. And then compartmentalizing the list. He'd always been good at compartmentalizing, far better than she was.

She imagined his list—finalizing his sermon, coping with church-related issues, making a plan to find her father. She knew Jack wasn't capable of just sitting back and waiting for Carson to show up. Added to all that, somewhere on his agenda, he'd feel personally committed to seeing that, after church, she and Madge went back to their safe house. Anything else, she hadn't a clue, but she bet it was worthy stuff, selfless stuff. Reverend Jack Vermillion was nothing like the self-centered, ambition-driven man she'd divorced. Even if she hadn't seen evidence of it over the past weeks, she would have beeen convinced after their conversation last night.

"Sunday is a busy day for you," she said. "I'm sorry Dad has complicated it."

"It's okay. I don't know how I can do anything anyway. He's gone and we don't know where. And yes, Sunday is busy, but I'm usually able to take a few minutes to eat lunch." He hesitated, and then spoke in a tentative voice. "I asked Jeanette to make enough for two. Will you join me? Just us . . . well, and Jeanette."

"I'd like that."

He clicked off. And in spite of the troubling reason for his call, she found herself wanting to smile.

CAMILLE WAS a little self-conscious as she settled into a pew with Madge for the eleven o'clock worship service, the first she'd ever attended. Her mother must have taken her to church before she and Carson were divorced, but Camille had no memory of those early years. Weddings and christenings didn't count, she decided.

They were singing a hymn when Madge was tapped on the shoulder by a uniformed policeman, who passed her a note. She read it, handed it over to Camille, and then quietly left. The dispatcher on duty that day, Camille read, had taken ill. Could Madge fill in?

Without Madge, Camille felt awkward and a little exposed, but she didn't have a chance to obsess over it. Her mother and Allen slipped into the pew beside her, clearly surprised and delighted to see her, and she relaxed. Minutes later Jack took his place behind the pulpit.

He looked strange to her in his vestments: flowing black robe, blue scarf, and a silver cross touching him at heart level. But two minutes into his message, she forgot how he looked.

She would forever remember that first sermon she heard Jack preach. She knew him to be a gifted speaker. The first time she'd seen him he was giving a dynamite PowerPoint presentation at a legal conference. He mixed humor and facts in a way that kept his audience with him. This was nothing like that. Not even close. Now, along with humor, a funny reference to his black eye, and biblical text, he radiated heartfelt passion for his theme: the importance of seeking God's purpose in one's life. Camille wondered if others in the congregation were as spellbound as she.

OUTSIDE ON the church steps, her mother took her in hand as she waited for Jack. She did her best to mingle but felt like a fish out of water until finally Jack managed to make his way through the crowd to her side. Still in ministerial garb, he looked handsome and self-confident, enough so that she guessed a few of his female parishioners might have a crush on him. It was a possibility she did not like.

She also wondered what people thought as he introduced her around, calling her "a very special friend." She noted that her mother and Allen looked on, smiling. But the crowd finally dispersed and Jack put out his hand, indicating the path leading around to the parsonage. For just an instant, Camille hesitated before falling into step with him. To go with him meant an important milestone had been reached in her heart and in their relationship. But she fell into step beside him although they walked without touching.

Inside, they found no sign of Jeanette. As Jack checked other rooms, he peeled off his robe, loosened his tie, and unbuttoned his shirt collar. By the time they reached the kitchen, he was comfortably casual and obviously surprised to find a table formally set with china, crystal stemware, silver place settings, beautifully embroidered napkins, and fresh flowers. A note from Jeanette informed them that chicken salad and a lemon meringue pie were in the fridge and warm French bread was in the oven.

"We're alone," he said with a wide smile.

"I bet it doesn't happen often that Jeanette leaves you unattended with a woman," Camille said.

"It never happens." He moved to the patio doors, checking one last place his housekeeper might be. "You have passed a more difficult test than the U.S. government requires of a CIA agent," he told her. "Looks like you've won Jeanette's heart." Crossing to her, he put his hands on her waist and spoke huskily. "You've had mine from day one."

She was silent a long moment, staring at a button on his shirt. She looked up into his eyes. "So what happens next, Jack?"

Jack, in turn, took a long moment to answer. "We're going to enjoy this nice lunch and then talk."

No, she wouldn't be able to eat with all that was on her mind and in her heart. "I've been doing some thinking."

Jack's smile faded and he let her go. A guarded look came into his eyes. "Should I sit down?"

"You may need to after you hear me out. There's so much to say, so much I never thought I'd even want to speak. To you, I mean."

He was absolutely still. She could see that he was braced for bad news, but she had to work through this the only way she knew how.

"This is not about the situation that's consumed us ever since your sister was murdered. It's about us. Personally. About our marriage. The divorce."

She paused, letting her gaze roam over his face. Seven years and the effects of an abundance of bad choices had left their mark. But it was still the face of the only man she'd ever loved.

She must have gone silent a little too long. Jack shifted restlessly, looking anxious. "You aren't going to stop there, are you?"

"No, there's more." She thought he might have been holding his breath. He let it out with a cautious nod, but he was still wary.

"I've spent the whole time since our divorce blaming you for everything that went wrong when we were married," she said.

"That's because I was—"

"Please, just listen." She waited several beats to pick up her thoughts. "I just couldn't deal with your alcoholism. On several levels. I hated that my husband was often drunk in private and in public. But instead of looking for solutions, I simply nagged you to give it up, to change. Looking back, I see there were options, but I ignored them. Even before coming here to Blood Bayou and being thrown into contact with you, I'd been thinking that I had options back then. I could have gone into counseling. I could have joined Al-Anon. Maybe those actions would have helped me help you. But instead, I was too busy trying to keep up appearances, trying to act as if nothing was wrong. Enabling you. Trying to present a face to the world that said, 'Look at us. What an attractive, successful couple we are and isn't our marriage lovely.'"

With her eyes downcast, she paced away from him, circling around the pretty table, intent on expressing what she felt. "The straw that broke the camel's back was David Bergeron and the horrible accident. I didn't even try to cope with that. It was so far beyond the meager tools I had to handle emotional trauma that I just walked away. It was a cowardly thing to do, abandoning you when you needed me most."

She stopped, looked over at him. He stood stock still with a stunned look on his face. "I guess I've surprised you."

He tried to speak but was forced to clear his throat to make it happen. "Yeah, I guess you could say that."

She faltered a little herself. Dredging up that time meant facing the darkest days of her life. Old pain. Tragedy. Shame. Failure.

She drew a deep breath and gave a little twitch of her shoulders as if trying to shake off the past. When she spoke again, her voice was clearer, stronger. "We talked last night about forgiveness. I've been unwilling even to consider forgiving you, though I've seen what you've made of your life since that awful, horrible day. I can never forget it, maybe that's impossible. But I'm working on the forgiveness thing, Jack."

"Camille—"

"No, wait. I'm not blameless here. I made mistakes, I was stubborn, I enabled you, but, most of all, I feel as if I abandoned you in a time of need and I'm not proud of it. Can you forgive me for all that?"

"Can I forgive you?" he repeated with a note of wonder in his voice. He moved to her, took her hands in his. "My sweet darling, there is nothing to forgive."

"There really is, Jack."

He gave a helpless laugh. "Then yes."

She smiled, touched by the look on his face: disbelief mixed

with joy and amazement. She backed away out of his reach and
went to stand behind a chair. "There's more I want to say." She
drew in a shaky breath. "I thought of it in your sermon this morning where you talked about finding purpose in our lives. Since
our divorce, I've been very busy trying to right wrongs in our
justice system. That's been important to me because I rely on the
law to give meaning and purpose to my life. But since I've been
watching you these weeks, I can see that you rely on your faith in
God to give meaning and purpose to your life. And anybody and
everybody can see the difference it has made in you. I'm awed."

"Don't be," he said. "I'm still a flawed individual. It's just
that I've been redeemed and that makes it less agonizing for me
to live with my past." When he saw her trying to process that
thought, he added, "Think of it this way, Camille. You practice
law, you try to right wrongs in our justice system, but I've come
to realize there's a higher calling—at least for me—faith. And
it's a better answer to the ups and downs of life and the law, as
well. Does that make any sense to you?"

"It does. Since you're a pretty good example of it."

He made a low sound, looking at her with his heart in his
eyes. "Do you have to be over there saying all this? I want to
touch you, Camille. This is something I worried would never
happen. So I want to hold you now, kiss you. I want to open the
door and give a happy shout that'll be heard all the way to New
Orleans."

She stayed where she was, but smiled and blinked a little
when she felt tears threatening. "So what I said makes sense? It's
all a little scrambled in my mind right now. But since it seems
like you make a lot of sense in just about everything you say
these days, maybe you'll be able to walk me through it."

"Nothing would make me happier." He paused a minute with his gaze on the table, and then looked up at her. "I've been thinking about something. I don't want to spook you, especially now that you've opened your mind and heart the way you have. I don't believe it was an accident that you came to see me after Luanne's murder, Camille. It was so out of character, not that you wanted to express sympathy, but that you'd speak to me, face-to-face. It had been seven long years with no contact between us and then, boom! you're knocking on my door."

She smiled. "Actually, it was the church door."

"Don't run screaming when I say this," he warned. "But I believe God meant us to be together, Camille. I believe we're fulfilling His plan for our lives."

"I know you said I shouldn't be spooked, but that comes close."

"But one day it won't." He spoke softly, but with certainty. "So can I touch you now?"

She laughed. "I guess so."

Before the words were all out, he strode across the kitchen, swept her up in his arms, and whirled her about, laughing joyously. "I love you!"

She was breathless when he set her back on her feet. And then she reached up and tenderly took his face in her hands. "I love you too."

In spite of the worries simmering beneath the surface in both their minds—Carson's sudden disappearance, Harlen's murder, and scariest of all, a killer stalking Camille—lunch was still a blissful affair.

Jack couldn't seem to stay in his chair. He kept rising to kiss Camille, to touch her hair, her face. She kept making protesting noises she didn't mean. At one point, when she accidentally clinked her fork against a fragile crystal stem, she gasped in horror. She held it up to the light, studying it. "This is beautiful. And so is the china and the silver. And the gorgeous embroidered napkins. Did all this come with the job?"

"In a way, I guess it did," he said, "thanks to your mom."

"My mom?" She did a double take. "My mother?"

"Yeah, Diana. After I'd been here a year or so, she decided that I needed respectable stuff in the house for occasions when I needed to entertain. At budget time, I really do need to entertain," he said with irony. "So, she started a little underground campaign. Next, a few ladies of the church threw a shower for me. I guess that's what you call it when you're given a ton of household gifts. It's what they called it. It was some party."

"A shower." Deadpan from Camille.

"Uh-huh." He waved a hand at the table. "And that's how I got all this stuff."

Camille settled back in her chair studying him thoughtfully. "You must have won their hearts big time." She lifted a sterling silver fork, "This is not cheap."

"Actually, I think it's an heirloom from one of the older ladies in the congregation who has no children to inherit it. I've asked, but she's never admitted it. And Diana's lips are sealed." He reached across the table and squeezed her hand. "You have a wonderful mother."

"Has she adopted you? That's what it sounds like."

"I should be so lucky."

Neither said much for a while, just sat gazing at each other as lovers do. But they weren't lovers yet, Camille reminded herself. And maybe it wasn't meant to be that they ever would be again.

Even though she loved Jack and probably had never stopped, she was still in the dark about parts of his life.

"I feel a little goofy," Jack said, resting elbows on the table. "I can't seem to stop smiling."

"I noticed," she said. "But if Jeanette pops in, I want you to act parsonly."

"Parsonly?" Still grinning, his eyebrows rose.

"Yes, first thing is to ditch that goofy smile."

"And you'll act like a proper parson's wife?"

"I wouldn't know how."

His smile slipped. "Of course you would. You'd be your natural self. You aren't seriously thinking there's a litmus test for the role, are you?"

"I think there probably is, Jack. First, there's my own personal faith journey, which as yet is unfinished. And I'd want to share your whole life, everything, but would you be willing to let me? I don't mean in the way that lawyers must hold sacred things told to them by clients. I wouldn't expect you to share personal problems brought to you by church members. But I sense there are parts of your life that you keep private. I don't see how we—"

She broke off as her cell phone rang. "Hold on. Maybe that's Dad calling." She quickly pushed her chair back and hurried to get to her purse before the call went to voice mail. Glancing at the screen, she gave Jack a glad thumbs-up. "It's Dad."

Moving toward the French doors, she spoke urgently. "Dad, we've been so worried. Where are you?"

"Never mind where I am. I got your messages. I'm just calling to tell you I'm okay and that you're not to worry."

She met Jack's gaze in distress. "Dad. How can I not worry

after what happened to Harlen Richard? Wherever you are, whatever you're doing, you've got to drop it and come back here. Better yet, tell me where and Jack and I will come and pick you up. You can stay with Jack. You'll be safe there."

"No, I—"

"Then Madge's house," she said insistently. "You can stay there. With me. We have police protection."

"No, Camille. I'll get in touch when I'm done here."

"Dad, this is no time to be stubborn!" Her voice rose with panic. She tried to think of a way to reason with him. "Look, if you're in trouble, let us help you. It doesn't matter what you've done."

"I think it does, honey. I've been pretty stupid and blind as well. And now I might wind up in worse shape than Harlen."

"Nothing could be worse than what happened to Harlen, Dad."

"There are some things worse than death, Camille. Just don't worry about me. I'll call you when I get this straightened out."

"Dad! Please don't—" She stopped. The phone was dead. She gave Jack an anguished look. "He hung up."

Jack took the phone from her and snapped the cover closed. "I take it he didn't tell you where he was."

"No."

"Okay. But that doesn't mean we can't figure out where he might be. Don't panic. Let's sit down and go over what he said, what you heard." He pulled Camille into an embrace. "Together maybe we can figure out where he's gone, and whether he wants our help or not, he's got it."

* * *

CARSON SLIPPED his cell phone in his pocket after talking to his daughter. He stood in the center of Harlen Richard's fancy kitchen thanking his lucky stars that there had been no alarm when he broke a pane in the back door and just let himself in. Now he had to find the man's home office. He knew Harlen frequently worked at home, so there was bound to be paper of some kind, something like the telltale document that Jack found lying about at the camp. He blamed Harlen for that carelessness. He was hoping to have a bit of Jack Vermillion's luck himself.

To get inside the grounds of the ostentatious estate, he'd ignored the yellow police tape strung around the gate and simply punched in the code no one had taken the precaution of changing. Corrupting a crime scene was the least of his worries.

He'd parked his car out of sight at the garage out back. It wouldn't be suspicious anyway, he told himself, as he drove the same car as Richard. Still, he wasn't much of a housebreaker. He'd run smack into those stupid wind chimes as he crossed the patio. The noise had nearly deafened him. Would Harlen have the usual kind? No, he had to have those expensive, big-bong things. And why hang them where folks crashed into them? Between that and nagging angina, he felt rotten.

The pain behind his breastbone persisted as it had for hours, after starting in the middle of the night. Indigestion, he'd hoped. Now he knew better. He pressed his fist to his chest but felt no relief. He'd taken a nitroglycerine tablet minutes ago. That made four so far that day. But nothing helped. He figured he was working up to a heart attack, but with luck it wouldn't strike before he found what he was looking for.

He made his way through the humongous house in search of Harlen's home office. Bound to be a safe too. He didn't have the combination to that, but again, with luck, maybe he wouldn't need it. So far, except for his heart acting up, he'd been fortunate.

He located the office and sat down behind Harlen's desk to rummage through the drawers when he had the strange feeling that he wasn't alone. He let his gaze roam over the room but saw nothing. Still, he was sure he'd heard something. His next thought was that Camille and Jack had figured out where he was. Maybe he should go through the house and check. He closed the drawer and was on the point of getting up to search the rest of the office when a man appeared in the door.

Carson jumped to his feet upon recognizing him and rushed into speech. "I can explain why I'm here. I know it's a crime scene and you're probably going to throw me out, but Richard was my business partner. I have a right to protect my interests."

"You don't have to explain anything to me, Carson. We're probably here for the same reason."

Carson stared at him, frowning. "What do you mean?"

"With Harlen out of the way, I need to do some tidying up. Just like you. And you owe me, you know that? I watched you bust out that pane in the door. What if the alarm had gone off? You'd be in a pickle then, huh?"

"You know how to turn it off?"

"I also know the safe combination." He made a nasty sound, clicking his tongue. "Harlen sure didn't want to give that one up."

Shocked, Carson sank down in the chair. "It was you. You killed him."

"It was him or me. And now it's you or me. We can't afford

for your nosy little girl to get her hands on certain documents, can we?"

"I don't know what documents you're talking about."

"Carson, don't play me for a fool. You and Harlen were partners."

"But I—" He stopped, gasping as chest pain intensified. It was hard to breathe now. It felt as if his lungs were being squeezed in a vise. But he needed to be sure he understood what he'd just been told. And then it dawned on him. "Are you Harlen's land man? But how could—"

"Harlen's? Like he never told you?"

"He didn't, no. And my daughter doesn't know anything." Blinding pain nearly bent him double in the chair. He was forced to wait a moment before he could speak. He meant to sound stern, but he could hardly breathe. "I want you to leave my daughter out of this."

"Hah! Don't I wish. I've done everything except personally escort her out of town, but she's too stubborn to give over." He smiled grimly. "However, she won't be a problem much longer. I'll take care of her after I get what I need out of that safe."

"No, listen—" Carson tried to get to his feet, but he suddenly found the pain in his chest too much. Weak now and sweating profusely, he fumbled in his jacket and pulled out the nitroglycerine. "I need—" He worked at the cap, but suddenly his fingers seemed all thumbs. He looked up, needing help. "Could you please—"

"No, I couldn't."

The pain was excruciating now, almost blinding in its intensity. "Please, help me . . ."

"Now this is a stroke of good luck, Carson, ol' boy. Looks

like something bad might be happening to you." He strolled over to a chair, hitched up his pants to save the sharp creases, and sat down. "I'll just wait awhile and let it happen. Save me the trouble of making a mess when I had to kill you."

Carson hovered on the edge of collapse. Every labored breath was agony. He thought of his cell phone, but this monster wasn't going to just sit and watch him call for help. He couldn't call for help anyway. He couldn't even pull the cap off his pill bottle. He was dying. He felt a sudden, fierce regret that his sins had found him out. And that Camille would be ashamed of him. It was his last thought before he fell into smothering blackness.

CHAPTER **twenty**

"THINK, CAMILLE. WAS there anything, any background noise, any sound you could identify while Carson was talking?"

"No, nothing. I've told you, Jack. You keep pushing and pushing, but it won't do any good if it isn't there." Unable to sit another minute, she jumped up from her chair and began pacing the small kitchen. "If you mean a bus or a train whistle or anything like that, no. My mind was focused on trying to reason with him."

She raked a hand through her hair in frustration. "I can't believe he doesn't realize how dangerous it is for him to be out on his own like this. Someone murdered his business partner, for heaven's sake! He could be next."

"He's well aware of that. Which is why he ran." Jack, propped against the counter, straightened as she passed, and stopped her by snaking an arm about her waist. "Think of it this way. Maybe he didn't want to drag you into his trouble. Maybe he wanted to protect you. That's pretty normal for a father."

"But I might have been able to help!" Added to the frustration in her voice was bewilderment. "I'm not some shrinking violet. I work with criminals every day. As he's usually more than happy to remind me," she ended on a bitter note.

Jack elected not to argue that. Instead, he tried bringing

their conversation back to the problem at hand. "When I got him settled in the bedroom last night, he was agitated. I tried to get him to tell me what was on his mind, but—"

"Other than the fact that he'd just discovered his business partner with his head almost severed by a murderer?" With a weary sigh, Camille leaned her forehead against Jack's shoulder. "Who wouldn't be agitated?"

His arms went around her, rubbing her back absently. "Back to the phone conversation," he said. "Did you hear any traffic? If he was in New Orleans, there's a lot of noise, street music, people. River traffic too. Tugboats, for instance. Their horns are distinctive."

"For the tenth time, Jack, I didn't hear anything. It was quiet. It was—" She stopped as something edged at her memory. Something . . . "Wait, wait. Chimes. I heard wind chimes."

He looked blank. "Wind chimes?"

"Give me a minute." She turned to him without really seeing him, still caught up in trying to pin down the memory. "I think I heard wind chimes. You know, at Harlen Richard's house he had those elegant chimes, not the tinkly stuff, but the incredible deep-toned kind. The expensive kind." She thought for a minute, then rushed on. "I noticed them when he took us through his house that day when—"

"I remember when."

"Uh-huh. Right." Her thoughts were galloping ahead. "But how could he be there? It's all locked up. It's a crime scene. He wouldn't be able to get in."

Jack was already moving. "He has the code to the gate. He told us that. Unless Raines remembered to order it changed, which I bet he didn't. Getting in the house would be a problem, but if I wanted to get inside, I'd just bust out a window and climb in. Even with a chance that I'd set off an alarm." He dug in his pocket for his car keys. "Come on."

LESS THAN fifteen minutes later, Jack pulled up to the closed gate. He sat hunched up to the wheel of his SUV, his fingers tapping impatiently. "Looks like someone's been here," he said to Camille. "They've removed the crime scene tape."

"Probably so as not to rouse suspicion," she guessed.

"Yeah. If it was left blowing in the wind, someone was bound to notice." He glanced at his watch. "Couple of hours yet to check it out. We should have time. After six-thirty it'll be a bit of a complication for me."

She gave him a puzzled look. "What happens at six-thirty?"

"The evening worship service."

"Oh." She paused, then repeated with dismay, "Oh! Of course. I forgot about it being Sunday." She bent her head, rubbing a spot between her eyes. "Can you see how totally unsuited I am to share your life?"

He didn't contradict her. "It isn't like we'll be sharing a life starting tomorrow morning, sweetheart. Before you make that commitment, you need to work through your questions about faith. And once your heart is right on that, I bet you'll find understanding and fulfilling the job of pastor's wife a piece of cake."

"A piece of cake?"

"Well, you've always been a quick study."

She laughed. "Let's change the subject. How are we going to get inside this gate?"

"We aren't." He put the SUV in reverse and checked the rearview mirror. "We have to find a place to park where we won't attract the attention of the cops. We're going to shinny right over the walls of this compound."

"Really?"

"Really. We don't have the code and we can't ask Raines for permission to enter the premises. I don't want to explain why we think we need to get in. Probably wouldn't let us in anyway."

He'd backed away from the gate while talking. At the corner he made a right turn onto a side street and parked. "If Carson has reasons for sneaking into the house, let's give him a chance to tell us why before the police are involved."

"Excuse me," she said as they got out of the car, "but have you noticed what I'm wearing?" She glanced down at her trendy skirt and strappy sandals. "This outfit is for Sunday church, not wall climbing or housebreaking."

"Not to worry. I've got a plan."

With Jack leading, they walked along the edge of the property looking for a place where the thick shrubs would serve as cover as they scaled the fence. "I didn't realize it was so high," Camille said, casting a worried eye at the twelve-foot edifice.

"Again, not a problem. I'm going to boost you up, then you wait for me to climb up beside you and then you jump down. I'll catch you. Piece of cake."

"Please don't use that term again." A piece of cake it was not. The wall still seemed gigantic. "Is this our only option?"

"Yeah, it's our only option."

So far they'd been lucky that the side street was free of traffic—not unusual, Jack told her, as it was a quiet neighborhood and it was Sunday. But, taking no chances, he chose a place to scale the wall that was well concealed by a thick ligustrum hedge. It proved to be sturdy enough for Camille to get a foothold, and with a boost from Jack she found herself on top of the brick wall.

In two minutes, he was beside her. "No time to enjoy the view," he said, looking down. Gauging the distance, he dropped with athletic grace to the ground, then turned to look up at her, spreading his arms wide. "Jump, sugar. Eight to ten I catch you."

She saw the gleam in his eye, and for a second she also caught a tiny glimpse of the wickedly reckless Jack she once knew. He was enjoying this!

"Here, catch these." She slipped off her sandals one at a time and tossed them down to him.

"No backing out now," he teased. "You can't go home barefoot."

She held her breath and jumped.

As good as his word, he caught her. For a few seconds, instead of setting her on her feet, he held her close, their bodies touching head to toe. With a low laugh, he buried his face in her hair and kissed her ear. "Don't you love it when a plan comes together?"

She burst out laughing. "Okay, big guy, let's see how the rest of your plan goes."

He was still chuckling when he bent to put her sandals back on her feet. "You're a good sport, lady."

Then, straightening up, he caught her hand. But instead of heading toward the house, he pulled her toward the outlying area of the grounds that wound down to the bayou. "Let's watch the house for a few minutes before trying to get inside. And keep your voice down when we get close. We don't want to announce our arrival. Just in case."

She gave him a quick look. "Just in case what?"

"Just in case it's not Carson in there but someone else."

The killer. Suddenly the search for her father wasn't just urgent. It could well be dangerous. She put her hand out and stopped him. "Listen."

"What?"

"The chimes. I hear the chimes. I knew it! Dad called from here."

"We can see the garage from here. He had to come in his car. I don't think he would have parked it out front." He took her hand and pulled her along with him until they had a view of the garage. There, parked in plain sight, was a black Mercedes.

"That's Dad's car." Camille said. "He must be in the house."

"We don't know it's his. Harlen drove the same make and model," Jack reminded her. He was frowning as he surveyed the back of the home. "Carson didn't have a key, so before we just march up to the back door, let's try to find how he got in. We don't want to surprise him. He may have come armed since he's breaking a law by being here."

"Dad wouldn't shoot us, Jack."

"Not intentionally, but let's not take a chance by surprising him."

"As for breaking a law, we are too, aren't we?"

"Yeah, but I'm telling myself it's for a good cause. When I have to explain it to June Raines, I'm hoping he'll see it that way."

"With any luck he'll never know," she said with feeling.

He put his finger to his lips. "Let's do it."

They were halfway across the patio when Jack spotted the broken pane in the back door. "Well, that explains how he got in," he murmured, as if to himself. "But I'm wondering why the alarm didn't go off. You'd think the chief would have left orders to arm the security system."

"Let me just call out to him, Jack." Obeying orders, Camille spoke softly. "He might not want us to find him, but if he knows it's me he won't have any choice."

"Okay, try it. But let me push the door wide open. I want you to stand behind me. It's better not to take any chances."

When he stepped in front of her, Camille saw him reach behind and pull out a gun from his waistband. "Jack! What is that?"

"A hymn book. What do you think it is? Now stay back!"

"Where did it come from?"

"From my past," he muttered. "Weren't you going to call Carson?"

"Is it legal for you to have it?"

"No, Madame Prosecutor. And if this escapade turns bad, I'll probably have to answer to June Raines for not giving it up. So now that we're up to our necks in crime, are you going to call your daddy or do I have to do it?"

It took her a minute to gather her wits. This was not the time or place to argue. But she'd never known Jack to have a gun even before he went to prison.

"Camille—"

"Dad!" she shouted. "It's me, Camille! Are you in there?"

Silence. She looked at Jack, eyebrows raised in question.

"Try again," he told her.

"Dad! Can you hear me? It's me, Camille! I'm coming in, Dad."

With the gun in his right hand, low and flush against his thigh, Jack motioned to Camille with a hike of his chin. "C'mon."

THE HOUSE was quiet, seemingly empty, Jack thought. That should have lessened some of the tension he felt but didn't. When Camille would have stepped up alongside him, he threw out his left hand to stop her. "If Carson's here, he would have answered you. I want you to wait outside while I check the house. Better yet, use your cell phone and call nine-one-one. June needs to know that there's been a break-in."

"No. Not before we know for certain Dad's not here."

"Camille, do as I say."

"I'm not leaving, Jack."

"I should have done this on my own," he muttered in frustration. But he had to admit that he couldn't be sure she was any safer outside unprotected than here beside him. Moving stealthily, they crossed the kitchen and the dining room. Jack couldn't shake the feeling that the house was too quiet; that something was wrong.

In the den, he saw Camille avert her eyes from the stained leather couch and carpet. Other than that, nothing was out of place, no muss, no fuss. The only damage they'd seen so far was the broken pane on the back door. Ahead, through double doors, was the formal living room and vast foyer. Jack was beginning to relax, telling himself his instincts, honed in prison, were overreactions.

"He doesn't appear to be here, Camille."

She stood looking around curiously. "Wouldn't he have an

office? You must have been here when Luanne—" She stopped, tilting her head. "Did you hear that?"

"I did. Stay here, and don't argue!"

Jack tightened his grip on the revolver and moved cautiously toward an area of the house they had not explored. He whirled about at a popping sound as floor tile inches from his feet erupted, spraying chards of Italian marble. He felt a stinging pain on his cheek, but his only thought was for Camille. He reached for her, dropped with her to the floor, then rolled them both toward a long skinny table and jerked at it to pull it down as a shield. He heard another shot. Then another.

Barricaded behind the table, he was breathing hard and bracing to ward off another gunshot when a crash sounded from somewhere distant in the house.

"That was the kitchen door!" Camille's voice was lowered to a scared whisper. "Someone just ran out the kitchen door!"

Jack turned and looked at her. He knew his eyes were wild. Someone had just taken a shot at them. She could have been killed. Rage roared through him at the thought. "Do I have to tie you up to make you stay put while I check?"

She reached up and touched his cheek. "You're bleeding."

He used the back of his hand to swipe at it. "It's nothing. I think whoever it is, he's gone. But I need to check."

"Okay. And I guess we should call the cops now." She rearranged herself and sat up. "It's a miracle, but my cell phone's still in my pocket."

"Two miracles in two minutes," he said grimly. "And yeah, call."

Jack's adrenaline was still up as he moved to the formal living where windows faced the side lawn. He jerked the heavy drapes aside and scanned as much of the grounds as possible. He saw nobody. On his way to another vantage point, he glanced back to be sure Camille was making the call. Her eyes were as big as her face, but she was calling.

"Nine-one-one?" He mouthed the question and got a nod.

Suddenly he heard a new sound and recognized it as the starting of a boat engine. By the time he reached a window with a view to the bayou, a power boat was cutting through the water, already fifty feet from the dock. Jack squinted, trying to make out identifying features of the driver crouched over the controls of the boat. Baseball cap, the brim pulled low on his forehead, substantial sunglasses. That, coupled with the turned-up collar of his jacket, obscured all facial features. Jack realized he would be able to tell June nothing useful. He couldn't even be sure if he was black or white.

He was heading back to Camille when he heard her anguished scream. Instantly he broke into a run, in full red-alert mode again. He stopped short at the door of a room they'd missed in their cautious trek through the house. Carson St. James lay in a crumpled heap on the floor. Camille was on her knees beside him in a panic, her hands moving frantically over his body. Her terrified eyes sought Jack's. "He's not breathing, Jack!"

He was at her side in four long strides. Going down on his haunches, he pressed two fingers on Carson's carotid artery but felt nothing. The man's face was a ghastly, sickly gray, his lips blue. Not a good sign, Jack thought.

"Call nine-one-one again, Camille! Tell them we need EMTs, Code Blue." He put his ear to Carson's lips, straining to hear any faint whisper of life, but again, nothing.

Beside him, Camille's trembling hands were trying to dial.

"He must have been shot, Jack, but I can't find where." Her voice was unsteady. "I couldn't turn him over." She put up a hand to stall Jack's reply. "Hello, this is Camille St. James. I just called. I'm still at the Richard estate." Her voice gave a little hitch. "My father has been shot. Please send an ambulance. And hurry!"

While she was making the call, Jack lifted Carson to search beneath him for a gunshot wound. Finding nothing, he lowered him so that he was flat on the floor again. "I don't see anything either, Camille. I don't think he's been shot."

"Then what?"

"I think he's had a heart attack. I can't find a pulse. I'm starting CPR." While he talked, he was tearing at Carson's jacket, popping the buttons off his shirt to bare his chest. That done, he interlocked his hands and rose on his knees and began the compressions: one, two, three, four, five, six, pause. "This is all we can do until help arrives."

THE AMBULANCE arrived inside fifteen minutes. Jack gave over to the EMTs, who immediately went into emergency mode assuming a heart attack. To Camille's heartfelt relief, they found a faint pulse, possibly thanks to Jack's CPR. But it was plain to her by the look of the medics that Carson's condition was grave. While she hovered on the sidelines watching anxiously, it was Jack who caught the full brunt of Chief Raines's indignation.

"Last person I'd expect to pull a stunt like this, Jack." Raines shot a hard look at Carson on the floor. "Breaking and entering is bad, but you busted right through my crime scene tape. You're letting your personal feelings take you down a dangerous road, my man."

"I know it was irregular," Jack said.

"Irregular?" June's mustache twitched with outrage. "I don't like reminding you, but you weren't always a preacher, Jack. For that alone, folks around here expect you to walk the straight and narrow." He hitched up his pants, warming to his lecture. "It'll tax my ingenuity to figure out a way to give you a pass on this."

Jack breathed a silent thank-you to God. "I appreciate that, June. I guess Camille and I were caught up in the urgency of the situation. After what happened to Harlen, she was worried about her dad's safety, so when he called and we figured out where he might be we took off. We should have called you. I take full responsibility. I won't be guilty of doing anything like that again."

Raines puffed out his chest, putting Jack in mind of a little rooster. "I'm going to take your word on that, seeing as you haven't taken a misstep in the time you've been in Blood Bayou, Jack. But I'll need a full statement from both of you." He glanced over at the busy EMTs. "Mr. St. James too, if he survives."

Carson was on the stretcher now but still unconscious. Camille stood with her hands pressed to her lips, almost as pale as her father. It was plain to both men that she was terrified.

"One more thing, June." Jack knew he was just about out of favors from the chief, but he had to try. "Can the statements wait until we get to the hospital and see what condition Carson's in? Camille may need to be there when he's admitted as next of kin. He may need emergency surgery . . . if he makes it to the hospital."

Raines considered, taking his time. "You sure you can't tell me anything about the shooter?"

"Precious little," Jack said. "Nothing helpful. As far as I

could tell, he appeared to be in good physical shape. He sure ran to that boat fast enough."

"What size was he?"

"I don't know, June. He wasn't overweight. Have your guys recovered the bullets? I think he got off several shots."

"They have, and that'll go to ballistics. But without a weapon, I don't see it helping . . . until we get him. Did you get a number on the boat?"

"Too fast. It was a fully rigged out craft, blue. An outboard, of course. That's about it."

"A hundred of those hereabouts," Raines said absently, stroking his mustache.

"True."

Seeing Carson wheeled out by the medics, Raines gave Jack a brisk nod. "Well, I don't see delaying your statements as a problem. Right now, you'd better go with Camille. She might need a preacher."

CHAPTER twenty-one

ONCE AGAIN, CAMILLE found herself in the hospital, fearful for the life of someone she loved. Carson was in critical condition and had been taken to the cardiology floor within minutes of arriving at the ER for open-heart surgery. She was torn between fear that he might die and relief that there was at least something to be done that might save him. Now she could do nothing but wait.

Jack, seeing the look on her face, put both arms around her. "He's in good hands, sweetheart. Best thing we can do now is pray that all goes well."

"I was so scared, Jack."

"Me too. It looked bad for a while."

"I'm so glad you knew what to do," she murmured, "and that you're here with me now." She was hanging onto him, drawing strength from him. Jack seemed so strong. In spite of the awful things that had happened lately, he was like a rock.

He led her to a small waiting room provided for families of cardiac patients. "I spoke with June Raines," he said. "He tells me he's reinforced the security at Harlen's estate. The safe was open and undamaged. Whoever was there had the combination. It was a timed safe, which meant it could only be opened as programmed."

"How can that be!" she exclaimed. "I can't see Harlen Richard voluntarily giving the combination to anybody."

"Maybe he would if someone held a knife to his throat."

She felt her stomach roll. Of course. And he'd been murdered anyway. She tried to put the grisly picture out of her mind. "What were you able to tell them about the shooter? I never had a chance to ask after you ran after him. Everything went out of my mind when I found Dad on the floor."

"I had only a glimpse. He had to have come by way of the bayou since he got away on a speedboat. It must have been concealed; otherwise we would have spotted it."

Camille felt a wave of exhaustion and sat down on an uncomfortable chair. "Are we in big trouble?"

"Maybe not, but the chief is pretty ticked off. At me especially. He'll want statements from both of us, but he'll wait."

"Did he confiscate your gun?"

Jack moved to a coffeepot and filled two Styrofoam cups. "He doesn't know about it. And with all that's happened I'm hesitant about giving it up."

He was thoughtful as he walked toward her with the coffee. "What is so frustrating to me is that this guy is on a killing spree and nobody seems close to figuring out who he is or why he's doing it."

Her hands shook as she took the coffee, grateful for anything that might warm her up. Why were hospitals always so cold? "Dad may have seen the killer," she said. "Maybe he can ID him when he's able to talk."

"That's a good reason for June to assign a cop to keep out unauthorized visitors," Jack said.

Trust Jack to think of that, Camille thought. The *new* Jack.

Sipping the coffee he'd thoughtfully provided, she watched him move to the door on the lookout for anyone who might give them a scrap of information about her father. At the same time, as people came and went in the hall, she noticed that he was often recognized, greeted warmly, respectfully. Amazing that she might be part of that new life with Jack.

She stood up abruptly and joined Jack at the door. It was too early to know anything, but sitting was impossible. "When Dad called us, he was in Harlen Richard's house. He was okay then. I wonder if the killer was there when he collapsed."

"There's no way of knowing at this point, but if he was, he's already murdered three people outright," Jack said grimly, "so he would have been untouched by a man in the throes of a heart attack."

When Camille shuddered, Jack pulled her close to his side. "That is strictly speculation, Camille. Don't torture yourself with what-ifs and maybes."

"We have to figure out who he is!"

But they'd been trying for days now and they were no closer to finding him than on day one. With her emotions in turmoil, she watched medical staff coming and going down the hall awhile. But no one headed her way with an update on her father. It was all routine to them, she thought. They saw life and death daily at its rawest, most elemental. How did they cope with that?

This time, as the elevator pinged, her face lit when a tall man stepped out of it. "Ray!" She turned to Jack, who was back at the coffee bar. "It's Ray Wyatt. He must haunt this place."

As Wyatt entered the small room, she met him with both hands outstretched. He hugged her, kissed her cheek, and stepped over to shake hands with Jack. "I just heard about your daddy," he said to Camille. "How's he doing?"

"I don't know yet, Ray." She glanced at her watch. "He's in surgery now. It's been awhile, but we just don't know what to expect."

Ray shifted his gaze to Jack. "How the heck did y'all get in Harlen's house?"

"How the heck do you know everything that goes on in this town?" Camille countered.

He smiled and lifted his eyebrows. "Sources, I got sources."

Jack moved toward them from the coffee bar. "Did your sources tell you that we hope Carson can identify the intruder?"

Surprised, Wyatt said, "No, I understood Carson was pretty serious when the EMTs got there. Did he say anything?"

Camille was shaking her head. "No, he was unconscious, Ray, but we hope when he comes around after the surgery he'll be able to tell us something. It's all we have to go on at this point."

"Like I said, tough luck." Ray moved to the coffeepot and helped himself to a cup. "Have you had a chance to check on Chester today?"

Camille's hands went to her cheeks in dismay. "I haven't even thought of him. That's awful. I'm just so—"

"I checked," Jack said, then shrugged at Camille's surprise. "According to the nurse, he's showing more and more signs of coming out of the coma. Any minute now he may wake up."

"If he does," Camille said, "maybe he'll have something to say that will shed some light. They won't admit it, but I don't think the police have anything much to go on." She stopped and snapped her fingers. "That reminds me, I really want to talk to Alafair. Hopefully I'll be able to do that in a day or two." She paused and brought both palms together beneath her chin as if in prayer. "Depending on how Dad does."

Wyatt set his cup on the counter. "Well, seems like things are in good hands here. I think I'll just go up and check on ol' Chester." He caught Camille's hand and squeezed it. "You take care now, hon. See ya, Jack."

She stood drooping a little when he left. "I wish someone would stop by and tell us something, anything! Waiting like this is so hard." For the tenth time she checked her watch, then gave a little gasp. "Jack! I forgot about your evening worship service!"

"I called one of my deacons and explained the circumstances. He'll take over."

"Is that okay?"

"It's okay," he said with a half-smile. When he tossed his empty cup and crossed to her, she went gladly into his arms. "Now would be a good time to pray."

AFTER AN hour and a half, there was still no word from the surgical team. The suspense was even getting to Jack. He had walked down to the nurses' station and asked if someone could tell them something. Usually there was a volunteer on duty to keep family members posted on patients' progress, but it being Sunday and Carson's surgery unscheduled, nobody was available. They'd just have to wait.

A few minutes later it appeared that his plea got results. A resident in green scrubs appeared in the door of the waiting room. Camille jumped up, eyes wide and fearful.

"I'm Dr. Fiske," he said, extending a hand to Camille first

and then to Jack. "Sorry no one has had a chance to talk to you. I understand your anxiety. The surgery is ongoing. It is as Dr. Hymel expected after studying the patient's cath films before surgery. It will be a multiple bypass procedure. He knew that going in."

"Is that unusual?" Camille wanted to know.

Fiske's smile was tight. "Not really. In fact, a single bypass would be more unusual. But your father is in good hands. Dr. Hymel is the best. And your father is holding his own. That's good. But he's not out of the woods. He's had a serious myocardial infarction."

"Heart attack," Camille murmured.

"Yes," Fiske said. "You probably have questions, but I'm afraid I don't have answers yet. Take a walk. Get something to eat. We'll let you know as soon as your father is sent to the recovery room."

"But he will make it," Camille said anxiously. "That's what you're saying?"

"There's just no way of knowing, but I repeat, he's holding his own." The smile he gave as he moved toward the door was sympathetic. "Now I must get back."

Jack saw that Fiske had not relieved Camille's mind very much. He took her by the arm and led her to one of the hard plastic chairs. She sat down gratefully. "Are you hungry? Could you eat something? We can go to the cafeteria."

She was looking at him but didn't seem to hear him. Her eyes were full of worry. "He's holding his own," she said, as if to reassure herself.

"Which is good news," Jack said.

"But he could die."

Jack wished he could deny that, but both knew it was true. "You'll feel better if you eat a little something." He held out his hand. "Let's go to the cafeteria."

She was shaking her head. "No, but if you'll go and bring something back, I'll try to eat. Maybe yogurt. I don't think I could swallow real food."

"Good girl." He gave her a hug and headed down the hall at a brisk pace. He didn't want to leave her alone too long. He'd tried calling Diana and Allen as soon as Carson was admitted, but he hadn't been able to reach them. Camille remembered her mother telling her after church they'd been invited to spend a few days with friends in Grand Isle. Allen was an avid fisherman. Apparently, they'd turned their cell phones off or they were somewhere without a cell. Madge, who would have been more moral support, was working. Except for him, Camille had no one. He vowed to change that once he'd brought her into his life as his wife.

IN THE cafeteria, as Jack waited in line, he marveled at where he was in God's plan for his life. Truly, the Lord worked in mysterious ways. His heart ached for Camille in all she was forced to endure lately. First, stalked by a nameless, faceless killer, now her father fighting for his life, and adding to her stress was the rekindling of their love. It brought joy, yes, but there were issues that added pressure: his calling, her faith questions, their rocky history. He knew she had concerns, she was entitled, considering everything, but he hoped—he prayed—she would be able to overcome.

"Sir? Sir! Your total is twelve dollars and thirty-six cents."

"What? Oh, sorry." With an apologetic smile, he paid the irritated cashier with a twenty-dollar bill, pocketed his change, and helped her sack up the fruit, yogurt, juice, and snacks. His departing smile was genuine. "Have a nice day," he said.

His smile lingered. In spite of all that had happened this tumultuous day, he just couldn't let go of the sheer joy of having Camille fall in love with him again. He had been granted the second chance he once feared would never happen and his heart wanted to burst with joy.

As he walked the twists and turns in the hospital corridors, making his way back to Camille, he turned his gaze to a window in time to see on the horizon a glorious, dazzling summer sunset. He stopped just for a moment as if he might actually see the face of God smiling at him, so awesome was this gift he'd been granted.

It was as he stood there counting his blessings that his cell phone rang. He shifted the sacks to get a look at the screen. He waited a beat or two after seeing the church parsonage number, reluctant to be torn from the wondrous mood he was in. But duty called.

"Hello, Jeanette."

His housekeeper wasted no time greeting him formally. "You are not going to like this, *cher*."

"What is it, Jeanette?"

"You had a call. On this house telephone. It was that woman, Angela Berthelot. She think I don' recognize her voice, but after five years, she mus' think me stupid as a *rabat*."

He'd never given Jeanette Angela's name, but he wasn't surprised that she knew it. "Angela doesn't think you're stupid as a cockroach, Jeanette."

"Humph! You keep on thinkin' that, *cher*. Me, I know what I know."

He turned away from the spectacular sunset. "Is there a message?"

"Don' she always leave you a message? This time, she tell me to tell you that it is urgent. That you mus' call her back right away."

He frowned. "When did she call?"

"Urgent means don' finish washing up dishes that were left on the table from lunch. So, three minutes."

"I'm sorry about that, Jeanette, but Camille and I were interrupted by an emergency. Thanks for calling. And thanks for making that beautiful lunch." He hung up before she had time for another pithy comeback.

Angela wouldn't send an urgent message unless she was genuinely concerned about something. He would have to put her off until Carson was in Recovery and out of danger. Who knew how long that would be, possibly even sometime tomorrow. But he couldn't leave Camille.

He moved to a bench in the corridor to make the call. He hadn't found the right moment to share with Camille his commitment to Sojourner. First he'd talk to Angela and then maybe during the hours while he waited with Camille for Carson's return from surgery, he could tell Camille about Sojourner.

Angela's phone rang only once. He heard the urgency in her voice with her first words. "Jack, thank God you called in time."

"What's wrong, Angela?"

"It's David. You wanted to be notified if he took a turn for the worst. This is it, Jack. In the last twenty-four hours, his kidneys have almost completely shut down. He's dying. That's not my assessment but Dr. Williston's. He says there's nothing we can do."

"Call an ambulance, Angela! Get him to the hospital now!"

"David has definitely nixed that idea, Jack. You know that. The two of you have had this discussion. He has refused any extraordinary procedures, including going to the hospital. He knows he'd be powerless there." She gave a heavy sigh. "He's an adult, Jack. It's his right to choose how to die." For a second, her voice wobbled. David was a great favorite at Sojourner. "His grandmother is with him, but Jack, David is asking for you. According to Williston, he could go any minute. You must come."

Jack's heart plummeted.

No, please, God, not now!

With his head bent, he held the phone in a death grip while his mind raced. He couldn't leave Camille. How could he make her understand? Then he felt shame that his first thought was for himself, not David. God had granted him redemption for his heinous destruction of that boy's life. David, God knows why, had forgiven him. But when he'd promised to put his mission at Sojourner above all else in his life, he had not thought he'd come to a place where he had to choose.

Don't test me this way, Lord!

"Jack? Are you there, Jack?"

"Yeah, I'm here." He pinched the bridge of his nose knowing he had no choice, and sighed. "I'll be about thirty minutes getting there, Angela. Tell David I'm on my way."

* * *

WHEN JACK left to go to the cafeteria, Camille gave herself a lecture. The doctor was right. Stress depleted energy. She wouldn't be of use to anyone if she fainted. She needed to eat something in spite of the fact that she didn't know if she could swallow.

She'd barely tasted anything at lunchtime, she'd been so enthralled with Jack and their newfound happiness. It was amazing how easily they'd reconnected. Although she had denied it for a long time, his absence after their divorce had left a hole in her heart, in her life. This time, they would share a deeper, more meaningful commitment, she believed that. She wanted to understand his faith. She wanted to share his belief. She was eager for Jack to show her the way.

"Ms. St. James?"

"Yes." She jumped up from her chair. But it wasn't a doctor. It was a woman in a tailored suit and carrying a sheaf of paperwork. Camille went toward her, frowning. "What's wrong?"

"I'm Sheila Dixon from Admitting. You're next of kin to Carson St. James?"

"Yes, he's my father."

"I see, well, he was admitted, as you know, in emergency status." She motioned to the paperwork in her hands. "You furnished some information, but considering the confusion at the time—"

"My father was in critical condition."

"Yes, so I was told." She touched the bridge of her glasses, straightening them on her face. "But I'm going to need a more complete file. I wonder if you could come down to Admitting and take care of that?"

Camille looked around. "Now?"

"I'm sorry, it is necessary."

"But my father is in surgery. I need to be here in case they need me."

"You'll be two minutes from this area. We'll let them know where you are, but I don't imagine it will be a problem. I understand your father is having open-heart surgery?"

"That's right."

"And he's only been in surgery an hour?"

"And a half. An hour and a half."

Sheila Duncan nodded knowingly. "I'm fairly certain that it will be at least that much longer, Ms. St. James. In fact, if you'll allow me to say so, taking care of this paperwork will be useful in passing the time. Time, as you've probably noticed, goes very slowly when a loved one is in surgery and you have nothing to do but wait."

Camille gave in. She pulled out her cell phone to call Jack and with a distressed sound realized the battery was gone. Nothing for it, she scribbled a note to him and asked an elderly couple in the waiting room to give it to him when he got back from the cafeteria. They had been talking with Jack about their son, who'd been in a car wreck. She wrote Jack's name on the folded note, handed it to the couple, and left.

JACK WAS distraught over what he had to do. Camille would have no one to be with her while she waited for Carson to come out of surgery. If he made it. There was always a chance that he wouldn't survive, he was that critical.

If it were anybody but David . . .

Camille was not in the waiting room. It was empty except for the elderly couple whose son was in surgery. The old man got up from his chair, moving creakily over to Jack, and thrust a note in his hand.

"This is from your wife," he said.

Jack didn't take time to set the old man straight, but quickly unfolded the note. He scanned it hurriedly and crumpled it in his fist. He tried calling her on her cell, but it went to voice mail. He couldn't leave without explaining where he was going and why. Glancing at his watch, he knew it would kill precious minutes to go to Admitting, but he had to. With a distracted thank-you to the old man, he rushed out of the waiting room and dashed for the elevator.

While descending to the first floor, he rehearsed what he'd say to Camille. Why, he wondered in disgust, hadn't he explained about Sojourner House to her before? But even if he had, would she see that it was his duty to go to David now instead of staying with her while her father was at death's door? Would she understand?

The elevator pinged and stopped.

He stepped out, casting another anxious look at his watch and hustled down the hall toward the Emergency Room. Since Carson was admitted in ER, he assumed Camille would be there. A part of him wanted to rail at the bureaucratic red tape required of patients, but it would only raise his blood pressure more.

Thank God it was Sunday. There were few people about and none of the bustling activity that characterized the hospital on a weekday. He looked again at his watch. He needed to be on the road. He didn't—couldn't—fail David now.

Around the next corner and he was in the ER. Unlike the

front entrance and halls, this was a busy place. Chairs were packed with individuals. At another time, he would have scanned their faces looking for folks who might be members of his congregations, but he couldn't take the time for that now. He strode directly to the admissions desk. A bespectacled woman in a severe suit looked up. "May I help you?"

He knew many of the staff people in the hospital but not this woman. "I'm Jack Vermillion. A few minutes ago—actually, I don't know how long ago it was—but Camille St. James left the surgical wing in Cardiac Care to come down here and fill out paperwork."

She pushed at her glasses to bring him into focus. "Oh, yes, Ms. St. James was here. As for how long ago—"

"Has she left?"

"Yes."

Jack felt like yanking her across the desk and screaming in her face. But all he did was ask as politely as he could manage, "About how long ago was that that, ma'am?"

"Oh, let me see. Not even five minutes."

He should have run into her on the elevator or in the hall. Where on God's earth was she?

"Is there a problem?" Severe Suit asked.

"No, no problem." He turned away, and then belatedly looked back at her. "Thank you."

He stood in the hall for a distraught minute trying to decide what to do. But nothing for it, he'd have to retrace what he hoped was Camille's route to the waiting room. Hopefully, he'd find her.

But he didn't run into her on his way back to Cardiac Care, nor did he find her in the waiting room. He tried her cell again and again it went to voice mail. He guessed what had happened. Her cell was out of juice. He was beyond feeling urgent now. He was beside himself. He patted his breast pocket where he usually kept a tiny notebook and found nothing. Next he checked his back pants pocket. Nothing. It was in his car. He looked around frantically for something to write on and spotted the crumpled note from Camille where he'd tossed it. Nothing for it, he'd have to use the reverse side.

"I'm sorry, do you have a pen I might borrow?" he asked the old gentleman.

"Right here." The old guy plucked it out of his breast pocket. "I keep it handy."

Jack mumbled thanks and began scribbling words to try to explain the inexplicable. He knew she would see nothing he wrote as justification for abandoning her in a crucial moment. But he had to try.

He finished it and walked over to the couple. "I'm Jack Vermillion," he said to the old gent.

"Milton Blanchard," the man said, rising to shake Jack's hand. "This is my wife, Mary." His wife nodded, but she was obviously worried, her mind elsewhere.

"You haven't heard anything about your boy yet?" Jack asked, while his mind screamed at him to leave. Now.

"No, sir. Not a word."

"I wonder if you'd do me a favor and give this to Camille when she returns."

"Your wife? Oh, sure." Blanchard took the note and put it in his breast pocket. "Be glad to do that. You look kinda worried. You two missing each other like this . . ." He shook his head but didn't seem to see a need to finish his thought.

"I am worried, sir. And I have to go, but if you'll give that to Camille, I'd appreciate it."

"I'll do that, Jack."

Jack backed away. Outside in the hall, he stood, uncertain. Still no sign of Camille. He looked again at his watch and rushed toward the elevator.

CAMILLE STOPPED at the elevator cupping a warm, fresh cup of coffee. She was eager to get back to the waiting room, hoping that the long ordeal of her father's surgery would soon be over. The clerk had taken her sweet time sorting through a mountain of papers that Camille had signed after barely scanning them. As a lawyer, she knew she should have been more diligent about checking what she signed, but there was no point. Her father had been admitted and now there was paperwork.

Careful not to spill anything on herself, she hitched the strap of her purse on her shoulder and punched the elevator for the second floor. She'd spotted the designer coffee wagon in the lobby earlier and after leaving Admitting, she'd succumbed to the temptation to take a second and get a cup to go. Sipping it now, she thought nothing was quite as delicious as coffee and cream, perfectly blended.

She found herself looking forward to whatever Jack had managed to get in the cafeteria. Jack. She took a deep breath. Thank goodness, he was here with her.

However, he wasn't waiting for her as she expected. She entered, frowning. A doctor in scrubs was sitting with the elderly couple. He spoke softly and Camille couldn't hear what he was saying, but it wasn't good. The lady was weeping openly. The old gentleman was pale and shaking. The doctor reached up and patted the arm of the woman. It was a gesture of comfort and sympathy. No mistake about that, Camille thought. It didn't take much insight to guess what had happened. Their son had not survived. Her heart went out to them.

Where was Jack? He'd returned from the cafeteria. Two sacks with food sat on a corner table. She backed out of the waiting room, feeling uncomfortable witnessing the tragedy that had befallen the couple. The hall was empty except for a lab technician wheeling a cart loaded with medication. She watched as the tech punched the security button that opened the double doors to the surgical wing. From the quick glance she managed to get before the doors closed, she could see nobody, nothing.

The doctor emerged from the waiting room looking grim and shaken. Camille didn't envy anybody having to deliver such tragic news. To lose a child had to be the ultimate loss. This was a time when Jack's calling would seem a godsend. But where was he?

She wandered down the hall, mostly to give the couple some privacy, but in a few minutes, they came out of the waiting room, he with his arm around his wife's shaking shoulders as she wept. He looked older than he'd appeared an hour ago. As she watched, they stepped into the elevator and left.

Where was Jack?

An hour later, he had still not appeared and there had been no word on her father. She wasn't sure which upset her more. She simply knew she felt crushed that Jack had taken off for some reason and hadn't bothered to tell her. She looked around the cheerless room with its hard, ugly chairs. Hard, ugly, *empty* chairs. She was alone. She might as well face it. Her father was at death's door in the operating room, her mother was somewhere out in the Gulf of Mexico fishing, her brother was back in Houston on business, Madge was working, and she was alone.

She sat down because her knees were threatening to buckle. and she didn't want to find herself on the floor with no one around to see or care. But she wouldn't cry. She had cried a river of tears over Jack Vermillion and she'd been a fool to think it would be different this time.

But she was just so bitterly disappointed. And hurt. If the situation were reversed, and Jack needed her, nothing would have taken her away from him.

At that thought, she drew in a deep, fortifying breath. Just because Jack wasn't here didn't mean she couldn't manage perfectly well without him. She could. She would. She'd done just fine without him for seven years. And she'd spent a lot of her childhood thinking no one cared and she'd been wrong. She wouldn't fall into that self-pitying trap today.

She looked at the sacks where he'd left them. She still needed to eat something. So she would. She grabbed a sack, but her hands were shaky. She fumbled a bit, but once she'd pulled out the yogurt, she opened it almost defiantly, grabbed a spoon, and took a mouthful—and could barely swallow it.

Okay. She set it aside. Later, she told herself. She then settled back in the viciously hard chair to wait for word of her father.

JACK'S PRAYER as he headed to Sojourner as fast as he dared drive was that he'd make it in time to be with David and that David was still able to know he was there. But as he drove, he worried about Camille.

A note was so inadequate to explain why he'd left. He told himself he would be able to make it right when he could explain in person. But lurking in the back of his mind was worry that any explanation would matter. The emergency with David was a good example of the many moments when, as a minister, he had to place his calling over his personal life. Camille had finally been persuaded to set aside the past long enough to consider giving him a second chance. That was a miracle in itself. But now he felt a crushing fear that she might not be willing to embrace his life fully.

He spotted Craig Williston's car in a spot reserved for the attending physician. Jack parked beside it, got out and headed almost in a trot to the front entrance. If Craig was still here, chances were that David was still alive.

Please let me make it to him in time, Lord.

Mattie Bergeron spotted him at the door before anyone else. David's grandmother was tiny and toughened by a life of hard living. She had coarse salt-and-pepper hair worn in a braid that hung almost to her waist. At one time she had treated Jack with a revulsion that made him feel lower than a snake. And he'd deserved it. Somehow they'd gotten beyond it. Today she met him at the door, her dark eyes red and swollen with tears and grief.

"I was afraid you'd be too late. But that boy, he's stubborn. He waited for you."

Jack moved to the bed, braced before this brave and supremely talented young man whose bright future he was responsible for snuffing out. David's eyes were closed and his breath shallow and uneven. Intervals between breaths were so long that Jack was alarmed. He took a thin, cool hand in his and moved his thumb gently back and forth over the bony knuckles.

"Dave," he said softly. "It's me, Jack."

Eyelids fluttered and opened. To Jack's amazement, David's cracked lips stretched into a semblance of a smile. "Knew you'd . . . come."

"You call," Jack said softly, "I come." He swallowed hard around the tightness in his throat and somehow managed a light tone. "What's going on, buddy? You been out drag racing again?"

David mustered the strength to roll his eyes. "Yeah, that's . . . what I been . . . doin'. Hit one-seventy on a . . . turn and totaled that . . . sucker."

"No pain, no gain," Jack said while feeling such fierce anguish in his heart that he wanted to wail. But he could not let it show, not now. This was David's moment. "They tell me you're thinking of sitting out the next race. Say it ain't so, Dave."

"I have . . . a bigger . . . more important . . . race."

Jack swallowed hard again. "Okay. It's your call, buddy."

Somehow, David managed to lift a finger. "One . . . question, Rev. I know . . . you have . . . the . . . answer."

"I don't know about that, but ask away."

"What do . . . you think it'll be . . . like . . . in Heaven?"

David's eyes closed, exhausted by the effort of speech. But Jack knew he was still there. That he was listening, waiting. Jack rubbed a hand over his face in agony at what his reckless irresponsibility had wrought. How was he going to live with himself when David died?

Finally his throat opened enough to enable him to speak. "I don't know what Heaven is like, Dave. But surely for you it is a place where you'll be whole again, healthy and strong and able."

"Yeah. That's . . . what I'm thinkin' too." He went quiet, still. Jack held his breath, afraid it was the end. But in a minute he saw another fleeting smile. "So I'll see you . . . there, Rev."

There was no more talk after that. David lay sinking deeper and deeper into that deathlike twilight as the hours passed. He seemed peaceful, accepting. Jack thought maybe he'd been right in refusing to be hooked up to machines that only prolonged his suffering when nothing would stop the inevitable.

Once or twice in the long night, he stirred. Once he murmured, "Ma Mattie!"

Mattie bent, tears coursing down her face, and pressed her cheek to his. "I'm here, darlin' boy."

Once he called Jack, who laced his fingers with David's that were now cold, so cold. "I'm here, Dave."

At sunrise the next morning David took his last labored breath.

CHAPTER twenty-two

BY THE TIME midnight rolled around, Camille was exhausted and wired by worry and too much coffee. She'd lost count of the number of cups she'd consumed, but she was back at the coffee bar when a doctor finally appeared.

"Ms. St. James?"

She instantly dropped the disposable cup in the trash and hurried across to meet him.

"I'm Dr. Hymel." He wore green scrubs and a cap printed with SpongeBob and his side-kick Patrick. He stood at least ten inches taller than Camille. She thought he looked more like a professional basketball player than a cardiovascular surgeon.

"Is the surgery over, Doctor?"

"It is. And your father is in Recovery. His heart was riddled with plaque and required five-part bypass surgery to alleviate major blockages. The man was a heart attack waiting to happen. Luckily, he came through the surgery as well or better than expected considering the delay in getting to him after he collapsed."

"But is he going to be all right?" she asked anxiously.

"He's critical, but he's holding his own." Hymel pulled the cap from his head and left it dangling on his neck by two strings. "It was obvious once we got in his chest that he's a smoker. He needs to give that up. Maybe you can suggest it." He gave a small smile. "Tell him if he wants to see his grandchildren, he'll have to quit."

"May I see him?"

"Not yet. He'll be in Recovery for a while, certainly until we feel he's able to hold his own in CCU. I want to prepare you. He'll look pretty sick. His heart was enlarged. That's what happens when it has to work too hard. It needed new blood and it'll get it now. He has an airway, meaning he won't be doing any talking for a day or so. We'll take that out as soon as possible and free him up so he'll be able to complain to his heart's content— no pun intended."

Camille smiled weakly at his joke. And it was all too probable that her dad would complain, considering his personality. "When you say he'll be in Recovery a while, do you mean for the rest of the night?" She glanced at a clock on the wall. "It's midnight now. Do you think—"

"No way to tell." He began backing away toward the door. It had been a long night for him too, she thought. "But we like to get patients out of Recovery as soon as it's safe. Any other questions?" He had his hand on the door frame, poised to go.

"Will my father be an invalid after this? Is the damage to his heart so great that he won't be able to resume working? He was not breathing, as far as we could tell when we found him. And a five-part bypass seems so drastic."

"I wouldn't assume his heart wasn't beating just because you couldn't detect a heartbeat or a sign that he was breathing." His smile became more genuine. "As for a five-part bypass, it is more common than you might imagine. In fact, I have many patients who have undergone multiple bypass surgery. Most resume their lives with a few restrictions. I'll discuss those with your father as soon as he's able."

"Thank you, Doctor."

"Get some rest yourself," he said on his way out. "You look as if you could use it."

Camille agreed, but no way was she going to leave until her dad was awake and settled in CCU. She pushed a couple of the chairs together, put her feet up on a third, and used her purse as a pillow, trying to calm her thoughts enough to relax, maybe even get a little sleep.

Thirty minutes later, she gave up trying. She stood, pressing her aching lower back with both hands. Her shoulders were stiff, she felt scruffy and in need of a shower, and she longed for something to read. Or at least something that wasn't outdated or dealing with a subject she had no interest in. She was idly sifting through the stack of moldy magazines when Madge stuck her head in the door.

"Hey, girlfriend."

Camille had never been so happy to see a person. Madge sauntered into the room with a large carry-all, which she dropped on a chair, then held her arms out for a hug. Tears threatened, so Camille closed her eyes and savored the embrace. She really needed a hug.

"I got here as soon as I could," Madge said in a sympathetic voice. "I had to work a double shift."

Camille fought against letting Madge see what a baby she was. She stepped back, turning to quickly wipe the corners of her eyes. "Thank you for coming," she managed.

"What are friends for? So how's Carson?"

"He's in Recovery. It was a five-part bypass. He's holding his own. That's their standard line, I guess. It's all they ever tell you around here."

"Well, that's better than the alternative." Madge looked around at the empty chairs. "Where's Jack? Harassing the help?"

"Jack's not here. He's gone."

Madge did a double take. "Huh? Gone where?"

"He didn't say." Camille moved to the door, hoping to see somebody with news. "He just disappeared. I had to leave for a few minutes and when I got back, he was gone. No word, no note, no nothing. Gone."

Madge stood with her hands on her hips, frowning. "He didn't say anything, didn't call? He wouldn't do that, Camille."

"If he called, I didn't get it. My cell is out of battery, but there are ways he could have let me know, Madge. Maybe it was some kind of emergency to do with his church." She put her hand to her mouth to hide her trembling lips. In a moment or so she had herself under control again and mustered a smile. "It's a good thing I don't really need anybody to hold my hand."

Madge was silent, her head tipped as she considered the situation. "You may not need just anybody, but you need Jack at a time like this. Whatever happened that he felt he had to leave, it has to be vitally important."

"Whatever." Camille shrugged.

"I guess you're mad."

Camille gave her a surprised look. "Well, wouldn't you be? My father lies at death's door with a massive heart attack. Surgery was required to save his life. It was touch-and-go whether he lived or died. He still might die." She released a mirthless laugh. "So I believe that a situation like that pretty much counts as something a minister understands. For a minister who claims to care about someone, it's hard to see why he'd . . . whatever, Madge. He's not here. That's that."

Madge apparently decided not to pass judgment. She dug in her purse and pulled out her cell phone. "Here, take my cell. I won't need it and you do. I'll take yours and charge it up for you at home." She bent to pick up the carry-all she'd brought with her. "I know how miserable these chairs are, so I brought you a pillow and blanket." She gave a cheeky wink. "From the jailhouse supply, so don't complain if they aren't quality stuff. I can't stay because I have to take the morning shift again. Melanie is still sick. And tomorrow morning on my way to work, I'll drop off a change of clothes for you. You can shower right here. I don't know if anybody told you that. It's a courtesy for family of patients in critical care."

"They didn't and thank you. And thank you for the phone, but won't you need it?"

"One of Blood Bayou's finest drove me over here and he'll take me home. He's instructed by the chief to stay. I'll be okay. And you'll be okay as long as you're here in the hospital."

Camille picked up a pillow and held it close. "Thanks for thinking of this." She wrinkled a nose at the chairs. "Those awful things aren't made for people. Makes you wonder who decides what furniture to place in a hospital waiting room."

"Someone who's never had to spend a night trying to get comfortable in one." Her look turned thoughtful. "I wish I could stay with you, but I just can't, Camille. I guess Diana didn't feel she could leave Allen?"

"They're fishing. In Grand Isle. She doesn't even know. We couldn't reach them."

"Oh, sweetie." Madge gave her arm a sympathetic squeeze. "Use that pillow, snuggle up under that blanket, and try to get some rest. I bet Jack will be back any minute now. He's probably worried sick about you."

Camille managed a weak smile. Wherever Jack was, he wasn't thinking about her. With a sigh, she sat back to wait for the end of the long night.

JACK WASN'T back, not even after dawn streaked the sky. But Carson was out of Recovery and settled in CCU. And by the time the sun was up on another hot summer day, Camille had showered and changed into fresh clothes. Her father was in a drugged, aftersurgery fog, the airway still in place, and mostly unaware of where he was and what had happened to him. She couldn't leave yet.

She still had not heard from Jack. Not personally, anyway. She'd been called down to the security office in the hospital early that morning to pick up her car keys. Apparently Jack had arranged for someone to deliver her car and park it in the hospital garage. It puzzled her that he chose not to leave her stranded without a car even though he'd abandoned her.

At eight o'clock, Madge's cell phone rang. Her heart did a little jump, hoping it was Jack finally getting around to calling, but of course he wouldn't know she had Madge's phone. Flipping the screen open, she saw that it was Alafair. "Hello?"

"Madge, this is Alafair."

"This is Camille, Alafair."

"Oh, Camille. Hi, how are you?"

"Okay. Do you need to talk to Madge?"

"Actually, I can tell you as well as Madge. I hope I'm not calling too early."

Camille stepped out of the CCU waiting area. "Not at all. Actually, I've been thinking about you. I intended to call you yesterday, but things happen."

"Really? Was it about Luanne?"

"Yes. I thought maybe you might have thought of something since Madge and I talked with you."

"That's why I'm calling. I don't know how I could have forgotten this, but I have something that you might be interested in." She paused and Camille heard water running. "I'm in my kitchen and my grandson wants a drink of water. Isn't that the way it happens? You get on the phone, they suddenly need a drink."

"You mentioned something of Luanne's?"

"It's a box of things that belonged to Stephanie Hill. She and Luanne were very close, you remember I told you that?" Another pause. "Charlie, don't shoot that thing in the house! Go outside! Sorry, Camille, where was I?"

"A box belonging to Stephanie Hill."

"Oh, yes. Let me explain. Stephanie had practically no family except for this distant relative—a lady—in Detroit, I think it was. Anyway, when she died, this lady cleared out her things because she needed to sell the house, you know? She just went through it like a white tornado."

"And what about the box?"

"Well, since Stephanie's best friend was Luanne, this lady gave her a lot of Steph's personal belongings, clothes and stuff. She knew Luanne didn't need it, but she thought she could give it away to people who might."

"So Luanne had this box?"

"Actually, it was several boxes. And no, I had them. Luanne was pretty cut up over Stephanie's murder and she didn't have the heart to even look at it. She used to give me lots of things. She was very generous. So she kind of shuffled through it and then she said I could have it all. Then I took it and dropped off the clothes at Goodwill. There wasn't much else in the last box that I was interested in, either. Letters and stuff. Pictures. There was some jewelry, but it was all costume. I let my granddaughters play with it." She stopped abruptly. "Charlie, I told you to play outside!"

She sighed. "Charlie spent the night with me and he got up this morning at five-thirty, if you can believe that."

"You were saying about the box?"

"The box. Yeah, I put the one with letters and pictures out in the garage and mostly forgot about it. This was five years ago, you understand. Then I was out there yesterday looking for something to entertain Charlie and spotted it. I thought you might want to look inside before I just toss it out, you know?"

A box of Stephanie Hill's personal letters? And photographs? It could be a treasure trove or it could be nothing. But Camille wasn't about to pass up checking it out.

"I definitely want that box, Alafair. But I'm at the hospital right now. My father is just out of open-heart surgery."

"Oh, my goodness! I'm sorry. Tell me where to drop this off—at your mom's house or wherever. I'll be glad to do that."

"Thank you. My car is parked in the hospital garage. I could meet you there as I'm just hanging around waiting. Would that work for you?"

"I'm on my way."

CHAPTER twenty-three

CAMILLE HAD NOT been able to tell Alafair where to meet her in the parking garage, since she'd failed to ask the security guard who'd delivered the keys for the exact location of her car. She knew only that it was on the third level. When she approached the young guard at the front desk, whose name tag read Will Peyton, he didn't know where her car was either, but he seemed agreeable to helping her search for it.

They were in the garage elevator going up when it opened on the second floor. Ray Wyatt was waiting. He looked surprised. "Camille, I didn't expect to see you here. Thought you'd be with your daddy. You going down?"

She put a hand on the elevator door to hold it. "No, up. My car is somewhere on the third level and I need to move it. But first Will and I have to find it."

The guard raised his hand. "Yo, Wyatt."

"Will." Wyatt's gaze shifted back to Camille. "You look more like yourself today. Mr. St. James must be okay."

"He survived, but we won't know for a while if he's okay. He still has the airway so he can't talk. It's not a problem right now as he wouldn't be able to talk much anyway. They tell me it'll be a while, depending on how well he does." Still holding the door, she added, "Are you here to check on Chester?"

"Your daddy first, then Chester. I swear that old guy is going to come around yet."

"But will he be able to tell us anything?" She sighed. "That would be something, wouldn't it?"

The elevator suddenly buzzed an alarm. Wyatt stepped inside. "I'll ride up with you and then go back down. Where's Jack? Did you leave him with your dad?"

She watched the numbers climb to the third floor. "Actually, I haven't heard from Jack since he left last night."

"No kidding? Must have been something real urgent for him to leave you. Man, he's like those German shepherds at Madge's house. Anybody looks wrong at you, he bristles. If he could bark, he would."

"You exaggerate," she said. The elevator stopped at the third level. She started out, but stopped and held the door. "Oh, wait, Ray, listen. You'll never guess what happened. Alafair Menard called and told me she has a box with some personal things belonging to Stephanie Hill."

"So?"

"She's bringing it to me. I guess I'll stow it in my car until I get a chance to look at it. I admit I'm curious about what's inside the box, but it'll have to wait until I can open it at Madge's house." She flashed him a smile as she turned to go. "Thanks for looking in on my dad. He may not be aware of it, but it's nice to know somebody cares."

WHEN CAMILLE left with the security guard to go to the parking garage, she just missed Jack, who'd parked on the ground level in the area reserved for physicians and clergy. He had spent the trip thinking of ways to better explain to her his Sojourner mission and what it meant to him. Why, he'd asked himself, had he left it so long? He should have shared it when he told her about his conversion in prison. Or over lunch when she had opened her heart to him. Why had he withheld a piece of his own heart?

As he approached the physician's entrance he saw Chief Raines talking to one of his deputies. He lifted a hand in greeting but didn't stop to talk. He was eager to see Camille.

Once inside, he took off in a brisk walk, passing Ray Wyatt going in the opposite direction. His greeting was polite and perfunctory. Wyatt's was similar. Jack had an idea that the detective didn't like him much. And if he were honest, Jack admitted that the feeing was mutual. Unlike Camille, he couldn't warm to him. Something about Wyatt just rubbed him the wrong way.

He arrived at CCU expecting to find Camille with Carson. But she was not at his bedside or anywhere else that he could see. Thinking she was probably in the waiting room, he headed in that direction. He found it crowded with a new crop of patients' family members, but Camille wasn't among them.

He stood in the hall feeling some unease. A door opened and he turned as a woman came out of the restroom. "Excuse me," he said, "but was there another person in the restroom? I'm looking for . . . ah, a dark-haired woman, about your height, Camille St. James."

"No, the restroom is empty," she said. "But I saw her earlier in the CCU, or at least I think it was the person you're looking for. But that was about an hour ago."

"Thanks."

Jack stood for a minute in indecision. Then he pulled out

his cell phone and called her. It went again to her voice mail. He wasn't surprised that she wasn't taking his calls. But where was she?

He headed slowly back toward the CCU, his mind teeming with possibilities to account for her being gone. Surely she hadn't put herself in jeopardy by leaving? Except for the Blanchards, the waiting room had been deserted when he left. Had the killer managed to corner her right here in the hospital? Had that idiot of a security guard failed to take her keys to her as he'd been told?

"Reverend Vermillion, are you here to see Mr. St. James?"

Jack took a minute to gather himself and answer the nurse. "Yes, but I expected to see his daughter with him."

"Oh, she's taking a shower, I think. She'll probably be back shortly. You can see the patient now if you want. I'm Ben, Mr. St. James's nurse."

"I'm Jack Vermillion, a friend of the family." Jack almost sagged with relief. Another minute without knowing where Camille was and he might have given the hospital staff something to talk about. Seeing the Reverend Vermillion freaking out would make good break-time stories.

As he followed Ben to Carson's bedside, the nurse chatted. In CCU, he explained, the ratio of nurse to patient was one to one during the first twenty-four hours after surgery. So until then, he alone would be seeing to Carson's needs.

"We removed the airway not too long ago. That's early, but the doctor okayed it. He's groggy but coming around in fits and starts. High on pain meds, but that's normal. Big guy like him with that barrel chest, open-heart surgery is really tough."

Jack noted on Carson's face the trauma of surviving a massive heart attack and major surgery. His features were haggard, his color a pasty gray. The lines that added character and gravitas when he was healthy made him look simply old now. For once he showed every day of his age.

Ben jiggled with the IV line on Carson's left arm connected to a plastic bag suspended on a steel pole. "He's been talking, but it's crazy stuff. Real agitated too. Meds do that to some patients." He paused, looking at Carson. "You know, it's funny. These guys, they can't leave their work behind even with a heart attack. Here he is a few hours after almost meeting the Grim Reaper face-to-face, he comes around and starts giving orders right and left. Talking about secret deals and maps, cussing his business partner, junk like that."

Ben wagged his head slowly, looking bemused. "Like I said, some folks don't tolerate drugs as well as others. But if we can wake him up again and get him talking, hopefully making sense, that would be a really good sign. Want to try?"

Jack knew what was unspoken: the possibility of brain damage. When the paramedics got to him at Harlen's house, they said Carson's heartbeat had been very slow and weak. While one had quickly administered oxygen via an Ambu bag, the other had installed an IV and delivered a drug designed to kick up his heartbeat. His mental capacity would be directly related to whether he'd received enough oxygen in time.

He touched his ex-father-in-law's right hand. "Carson. Carson, can you hear me?"

Carson made a wordless sound but did not rouse.

Jack leaned closer and tapped a limp hand. "Carson, you need to wake up. It's Jack."

Carson groaned and stirred, then winced with the effort. His eyelids fluttered. After a moment or two, he quieted and seemed to drift back into nothingness.

"Don't give up," Ben said.

Jack tried again, this time speaking with more strength. "Carson, you need to wake up. Come on now. Talk to me. You've had some surgery. You're okay now. Wake up, Carson."

Carson made another sound, more agitated. His eyelids fluttered as if he struggled to swim up out of a drugged oblivion.

"Come on," Jack urged softly, "Come on, Carson. Rise and shine."

His eyes finally opened to mere slits. He blinked several times and seemed awake. For a beat or two, he had the clearly confused look of someone in a strange place trying to figure out where he was. Jack, watching, could tell when full cognizance dawned. The confusion in Carson's eyes suddenly became alarm. He brought his hand up, jerking at the lead-in to his IV and nearly pulling it out before Ben quickly moved to prevent it.

"Carson!" Jack said. "It's okay. You're in the hospital. Look at me. You know who I am?"

"Pain," he whispered, closing his eyes. "Jack." And then his eyes snapped open, sought Jack's. He spoke weakly. "Jack, the land man. It's the land man."

"What? Say again, Carson."

He groaned. "Pain. My pills. I need—"

"I'm giving you something to ease that pain now, Mr. St. James," Ben said in a clear voice, one practiced in penetrating a drugged fog. He tapped the hypodermic and pushed the plunger.

"Wait. No." Carson tried lifting his hand, but only managed to move his fingers. "The land man killed them . . . every one . . ."

Jack was riveted. His voice urgent, he leaned over, his face almost touching Carson's. "Killed who, Carson? Don't go back to sleep! Killed who?"

"Camille. He . . . kill Camille. Stop . . . him . . ." He fumbled for something, tangling his fingers in the sheet.

Jack reached for his hand and was surprised by the strength of his grasp. "Stop him . . . Jack."

"Who, Carson? Who is it?"

"Harlen . . . land man." He managed to twist his mouth in a weak look of disgust. "Big . . . secret."

Jack spoke firmly. "Tell me the land man's name, Carson."

"Cop . . ."

Cop? Jack thought a minute. The chief? June Raines? His heart skipped a beat. June was in the building. But somehow . . . no, not June.

Now the narcotic in the drip was kicking in. Carson was still mumbling, fighting the drug, obviously agitated. Jack bent down close to try to make out what he was saying. A name. Jerking back in shock. Could it be?

Ben spoke softly, "He's under, Reverend. Sorry. If I'd known . . ."

But Jack heard only a roaring in his ears. Stunned, he straightened, while the name reverberated in his brain.

He knew. He knew when Carson mumbled, "Cop," he knew. What a slick character. What a soulless devil. And he was in the building right now.

He blinked rapidly in agitation and gave a shake of his head to clear it. "Camille," he said to Ben in a dazed tone. "Where is she? Where did she go to take that shower?"

Ben was looking at him strangely, but Jack had only one

thought in his mind. Getting to Camille. "The shower room, Ben! Where is it?"

"Straight out of the CCU," Ben told him. "Take a left at the end of the hall. There's a nurse's station. They'll direct you."

Without another word, Jack charged down the hall. He barely restrained himself from breaking into a jog. He reached for his cell phone and dialed the Blood Bayou PD. He got Madge, who was on duty, who passed him to the deputy chief, a new man who'd been recruited from New Orleans. Jack explained what Carson said and got a skeptical reaction. But the deputy chief promised to send Patrick Duval. Jack clicked off feeling some relief, knowing he wouldn't have to tell Duval how urgent the situation was. He'd know.

Now, rounding a corner in the hall, he ran smack into a lab technician pushing a cart with medication and blood samples. Glass tubes tinkled against one another and a metal pan crashed to the floor with a terrible racket. He picked himself up and helped the dazed lab person to her feet. Backing away, he apologized sincerely, intent only on reaching Camille. On keeping her from innocently walking into certain death.

Three people manned the nurse's station. All three looked up in surprise as he appeared, wild-eyed and breathing hard.

"Why, Reverend Vermillion," said a red-haired nurse, a member of his congregation. "Is something wrong?"

"My wife . . . ah, Camille St. James. They told me she was in the shower room."

Another nurse spoke up. "No, Reverend, she was here, but that was a good half hour ago. She seemed anxious to get back to her father in CCU."

Fear made his reply sound harsh. "She's not there! She never made it back there." He calmed himself. "Did you notice whether she took the elevator?"

"She did." This from the redhead, whose name Jack could not remember. "She mentioned going to the garage. Maybe she decided to—"

But he didn't wait to hear what the woman thought Camille might have decided. The garage was three levels of dark, dangerous territory, the perfect place to ambush a lone woman. Without another word he turned, and this time, he didn't just hurry, he ran flat out.

CAMILLE MOVED her car to a parking place on the first floor of the garage, but not as close to the elevator as she would like. In fact, it was in the corner farthest from the elevator. Still, it beat being in the upper tiers of the high-rise. She felt fairly comfortable being on ground level and clearly visible. At night it was way too dark and deserted on higher levels.

Will stayed with her as she waited for Alafair, who appeared about five minutes after she parked. He unloaded the box willingly and placed it in the trunk for her. And while Will stood nearby, Camille and Alafair chatted, but Charlie, the rambunctious grandson, made conversation difficult. Meanwhile, Camille was dying of curiosity about what she might find in the box. Unable to help herself, she opened it right from the trunk with Alafair at her elbow. Letters, she saw, or rather cards, lots and lots of greeting cards among other odds and ends, but mostly paper.

"Charlie!" Alafair grabbed the boy as a car cruised pass. "Are you trying to get hit by a car?" She gave Camille a helpless shrug.

"I can't have a conversation with him darting in and out of traffic. Even in a parking garage. We have to go."

"Thank you for bringing the box," Camille said.

"Glad to do it. And I hope your father will be okay. 'Bye now."

As Alafair drove off, Camille reached up to close the trunk lid, but the temptation was too great. She'd just take a little peek at one of the letters.

The first thing she picked up was a greeting card. Written on the envelope, *To My Sweetheart,* in flowery script. And inside, hearts and pink roses and fat little cupids. Camille frowned. Odd. When investigating Stephanie's murder, the Truth Project had been unable to find anyone who might be considered a romantic interest in her life. Camille's gaze shifted to the signature.

R.

She stood perfectly still, staring at the initial. Behind her, Will's radio squawked. Still focused on the *R,* she barely heard the exchange as Will and a dispatcher talked.

"Ms. St. James, I'm going to have to respond to this," Will said. "Some crazy in the ER is acting up. Probably a druggie. You want me to walk you back inside first?"

"No . . ." She was still holding the card, thinking. Without looking at Will, she moved her hand in vague dismissal. "No, you go ahead. Thanks."

"You sure?"

"Uh-huh." It was midmorning. People were coming and going everywhere. "I'll be okay."

She'd never taken her eyes off the card. But now she put it down and picked up another. This one a valentine. More hearts and flowers. A sappy verse. And the words *I love you,* scrawled in a masculine hand and signed, *R.*

R. Nothing more.

Fascinated now, she opened half a dozen cards. All were from the same person, Stephanie's lover, apparently. All gushed declarations of undying love. With lots of pretty explicit sexual innuendo. The woman had definitely been romantically involved with "R."

There were old bills and various business papers, but only a few letters, none from her lover. Most were from a grandmother Camille assumed was deceased, as the dates were long past. A few were from the sole relative in Detroit who'd disposed of her personal belongings.

But somehow reading Stephanie's personal cards and letters gave Camille an uneasy feeling. Was she invading the dead woman's privacy? Was her interest in the contents of this box legitimate in light of Luanne's murder? She knew in her heart the two were linked, and her qualms weren't enough to overcome her curiosity.

Next she turned up a small leather case. She recognized it as identical to one she used for her own hand-held recorder when she was in the field without her laptop. The batteries were probably too old, she thought, but she pushed Play anyway. She was not surprised when nothing happened.

Camille's recorder was in the glove compartment of her car, but as she was considering whether to try playing the tape on her own machine, she spotted an envelope from a photo processing lab. She set the recorder aside and opened the envelope, then turned to glance around the garage. She'd been so caught up in sifting through the box she'd almost forgotten where she was.

But there were still people coming and going and cars cruising slowly, for parking spaces.

Reassured, she propped herself against the trunk and pulled the prints out. She'd just take a minute, as she needed to get back to CCU. The first photo was Stephanie in a bikini, trendy sunglasses, and a wide-brimmed hat. She was standing at the controls of a blue, tricked-out pleasure craft docked at a pier. Blood Bayou, Camille guessed, and looked at the next shot. Stephanie again, same boat, same bikini. And again and again. A pretty, dark-haired woman with voluptuous curves smiling happily at the person taking the pictures.

"Must have been that sexy lover," Camille murmured. "Mr. R. Whoever."

She turned up the next print and her heart stopped. The person smiling into the camera was Ray Wyatt.

CHAPTER twenty-four

CAMILLE'S MOUTH DROPPED and her hands fell to her sides. Ray Wyatt was the mysterious "R"? Stephanie Hill's lover? Camille stared in space, trying to wrap her mind around that incredible fact. But one undeniable fact stared her in the face: Ray had joined the Truth Project team to work the Stephanie Hill case without revealing he'd been her lover. It had been Ray who volunteered to search for anybody with an intimate connection to Stephanie, and he claimed he found nothing.

Camille felt blindsided, beyond shock. The Truth team had been dazzled by Ray Wyatt. They'd considered having a veteran homicide cop from New Orleans a terrific asset. They'd rejoiced at his timely appearance to help gather evidence and free the man falsely accused of a brutal murder. Why would he do that?

She did not want to believe what she was thinking.

BECAUSE JACK had no idea where Camille's car was parked in the garage, he went first to the security office, hoping to find the guard who'd delivered her car keys. Hopefully that would be the same person who parked the car.

The office was empty. He stood in the doorway for an agitated moment, staring at the empty desk. Where was everyone, for Pete's sake? Frustrated and growing more anxious, he turned to leave and for the second time in ten minutes collided with a hospital worker. It was a janitor with a mop bucket on wheels. Neither of them went down, but the bucket was upended.

"Sorry," Jack muttered, steadying the elderly man. "I didn't see you."

"Okay, Reverend." The janitor grinned. "Looks like you're in a big hurry."

Jack set the bucket upright and pushed a hand through his hair. "I was looking for the security people."

"They're all in the ER." He began mopping the wet floor. "Big commotion over there. You never can tell if some wigged-out folk gone and pull a gun. They want drugs, you know."

Jack thanked him and hustled toward the ER. He was torn between going to the garage and tearing up and down the aisles looking for Camille or the more logical option—finding the guard who knew the location of her car. On the other hand, he only had the word of that nurse that she was going to the garage.

He decided to try calling her again. If he kept trying, she would have to pick up eventually. He reached to get his cell phone from the clip at his belt. Missing it, he looked down to check. The clip was gone. And so was his cell phone. He must have lost it in one of his two collisions. Without it, he wouldn't know if Camille was trying to call him. He turned his face up to the ceiling, wanting to howl in frustration.

He broke into a run but was forced to stop short at the ER. The entrance was blocked by two police cars, blue lights flashing. A dozen people had been removed from the waiting area and herded to a location the cops deemed safe until whatever was going down in the ER was over. Chances were he wouldn't be able to talk the cops into letting him go inside. At any rate, he couldn't take the time, and time was of the essence now.

Jack ground his teeth in frustration and escalating fear for Camille. He would have to search the parking garage without knowing where her car was parked. It would take a few minutes before a couple of BBPD cops would arrive to help, assuming Duval followed through on his promise. And if he had to search on his own, he'd need his gun. He blessed his decision not to turn it over to Raines.

STILL REELING at what she'd learned, Camille closed the trunk and hurried around to the driver's side. She climbed in behind the wheel, leaving the door open. Inside the glove compartment, she pushed aside a metal flashlight and pulled out her recorder, popped out a used tape, and substituted Stephanie's.

The first few minutes on the tape were of poor quality. It was business-oriented stuff, a group of people complaining about workplace rules. Maybe Stephanie considered it useful to record the meeting, intending to refer to it later. Disappointed, Camille was on the point of clicking it off when abruptly, a voice spoke loud and clear.

Stephanie Hill stated her name and the date, "This will be an attempt to record a conversation with NOPD Detective Ray Wyatt," she said into the microphone. "I suspect Ray committed arson and murder in his off-duty job as a land man buying property for investors." The tape went silent.

In a panic, Camille checked that it was still running. In seconds, talk began again, but it was difficult to hear, as if the machine was too far away from the subjects speaking. Camille adjusted the volume and recoiled in distaste upon hearing playful banter between lovers. In spite of the provocative remark about murder and arson, she had no stomach for listening to that. She started to shut it off, but suddenly the sound quality improved, as if the recorder had been moved. No more playful banter. Now it was simply two people talking normally.

Camille listened, transfixed. If this was pillow talk, it wasn't lover-like at all. The person being recorded would never knowingly have permitted it. On the tape, Stephanie was cleverly coaxing Ray Wyatt into admitting that he'd once set a fire that resulted in a man's death.

Camille was amazed at Stephanie's audacity. Had the woman not realized how risky it was to know Wyatt's deadly secret? Had she paid with her life for knowing it?

So utterly absorbed was Camille in the drama unfolding on the tape that she was taken by surprise when the passenger car door was suddenly jerked opened and Ray Wyatt slid into the seat.

"Whatcha' got there, *cher?*"

Fear slammed into her with deadly force. For three seconds, she was too stunned to scream. Or move. And in those precious, lost seconds, Wyatt pressed the blade of a knife to her throat.

Terrified, Camille strained against the seat back to escape the sting of the blade. "Ray! What—"

"Shhh." He touched her lips with one finger, then spoke in a conversational tone. "Sorry, babe. But in critical moments like these, I like a little privacy." Holding her terrified gaze with an evil smile, he leaned across her and closed the door. The tape recorder, which had fallen from her fingers to the floor, was still running. Wyatt's expression was amused as he listened to his own voice describing to Stephanie Hill in detail how he'd committed murder.

"*You* were Harlen's land man," Camille said in a shocked whisper.

"Harlen needed that property," Wyatt explained offhandedly. "But one old fool refused to sell. Stubborn as a mule. We had no choice."

"Harlen," she repeated. "Not my father."

"Nah, your daddy didn't want to know inconvenient details, but he's greedy, so he was happy to be an investor." With the knife still at her throat, he bent to pick up the recorder and shut it off.

"Enough of that. I'd leave it on for your enjoyment, but you won't get to use it, so what's the point? When they find you—if they ever do—you won't be able to tell what you heard." He was shaking his head regretfully. "I really didn't want to have to do this, Camille. But you just wouldn't quit."

Her eyes cut to the rearview mirror, where she could see people and cars coming and going.

"You looking for somebody to help, *cher*? Forget it. You have no chance to get out of this car alive."

"What are you going to do, Ray?" Terror made her voice quiver.

He sighed dramatically. "It's obvious, isn't it? I'm going to have to kill you."

Abject fear. She knew now what that meant. With his knife blade stinging her throat, she was so afraid she could hardly breathe. But her mind was racing along with her heart. Panic would not help her. She had to calm herself enough to think.

She had to stall him. She managed to control the tremor in her voice to ask, "It was you who killed Stephanie and Luanne, wasn't it?"

"Well, you finally got it." He made a sound with his tongue and teeth. "Dang, Camille, a couple times there, I thought for sure you'd figure it out. My good luck you got distracted with your ex."

She had to keep him talking. "I want to understand why, Ray," she told him. So long as he talked, she would stay alive.

"You heard it on the tape. Me and Stephanie had a good thing going. I thought I could trust her." He actually sounded hurt, but his voice hardened as he added, "But she's like every other woman on the planet. You give them a chance, they stab you in the back."

He was looking at Camille, but she didn't think he really saw her. In his head, he was somewhere else. Maybe he truly felt something for Stephanie. Not love, definitely not love, but something.

"I turned the world upside down looking for that tape," he said, shaking his head in disgust.

"How did you know there was a tape? Surely Stephanie didn't tell you she had it." However, Camille was thinking if the woman was reckless enough to record Wyatt admitting to murder, she just might be reckless enough to tell him for reasons of her own.

"She had a crazy idea to blackmail me," he said in disgust. "No woman tries that stuff with me and lives to tell it." He moved the knife blade against her throat. "After that I actually enjoyed killing her."

So much for thinking he might have loved Stephanie. "Did

you think Luanne might have the tape?" That would explain why he killed her.

"Nah, when it didn't turn up, I figured it never would. I thought that cousin of hers in Detroit had probably tossed it when she was clearing stuff out to sell the house." He winked at her, mocking. "Lucky you for finding it."

"But what about Luanne?" Camille said. "You didn't even know her—or did you?"

"Only through her old man. Like I said, we had business ties."

Business ties. His term for the dirty work he did for Harlen. She controlled a shudder. "If you didn't think Luanne had the tape, then why did you kill her, Ray? Did she know something?"

"That dingy broad? She didn't know diddly about nothing. No, babe, the reason you've had so much trouble trying to figure out why she was killed is because you never put all the pieces together—I mean, the crucial pieces." He moved the blade hideously close to her eye and began gently stroking her cheek. "See, it's like a puzzle. Now think. Why would some other Blood Bayou babe have to die?"

How could she think? She was so terrified that she could hardly breathe, let alone think. "I don't know, Ray," she managed to say. "Tell me."

"It was pretty cool." He relaxed suddenly and smiled, settling back a bit. Using the knife as an admonishing finger, he wagged it at her. "You're gonna be mad at yourself when you hear. It's simple, really."

She swallowed with relief that the knife wasn't at her throat or her eye. Though it hadn't stopped her teeth from chattering. She clamped her jaw to be able to say, "Simple?"

"Think. When you let Chester out of jail, another woman had to die so folks would think he was guilty of Stephanie's murder after all." Wyatt looked lovingly at the knife in his hand. "It could have been any woman. I mean, if Chester had been hired by your mother, she would have been the one to die."

She was horrified at the thought. The man was a psychopath. He was utterly without a conscience. How had she not seen it?

"As for ol' Chester, he practically invited his own downfall by coming back here in the first place." She tensed with terror as he leaned over and casually brushed her hair back from her ear with the knife blade. "After I killed her, I had Chester lined up to go inside the gate and do some yard work. I knew he'd find her." He looked evilly satisfied. "He did just what I thought he'd do. Ran over and tried to help. Stupid sap. Got her blood all over him."

"I think I understand," she said, trying not to watch as his thumb stroked across the business edge of the knife blade. "And then you made the anonymous call to BBPD."

"Cute, huh? You would have figured it out sooner or later, smart gal like you." He flashed another wicked grin. "To tell the truth, I was worried that you would before I could take you out."

She didn't need to ask if he was the one who crashed Jack's car in the bayou, but to keep him talking seemed her only chance of escape. "That must mean that it was you who tried to drown Jack and me in the bayou," she said.

"It was worth a try. I preferred getting to you at Madge's house, but I couldn't get past those monster dogs she keeps. I would have put a bullet through the one who chased me, but I was running and it put my aim off. So, in a way, you've forced my hand." He shrugged and added with macabre regret, "Now I have to do what I have to do."

"Ray, be reasonable," she said in a pleading tone. "You can't get away with this. Look around you. There are too many people."

"Not so much at the moment. Besides, there's nothing suspicious about two people sitting in a car. Trust me, nobody will have a clue."

Trust him? What an obscene thought. She tried another tack. "Jack is on his way right now. We were to meet in the garage."

"Liar, liar, pants on fire," he said softly, again wagging the knife horribly close to her face. "Jack is somewhere in the hospital tearing the place apart looking for you. Last I saw, he was at the ER. And in case you're thinking security guards, they're all busy looking for a bomb." He gave a satisfied smirk. "I needed to create a small diversion, give myself time to get to you and your daddy. I knew everybody would scramble down there. So, no security guards, no Jack, no help."

She almost cried out loud. Her father lay helpless in the CCU. After Wyatt murdered her, he'd go after Carson. And then, of course, Chester. She could not let him do this. But what could she do?

If Jack were here, he would say it was a good time to pray. But the thought of prayer was so new to her. So untried. Would God even listen to a person like her?

Please, God, tell me what I can do.

It was a plea sent in sheer desperation. And it didn't surprise her that no miraculous light suddenly broke over them. No guardian angel appeared on the hood of her car. She felt tears of despair welling in her eyes.

"It's show time, *cher*."

"Wait. Just tell me this, Ray." She had to keep him talking. "What happened to you? You're a police officer. You've spent your life protecting people. You have so much experience in catching criminals. Now you are one. Tell me what happened. I think you owe me that much."

She thought at first that he'd ignore her, but then he cocked his head, looking at her. "You can't guess? Money, Camille. I spent twenty-five years at NOPD and I've got a pension that barely puts gas in my truck. Harlen Richard paid me ten times that. He was a cash cow that was gonna keep on giving."

He paused and suddenly put the point of the knife under her chin with just enough force to sting slightly. "But you had to mess it up, Camille. Nothing to do but you had to spring Chester. It was over for you after that."

By the look in his eye, she realized he craved the sight of her blood. It was a terrifying thought. She wondered how long he'd be able to control that craving.

He gave a hitch of his chin. "So start the car now and let's cruise on out of here."

"The keys," she managed to say through a dry throat.

"What?"

"In my purse. On the floor."

He hesitated, giving her a sharp look, but then he took the blade away. "Get it."

Looking at him and moving cautiously, she bent and reached blindly for her purse. Once she had it, she unzipped it with shaking hands and fumbled through the contents in a search for the keys. In vain. "I can't find the keys, Ray."

"Don't be an idiot, Camille. I'm about out of patience." The first hint of irritation crept into his words. "Do what I tell you. Get the keys. Start the car."

She brought her hand up to protect her throat. "I'm serious. I think I must have left them in the trunk."

For a beat or two, real rage flickered in his eyes. "I want to see that purse!"

Moving gingerly, she held it out to him. Instead of taking it, he gave an impatient shake of his head. "Dump the contents on the dash."

She did as he ordered. A host of stuff littered the dash, but no keys. Her heart leaped. He had a problem.

He exploded in a violent burst of profanity. Camille shrank back as he raged. "You are so stupid! Just like a woman, walking off without her keys!" She flinched as he slammed the purse to the backseat and hit the dash hard with his fist. "I should slice you open right here and now! From day one you have been a gigantic pain in the rear!" He cursed again.

Camille watched warily, wondering if, instead of her purse or the dash, she'd be the object of his rage next. Would he kill her right here in the car? But finally he seemed to calm a fraction and rein in his temper. He drew a long, deep breath.

"Okay, here's the plan." Although still furious, he spoke in a controlled voice. "Crawl over the console. I want you to get out on this side. Then we both walk back there and get the freaking keys."

Crawl over the console? "Come on, Ray." She gave him look of disbelief.

"I mean it!" He slashed at her with the knife, missing her cheek by a hair. "Get over here!"

Terrified, Camille began the awkward transfer from the driver's seat to the passenger side? Anybody watching would probably assume they were lovers behaving inappropriately. It was a sickening thought.

Ray was out of the car when she reached the passenger seat. He motioned her out with a jerk of his head and the instant her feet touched ground, he was directly behind her, the knife point piercing the fabric of her shirt and pricking the soft flesh at her waist. Another spot where she would be bleeding. Worse, it would take only slight pressure to sink the knife fully into her and she would die.

"Don't try any tricks," he ordered in a menacing voice. "We're walking to the trunk, where you will remove the keys. You'll get back inside the car the way you got out, over the console. I'll be beside you. Start the car, back out, and drive out of the garage slowly. Do not mess with me, Camille. You will not live to tell it."

With the knife as a stinging reminder, she did exactly as told. But he took a big risk in letting her out of the car. Her mind raced frantically to come up with a way to use the chance that, somehow, had been given her. Was it God?

The space between her compact and the SUV parked next to her was a tight squeeze. But her eyes were busy, madly searching for help. How, she had yet to figure out. To anybody who might notice, there appeared nothing suspicious about them.

But there was no one in sight. This particular area was deserted, not even a moving car. She felt a wave of despair. Did everything work in this monster's favor? No. She remembered the keys. Leaving the keys in the trunk was a miracle. She needed another one.

JACK BURST into the garage as if the hounds of hell were chasing him and dashed to his car to get his gun. He gave a frantic look at the cars nearby on the off chance that Camille had parked in a clergy space, but there was no sign of her compact vehicle. He realized it would be dwarfed by larger vehicles anyway, meaning he'd have to check up and down every aisle. To quell the panic that raged in him, he breathed a heartfelt prayer.

Please, God, let me find her. Let her be unharmed.

He was convinced that Wyatt was in a state that psycho-pathic killers inevitably reach when bloodlust and panic over-come their cunning ability to function normally. He had to be approaching meltdown considering the events of the past twenty-four hours. Logic and caution would be beyond him. So, if he managed to get to Camille, he would surely not hesitate to kill her.

The thought was enough to send him in a dead run up the ramp where visitor parking began. Chest heaving, he stood sur-veying the sea of cars within his line of vision. No sign of Ca-mille. He forced himself to begin a methodical search.

CAMILLE, THINKING feverishly, delayed reaching for the keys hanging from the trunk lock. She realized that Wyatt could not kill her out here in plain sight. He needed to force her back into the car and drive to another location, taking the box and audio tape. A scream was her best option, maybe her only one. It would echo all over the cavernous garage, but would a scream push Wyatt over the edge? Would she live to run?

"Take the keys," he growled at her.

Her hands were shaking so hard she didn't know if she could pull them from the lock. Seeing her hesitation, Wyatt gave her an impatient nudge with his knee. The point of the blade pricked. She winced at the sting. More blood. It was effective in moving her. She pulled the keys out slowly, taking surreptitious looks in frantic hopes of seeing someone.

Please, God, please. Help me.

She looked at the keys in her hand and it occurred to her to simply drop them.

Wyatt cursed as they fell to the concrete and instead of ordering Camille to pick them up, he bent to do it. It was her chance. With a piercing scream, she darted away.

Camille's scream galvanized Jack as nothing else could. In one leap, he charged in that direction. At the first aisle, his gaze moved frantically, searching. Nothing was visible, but at the next, he thought he caught a flash of color. The barrier posed no problem. He took it in a broad jump that would have done credit to an Olympic athlete.

"Camille!" he yelled.

"Over here, Jack!"

Following the sound of her voice, Jack barreled up the incline just in time to see Camille darting between two parked cars with Ray Wyatt running after her. He would have her cornered, Jack realized. But he knew he would not be able to reach her before Wyatt.

"Don't come any closer, Jack!" Wyatt yelled. "I've got her."

Jack slowed to a walk, his heart slamming in his chest. Wyatt stood in the middle of the aisle with Camille in front of him. His left arm was tight around her waist. In his right hand, he held a knife at her throat.

"I said stop, Jack! I mean it!"

"I hear you, Wyatt." He spread his arms wide to appear submissive.

"We're leaving, Jack," Wyatt told him. "If you try anything, I'll kill her right here."

Camille was pale, eyes wide and terrified. Wyatt's wrist was blocking her airway. Jack heard the raw sound as she struggled for air. In a controlled, reasonable tone, he said, "Wyatt, Camille can't breathe. Ease up, okay?"

"You stay back, I'll ease up."

Jack trembled with the effort of holding back. He wanted to charge forward, hurl himself at Wyatt, tear him from limb to limb, crush him. He struggled to control the rage in his heart and the terror pulsing in his head. He spoke again, his voice low and nonthreatening. "You don't want to hurt Camille, Wyatt. She's a friend. She has done you no harm."

Wyatt gave a derisive snort. "No harm? Digging into murder cases that were best left alone did me no harm? She's been nothing but harm!"

"Okay, okay." Jack put up both hands, palms out, and took another step. He knew Camille's eyes were on him, but he didn't look at her. Couldn't look at her now. "Let's stop and think, Wyatt. What will you gain by hurting her?"

"I'm using her to get out of here. Then I'm leaving this miserable place."

"Don't you have a problem? You're in a parking garage. You can't get out. The place is crawling with cops."

"They're preoccupied. As I planned." He began dragging Camille back to the car. Needing to gauge distance, he took a quick glance behind him. Giving Jack a chance to move forward. Still, it was not enough. He met Camille's eyes then and realized she was trying to give him a message.

"Wyatt, I don't think Camille can breathe. You'll have to ease up or she won't be able to make it to the car."

Wyatt's laugh was short. "Oh, yeah, thank you for that helpful advice, Jack. Must be the preacher in you."

Camille made a thin, helpless-sounding cry and went limp. Wyatt made a wild grab for her as her body began to sink to the ground. But as she was a boneless, dead weight, he couldn't keep her upright.

Wyatt's distraction gave Jack the chance he needed. He sprang forward as Camille scrambled on her hands and knees out of Wyatt's reach. Without his hostage, the detective gave an enraged bellow and came at Jack with the knife. Jack pivoted sideways as the blade slipped past, missing his belly by a hair. Off balance from the lunge, Wyatt's arms flailed wildly as he tried to stay on his feet. Jack seized the man's wrist and twisted with all his might. The knife fell to the ground.

Camille scrambled from behind a car and scooped it up. She had it in her hand when Jack yelled "Run, Camille!" She ignored him and slung the knife in a tall arc over half a dozen parked cars.

Wyatt pulled away, then charged Jack again, but Jack sidestepped before Wyatt could grab him. Jack threw all his weight into a hard punch to the man's kidneys. Wyatt staggered but didn't go down. He turned and charged Jack again. But, weakened by the punch, Wyatt was slower and more awkward. Jack hit him solidly on the jaw. The man's head snapped back. Wyatt was stunned but didn't go down. Jack threw a hook that caught Wyatt on the left eye. Jack followed with a hard punch in his stomach.

Wyatt was up again and rushing him. Jack prepared to meet the full force of the attack. The two men went down in a wild tangle of arms and legs. Camille dashed to her car and rifled through the glove compartment. Moments later she returned carrying a long metal flashlight.

Jack and Wyatt were now upright, locked in a ferocious battle. Wyatt pulled away and Jack planted a fist in the man's stomach, but it failed to take him out. Wyatt responded with a blow that glanced off Jack's nose. Blood spurted and poured down his face.

"Get out of here, Camille!"

Jack's two-second distraction gave Wyatt a chance to cock a foot back ready to kick him. Camille rushed forward with the flashlight raised high and brought it down on Wyatt's head with all her might. It landed with a loud *cr-r-raa-ck*. The detective went down like a felled tree.

In a flash, Jack had his belt off using it to bind Wyatt's wrists. That done, he stood up, his chest heaving, and gave Camille a fierce frown. "I told you to get out of here."

"And leave you to be killed?" she said with hands on her hips.

He swiped at his nose and came away with a bloody hand. "How?" He removed a handkerchief and pressed to his nose, he added, "If you noticed, he didn't have the knife anymore."

"But he might have picked it up again, so I threw it down there somewhere." She waved an arm to show him, but her voice had begun to shake. She opened her mouth to say something else, but instead her face crumpled like a little kid whose puppy had been run over.

"Come here." He drew her up close and pressed her head to his chest.

"He's the killer, Jack. He was going to kill me. He told me he was going to kill me."

"I know."

"And Dad and Chester. He's a monster."

"Yeah." He stroked her hair while trying to stifle the rage still roiling inside him. "But he underestimated my girl," Jack said, hugging her a little tighter. "Clever of you to faint."

She was still trembling but managed to straighten her spine. "I did not faint. I pretended to faint."

He knew that, but getting a rise out of her was a tactic to chase away her fear. "But the best part was when you beaned him with that flashlight."

"I wanted a baseball bat," she said grimly, "but there wasn't one handy."

Amazingly, he found he could laugh. It was weak, but it was a laugh. And he was relieved that Camille's voice had lost some of its tremor too, so hopefully the terror of her ordeal was fading.

"But promise me the next time we're in a situation like that, you'll leave when I tell you."

"Here's what I promise: I promise never to get in another situation like that." Then, drawing a long, shaky breath, she pushed away. He knew by the way she refused to look at him that she suddenly remembered how—and why—they'd parted last night. In the first rush of relief after a terrifying ordeal, she'd turned to him. But she was still angry. He was anxious to deal with that, but would she give him a chance?

That was when he saw a trail of blood running down her throat. "You're bleeding! He hurt you!"

She touched the soft flesh under her chin. "He couldn't resist using that knife; just a little prick here and a little prick there. It's nothing really." But when she glanced at the blood on her fingers, her tummy took a little tumble. She had come very close to dying.

Jack thrust his own bloody handkerchief into her hands. "I'll kill him. I swear I'll kill him." He skewered Wyatt with a fierce look. The man had regained consciousness. "You'd better hope they lock you up somewhere far from here, Wyatt."

In spite of getting the worst of their fight, Wyatt was defiant. "Give me another five minutes and I'd have cut her up a lot worse."

Camille restrained Jack with a hand on his arm. "Don't, Jack. He'd like nothing more than to provoke you into doing something that might be a blot on your name. Don't give him the satisfaction."

But Wyatt wasn't done taunting Jack. "It ain't over yet, preacher. I've got friends, so you better watch your back. And that includes your sweetie," he added with a hitch of his chin at Camille.

"It is over, Wyatt," Jack replied. "And you'd do well to watch your mouth now." If Raines didn't show up soon, the way he was feeling, he didn't know if he could keep from resorting to behavior unbecoming to a minister, no matter what the damage to his reputation.

The eyes of both men were locked in grim combat as two black-and-whites hurtled into the garage entrance with sirens screaming and screeched to a stop beside Jack and Camille.

"At last, the Keystone Cops," Camille murmured.

Jack grunted as Chief Raines stepped out of the car. He was glad to see him, but it was only by the grace of God that they weren't too late.

With an officious nod of his head, Raines directed two cops to Wyatt. "Cuff him and put him in the car," he ordered, then turned to Jack.

But before he spoke, Jack reached behind him and pulled a gun from his waistband. Holding it by the barrel, he handed it to Raines.

"What's this?"

"A gun, June. I'm turning it in. Officially."

Raines' eyebrow rose skeptically. "A little late, isn't it?"

Camille, who'd been standing back with uncustomary reticence, made a squeaking noise and stepped up to Jack. "You had a gun all this time and you didn't think to use it when Ray had a knife at my throat?"

"I did. But I couldn't take a chance that he wouldn't freak out and use the knife before I had a chance to pull the trigger. He knew his game was over, but he hated you enough to take you with him."

"Would you have pulled the trigger?" she asked.

"In a heartbeat."

"A moot point," Raines said. "It is illegal for you to have a gun in your possession, being a convicted felon and all." He studied his nails. "Good thing you turned it in a few years ago."

Camille couldn't believe the way BBPD did business. Starting at the top. But this time she wasn't in a mood to quibble. She handed Raines her car keys. "There's a tape in my recorder and a box of evidence in the trunk of my car," she told him. "It's information you'll need to build your case against Wyatt."

"Why, thank you, Ms. St. James."

"Please drop my keys off at the hospital information desk," she said. "I'll pick them up when I leave tonight."

"It'll be my pleasure," the chief said.

Jack and Raines watched Camille stalk off toward her car. When Jack took a step to join her, Raines put out a hand and stopped him.

"Sorry I didn't get here in time to stop Wyatt before he got to Camille." He gave a helpless shrug. "Your message came into the station and was passed to my new deputy chief, who passed it to Duval, but it took awhile. Even if my deputy didn't know you, you'd think any citizen in jeopardy on hospital grounds would have built a fire under him." He shook his head. "Maybe I'm expecting too much." He paused a moment, then, "I owe you one, Jack." He sent a glance toward Camille, rummaging in her car. "I never thought I'd be saying anything like this, but your lady has some fine investigative instincts. I guess I should have paid more attention."

"He would have killed her, June." Jack took another step toward Camille. And again the chief stopped him.

"Hold on," Raines said. "I never got a statement from you and Camille after the incident at Harlen Richard's house. That makes two statements you owe me now. When do you think it would be convenient to drop by and take care of that?"

"Can't it wait, June? Camille's dad is in CCU at death's door. I have to stay with her. We'll try to get around to the department as soon as he's out of the woods."

"Of course, of course," Raines said, smoothing his mustache.

"We're here to protect and serve, apparently at your convenience."

Jack chuckled. "Thanks, June."

Before Raines changed his mind again, Jack strode to Camille's car. "I'm going up to CCU with you," he said.

"Okay," she said coolly. "Maybe they can clean that blood off your face. I don't want to look at it while you explain where you were last night."

CHAPTER twenty-five

CAMILLE FOUND HER father awake in CCU but agitated and uncomfortable. His anxiety was greatly relieved when he realized that Camille was safe, that Wyatt was in custody and no longer a threat to her or anyone else. She stayed at his bedside for the allowable quarter hour, but after a few minutes he drifted off to sleep. Ben, his nurse, assured her that restful sleep was the best thing for him.

He walked with her out of earshot of his patient. "Since coming out from under the anesthetic, Carson has been too worried about you to be able to get the kind of rest he needs. Pain meds put him under briefly, but he fought it. Not a good thing."

"I'm going to stay with him until he's out of the woods," she said.

"That's up to you but not necessary now," Ben assured her. "He won't even know. Now that his mind is at rest, he'll be out for several hours."

"I'm staying anyway."

"No offense, Ms. St. James, you look like you could use a few hours sleep yourself." Ben glanced beyond her to Jack. "Can you talk her into going home and getting some rest?"

Jack shrugged.

"I can sleep here as well as anywhere," she said.

Ben lifted one eyebrow. "On those chairs out there?"

"You should heed good advice," Jack said. Standing behind her, he put his hands on her shoulders and began massaging her.

She froze at the touch of his hands, and then in spite of the fact that his fingers had homed right in to the worst of her aching muscles, she shook him off and turned to Ben. "Thank you for the wonderful care you're giving my dad," she said, handing him a card from her purse. "If anything happens, anything, here's my cell phone number. Call me, please."

"I will," Ben said. "Now, you get some rest."

Jack followed her as she left CCU. "Let me drive you to Madge's house," he said. "She'll be off at eleven and even though you won't need security anymore, you won't be alone. I could use the time to explain myself. I guess my note wasn't clear."

"All I know is I came back to the waiting room and you were gone. Out of simple courtesy, you could have told me . . . What note? I never got a note."

They were at the elevator. The doors opened to reveal an orderly with a bedridden patient. Jack and Camille stepped inside, she nodding politely. Jack was uncharacteristically mute. She gave him a quick glance. He seemed shocked, but neither spoke as the elevator started up. "We're going up, not down."

The elevator stopped on the next floor and the orderly wheeled his patient out. When the doors closed, Jack pushed the button for the ground floor before Camille had a chance and then rushed into speech. "I left a note, Camille. I gave it to Mr. Blanchard, who promised he'd see that you got it."

"I don't know anything about that." She watched the light on the elevator indicating floor levels and then remembered. "Was that the elderly couple in the waiting room?"

"Yes. When I got voice mail on your phone, I left a note using the back of your note. I couldn't find any paper. I let Blanchard know it was important that you got the note." He was frowning. "I'm surprised he forgot. He seemed reliable."

"Their son died."

"What?"

"I got back from filling out those papers and a doctor was with them. From the way they reacted, I think he was giving them the bad news just as I walked in. They left a few minutes later."

Jack pressed a hand to the back of his neck. "Well, that explains a lot."

"Not to me."

The elevator doors opened, and Jack followed Camille out and across the lobby. "If you won't let me drive you home," he said, speaking in a low, intense tone, "will you let me follow you in my car to Madge's house? I need just a few minutes to tell you what happened, why I had to leave. You have to know I wouldn't be so thoughtless as to walk off without a word if I didn't have a good reason."

MADGE'S DOGS were ecstatic at the arrival of two favorite people. After they both greeted them, Camille suggested going out on the back porch to hear what Jack had to say. She wasn't feeling particularly hospitable and the mosquitoes would probably feast on them. That would keep his explanation short.

Jack must have had the same notion. He turned on the ceiling fan. "It should keep mosquitoes from eating us alive," he said.

She went straight to the swing and sat down, her gaze turning naturally to the bayou. Night sounds abounded, crickets, the low hoot of an owl, and her favorite—a bullfrog's croak. While she looked, a fish broke the surface of the water, leaving an ever-widening ring. She understood why some people chose to live on the bayou. It was peaceful and serene. Sometimes.

Jack stood at the porch rail, hands in his pockets. Something about his profile as he looked out at the bayou stirred emotions she needed to resist. Would she ever be able to do that? she wondered. In spite of their troubled history, in spite of the reasons she now believed they were ill suited, she still found Jack deeply appealing. And in spite of everything, she still loved him. Why was love so perverse?

"How did you find me today?" she asked. If it hadn't been for Jack, she would surely have been Wyatt's next victim. She owed him for that.

He turned to look at her, letting his eyes roam over her face. "Carson came out of the anesthetic talking about Wyatt being the killer. You needed to be told, but I couldn't find you anywhere. Finally, a nurse said that you might be in the garage. I'd just entered the first floor when you screamed. If you hadn't, I don't know how long it would have taken me to find you."

"You saved my life and I'm grateful. But it doesn't change anything about last night when you left me alone at the hospital."

He crossed the porch and took a chair facing her. "I need to explain why I had to leave you, Camille."

"I'm guessing it has to do with your church. Your life is your ministry. I was right to worry that I'd be woefully inadequate I'd be as a minister's wife. What it boils down to is this: You can't be happy without your ministry. You can't even be whole without it. So when your personal life conflicts, you're going to choose your calling every time. And that's as it should be. I was unprepared for such a holy commitment."

"It wasn't my church."

But she didn't hear him. She was caught up in her own angst. "I was scared to death, Jack. Can you understand that? My dad might be dying. I needed you. And poof! You were gone. A good minister's wife would know and accept that."

"It wasn't just that I was needed elsewhere," he told her in a pleading tone. "David Bergeron needed me."

"David Bergeron?"

"Yes, that's what I've been trying to tell you."

"Do you mean the David Bergeron that you—" She stopped. "David, who is now a quadriplegic? That David?"

"He's been at Sojourner House for several years. It's a rehabilitation facility."

"I know what Sojourner House is. I didn't know that David was there." She studied his face in the soft darkness and saw sadness and regret and guilt. "Well. Now I understand why you have such a strong commitment to the place."

"Not to the place, Camille, but to the people. And especially to David."

Penance, she thought.

"You'll find this hard to believe, but David and I became friends. We pretty much had a standing date at Sojourner."

"You and David are friends?" She couldn't hide her astonishment.

"It took awhile. He was an angry, difficult patient. He wanted to die." He glanced up at her. "I did too, every time I looked at him."

He wasn't alone there. She had struggled with her part in the tragedy of David Bergeron. It haunted her that she'd set his appointment on a weekend afternoon, knowing Jack would likely be drunk. Anything could happen when Jack was drunk. She, better than anyone, knew that. And yet she'd arranged for David to come over.

Jack let his gaze drift again to the still, dark bayou. When he spoke, it was in a distant voice. "We had a lot in common, David and I. He came from an alcoholic father and a mother who was bipolar and addicted to drugs. Like me, he didn't have much guidance as a kid. But, unlike me, he didn't fall into the trap of addiction. He focused on making something of himself. He knew the road his father took was wrong and he had the grit to resist it."

"When I met him," Camille said softly, "he'd already aced high school. He wanted to get a leg up on a couple of college courses. His ultimate aim was law school. He had such a promising future."

"And I demolished it." Jack pushed up from his chair, his eyes tortured. "I will never be able to forget that. The price David paid for my reckless stupidity will always be with me." He drew in a long, unsteady breath. "It was after I got out of prison and finished seminary that I realized I might make a difference for other young people with catastrophic injuries. It was one small way I could try to make amends."

"I understand now how you were familiar with that back road when we crashed into the bayou."

"Yeah. Sojourner is not far from there. I should have told you the reason behind my commitment to the organization and to David. I don't know why I didn't. I'm sorry."

"Water under the bridge now, Jack." She wasn't going to let him load her up on guilt. His hands gripped the railing hard.

"I had to go last night because David was asking for me."

"You don't have to explain anything. Really. I absolutely understand."

He didn't seem to hear her. "I wish you could have known him, Camille. He loved video games and he played brilliantly. He beat me almost every time. And NASCAR. He was passionate about NASCAR. I promised to take him one day." His voice, low and unsteady, shook a little. "But he never got strong enough to go."

She was touched in spite of herself. Only the hardest of hearts could doubt he was in pain. "How were you able to bear that?" she asked.

"He's been plagued with infections, pneumonia, bedsores. Quadriplegics have so many health problems." He looked off in the distance, frowning. "You wonder how they don't go crazy. I probably would."

She wanted to speak a word of sympathy but couldn't form the sentence. She hardly knew what she felt.

He cleared his throat. "Lately, his kidneys began to fail."

Her eyes narrowed. "So, last night, did you have to go because—"

"Because Angela called and said David was asking for me." Jack turned then, forcing himself to look at her when he told her. "He was dying."

Camille's lips parted soundlessly.

"He was so incredible," Jack said softly, as if seeing it all again. "Tough and brave and funny, and just so sick. He was barely able to breathe and he was still joking."

Listening, Camille had both hands pressed to her lips.

"He died early this morning."

"Oh . . ." Her eyes filled so that Jack's profile blurred against the moonless night.

"He wanted to know what Heaven was like. He asked me to tell him." Jack gave a short, bleak laugh. "Like I, of all people, would know."

"What did you say?"

"I promised in Heaven he'd be strong and whole and able to do whatever his heart desired."

She stood and, because she couldn't stop herself, went to him and slipped her arms around him. No matter their differences, this was a tragedy they shared. Jack reacted by clutching her close against him. With her cheek resting at his heart, she murmured, "I'm so sorry. It must have been so hard for you. And I made it worse. You should have told me, Jack."

"Yes, I should have, not last night, but long before now. And last night, instead of a note that could go awry, I should have found a way to be sure you knew." His voice was broken. "When I got back to the hospital and you were nowhere to be found," he said with his face buried in her hair, "I was afraid that God was going to take you away from me too."

"I'm not an expert in this faith thing. But I don't believe God works like that."

"I've never been as terrified as when Wyatt had that knife at your throat."

Something that had been a hard and tight knot around her heart eased. She took in an unsteady breath and spoke softly, "I needed a guardian angel and you appeared."

"I'm no angel," he told her. "I've made so many mistakes and hurt so many people it's a miracle I'm even allowed to go inside a church. Let alone pastor one."

"And I'm so selfish and self-centered it's a miracle that I'd think for a minute I could be a pastor's wife."

He went as still as the bayou before a storm. Leaning back to get a look at her face, he said, "Sometimes I don't work on my sermons until Saturday."

She was smiling faintly. "When I lose my temper, I sometimes swear."

He began to look amused. "The organist has no talent, but I lie and tell her she's great."

She flicked a little speck off the front of his T-shirt. "I have a problem with jealousy."

He regarded her blankly.

She pushed completely out of his embrace and walked to the porch railing. Turning to look at him, she said, "I heard that you have a special fondness for the woman who runs Sojourner House."

"Angela." Really enjoying himself now, he moved a little closer. "It's true, I do."

"So if there was a man I had a special fondness for, wouldn't you be a little jealous?"

"If he was as old as Angela, no."

She tilted her head, eyes narrowed. "Which is?"

"Probably about sixty-two."

Her eyes widened. "Is that the truth?"

"Enough of this." He reached out and hauled her into his arms, holding her as if he'd never let her go. "We might be flawed in a few ways because we're human, but we're perfect for each other. And you will be perfect as a pastor's wife."

"I have a long way to go, Jack. You'll have to help me, guide me. I'll be a total screw-up many times, but I promise I won't have another meltdown like I did last night." She reached up and touched his cheek. "And you have to promise you'll tell me the important stuff as it relates to us. Your commitment to Sojourner House would definitely fall into that category. Don't shut me out, Jack."

"I promise." They stood swaying, both marveling over the wondrous end to this incredible day. His lips brushed her hair and his voice grew gruff with emotion. "I'm going to make you so happy."

Her lips tipped up at the corners. "I know. I'm looking forward to that."

He drew back to look at her. "Does that mean you will marry me again? I mean, eventually, when you're comfortable with who I am and what you'll have to take on to be my wife and when you've worked your way through your own faith journey. Will you marry me then?"

She gave a careless lift of her shoulders. "That's the only way we can have children, isn't it?"

For a second, he seemed almost unable to breathe. She saw in his eyes a mother lode of emotion: joy, amazement, disbelief, gratitude.

"How many would you like?" he finally managed to say.

"As many as the angels see fit to give us."

With joy in her heart, she let him gather her close as a new moon broke through the clouds above the bayou. "How long do we have to wait?"

"Depends," she laughed softly. "Do you know a good preacher?"

About the Author

Karen Young, with more than 10 million books in print, is the *USA Today*–bestselling author of 34 novels. She is known as a spellbinding storyteller who writes with sensitivity about issues facing contemporary women. She has been nominated three times for the Romance Writers of America Rita, which she won in 1993 for *The Silence of Midnight*.

It is her belief that good inspirational fiction is not about simply adding a religious component to a book—it is so much more. In many novels, the elements of spirituality and faith are mostly absent in characters facing life's inevitable pitfalls. Karen believes that showing her characters' faith journey, in addition to the physical, intellectual, and emotional aspects of their lives, enhances and adds meaningful depth to her books.

Karen lives in Texas. She loves to hear from her readers, and you can learn more by visiting her website: www.Author KarenYoung.com.

MISSING: MAX

by
KAREN YOUNG

Enjoy this excerpt from Karen Young's next novel,
Missing: Max—available spring 2010.

CHAPTER ONE

SOME PEOPLE, JANE Madison had often heard, have premonitions about calamity before it strikes. But Jane would later recall that she'd felt only irritation when her cell phone rang as she stood in line waiting for fast food. In fact, she decided to ignore the call when she saw it was Melanie. Her stepdaughter probably wanted to change her order, but after standing for more than twenty minutes in line, Jane was finally next, so changing was not an option.

The teenager ahead of her turned suddenly, loaded down with multiple orders of fried shrimp, calamari, and beer, and nearly crashed into her. Not for the first time that day, Jane wished she were elsewhere. Ordinarily, she gave a pass to Mardi Gras Day in New Orleans, but Melanie was at the age to be enthralled by the uninhibited and often near-depraved behavior all too common at the event. So Jane had reluctantly agreed to take her, even though it meant having to take Max.

The other possibility for Melanie's call was that Max was awake. If he was, Christine would know what to do. Having her best friend along made the day a bit more tolerable for Jane.

It was because of eight-month-old Max that Jane would have preferred skipping the parades that began midmorning on Mardi Gras Day and lasted until midnight. They would head home long before festivities ended, of course, but until then, she would just have to make the best of it. Teething had made Max cranky and restless lately, but so far he'd been surprisingly docile, just watching the goings-on around him from his stroller. Kyle, of course, had been unavailable to take his daughter to the parades even though he'd promised he would. Work intervened, as it did so often with Kyle . . . even on holidays.

Her cell phone rang again. Apparently, Melanie wasn't giving up. Now loaded down with two large bags and three soft drinks, Jane looked around for a place to set everything down, but there was nothing, just hordes of people, literally a crush of humanity. Grumbling, she turned back to the vendor's cart and with a murmured apology transferred the load to his counter and fumbled to click her phone free of her purse. Sometimes Melanie could try the patience of a saint. "What is it, Melanie?"

"Mom, Max is gone!" the girl cried. "You've got to get back here! He was asleep in his stroller a minute ago and now he's disappeared!"

Jane shifted to allow an impatient customer access to the vendor's condiments. "What do you mean, he's gone?"

"Just that! Didn't you hear me? He's disappeared." Melanie's voice caught on a sob. "Hurry! We've looked everywhere, but there are so many people!"

"How could he be gone?" She was used to Melanie overreacting. Even the girl's friends called her a drama queen. "Let me talk to Christine."

"She's not here. A lady fainted and she went into the hotel lobby to help and Julie and Anne-Marie were here and we were talking and Max was in his stroller under the balcony just where you left him and then he was gone!" She drew a shaky breath. "Mom, I'm so scared."

"Christine didn't take him with her?"

"No, no! Listen to me!" Melanie's voice went up another notch. "I'm serious, Mom. He's gone. Someone took him and his stroller and everything!"

Jane felt the first real stirrings of alarm. "Don't leave," she ordered. "Stay where you are, Mellie. And don't hang up. I'm on my way." Food forgotten, Jane hurriedly headed back the way she'd come. As she plowed through the crowd, people took one look at her face and shifted out of her path.

"I can't just stand here and wait, Mom!" Melanie said in a shaky voice in Jane's ear. "We're going to Jackson Square."

"Jackson—why?"

"Don't you remember? We saw some policemen there when we were trying to find a place to— Never mind, Mom, I'm going there. I have to hurry!"

Jane barely managed to avoid crashing into a man outfitted in Native American garb, complete with a full feather headdress. Considering some of the bizarre costumes she'd seen today, his was almost tame. With a muttered apology, she stepped around him, keeping the phone pressed to her ear. "Don't go any further until I get to you, Melanie."

"There's a cop on a horse! I'm going over."

"Okay, but don't hang up," Jane ordered. Police officers mounted on horses were able to push through the crowds. And they were easy to spot. "When you reach him, stay there."

Melanie gulped and burst into wild sobs. "Mom, I don't know how it happened! We were all just watching the floats and—"

"Just calm down, Mellie. You can tell me when I get there." Surely there was a logical explanation. Babies didn't just vanish, although in a teeming crowd, it would surely be easier than— She stopped herself. She would not go there. She would not think the unthinkable. "Can you see Christine?"

"Not really. I told you, she went into the lobby. I mean, I saw the EMT's trying to get through. The lady who fainted is inside and so is Ms. Christine."

Christine was the practice manager for a team of internists. Although she'd had no formal training as a nurse, she would certainly know what to do if someone fainted. "I can see the EMT unit now, Mellie. I'm going to stop and talk to Christine just to be sure she didn't take the stroller."

"We saw her run over to the lady, Mom! She didn't take Max."

"I'll just double-check."

The sidewalk was choked with people, but Jane finally reached the hotel where the EMT ambulance was now loading the woman inside. Spotting Christine, Jane tried forcing her way through the crowd, but she was quickly blocked by a policeman.

"Ma'am. You'll have to stay back and let these people do their jobs."

"I understand, but I have to talk to—"

"I'm sorry, but you can't talk to anyone just now."

Jane craned her neck to look around him and managed to catch Christine's eye.

Christine's gaze went wide with surprise. "Jane. What is it? What's wrong?"

"Did you take Max with you?" Jane called over the cop's shoulder.

Christine looked confused. "Max? No. What—"

"He's gone. Watch for him or his stroller. And call my cell when you're done here. I've got to go." Then, to the policeman, "Please alert the police. Now. Tell them my baby has disappeared."

Without checking to see whether the cop responded, Jane surveyed the sidewalk fronting the hotel where she'd left Melanie with Max. It was still choked with people cheering madly as the parade floats lumbered past. She looked about anxiously. There was no sign of Max or his stroller.

She put a hand to her heart and breathed a fervent prayer. *Please, God, don't let this be happening.*

Turning, she headed in a rush toward Jackson Square, a full block away. As she pushed through the reveling crowd, she told herself that Melanie's reaction was typical teenage hysteria. Still, there was a sick feeling in her stomach. The possibility that Max really had disappeared was simply too frightening to be real.

Finally, she reached Jackson Square. In spite of the fact that she was still connected to Melanie on the cell phone, she wasn't able to find her right away in the people milling about. She drew a desperate breath. How would she find Melanie in this crowd? Above her, the three tall spires of the St. Louis Cathedral reached high in a sky that was so clear and blue that it almost hurt to look at it. Again, she breathed a prayer. Where was Melanie? Then, there she was, standing on the steps of the cathedral speaking frantically to three uniformed policemen.

Thank you. Thank you.

One cop held the reins of a horse, which stood patiently, unfazed by the rowdy crowd. Melanie's friends hovered near her, looking frightened. As Jane approached, she could see that

Melanie was crying, gesturing with her hands as she talked while her eyes anxiously scanned the area. Jane's hope that this was all a mistake faded. Down the block on Bourbon Street, floats lumbered past, but in the parklike square, choked with hundreds of people, how would they be able to find a baby, even in a stroller?

Like Melanie, her frantic gaze swept up and down the thronged square. But there were so many people, so much confusion. Shops were closed, sidewalks jammed. Streets leading off the square were blocked off to accommodate the crowds. Balconies groaned with the weight of people lucky enough to have access to a balcony. There was an occasional stroller, Jane noted, but none was a familiar blue with yellow plaid trim. With her heart beating frantically in her chest, she approached Melanie and the cops, two men and—she saw now—one woman.

"I'm here," she said, as Melanie launched herself into Jane's arms. Looking over the girl's head, she asked, "What happened? Where is my baby?"

The policewoman spoke. "Are you Mrs. Madison?"

"Yes, yes."

"Mom, I've told them we shouldn't waste time talking! We need to be looking for Max!"

Jane caught Melanie's arms and angled back enough to see her face. "Mellie, be calm for a moment. Please. Let me talk to these people."

"I'm Officer Cox, Mrs. Madison," the woman said, extending her hand. Jane shook it, nodding mutely. "We've talked to Melanie trying to get details of exactly what happened. Maybe there's a logical explanation. She tells us that there was another adult—"

"Christine O'Brian," Jane said, nodding. "I just spoke to her. She's over there with the EMT's and the woman who collapsed. She didn't take Max with her."

"And there was no one else with you today? No one who might have felt it okay to take the baby?"

"Without asking me?" Jane stared at her. "No, of course not."

Cox pulled out a small memo pad. "And how old is the baby?" she asked, pen poised.

"Eight months. He has b-blue eyes and blond hair." Jane swallowed, struggling to keep calm. "He's wearing a red shirt and denim overalls. White sneakers. He's in a stroller. Navy blue and yellow plaid."

"Could he have crawled out of it?"

"He couldn't have climbed out on his own. He—" She turned to Melanie. "Max wasn't out of his stroller, was he?"

Melanie's face crumpled. "No, he was asleep. Just the way he was when you l-left him with m-me, M-Mom." She pressed the fingers of both hands against her lips. "I'm so scared, Mom!"

"We'll find him, Mellie." Jane squeezed the girl's shoulders gently before turning back to the cop. "Have you alerted other policemen? Is someone looking? How could a baby in a stroller just disappear?" But even as she asked the question, she knew the answer. The stroller didn't just disappear. Somebody had been watching and when Christine left Melanie in charge, the teenager had become distracted by the parade and the sheer frenzy of Mardi Gras. Someone had seized the moment to take her baby.

That was the moment when Jane's concern escalated into real terror.

"I've alerted the units in the area, Mrs. Madison," Officer Cox said, touching the radio attached to her belt. "We're sending out a B.O.L.O."

"B.O.L.O?"

"It means be on the lookout." She spoke briskly into her radio and received a squawked response that was unintelligible to Jane.

As they stood isolated by the trauma of a missing child, people milled about enjoying Mardi Gras. Some were in costume, others not. Many drank from open beverages, which was allowed in New Orleans. Some were drunk, but most were simply reveling in the abandoned spirit of the holiday. Jane's gaze strayed beyond Jackson Square where the river formed the east boundary of the French Quarter. Kidnapping a child on a day meant for celebration seemed obscene. While mingling with the crowd that day, had she looked into the face of the person who'd taken Max?

"Approximately how long has it been since you actually saw the baby, Mrs. Madison?"

Jane struggled to focus. "Twenty—maybe thirty minutes, no longer. I left to get food." She looked at Melanie. "How long after I left did Christine leave to help the woman, Mellie?"

"I don't know. Pretty soon, I guess. You weren't even out of sight."

"Meaning it could be as long as thirty minutes, give or take," Officer Cox said. Without stating the obvious, both knew a person could travel half a mile in that much time. Even in this crowd.

"We've got to find him!" Jane felt panic rising in her chest, heard it in her voice. She stopped, drew a breath to try and collect herself. With her hand on her heart, she spoke again. "I'm sorry. This is just . . . so— It can't be happening!"

"Please. Come with me." Cox caught Jane's arm and guided her toward the cathedral. "We'll be able to talk away from the crowd." She turned to Melanie. "Come with us, Melanie."

"I know you're frantic with worry," Officer Cox said as they headed for the steps of the cathedral, "but there are literally hundreds of uniformed policemen on duty today and all have been alerted. They'll be looking for the stroller you've described. If they spot one like it, they'll stop and check. They'll call me. Meanwhile, let's try to reconstruct what happened. There could be a very logical explanation."

"Like what!" Jane cried.

"Someone could have wheeled it away by mistake. Many of these strollers look alike." The possibility was so ludicrous that Jane didn't bother contradicting her. No parent on the planet accidentally claims a stroller with a strange baby in it.

Jane's cell phone, still in her hand, rang. Hope bloomed in her chest. Maybe, just maybe—"Hello!"

"It's Christine. Where are you?"

"At Jackson Square. Heading to the cathedral. Did you see any sign of Max?"

"No. I heard you say he'd disappeared. Are you serious?"

"Yes. Oh, Christine, I can't believe this."

"I'm on my way, Jane. I'll find you. Meanwhile, I'll be praying."

Turning from Jane, Cox spoke to both cops standing by. "Head over to the hotel where the baby was last seen. People who have set up on the sidewalk to watch the parades might have noticed something."

"I'm here, Jane." Christine, breathless from running, slipped an arm around Jane's waist and gave her a reassuring hug. "Thank goodness I was able to find you. What in the world is going on?"

"Someone has taken Max," Jane said. "This"—she turned to Officer Cox—"this is my friend who was with Max and Melanie when I left to . . ." She trailed off, swallowing hard.

"Surely—" Christine broke off. "What—how—"

"We're working on that now," Cox said, then refocused on Jane. "Are you certain the baby was inside his stroller when you left?" she asked.

"Yes, of course. If you're thinking that he could have been missing then and I wouldn't know it, it's not possible. I checked to see that he was sleeping. He's teething and grumpy. I knew if he woke up they would have trouble pacifying him. He would want . . . me." Her voice caught. Now was no time to break down. Closing her eyes, she gave herself a mental shake. "He was asleep in his stroller when I left," she said emphatically.

"Mom, let's call Dad."

Melanie was very close to hysteria. As always when she was distressed, she wanted her daddy. Christine recognized the signs and slipped a comforting arm around the girl's waist. Jane gave Christine a grateful look. With every passing minute, Jane was feeling the need for Kyle's support, too. In a crisis, he was rock-solid.

"Max was definitely asleep in his stroller when I left," Christine said.

With the policewoman leading, they arrived at the cathedral. The steps were shallow and worn with the footsteps of the faithful for more than three hundred years, and wide enough to accommodate a crowd of people. A single look at the cop's expression and people parted like the Red Sea to let the group through to enter. Although an attendant stood guard to keep people out of the sanctuary during Mardi Gras except for regularly scheduled masses, he opened the door for Officer Cox and moved aside to give them access to the narthex.

Inside, the sudden hush was almost eerie to Jane. She glanced toward the altar with its display of religious symbols and quickly turned her back to focus on Officer Cox. She was not a religious person, although for the past few months, Christine, who was active in her church, had been urging Jane to explore the lack of faith in her life.

Cox spoke first to Melanie in a briskly professional voice. "Try and recollect anything unusual you might have noticed, Melanie." Jane guessed her tone was intended to steady Melanie enough to focus her thoughts. "Was there anyone who appeared out of place or suspicious-looking?"

"I-I didn't see anything or anybody like that. I mean, what was there to see? We were talking, we were all watching the floats, and when we turned around, Max had just . . . disappeared!" Her voice climbed as panic overtook her.

"Tell you what." Cox touched Melanie's shoulder. "Let's sit down over here on a pew to talk. All of you." With a tip of her chin, she indicated that Melanie's friends as well as Jane and Christine follow. But Melanie shifted free of the cop's touch, rejecting the suggestion. "We shouldn't be talking at all!" she cried. "We should be looking! We should block off the area! We should go inside bars and any place that's open! We should stop people and ask if they've seen Max! Whoever took him will get away if we don't do something to stop him right now!"

"We are doing something, Melanie," the cop said calmly. "We're doing all we can in this crowd. The incident has been reported. As we speak, officers are on the lookout for Max, but we can't 'block off the area,' as you suggest. It's not possible on Mardi Gras Day." Her tone turned brisk again. "Now. Let's each of you go over the past half hour once again to be sure we haven't overlooked something. You first, Mrs. Madison."

Jane drew a deep breath. Inside she was as agitated as Melanie and wondered how long she could keep from falling apart. "We stopped at the sidewalk in front of the hotel to watch the parades. I left Max with Christine and Mellie, who had two friends with her. There was a huge crowd of people milling about, of course. But beneath the balcony of the hotel, it wasn't quite as jammed." She looked at Christine. "Right, Chris?"

"Yes. And the stroller was right there when I left to go to the woman who fainted."

"And you noticed nothing unusual?"

Christine tried to think. "No. But I was there only another minute or two after Jane left when I saw the woman collapse. I told Melanie to watch Max and went right over."

Sharon Cox turned to Melanie. "Tell me exactly what happened from the time Mrs. O'Brian left."

"It was—" Melanie stopped with a guilty look at Jane. "Some guys we knew were on a float that was passing by and the parade stopped, right there. You know how it is, everything's moving and then it's not. It was only for a minute, Mom, honest." Her lips trembled as she met Jane's eyes. "They said when the parade was over that they knew someone on Bourbon Street who had rented rooms with a balcony and they were going to watch the rest of the parades today from up there. They invited us, too. So then it started up again and they left and we turned around and Max was gone!"

"This is the first I've heard about boys on a float," Jane said sternly. "Did you just forget you were responsible for your baby brother?"

"No, Mom." Melanie dashed at tears in her eyes. "I swear to you, it was only a few minutes."

"But long enough for someone to steal Max." Jane knew her words hurt, but her concern was for her baby now, not for Melanie.

"Mom, please call Dad! Please. We need him. He'll know what to do."

Until a few minutes ago, Jane had been hesitant about calling Kyle in case the whole thing turned out to be a false alarm. But now, with her stomach in a knot and her mouth dry with fear, it didn't look to be a false alarm. She shot Sharon Cox a questioning look.

"It might be a good idea to call your husband, Mrs. Madison."

Today, Kyle was working in the downtown offices of his firm on Poydras Street. He'd driven in with Jane, but after dropping her, Christine, and the children at Canal Street, he'd taken the car one street south to the high-rise on Poydras and parked in an executive slot to "take care of a few details," leaving Jane to deal with their children and the "fun" to be had at Mardi Gras. On a good day—not Mardi Gras—he could walk to Jackson Square in fifteen minutes. Today, it took him more than thirty minutes after Jane's call to reach the St. Louis Cathedral.

Jane, waiting anxiously in the narthex of the church, sprang up when he appeared. She'd given him few details except to say that it appeared Max had gone missing in the crowd. He wanted details, but there were none. God knows, she'd wade through fire to be able to furnish details.

Now his fierce gaze swept past Officer Cox's serious face and Melanie's tear-drenched cheeks to lock onto Jane. "Has he been found?"

"No."

"My God." He looked as if he'd taken a body blow. "There has to be a mistake."

"We've looked—" Jane paused. "They've fanned out to search as best they could, Kyle, but the crowds are so monstrous. They haven't turned up anything. It's as if he just disappeared into thin air."

"That's impossible. He must still be here somewhere. Getting away in this crowd without someone spotting him would be difficult. You did say they put out a bulletin describing his stroller?"

Sharon Cox moved to them, putting out her hand. "Mr. Madison, I'm Sharon Cox, the investigating officer." With a brief nod, he shook her hand.

"Now that you're here, I'd like to suggest we go to the police substation. It's a better place to talk. Once we're there, I'll explain—"

"I don't think we should leave. And what's to explain? We should be combing the area, knocking on doors, questioning people, looking into garages and courtyards. Somebody is bound to have seen something." Glancing outside, he raked a hand over his hair. "This is a nightmare."

"Everything you mention is being done, Mr. Madison. NOPD

is on the scene—has been from the start—but we're hampered by the crowd, as you might imagine. What we're trying to do just now is to piece together exactly what happened."

"How can you be certain he's nowhere nearby?"

"I can't say that with certainty," Sharon said. "But we've found no trace of him. No one has seen anything suspicious." Like Kyle, her glance strayed beyond the narthex to the reveling crowd outside. "At least, they've seen nothing that might be construed as suspicious beyond ordinary Mardi Gras madness."

"It's all my fault, Dad!" Melanie cried suddenly. She looked as if she wanted—no, needed—a hug, but something about Kyle kept her from throwing herself into his arms.

"Max was with Melanie and her friends," Jane explained, trying to keep the tremor from her voice.

"With Melanie?" Kyle frowned darkly. "Why was he with Melanie? Where were you?"

"They were keeping an eye on Max while I went to get lunch from a vendor. Besides Mellie, there was Julie and Anne-Marie. I thought—"

"You left our son in the care of a bunch of teenagers to get junk food?"

Melanie made a distressed sound. "Dad, just listen. Please."

"Hush, Melanie." Kyle waved the teenager quiet, but his gaze was fixed laser-sharp on Jane. "I'm waiting to hear what happened, Jane."

"You can't say anything worse to me than I've been saying to myself, Kyle. The kids were hungry. I went to get food. Christine was with them. It never occurred to me that anything like this could happen."

"Christine?"

"Yes, but there was a medical emergency. A woman fainted. Christine went to lend assistance. She—" Jane stopped, reluctant that she might seem to be casting blame on Melanie.

Kyle's steely gaze turned to his daughter. "So how could Max disappear if you were watching him?"

Melanie began crying again. "We—we got talking and suddenly the parade stalled and this float was right by us and it had some guys we knew from school on it. They were laughing and carrying on and everything. They threw us tons of beads and stuff. It was just for a few minutes, Dad. I know I shouldn't have taken my eyes off Max! I should have stayed right by him, but I thought he was safe on the sidewalk right beside me!"

"Clearly he wasn't beside you," Kyle said.

"But he was only a few feet away, honestly." She covered her face with her hands. "I mean, I don't know how long it was, but when we looked he was gone!"

Jane moved to her and wrapped an arm around the girl's shoulders. Inside her own heart was frozen with terror. "Don't, Mellie. You'll make yourself sick."

Kyle stood with his hands on his hips. "Can you estimate how much time passed before you noticed your baby brother was gone?"

When Melanie seemed unable to talk, Cox spoke up quietly. "We've covered all that, Mr. Madison. The parade stalled for about five minutes, so I don't see how it could have been much longer than that."

"But more than long enough for someone to take the stroller and melt into the crowd, then head for only God knows where," Kyle said in a flat tone.

"Possibly."

"I'm sorry! I'm sorry!" Melanie cried. "I didn't mean this to happen. I'm so sorry."

Jane drew the girl closer. "We know, Mellie. And we'll find him. You'll see. We will." She looked up into Kyle's eyes, her chin tilted. "We *will*!"

They all turned to look as the cop who'd been mounted on horseback appeared, moving reverently into the sanctuary of the church. His glance skimmed the Madisons before moving to Sharon Cox. "NOPD has found the stroller."

Jane pressed her fist to her heart. "Oh, thank God!"

The cop gave her a sympathetic look. "I'm sorry, ma'am. The stroller was abandoned . . . up on the Riverwalk." In one hand he held a tiny sneaker. "This is all we found. There was no sign of the baby."

FICTION YOUNG
Young, Karen.
Blood bayou /
R0112240155   FAIRBRN

FAIRBURN-HOBGOOD PALMER

ATLANTA-FULTON COUNTY LIBRARY

R0112240155